SURGE

BOLT SAGA: VOLUME FIVE
PARTS 13 - 14 - 15

ANGEL PAYNE

D1258469

SURGE

BOLT SAGA: VOLUME FIVE
PARTS 13 - 14 - 15

ANGEL PAYNE

WATERHOUSE PRESS

TABLE OF CONTENTS

For the two who surge my world with such joy:

Thomas and Jess.

You are my lights. You are my world.

SURGE

PART 13

PROLOGUE

REECE

Ever wonder why there's no superhero named Really Fucking Furious?

Maybe there is now.

I'm standing beneath a sky filled with Indian Summer stars, on a crisp and chilly night, in the middle of Malibu Canyon. In front of me is a twenty-foot vertical swath of blue fire, newly gashed into the side of one of these beautiful granite cliffs.

By guess who?

You got it. The new superhero on the block.

Just don't call me Bolt anymore.

I'm that *new* asshole, remember? Really Fucking Furious. The one with the name that really fits right now, considering how every cell of my blood is a cauldron of rage and I'm ready to use those stars as lightning bolt target practice right now. There's enough electric fire in me for all of them. Enough rage to take out the next galaxy over, as well.

But even if I pulled it off, the truth wouldn't change. The glaring certainty that crawls all over my conscience, gleeful maggots on the raw flesh of my psyche. The leeching reality at the hottest core of my anger.

I'm most livid with myself.

For getting complacent. Crap, even...comfortable.

What the living fuck?

But just thinking it, I recognize the truth of it. I've deluded myself that all the discipline and diligence with Emma's training over the last two months has been enough for preparing ourselves and has even been mentally good for me and the team. Yeah, I finally took a couple of beats to breathe, and I even took part in some of Emma's plans for our wedding. I'd assured myself that we all deserved at least a small break after everything that went down in July. That we'd fucking earned it.

It was never ignorance—God knows, after everything the Consortium already put us through, I knew better—but more like a fast repose. A staycation from our constant diligence. We'd infiltrated the Consortium's Palos Verdes compound and taken out the better part of their elite battalion there. We'd caught Faline *inside* her fucking hive. Hadn't that earned us more than half a second to catch our collective breaths? We figured those bastards needed to lick their wounds, giving us a break for at least a few weeks.

Once more, the Consortium beat us to the fucking buzzer.

They weren't licking anything.

They were planning.

Faline was planning.

And I was too goddamned soft to see it.

I wanted to believe that we could finally catch a break. That for just a few months, Emma and I could train our bodies, revel in our love, and indulge our passions by day—and by night, sleep without constantly stressing over what Camp Consortium had up their sleeves for us next.

"Zeus."

I whirl to my right as her voice, invoking her favorite nickname for me, brings a jolt of midnight sun. In the case of the woman I love, the expression isn't just mushy imagery. Her skin pulses with a faint golden light as she picks her way through the rubble to me, easily stepping into the embrace I open for her. Once I've welcomed her into my arms and drawn her close and tight, she leans back to brush off the smaller rocks still clinging to my formal vest and shirt. Not that I'll ever consider wearing these clothes again. Not after the nightmare of tonight.

"You feeling any better?" She looks ready to smile, but the expression doesn't make it past a valiant quirk of her lips. She hopscotches her gorgeous blues, now filled with concern, from me to the cliff and back again.

Before responding, I gaze deep into those brilliant, sapient depths. *Dear fuck.* Will her stare ever cease to string me up like a gutted ox? Drive me crazy mad with the need to clutch her close, kiss her forever, and do other wild animal things? Yes, even now. Maybe especially now. Anything for the sake of keeping her this close now. This safe forever...

The task I've already failed so miserably at.

And here I am, back at the beginning.

Nice to meet you, breathtaking lady. My name's Really Fucking Furious. And yours?

"Reece?"

Clearly she's not accepting my interior rant as her answer—though I'm pretty damn sure she's discerned most of it, judging by the little pinches developing between her eyebrows.

"Why don't *you* tell *me* how I'm feeling?" I thread it with sarcasm, hoping the levity will do us good—but once more, that's a big *F* on my report card. Still, my woman takes an admirable run at an answering laugh.

"I think your halo's too red to dignify that with an answer," she says, taking in the energy around my head that only she can see.

"I'm sorry." It spills out of me fast, but I quickly realize how much more it means. How much of a world-class, grade-A, supersized mess it has to really cover.

And suddenly, three syllables aren't enough.

"I'm so sorry, Emma."

Nor are double that number.

But I'm damn sure even thousands won't be, even if I had the right words at the ready—which I don't. Right now, I have only this. Only me. Only the words I can utter, from the wells of my remorse and fury, shoved through the filter of my ragged heart...and hope that somehow she feels it all as I offer it to her, like a kid who's brought a box of rocks for a queen.

But I can't do any better. I can't do any more.

Some "Savior of LA" you've turned out to be, Richards.

Right. The "savior" who stands here, so undeserving of the woman who wraps herself tighter against me, arms around my neck and curves pressed to every rigid edge of my body. Who stands on tiptoe to crush a full kiss across my numb lips, not emitting a single whimper as the balls of her feet audibly crunch into the gravel.

"*Reece,*" she rasps.

"What?" I snap.

"We're going to be okay." Another kiss, in two parts. She gently caresses the corners of my tight lips with the gentle magic of her own. "Even this is going to be okay."

I pull in a determined breath. Savor how her light, natural

scent invades my senses—and calms my rage. I treasure how her touch renews me and inspires me to reach for self-forgiveness. But most of all, and only for a second, I really believe everything she's just said. I really imagine that since the woman sparkles like the Yellow Brick Road, maybe she does know the way for everyone to get back home now.

"Damn it," I finally grate. "I want to believe you, baby..."

"Then *do*." She whispers the assertion into the center of my chest while tightening her grasp on my shoulders, pulling herself closer. "We'll get through this just like we've gotten through everything else. We'll do it together—now more than ever."

I indulge a fuller inhalation. It's necessary. I need more room to accommodate the power she's literally blowing into me with the words. The magical might of her belief, coming from that awestriking inner strength of hers, pushes me to up my game...so I can do the same. I'm the one on the billboards as the superhero, but this woman is the one who's shown me how it's really done.

But not with special bolts, laser blasts, or glowing fingers.

With heart. With fortitude. With faith. With the knowledge that when one's purpose is true, the path is worth forging—no matter how thick the darkness.

And now, she needs that same force from me. She *deserves* it.

"You're damn right, my beautiful Velvet. And I'm damn smart for knowing it this time." I offer the certainty of the words, along with the steadiness of my hold, as I gather her even closer against me. "For knowing it *always*."

I kiss her with slow but thorough adoration and clutch her even closer. Even tighter. Will it ever be close or tight enough?

I want to spend my entire life trying.

Our entire life.

As we pull apart by a few inches, I behold the bright sheen drenching her eyes. "Damn straight, Bolt Man."

But even as she declares it, the ghost of Really Fucking Furious flies in again, threatening to take a fresh perch across my shoulders. I fight the bastard off by kissing my woman deeper, battling to pull more of her astounding strength into my muscles, my bones, my whirling chaos of a bloodstream. The act is so dickishly selfish—right now, *she* should be taking all of this from *me*, not the other way around—but I vow to put the energy on a regenerative loop between us.

Together.

So surprise, surprise; the woman may just be right. Maybe we *are* going to do this.

With heart. With fortitude. With faith.

With love.

As one. *Together.*

Dear fuck, I hope so.

I pray so.

CHAPTER ONE

EMMA

Eight hours earlier...

"Yes. Yes. Yesssss!"

The shouts from my fiancé, guttural and primal and joyous, stoke a fire inside me like I've never felt before. I stretch to fulfill their demand, using Reece's beautiful baritone as my fuel, digging into wells of strength I never knew I possessed— and quite possibly didn't—until now.

The fire swells from my center. Takes hold of my nerves and tendons. Rides the fast lane of my bloodstream, bringing a sting of pain but a rush of power at once, until erupting off my lips as a long, scorching shout. I almost don't recognize the sound. Is that me causing birds to burst from the Malibu Canyon shrubs with the force of my roar? Is that my throat producing the badass war cry echoing back off Rindge Dam's hundred-foot face and along the massive canyon walls around us?

Holy shit. That *is* me.

And I sound pretty freaking awesome.

Kind of like a Valkyrie and a Jungle Queen decided to have a glowing love child. And why the hell not? I go ahead and take that description to heart, bursting with golden light that washes every surface I pass.

Best of all, I sound like a woman who's at last able to keep up with her superhero lover.

While becoming this way wasn't my choice and was officially the worst hell my body has ever been through, I'd be first in line to do it all over again.

To get to this heavenly moment?

Oh, hell yes.

The thought spreads a wide, joyous smile across my lips as more cells in my blood burst open, intensifying my light. I watch the illuminating impact on everything around me. Concrete and cliffs, bushes and trees, cascading water, and even the fading graffiti along the dam's walls are all transformed by the gilded light that emanates from my gaze and my palms.

"That's it!" Reece bellows. "Yes, baby. Do it!"

I toss back my head and laugh, at him more than with him, but I can't help myself. The man makes me delirious, now more than ever. He fills me, inspires me, lifts me...

And thank God for the lifting.

And not just in the pretty poetic way. Or even in the hot erotic way. Though *both* those ways are worth a hundred sonnets and sighs apiece, this is in the beyond-crazy way.

The is-it-a-bird-or-is-it-a-Crist way.

Yes, seriously.

Yes, unbelievably.

I'm flying—and this man's astounding energy pulses are my wings.

But his superpowers are just the beginning of his pure, epic hotness.

Even from nearly a hundred feet up, the man is a burnished, bulging fantasy come to life. His long, leather-encased legs are braced to the canyon floor below, while every striation of his bare, chiseled torso is well-defined from the effort of stretching his arms up toward me. His long, confident fingers spread wide, evenly distributing streams of electrical energy from the centers of his palms to support my weight like invisible waves beneath a transparent surfboard.

Cowabunga, Team Bolt.

He carries me even higher on a rush of air that hums and crackles, just like the exhilaration surging my senses and speeding my heartbeat. The more the excitement floods my veins, the brighter my power manifests. I know that as truth by taking in my own sprawled fingers, aglow with thrumming gold light that changes the very air through which I sweep them. But my favorite confirmation is in the sight of the birds that are brave enough to cavort around me, chirping and squawking, trying to figure out the new creature in the 'hood.

But I'm not here for the aviary brunch bunch.

I'm here to hone my focus. To dig deeper into my psyche. To summon even more potency for my powers: the blinding light and searing heat cascading through my bloodstream thanks to a decision I made more in a twist of desperation than any clarity of wisdom. Going after the world's biggest psycho bitch was probably the stupidest move of my existence—as Faline Garand herself reminded me when she turned the tables on Angelique, Wade, and me during what was supposed to be our quest to kill her. God only knows what other Consortium-style "fun" the woman's been able to download into her system since then.

Which means our nightmare is far from over.

Which also means that if Reece and I don't want to end up back on the woman's lab table—or worse, seeing one of our friends as Faline's next experimental rat—exercises like this aren't just recreational.

They're essential.

I can't ever forget the hopeless nightmare.

The helpless pain.

The evil I'll never stop pursuing, as long as I can still move and breathe.

A worthy credo—though it's been embedded in my soul since the first time Reece relayed his full experience at the hands of the Consortium. It's been nearly a year since the rainy afternoon in New York when he shared every detail, but the horrors echo in my mind like I heard it only yesterday. The soft horns of the boats out on the Hudson. The spatter of the rain on the windows. The muted tumult of traffic and crowds from the streets below. But most clearly, the grit Reece fought to dilute from his voice as he told me what they'd done to him... how they'd done everything they could to dehumanize him.

His determined composure was the only calm aspect about those moments of awful confession. Inside my heart, a protective fury began to rage like none I'd ever known. It was scary—and to this day, still is—but in other ways, it's grown into my version of a spiritual home fire. The anger is easier to keep aflame than its alternative.

Fear.

Especially at moments like this.

Reece's triumphant baritone consumes everything in the canyon, including me. His power isn't just lifting me from below anymore. It's flowing through me, mixing with the power I keep letting in, until my psyche is nothing but sun and my senses are pure light. Between one scalding heartbeat and the next, cognition and hesitation sear from my consciousness. I'm nothing but energy and instinct. I follow my outstretched arms, needing to ride the wind that flirts with my fingertips and kisses my smiling lips.

"You're there, Velvet." Reece's bellow is full of celebration. "Fuck *yes*. You're there!"

I drop my sights from the cloudless sky, letting out a soft laugh to match his jubilation. For the first time in our countless training sessions, we've gotten the mix right between his power and mine—and now my feet are even with the top lip of the dam.

"Holy crap!" I call back. "Look what we did!"

My words ping around the canyon walls, mixing with his exultant shout. "Fucking right we did!"

I don't dare look down to acknowledge him this time. When a girl's about to step off onto a curved concrete lip that's barely a meter wide, she needs all the visual focus she has.

"Perfect, baby. You're doing great." Though Reece is still joyous, a deeper thunder rumbles through his voice. Oh, *God*. When he starts sounding like the human version of these cliffs, my senses turn the texture of the sediment that's collected behind the high end of the dam, only without the picturesque trees that have taken root there.

"Shit," I mutter beneath my breath. "Shit, shit, *shit*." But thankfully, I'm able to shove aside the arousal, steady in my main purpose again. I'm here, I'm pumped, and I'm ready to take on the next part of my training course like the badass goddess that I am.

That I need to prove myself as...

No.

That I am.

Now that my inner cheering section has my back, I square my stance and fully face the six wooden "bad guy" cutouts

Reece has positioned between here and the spillway on the other side of the dam.

"You're doing great, beautiful!" The man's mighty baritone, always my ultimate inspiration, blazes up to me with perfect timing. I breathe in, welcoming more of his fire in my mind, my muscles—and every pore pulsing for him in ecstatic, electric love.

"Fry those fuckers where they stand, baby." But his energy doesn't dilute his voice's defined dip into lustier registers. "And then come back to me for your equally hot reward."

I spurt out a laugh. Toss aside my pretend battle batons before calling down, "Nothing like a not-so-subtle incentive, Mr. Richards."

Reece's chuckle is uniquely audible due to the natural echo chamber we're in. "Since when am I subtle with you, Miss Crist?"

I seesaw my head and crack my knuckles. "Valid point." Coming from the man who delivers the best rewards on earth— namely the kind that leave my throat raw from screaming and my sex numb from a thousand jolts of ecstasy.

But the guy's cutout building skills...

I seriously need to talk to him about leaving this stuff up to Wade and Alex. But before that happens, I need to get through *this*. And before *that* happens, I need to make sure I'm not laughing my ass off. So I tuck my head down, quelling a snorty snicker. And another. Oh, dear *hell*. My man has painted these big wooden "bad guys" so badly, they resemble *South Park* characters instead of legitimate Consortium henchmen.

No. Really.

I lean out a little, assessing the thick wood shapes. Though the obstacles increase in height and thickness down the line,

I still swear the fourth one down the line is Bebe. That, or a really bad piece of Sawyer Foley concept art. It could go either way.

As thoroughly as I'd love to jibe the man I love about exactly that, the silent conclusion is as far as I can take the ribbing. It's time to get to work. *Real* work. To apply myself fully to this "mission" as if it's the real deal—and that means viewing the cutouts as if they're really Consortium soldiers, not cute pieces of wood painted to look like TV youngsters. I have to start thinking like a warrior myself.

To turn Cartman, Stan, Kyle, and even that really funny Bebe into enemies who have been ordered to exact some deep damage to me.

All of them—except the cutout waiting at the end.

She's special, as symbolized by the care that was obviously spent on painting her big catlike eyes and red feline smirk. And even though he didn't bother with the sleek black hair and the matching latex catsuit, I already get the reference.

And I'm prepared to take Faline Garand all the way down.

To make up for the first time I was given the chance to do so—and freaking blew it.

I had the bitch. Dead to damn rights. Splayed beneath me, helpless as a fish on a pier. That should have resulted in her being dead in other ways too, but it hadn't—and as understanding as Reece was, and still is, about my lapse, I've already looked into his mind a thousand times about what has to happen in the aftermath of it.

There can't be *another* aftermath.

Right now, I can't even fathom what that would look like—considering Faline's decided *she* needs to be a member of the electric mutants club too. The powers she displayed back in July, from throwing an invisible web on the air to some advanced levitation moves, was more than enough proof for us all. But I doubt the woman is going to settle for simply making Rice Crispy treats for the team's fundraiser. She's probably already changing the T-shirts from *Team Bolt* to *Team Bitch*.

But that's never going to happen.

Which is why I get to work.

With all the instincts he's been teaching me to unlock inside. With every cell of my blood and force of my soul, abandoning the woman known as Emmalina Crist. I have to access something new. *Be* something new. An entity of primal purpose and cold intent, despite the fire I must access to bring it to life. In many ways, a creature that was born on that rainy afternoon in New York—for every time I must go to this mode, I start with that wrath-filled woman. She rises inside, helping to push back doors in my psyche until I reach the inner sanctum where the cauldron of my hottest rage burns.

From there, it boils and sluices into my blood.

Which twists around my bones.

Which fires into my muscles.

Which propels me forward along the top of the dam, undaunted and unafraid and unstoppable.

Which fires every long, lunging stomp I take in my badass boots, facing off to the line of enemies before me. And now, they really *are* enemies. I don't know the difference anymore. My mind shows me a mob of grimacing Consortium goons, and the firestorm through my whole body confirms that truth.

At my center, a white-hot nucleus burns brighter and bigger than ever before. It rolls furiously back over itself, spinning faster and hotter, like one of the Ground Bloomer fireworks I loved as a kid. But this thing isn't like a pretty colored flower. The sparks flying off its center are like shrapnel, nicking my ribs and clawing my guts. I cry out, protesting the assault, but I already know it's no use.

The invading energy is *mine*.

"Yaaaaaaahh!" I scream it as fire rages up every inch of my throat, making no other sound possible. As I repeat it, tiny sparks dance off my tongue and flicker at the edges of my gaze. I blink away the distractions, staying true to my fiery focus, and zero in on my first target.

And take a surging stomp closer.

Closer.

My chest turns into a hot bellows. My blood reaches critical temperature. I direct my arms toward the first asshole in the lineup, jacking one side of my mouth into a deceptively friendly smile. Reece's approving grunt comes through our comm line. He's watching every move I make; I feel the intensity of his scrutiny as clearly as if he's pulsed himself all the way up the rock wedge. If he sees me conveying anything other than a façade of "Superhero Zen," the man's going to let me know it, my concentration be damned.

But I'm on my game today.

Yes. *Yessss*.

I'm a glowing goddess.

A supercharged seraph.

A bolted, badass bunny.

And *ready* to take out this line of assholes and stand face-to-face with the bitch who runs them all.

Heat fills my arms, stinging my veins and glowing through my skin, before it collects in the center of my palms and then surges out through my fingers like rays of surreal sun. Only then do I feel it sneak into my grin as well, adding to the euphoria of my electrified high.

"Someone call for a pizza?" I quip at the first henchman—right before whipping my fingers up as if flicking off peanut butter. But the gold stuff in the air isn't Jiffy Extra Crunchy. They're balls of pure heat. The globs smack hard into the thick wood, melting it away like acid through steel, until all that's left is a pile of smoking balsa chunks.

Asshat Number One, down for the count.

Before I even step over the rubble, another burst of heat forms between my ribs.

And just like before, blasts out along my limbs.

Collects in my hands.

Sizzles out my fingers.

I lift a confident smile at the second baddie of the obstacle course. This cutout is bigger than the first one, and deliberately so. I'm not surprised, because Reece has already trained me not to be—the same way I know he's watching me and scoring me now not just based on *how* I tackle the "enemy," but *where.* Every combatant I face will have a different center of gravity and a different way in which it's handled.

Which I get a giant taste of now, as the bull-sized bruiser comes at me with full-throttle speed and fire-breathing fury. No; really. Reece has mounted the cutout on a rolling base so it coasts along a short length of slanted track, causing it to pick up speed with every inch it covers. And yes, he's even rigged the cutout with smoke blowers, just to make things more fun.

But I don't try to charge through the fog.

I crouch. And then wait.

And wait. And wait.

So the patience game is more excruciating than I thought it would be. But I'll deal. I *have* to. My blood burns to attack, but I let the bull loom bigger and bigger and bigger, until the second he's about to bash into me.

I dip back and to the side, leading with my shoulder and head. Within seconds, I've robbed the "attacker" of his prize like a toreador sidestepping a rushing bull—

Only this bull doesn't have time to recover and come snorting back around for more.

Thanks to the heat I've directed at the front of the short track, the wooden beast rolls off the end of the rails, down the steep slope of the dam, and all the way into the dark jade water below. I watch the lagoon swallow up those half-dozen chunks with a winsome shrug and a sarcastic murmur. "You didn't play nice, buster. No pizza for you."

Surprise, surprise—there's no pizza for Cutout Jerkface Numbers Three, Four, or Five either. Two of them come at me at once, equipped with whirling battle knives mounted on spinning wheels, forcing me to access a lot of the close-quarter battle moves I've been learning from Sawyer Foley over the last two months. Despite the extensive prep from the guy, whom I've now determined to be either former special ops or ex Assassin Brotherhood, it's difficult to dodge both rivals at once—thanks once more to Reece's "just for fun" innovations. Since each cutout hulk is also equipped with a turbo air fan, they wobble and squirm more than the average five-layer balsa plank. Then there's the way they're harshing the mojo of my magma bombs with their violent crosswinds.

Finally, after dropping to my belly and pushing the heat *up*, I'm able to weaken the metal track beneath at least one of them. With another "*Yaaahhh,*" I curve the softened metal with a bunch of hard kicks, forcing Jerkface Number Three to gore the crap out of his successor.

"Silly assholes," I rasp between hard breaths, recovering on my back. "You want two for one *and* free extra cheese? On a Saturday when UCLA is facing off against USC?"

No pizza for them either.

But it looks like Cretin Number Six wants the extra-large everything pie, with comped garlic knots *and* Mountain Dew—and is also refusing to take no for an answer. This asshole's taller than all the rest, but that's not what has my spine tensing and my neck hairs prickling. That comes from the gazillion bullet-sized holes drilled into the slab. There's hardly enough balsa left to keep the cutout's structure intact...

And I'm damn sure I know why.

But I sure as hell don't like that I do.

Because as soon as I pivot and start marching closer, all of my instincts are validated. Reece turns on the floodlights *behind* the cutout. The glare's so bright I can't see my own feet, let alone where I'm stepping. The damn things are likely showing up on a few satellite feeds from Mars itself. I'm plunged into a sensory deprivation tank, everything sucked away by light instead of darkness. After a few seconds, there's no denying the urge to fight it—

With a sun flare of my own.

I take a second to breathe deep. To focus fully.

My mutated blood doesn't let me down. It answers with atomic intensity, turning my center into nothing but white and gold light. It's permeating and excruciating, ripping out a war scream that makes my earlier cry sound like a baby's babble. I struggle to keep my hands extended, fighting past the crushing craving to coil my fingers into fists, even as the light strands between my fingers thicken to the texture of full webbing.

Webbing?

Okay, kids. Full stop.

I raise my hands to see sizzling strands looping back and forth between my stretched fingers. But the power—*my* power—doesn't stop at the webbing. As I watch, nerves racing and breaths pumping, the jolts combine and extend, taking over my fingers and making my nail beds look like pressed stars.

No.

"Pressed stars" is a cute name for nail polish. Now is no time for cute. I feel more like a walking tractor beam now, complete with the crazy-ass variations on my overall balance and perspective.

Including the way my power flows *in* as well as *out.*

But is that necessarily a bad thing?

By the time I'm done asking it of myself, I'm already figuring out the answer. I stop, not even trying to take any more steps, while pushing my hands up and out again, letting my cells experiment with the back-and-forth dynamic of the energy. The tactic is either a signature on my death warrant—overloading things on the "in" valve could be as dangerous as overflowing everything outward—or a breakthrough that'll become a valuable secret weapon for Team Bolt. I'm banking on the latter, staking my tactic on the philosophies from Sawyer's Jiu Jitsu lessons. *Observe. Conserve. Counteract. Counterbalance. Then control...*

Only in my case, there's an extra step. An important one. "Absorb."

As soon as I whisper the word into existence, my body recognizes it.

Embraces it.

Enacts it.

The nets between my fingers begin to vibrate. Then hum. Then sing.

Weirdly, that *is* the best word for it.

I feel a smile breach my lips as the music intensifies, like Andalusian flutes mixed with electric harps, a sound that's space-age but primitive at the same time. I look up in wonder. Is the canyon itself singing the harmony? I swear, as I watch the wind in the trees, that they're swaying in time to the otherworldly rhythm.

As it resounds louder...

Plays bolder...

Surges brighter...

Sucking up every spectrum of light in its path.

Holy shit.

Even the natural light.

In the space where the cutout just was, it looks like some nature spirit has walked in and washed the scene with a giant spectral paintbrush. There's literally nothing there—or so it seems.

I walk forward, my hands still webbed. I stop as soon as my outstretched fingers ram into the hole-ridden cutout. The only parts of the obstacle I can see now are the two places I'm still touching. As soon as I retract my hands, they disappear again.

"Holy..."

"Shit." Reece, freshly completing his pulse-and-bounce up the face of the dam, finishes with a shocked flourish for us both. He steps over, nearly facing off with me. Mirrors my open gape with every carved angle of his bold face. Pushing harsh, heavy breaths in and out of his bare, hewn torso—

That, thanks to the large cutout between us, I shouldn't be

able to see at all.

Not that I'm actually *complaining* about the view, but...

"Reece?"

He's attempting to do the same thing I just have—except when he taps at the wood slab, nothing happens. He looks like a Montmartre mime, if France bred mimes who wore nothing but shitkickers, black battle leathers, and burnished eight-packs.

"Emmalina. Holy hell."

More astonishment clearly dives over him, imparting more of the mime hunk vibe. His jaw works up and down, but no sounds come out.

Finally he stammers, "You...how the *hell* did you..."

"You think *I* know?" I grimace. My hands are really starting to hurt. The rest of me feels like hell's magma core.

"You...you sucked in all that light. Made it a part of you. And then the whole damn thing—"

"No shit."

"Velvet?" He's traded out the amazement for apprehension. "Em, are you—" And in one second of lightning speed he's at my side, cradling my crumple to my knees. "*Fuck.*" He lowers with me, gathering me into his lap.

"It...hurts," I mumble into his chest. *Damn it.* Of all the times for the man to smell so freaking good. Sunshine and sweat are such an intoxicating mix with his masculine musk, the only detail I can stand to commit to consciousness before another wave of agony hits me.

"Crap."

I force my head to tilt up. "What does *that* mean?"

"Sorry, baby." The resignation on his face copies the intent of his tone. "You've just had the chance to train new muscles, if that makes any sense."

"Kind of." He's speaking more to Lydia's wheelhouse now, not mine.

"Think of it like prepping for a marathon and getting past your first ten-mile mark."

"Do I have to?"

His answering smile, so tender and concerned, almost makes me regret my glare. "Damn it, Emma," he murmurs. "I really am sorry. I was hoping the mutation wouldn't affect you like it did me, but..."

"No such luck?" I attempt a laugh, but there's going to be no good fortune with that either. Before I get much further, the magma from hell rises over me again, claiming me with twice its awful fire. "Oh, fuckity-fuck-*fuck*!" But just as fast, my teeth are clattering and every inch of my body is racked by shivers. And I thought the hangover after Duncan Black's Halloween party was the worst I'd ever feel in my life.

"It's okay, baby." As Reece croons it, I'm aware of him cradling me closer but then fully rising. The canyon, so much my bestie a minute ago, is now a sickening collection of weaving colors and textures. "Don't fight it. That makes it worse. Let it happen. I've got you. *I've got you.*"

His last few syllables are noise after the five I fixate on in horror. "Just let it happen?" I spit, enduring a fresh fire infusion to my blood. "Are...are y-y-you f-f-f-freaking kidding me?" And then the ice again, turning all my fevered sweat back into ice.

"You're going to be okay." That, along with the doting strokes he keeps running along my forehead, will land the guy a walk-on nurse gig in some soap opera but doesn't answer my question at all. He lowers me to the cliff wedge between the dam and the spillway before finding a crag to lean my head and torso against. While the view is better—I'm able to watch as he efficiently removes my boots and sends me reassuring smiles—it in no way relieves the alternating waves of hellfire and ice torture continuing to play chicken with my blood.

"St-Still doesn't f-f-feel all right," I spew back.

"I know." And in all the lower registers of his voice, I hear that he really does.

"C-C-Crap," I manage to get out. "Is...is this what *you* go through all the time? Every time you p-p-put down assholes, *this* is how karma pays you b-b-back?"

He ticks up a lopsided smile. "It gets easier. I promise." And then adds to his irresistible spell by rubbing the balls of my big toes, nearly making my eyes roll back in my head from bliss. I'm so fast and far-gone to the bliss, I nearly don't hear him adding in a quiet growl, "Just not the first time."

I *nearly* don't hear.

Thank God enough of my psyche does that I jerk my head back up, spearing him with a glare and then charging, "And what does *that*—" But I'm slamming my skull back against the rock just as fast, as I comprehend everything he's been trying to prep me for.

Everything.

The war of my mind and logic, needing some semblance of normalcy again, battling the violent protest of my blood and instincts for exactly the opposite. Somewhere in the middle, my body tries to make them all talk nice to each other but pays the price with another blast of painful heat. A raging, blistering need that refuses to go away, incinerating my system in a frantic search for something—some*one*—to decimate without destroying. To conquer without killing. To take over without taking out.

And for the first time, I really understand why Reece did it all in the first place. Why Bolt *had* to happen. Why he looked the way he did on the night we first met, giving off the energy of an animal barely tethered...of lightning hardly harnessed.

"Oh, my God."

I turn my head. Reach out toward the beautiful face somewhere above mine. I need to tell him all of this—*right now*. I need to tell him how I finally understand and finally *know*...

But words aren't happening. Only the heat is. More and more of the insane, infuriating heat, like a parasite on fire inside me. Only Reece makes the ordeal a little more bearable. Thank God for him. He's my sanity, my guide, my partner. And yes, he's the superhero who kneels over me, serving me, still pressing his magical thumbs into the balls of my toes. He's also the man who gazes back at me with those all-knowing, all-seeing silver eyes. He comprehends so much...and because of that, offers me everything *he* is without fear.

I love him so damn much...

"You're going to be okay."

Now he's the leader who tells me that again and again and again, as sure as assuring me the sky is blue, even as the netting between my fingers sets the air aflame. Even as that fiery energy keeps hissing and snapping at the air like a wicked, starving beast. Even knowing that if I touch him with my hands in this condition, I could burn him...permanently mark him. He tells me that, knowing that if he doesn't, I might go insane from the conflict in my blood—

And the need inside my body.

He tells me that, knowing how deeply and fiercely I need *him*.

In so many damn ways...

CHAPTER TWO

REECE

I'm not afraid.

Fuck. I should be. Her solar-strength finger nets, likely manifested by her adrenaline surge from the obstacle course, are an astonishing new development. Clearly as much for her as for me. I knew it from the second she made the cutout disappear. Witnessing the shock on every inch of her face through that newly transparent space was nothing short of a revelation for my heart and triumph for my spirit.

And regrettably, a shock I could only indulge for all of two seconds. After that, every thought and instinct retrained on her. *Only* her. It had to be that way because I recognized all the signs of the power surge in her—the dilation in her eyes, the drop of her jaw, the sheen across her skin—and knew what was coming.

Knew it because I've been there before.

The first trip to hell.

The trip I'd desperately prayed she would be spared.

Even as the days after her transformation turned into weeks and then a month. And then two.

Throughout it all, I've pushed her harder in the training sessions, confident that I could. Knowing that I need to. Knowing *she* needs me to. Witnessing the growing regret in her eyes with every replay she runs of her confrontation with Faline and kicks herself for letting the witch get away. Flogs herself for not delivering a larger blow to the Consortium when she had their key leader in her grip, despite the fact that it was her first time ever with another person's life in her hands.

Despite the fact that *everything* she did that day had saved my existence.

Despite the fact that in doing so, she'd permanently changed her own.

So yeah, I'm going to fucking be here for her, no matter what direction the fallout takes. Though if the surge hits her as it did me—and that's a big *if* when messing with a person's bloodstream—then this "sacrifice" won't be a horrific one.

But Emma still doesn't believe that. Her eyes are wide and crystalline with dread. She battles to fold her fingers and shocks herself with her own searing currents. Plus and a minus for me there, since I know how much pain she's deliberately delivering to her system—though at the same time making her body writhe against the cliff's edge in gorgeous, flawless ways.

"It—it won't shut off," she cries. "D-D-Don't come near me, Reece. I—I can't—"

"Ssshhh." Okay, so I sound ridiculous, but aside from outright ordering her to calm down—an impossibility, if her power is backing up and building up as I think it is—it's the closest pacifier I can think of. The nearest thing to a timeout I can secure, for the few seconds I'm going to need to verbally walk her through this process. At least as much as I can while we're perched on a hundred-foot-high wedge of rock in the middle of Malibu Canyon. "Don't talk, Bunny. You need to just listen to me, and we'll get you through this, okay?"

"No!" she spits at once. "Not okay, damn it!" She bucks

her hips. Coils and uncoils her fingers. Even tries blowing on them, though her desperate air just fans their heat like a forest gust on campfire embers. "It—it burns. It hurts. It— God, it—"

"Aches?" I supply it only because I need her to focus on my voice instead of hers—on a force other than the one attempting to rip her apart from the inside out. But I also say it because I need to watch her reaction. To gauge the intensity of her fire.

"Yes. *Yes*. Aches!"

And as soon as she punctuates it by flinging her back, exposing the taut and sweat-drenched V of her neck and cleavage, I have my answer.

She's past *fire*.

And right on to *lust*.

No. She's bypassed that too.

The woman is thoroughly entrenched in *need*.

Well, shit.

I go ahead and mutter it aloud, though it's hardly the timeout I was hoping to grab this go-round. The truth is, there's *no* more time here. Certainly not enough for thinking, assessing, and mapping out a worthy action plan. My incredible woman clarifies that point with astounding efficiency—in the form of a long, erotic moan that careens everywhere it can in my cock.

"Reece! Oh holy crap, I'm burning up!"

She undulates so passionately, I have to dig a hand into her waist to prevent her from sliding off the rock. "Emmalina. My brave Bunny." The endearment doesn't do a damn thing to calm her. "I know, sweetheart. I know it's bad."

But do I? I scour my memory for the first time this happened to me. It was after I'd lifted a whole car with a steady pulse. It'd been around three a.m., off the Main Street Bridge in downtown. The driver had fallen asleep at the wheel, run off the road, and landed in the dry river bed. The sedan pinned a bunch of runaway teenagers camped there for the night. It'd been the first solid Bolt did for the world that made me feel great instead of grungy—until the backup surge hit. I felt like a dozen lightning bolts lap danced for me at once. If they'd been tangible, I probably would've screwed all of them too. Ruthlessly. Consecutively.

"You *don't* know." Emma's scream banishes even the wind from our clifftop. "If you knew, you'd—" She slides her hands, still sizzling, down to the space between her legs. She spreads them wide before stroking herself, burning away the leather, nearly turning her training leathers into a pair of chaps. Except that underneath, she's not wearing jeans. She's not wearing *anything*.

"Jesus," I croak, partly from bewilderment but mostly from raw arousal. At once, I collect my composure enough to grab her wrists, preventing the woman from burning herself down there with a second grab, though I'll be damned if I can look away. Her pussy has never looked so succulent, swollen, and sweet. It's never smelled so lush, fruity, and delicious.

"Don't need him. Only you. *Please*, Reece..."

Her husky entreaty exacerbates the pounding pressure between my thighs.

"Fuck," I mutter. "Oh, holy *fuck*."

The woman of my dreams is spread, bared, and begging for me to plunge inside her...

Atop a hundred-foot crag.

In the middle of Malibu Canyon.

In the middle of the afternoon.

But as I've so clearly reminded myself, I can hoist at least a couple of tons with my hands alone. And if I shift Emma just to the left, so just her torso hangs over the side of the rock, I can anchor my knees into the natural indents here...and here...

"Holy. *Christ.*" My snarl erupts from my nose as much as my lips, watching as the center of her body is angled up courtesy of the rocks on the crag. As she moans in obvious pleasure and opens her legs even wider, her sex is turned into an offering fit for a king: a red, delectable fruit with the richest, rarest pulp on the planet.

"Already *told* you. Tell him to clock the hell out." Emma issues it with a sultry expression, come-hithering me through the thick fan of her lashes while using her incredible obliques to keep her upper body raised in midair. *My Wonder Woman.* She isn't one speck afraid of the fact that she's dangling a hundred feet up in the air, her gaze glimmering as bright as the sun rays on the reservoir waters as she reaches to melt away the top button and zipper of *my* crotch. "Just you, my beautiful Zeus."

"Unnnhhh." Yeah, it's exactly how I answer her. Yeah, because right now, it's all I can manage. Because all I can comprehend or care about is how goddamned good it feels when my erection springs free from its leather confines, growing and hardening as it stretches for the treasure for which it was supremely created.

The moment Emma lands her gaze on my flesh, the brilliant threads between her fingers are joined by the bold glow beneath her skin. Even the strands of her hair turn lighter, flowing on the wind like blazing white feathers as every exposed pore of her skin becomes a blazing phoenix in its own right. She lights up even brighter as I settle between her legs, jostling the glowing drop at the tip of my sex into the pulsing folds of hers.

"Oh, holy ssshhh..." And she's lost to a high, delirious scream as the electricity in my juice seeks out all the receptors in hers, giving her a front-of-the-line pass for the climax coaster. It's only the first of many I plan on giving to her breathtaking body, her magnificent mind, her cosmically perfect spirit. Now more than ever, her pleasure is my everything...her ultimate desire my destiny.

"That's it, baby," I coax. "Ride it out. Soak all of the pleasure in. Everything I have for you. Everything I *am* for you."

Emma shudders, finally relaxing her abdominals and letting her head and shoulders fall backward over the crag's edge. "And everything I am...for you." Her sigh matches the limp abandon of her body, though I'm positive the little minx knows exactly what she's doing. Precisely how her new position raises her most tender parts even more. How thoroughly I can see every dazzling trickle on every layer of her spread blossom, surrounding the plum-colored depths at her slickest, tightest core.

"Soon, Little Velvet." How I summon the composure for the murmur might remain a mystery until the day I fucking die. "Soon. I promise."

She erupts into an impatient snarl, helping and hurting her cause at the same time. If the matter was up to my eyes and imagination, I could crouch here and savor the sight of her wet, quivering pussy for at least another hour. On the other hand, my cock has all but disowned me out of pure frustration. Emma is ready to fully side with the bastard, even after I stretch out my fingers and pulse the air beneath her, straightening out her body.

As she lifts her head, aligning our stares once again, she

grits, "You're a teasing son of a bitch, Reece Richards."

I extend my other hand and pulse again, lifting her head and shoulders a little higher. I need to see more of her. More of her incredible breasts, still respectably covered by her leathers but straining their confines. Higher up, the cords in her neck glow like polished gold ropes, consumed by her aroused gulps. Even higher and best of all, her gaze is a pair of liquid flames, blue and gold intensity that captures and conquers me.

"And you're my perfect little sun flare, Miss Crist."

The flames in her eyes grow hotter. "Maybe I am." She juts her jaw higher, defiant and radiant, while nudging the center of her body closer to the raging rod at the middle of mine. "But you know what they say about flying too close to the sun, don't you?"

"I'll take my chances." It's nothing but a grate on my lips—because she's nothing but fire around my cockhead. Fuck, *fuck*. Just the outer edges of her intimate walls feel so good...

"Even if you might get burned alive?"

"Worth it."

A tiny tremor overtakes her lush mouth. We've traded the expression back and forth since the beginning of our love story: two simple syllables that have grown to represent so many more. It's our version of "shut the hell up," "you're not talking me out of this," and "do you want Faline Garand taking me out instead?" all rolled into one. But there's one expression it stands for more than all those others combined.

I love you more than my own life—and this is me proving it.

I've lost track of how many times *she's* already demonstrated it to *me* the last fifteen months—not just in the obvious ways, like moving in with me and letting me beat up shitheads for her. There are the ways no one else has seen yet.

The day she climbed into a shower stall with me despite how I'd turned the whole thing into a miniature electrical storm. The night she went to a Paris soiree with my family, not knowing if the whole party was a secret trap orchestrated by my father. And a night barely three months ago, when she followed me out to a canyon a lot like this and nearly died in the name of giving me pleasure to ease my pain.

Offering herself to me.

Giving herself to me.

Risking so much for the mutant she fell in love with...and continues to keep loving with so much of herself....

And yet now, asking if *I'm* afraid of catching on fire.

Doesn't she know I'm already *on* fire? That I have been from the moment I first saw her?

Or maybe we're past the words.

And it's simply time for action.

"Reece!" The word erupts from her in a high, breathy sigh as I slide into her. The friction of our bodies creates a visible glow, even in the bright golden ribbons of late-afternoon light. My senses shine just as brightly, infused with the ecstasy of being part of her...one with her...set on fire by her. "Oh, God. Oh *yes*..."

"Damn." I cut her off with the growl emerging from the depths of my gut as I roll my hips, ordering myself to draw this heaven out a little longer. If we've learned any lesson together, it's to venerate every moment we possibly can, and fuck, is this one worth venerating. I focus on everything about it—the wind in her long ponytail, the desire in her azure eyes, the way her torso flows along on the air, controlled by the nuances of my pulses—before husking, "You're so beautiful. My fiery, fuckable angel..."

"Yours," Emma cries out. "*Yours*, my perfect god."

Every note of her voice is a new burst of flames through me—bubbling through my blood...fulminating through my mind...swelling in my cock. I'm a goddamned forest fire, and I've never loved the conflagration more. "Again," I demand from tight lips, feeding myself into her a little deeper. "Say it again, baby."

"Yours." She knows what I need—and the desperate, throaty declaration I need it in. "Always, forever...*yours*."

"Yes. Yesssss." The ache in my thighs becomes the pressure in my buttocks and balls. I've tried so damn hard to draw this out, to give her a string of climaxes before blowing my wad, but she's too goddamned delectable, riding the air above my energy as she rides every throbbing inch of my erection. It's so good. It's *too* good.

"Oh, *Reece*!" She flings her hands back as if punching them into pillows, only the cushions beneath her are stitched by electricity. *My* electricity. Because of that, something incredible happens every time her luminous knuckles land atop my pulsing bolsters.

The jolts zing straight to my blood.

Then my balls.

Then up my shaft.

"Holy *Christ*!"

Which has now, I swear to fuck, turned into a slave to the demand to mate with her. To fuse with her. To fill her and rut with her and worship her and fuck her. To take her as hard and as deeply as I can, helping my cause by hooking my energy around her shoulders and yanking her body back over mine in fast, brutal strokes. She throws her head farther back as I continue the rhythm, as old as the cosmos and as savage as the stars, panting and moaning in time to the flashes that erupt from our primal poundings.

"So...good," she cries out at the same moment her weeping walls clench harder around me. "Perfect...God. Don't...stop."

"Never," I snarl. "*Fuck*, Emma. Never!"

"I...I love you."

"And I worship you."

"Ahhhh!" Her scream seems to spark the air as her stretched hands do, the vibrant nets between her fingers incinerating tiny leaves and dust motes drawn by the vortex of our passion. "Ahhhh! Y-Y-You're going to...going to...make me—"

"Damn straight I am." I sound like a marauding beast, but I don't care. Isn't the growl part of the deal for the real superheroes anyway? Along with the cape and the night shadows? Well, I'm not doing a fucking cape, and I don't need shadows when I have this white-gold goddess in my arms, around my body, throughout every corner of my heart. "Give it to me, Emma. My sweet flare. My perfect fire. *Give it to me*, woman. Now!"

Her mouth opens on a wordless scream. Her hands, arched and extended, are surrounded in circles of gold light. Her body trembles like glass being cracked by the sun before gripping me like a supernova star sucking in the atmosphere. I'm as lost as that air, absorbed and absolved, vanished but vanquished, drained of all my light but exploded into so much more at the same time. Pure power. Pure completion. A jettison that starts at the top of my spine, plummets to the middle of my ass, and then rockets out of my cock with heat I've never known before.

I'm a new star.

A reborn cosmos.

"A fucking miracle." I blurt that one out loud for a couple of reasons. First, to validate I'm still capable of speech. But second and most importantly, so I can double its purpose: to give it back to her as the utter worship it's intended to be. I'm only a miracle because this woman's believed it of me—and believed it's always been *in* me. And never, through all of the madness and turbulence and bizarreness that's come along with our incredible, unforgettable love affair, has she ever wavered in that conviction.

And so yeah...the words. Just for her. From the dazed, amazed, miracle-bright depths of my spirit.

Right this second.

On this perfect day.

In this indelible brightness, as I slowly bring her back up and then secure her against the rocks again. As I stretch out, tangling our legs and relocking our stares and meshing the fingers of our free hands. Yeah, despite the sparks that linger between hers, and even after those sweet little fireworks manage to pop and sizzle their way down into my cock, making it instantly jolt back to life again.

As soon as the fucker punches at Emma's thigh, she parts her lips on a cute bell of a giggle. "Is somebody really not done being bolted today?" she quips.

I nuzzle into the delicious dampness between her jacket collar and her neck. "Am I *ever* done when it comes to you, little Flare?"

She grumbles softly. "Hey. What happened to *Bunny*?"

"And *Velvet*?" I prompt.

Her growl turns into a pleased hum. "Oh, good. You didn't forget."

"Never." I nip and bite my way up to the creamy curve of

her ear. "And I never will, either." I trace the edge of the pink crescent with the tip of my tongue. "My velveteen bunny still sits on her rightful throne in my heart and always shall."

During my assertion, she delves her fingers into my hair and massages my scalp with mesmerizing pressure. I struggle to focus on her words instead of that magical touch as she murmurs, "Only right now...we're not in the throne room?"

"Oh, we're still there, baby." I breathe in, concluding this is by far my favorite scent of hers so far. Coastal sage, wild wind, and satisfied woman, with an overtone of smoky sunshine. Jesus, how I want to fuck her again—but if my instincts are right, we've likely been out here longer than we originally planned, which means we're already late for the rest of the day. Normally even that wouldn't deter me, but today *is* today...

Forcing composure to my voice and an imaginary ice bath for my cock, I insist, "I think the throne room just needs a minor expansion."

"Hmmm." Her reply is defined by curiosity. "An expansion? Does Flare need that much space?"

"Hmmm." I repeat it, figuring her sultry vibration is worth reciprocating. "Flare needs to be picky about where her stuff goes."

She sniffs. "She sounds like a world-class bitch."

"Nah." I pull away far enough for her to see my sly smirk. "She's just a budding superheroine."

Her gaze is such a sudden pop of color, I'm too late to stop the new fireworks it sends to my cock. "A superh—" Just as quickly, the explosions melt and become big, gleaming tears. "I'm...I'm getting a badass name now?"

I toss a mock glower. "What? *Bunny* isn't badass?"

"Don't be a teasing bastard, Richards." She smacks my

shoulder but then squeezes out more of those gorgeous tears. And just like that, the boulder of emotion I've been sidestepping is a linebacker of lead, taking my soul down in one rush.

Somehow I manage, muttering around the giant fucker. "Haven't been teasing you, Miss Flare." As I use a thumb to swipe away some of the wetness from her cheek, I turn my stare tender but serious. "*I* think it fits." Holy fuck, probably more than she realizes. "But if you don't like it, we can—"

She cuts me short with a fierce, fast kiss. "I love it." And then another. "And I love *you*." But finishes with another soft sob. "Oh, God. Sorry," she blurts. "I'm a mess today."

My turn to initiate the kiss, though I'm more tender about our contact. "Well, today isn't like a lot of others." I brush her lips again. "In *a lot* of ways."

She laughs through the tears. "You're really right."

"I usually am."

"Nervy beast."

"Brilliant beauty." I take her lips with mine again, decidedly less of a gentleman about it. That's because there's a new message attached to it. *You're so perfect and you're so mine, Emmalina Crist. Especially now. Especially today.*

But as I pull away, I already see another thought tugging at her. Before I can query her about what's important enough for her new train of thought, she rasps, "So...is this what it feels like for you too? All the...heat?" She blushes, clearly having thought of a better word for the feelings.

"You mean all the lust?" I chuff as I fill it in for her. "The skin-stretching, blood-frying, gut-ripping—"

"Okay! Yes! All right!" She relents with a giggle. "The lust. *There*. I said it—though not before *you* made it sound like a freaking horror movie, mister."

"Oh, I had a bunch of stuff prepared about my impressively romantic cock, but this cute little sun flare came along and..." I snicker as soon as she does, ending the mirth with a succession of soft but wet kisses. I seize the opportunity with each contact, lingering longer and longer until I'm finally pushing all the way inside her warm, welcoming cavern and twisting my tongue against hers with passionate adoration. I don't let up until the woman is a moaning, sighing mass of mush beneath me—and admittedly, I'm shaking with need too.

Only when she deliberately pulls away, catching her bottom lip beneath her teeth, do I realize how well the game's been played on me, instead of the other way. But there's barely time to process that and let a confused scowl take over, once the mischievous bunny exposes her ultimate purpose.

"So...now that Flare has an official name and all..."

I almost laugh again. The woman is nothing if not persistent. "She still doesn't get to go public, baby," I rebuke as diplomatically as possible—expecting and receiving the backlash of her pout-twisted lips.

"But we'll have everyone together today, and—"

"Yet another reason why she stays a secret," I counter.

Emma huffs. "But media will hardly be an issue since we're only allowing the two photographers, and we've already asked everyone else to damn near relinquish their cells during the ceremony and reception. We can just ask them adamantly again, and—"

"Baby, even if we do, it won't matter. You know this as well as I do. We've vetted everyone attending or working this thing, but all it takes is one whisper in the wrong ear, or one photo 'accidentally' leaked, and the internet will combust quicker than an Outrider slamming a Wakandan force field." I stroke my fingers into her hairline. "I'm not going to sacrifice your safety in the name of your excitement."

Her pout becomes a glower. "But you gave me a new *name—*"

"And I'll be happy to put it on a T-shirt. Hell, I'll order them for the whole team. But right now, we're the ones controlling this narrative, and that's exactly what I intend to do. Clearly, Faline has advised the Consortium to lie low as she baits us with silence. Either that, or she has purposely kept the full reveal from them. Either way, those fuckers have been abnormally quiet, and I want to enjoy the scenic stillness for as long as we can." I allow my head to swing slowly back and forth. "I guarantee you, that bitch won't let things be peace, love, and Bob Marley forever. When she disrupts again, we all have to be on our A game." After tangling my hands deeper into her hair, I pull her in for a closer embrace, simply cherishing her softness and nearness. "But just for today, I don't want to worry about the fucking game."

Today isn't about the game score.

Because today, I've already won.

And I sure as fuck plan on celebrating that as thoroughly as I can—no matter how tightly she sets her jaw while pulling away. "I refuse to stay on the bench forever, damn it."

"*Emma.*" I emulate her obstinance. "It's only been two and a half months. And *I* trained—"

"For at least six," she injects along with a heavy sigh. "And wished you'd had even more time. I know. I *know.*"

"So you also know the rest of this drill," I counter. "I've also already acknowledged that I didn't have the extra information and resources that you do. Between everything you've learned and applied from Foley and me, you're already eons ahead of where I was at this point."

"And yet you still order me to stay under glass." An accusing gleam enters her gaze. "Glass I'm capable of turning to sand, by the way."

I notch two fingers against my temple. "Duly informed, ma'am." Then let my gaze drop to the ruined hardware that used to hold my pants together. "And damn, was the enlightenment fun."

As I hope, she finally softens. A little. "That's me," she grumbles nonetheless. "Just a barrel of fun. When you're finished, be sure to put me back on the shelf between the Twister set and the Gamerverse Pops."

"*Never.*" I dip my head, forcing her to view the determination in my gaze and feel the surety of my grip. "You're not meant for the shelf, lady." I slide an urgent kiss from one side of her mouth to the other. "Not now. Not ever."

As soon as I lift my lips back up, she demands, "Then when?"

I refrain from kissing her again. At this point, it'd be just a mollification. "Soon." And though it's not, she clearly takes it that way. "I *promise*, baby. Very soon."

She ropes down my gaze with the force of hers. Holds me hostage as she scours my whole face with her probe, which should have me twitching like a worm on a hook but doesn't. Her intensity is my consolation, my support. My shelter. My sanity.

At last, she speaks again. Just a whisper, though the calm assurance of it is enough. "Soon."

"Soon," I repeat, brushing her forehead with my lips. "Just not today, okay?" Then lift away only by an inch, filling my stare with the dark-turquoise magic of hers, and suffuse my senses with her sweet scent all over again. "For today, just let me have Emmalina Paisley. And in return, I'll give her all of Reece Andrew. No Bolt, no Flare, and no world that wants a piece of them." I let a few flyaway strands of her hair sift through my fingertips. "Just us, my beautiful girl."

Slowly, she recaptures the lush pillow of her lip between her teeth. Adorably, she swipes at a windborne leaf lodged in my hair. "Just us, hmmm? Kicking back, cruising through a So-Cal Saturday?"

I break into my finest shit-eating smirk. "Something like that."

"Grabbing some smoothies and watching the longboarders on the waves?"

"Something like *that* too."

"Maybe later on, getting some beers and calamari at Moonshadows and rate the pick-up lines we overhear?"

I chuckle. "*Definitely* something like that."

"Well, I like the sound of all that too, mister." With a slow, sultry smile, she ropes her arms around my neck. "But there's just one eensy-beensy thing we have to do first."

"Killjoy." It's tougher than I expected to make my grin fall. I don't want to scowl at her, even if the expression is completely feigned. "All right, then," I drawl. "What 'eensy-beensy' thing might that be?"

To my combination of delight and dread, she plays along with my reticence. As she lifts her head to caress her lips along mine, she's practically wincing. As we tangle our tongues, her moan is real. And as she finally drags away, she tilts her head with a sweet but tantalizing pout. "We sorta-have-ta show up at our wedding."

"Damn." I bask in the warmth of her giggle as I toss out a

really fake glower. "Is that today?"

She drops the pout for a nonchalant shrug. "Hey, if you want to go get beers instead..."

I cut her off with a hard and deep kiss, adding enough ruthless tongue to make sure she knows I'm not kidding around this time. Several minutes later, once I relent and release her again, I capture her gaze once more. "We may be doing this late, but we're doing it, woman." As I vow it, even the sun that's lent her its power seems to agree, turning a deeper shade of gold in her hair and in the tips of her eyelashes. "I can't wait another day to truly make you mine."

She cocks her head to the other side. "And to truly become *mine*?"

Emotion suffuses my chest. Pure light invades my senses. The answer I give her for that is the easiest sentence I've ever spoken in my life.

"That happened a long damn time ago, baby."

CHAPTER THREE

EMMA

About a mile after turning his M8 off Mulholland Highway and onto a private road twisting through rolling citrus groves and flourishing vineyards, Reece eases the car into a parking space next to a stunning two-story ranch house. Of course, the place is rich with California touches—the indigenous succulents in the planters, the white paint accents along the rails, the stylish flatstone pavers comprising the walkways—but it still feels like a world apart from LA, and even the ridge. In short, exactly what we were seeking. A place that feels like a new land for the start of our new life together...

It's going to be a perfect day.

The conclusion fills me with so much joy, I bounce out of the car and into Reece's arms before he can make it all the way over to open my door. He rumbles out a laugh as I pepper his jaw with joyous kisses, uncaring that we look like the ending of the schmaltziest romantic comedy ever made. God, what I wouldn't give for a day filled with nothing but rom-com hijinks.

"Fashionably late, hmmmm? Well, aren't you two right on trend?"

With my arms still around the burnished cords of my man's neck, I whip my gaze around toward the figure who's appeared on the house's sprawling side porch. "Well, hello to you too, Princess Purple Pants."

Lydia hurls a mock glower. "For that, you don't get even an obligatory *Congratulations*." Still, she underlines that with a little laugh. I'm not sure how to interpret the sound. It's a toss-up between her you're-so-busted grin and her you're-so-screwed drawl. Either way, I shake off the discomfort as soon as she inadvertently brings it. Nearly as fast, I attempt to scoop out the rest of the rock bits from my hair. But do I really expect to have more success with the task than I did during the drive over from the dam?

Not that I claim, or even want, the right to complain. I was the one who ordered Reece to keep the top down as we sped here. California afternoons like this were why he paid to have the M8 customized in the first place. The sunlight is the color of spun gold, swathed across the sprawling hills and vineyards in a stunning visual tapestry. The air is spiced with a little ocean, a little eucalyptus, and a lot of star jasmine. If I lean over, I can peek at the catering staff, their shirtsleeves rolled up as they set the tables for our reception.

Our reception.

Oh, God.

For some crazy reason, though we've already been here a few times before to solidify the arrangements, the truth of this moment starts hitting me in full force. Yes, right here. Yes, right now. Maybe it was why I begged Reece to take me out for training instead of a quiet lunch today. Why I'd known if we sat in a restaurant for a few hours, I'd be climbing the walls with restlessness. Why I'd gone on about how the Consortium likely isn't taking the day off, so why should we? That the world isn't going to stop just because of one wedding...

Ohhhhh, holy hell.

Our wedding.

Reece's deep laughter jerks me back to the moment. Though it still feels like I'm experiencing everything through a weird layer of gauze, the brilliance of his full smile is more dazzling than the crisp afternoon sunlight. A miracle. That's simply what the man is. A magnificent miracle.

"...all good, anyhow." The last part of his statement to 'Dia actually penetrates my fuzzy brain. "Because at this point, *congratulations* would just be premature. But you can have a hug for the sweet thoughts, anyhow."

"Ohhhh no, you don't." Lydia juts out both arms, warding him and his lingering mud clumps away from her swishy rose-gold gown, its soft-pink hues matched by the tiny flowers that have been braided into her hair. "I love you, brother, but not whatever you've been rolling around in."

"Whatever, *sister*." Reece cracks a new grin, already showing how much he enjoys getting to use the word. "Bet I can find someone around here who doesn't mind *rolling around* with me a bit."

"Oh, blergh! Noooo, not now!"

But my sister's protest isn't quick enough on the mark. All too swiftly, Reece is boldly scooping a hand around mine and then tugging me close. And then closer still as he slides his mouth down over mine. And in the space of one second gives back the orbit for my sun and the ground wire for all of my electrons. *This. Here.* The connection of our energies, bound by the simple contact of our skin, sizzling every drop of my blood but stabilizing every edge of my composure. He's my center. My reason. My destiny. My *more*.

My life...

And, so blissfully soon, my husband.

An assurance that rings through me with such surety, I think nothing of the wicked laugh I get to toss 'Dia's way as soon as the man lets me have some room to breathe. In return, my sister teeter-totters her head, ensuring the twilight wind turns her strawberry-blond waves into a curly halo around her impish smirk. "Go ahead, baby girl. Have your gloat now. I'm already popping the popcorn to watch when the tables are turned—especially because it's damn clear why the two of you are this late."

I blush furiously. Even Reece has the grace to color, if only for three seconds. It's hard to tell because his skin is so beautifully burnished by our hours in the canyon, but Lydia nonetheless preens in her triumph.

"I just need to know how the hell you two pulled off this role reversal thing," she charges, folding her arms—a good thing, allowing me to mirror the stance.

"Excuse me?" I volley.

"Role reversal *huh*?" Reece blurts at the same time.

"You heard me," Lydia rebuts. "Now come on, give it up. How is it that your maid of honor and best man have been hard-up, moony-eyed, and trapped at opposite ends of this place for three hours, while you two have been out—errrmmm..." Her stare narrows as she reaches up, pulling on a hock of my hair before gingerly extracting a small bit of something from it. "Doing whatever it took to get freaking bird feathers in your hair." She goes on, even as I snatch the tiny feathers from her, "And what's this schmutz all over your shoulder? Cement residue?"

I blush even deeper before deadpanning, "I could tell you, but then I'd have to kill you."

Reece follows my quip by barking out a laugh. "You should

see the pants we had to ditch."

"*Not* helping," I mutter.

"See?" Lydia jabs one pointer finger at him. "I *told* you keeping spare costumes in the cars was a good idea!"

He stiffens. "Not fucking *costumes*."

"And still not helping, kids," I cut in. "*Either* of you." Though both of them clearly don't buy a word. Honestly, I don't either. My heart has wrapped around the truth of all this along with my mind, so even if the ranch's exotic animals got out of their pens and decided to have a fun time at the reception for themselves, I'd be a happy loon as long as they left the minister standing for the ceremony. However it happens, if I can leave this place as Mrs. Reece Richards, there's nothing *anyone* can do to yuck my yums today.

"Emmalina. Paisley."

Not even Lauren Crist appearing on the back porch and spewing my name as if it's become *Beetlejuice,* only without the magical help. Or maybe *with* it. They summoned that guy because he was good at scaring everyone away, right?

Only that's not right either, because I'm *not* scared. Oh, everything's here that I should be dreading—that I *have* been anxious of since we left the dam—but suddenly, Mother's disapproval and disappointment aren't the duality of disaster that had me anxiously checking the time and psyching myself into my special dealing-with-Lauren Zen space.

"Hello, Mother." And just like that, the Zen is with me. No, it's not—because I suddenly realize I don't need it. I'm able to look at my mother now with a glow of real love, not mixed up with a need for her approval. The force of it inundates me, feeling a lot like those critical moments in the lab back at the ridge, when Fersh and Alex aimed the force of the sun at me and filled me with new power. Except that this doesn't hurt as much—unless I count all the tangled-up rocks I keep trying to finger-comb out of my hair. "Wow. You look fantastic."

So there's usually not a day when she doesn't, but I can tell she's taken extra care to make sure all the wrinkles have been tamed and all the hair is in place. She's wearing an elegant sheath from her favorite designer, St. John, with a deep V-neck and cap sleeves, in a shade slightly darker than Lydia's dress. In short, it's a look designed to make everyone question how she can possibly be the *mother* of the bride—and "everyone" is such an eye-popping list. To her perception, and probably a lot of the outside world's, it's close to a hundred of LA's and Hollywood's A-Listers—but to Reece and me, they're people like us. Working hard at our jobs every day, though we just happen to be doing it very much in the public eye.

"She's right, Mom." Lydia steps back, admiring her from head to toe. "You're stunning."

Mother discernibly mellows. The glow around her head, visible only by me, softens from crimson to pink. I wonder if she's ever been at a true contented gold, even as the color switches back and she returns to her previous business of scrunching her nose and clearing her throat. "Well, I'm not the one getting married." It seems to be her motivator for forcing her sights back to me—though clearly, she questions herself for doing so. If her rough huff doesn't convey the point, the double eyeballs to the back of her head do the trick. "Oh, *Emma*. For the love of—are you pulling *rocks* out of your hair?"

For reasons beyond my control—and apparently, my sanity—I spurt out a laugh. "Errrmmm, seems so." I peer at the brown bit between my fingers. "Though this one looks like a twig...of sorts. Or chipped bark? Or shredded rust?"

Mother escalates the huff to an outraged choke. "Now you're just being lippy."

Reece ducks his head until a bunch of hair falls over his forehead and then mutters, "And here I thought it was a *good* thing when your lips get involved."

Thank God my answering snicker gets swallowed by the next stage of Mother's rant. "You do realize that your wedding invitations say six o'clock, right? *Six o'clock*, Emma—as in, twenty minutes from now. That means no sleek up-do and whatever magic Corinne can pull together with your makeup. She's the best there is, but she's still not a miracle worker. And please, please, *please* tell me you remembered to pick up the roses from Muguet. They called at six this morning to confirm they received the custom order from Holland, and they were clear that the flower food in the vials had to be—"

She cuts herself off with a huff, taking a defined turn toward horror as soon as I grimace and jab a hand through my hair—revealing I've already chipped most of my nail polish. Which was—surprise, surprise—as specialized a project as the bouquets.

"Oh, Emmalina Paisley."

Though with that, she unwittingly gives Reece the biggest chance he's ever had to be my true superhero.

"Lauren. Please. All of this is on me." As he moves forward with decisive steps that scream *I am Alpha*, he steals back one of my hands—and every shred of my libido. "I didn't see my girl all day yesterday"—thanks to the last-minute spa and night club thing Mother insisted on planning as my bachelorette party—"and I was feeling a little...needful."

His sultry murmur draws me in and mesmerizes me to the point of stupid—almost making me forget that his "need" was practical as much as lustful. Not only did we sneak in the extra training session, but our travel time out to the dam gave him a chance to fill me in on Alex and Fershan's reconnaissance trip to the seaside villa in Monterey he's picked out for our honeymoon getaway.

Addendum: the absolutely *perfect* place he's picked out. I fell in love with the villa upon seeing pictures of the place, which sits right on the shoreline with its relaxed, modern lines. The décor is a blend of creamy modern luxury with rustic driftwood accents and has a huge king bed in the master that I *already* have wicked plans for.

Yes...five days' worth of plans.

Yes, worthy of the naughtiest honeymoon memories.

Yes, worthy of the most incredible man who ever zapped his way into my life, charmed his way into my heart, and loved his way into my soul.

Now knowing that the guys have installed additional security around its perimeter, identical to the system we've got in place out at the ridge, I'm damn ready to be done with the wedding foof-fest and move on to the part of the adventure that really matters. Pampering my superhero with all the wanton, wicked, supersized sexiness he can possibly handle.

Yesssss...

But somehow, despite how ready my Zeus looks for exactly that, I keep my outward demeanor on the dignified side of things. Yes, even as I manage to murmur, "Errrmm, yes. Needful..."

And just like that, he and I are back to our hottest, steamiest interpretation of the word. But he's going for it, and so am I. Greedily. Shamelessly. Openly basking in his husky thunder voice, his hot lightning gaze, and his fire-in-the-rain touch, which flows through my veins like liquid gold.

I swallow hard, fighting to keep its sweltering glow from bursting out of every pore in my body. While I hate him for the torment, I've never loved him more for adding "needful" to my favorite words list. It's right up there now, along with classics such as *macaron, alphabet, riverboat*, and an oldie but goodie, *golf course.*

"Oh, my." Mother's mutter jolts us back to the present—though as always, Reece doesn't give away a single tell about the tripled heartrate I feel in the pulse at his inner wrist. The man, still breathtakingly suave even in his leathers and a faded Eagles T-shirt, simply sweeps my knuckles up to his lips before throwing his devastating stare at Mother.

"Goodness is certainly right," he says. "And exactly what you've given me in this perfect piece of the sun."

If there's anything left of my mother's ire—as well as my vow not to talk him into a detour at the coat closet before Corinne gets her hands on me—he quashes it by circling those gorgeous grays back on me, turning my hand over, and kissing the center of my palm.

"Oh, *my*," Mother reiterates.

"Gag me with a takeout spork," Lydia mutters.

"Well, here comes the bride at last!" A new voice breaks in—though as we all look to the petite blonde with the trendy glasses, cigarette capris, and statement heels, Reece leans over and tucks me close, as if bidding me an affectionate goodbye.

Instead, the cocky hunk murmurs for my ears alone, "Already handled, Miss Corinne. Times three."

I giggle, glad for the chance to be distracted by Corinne's explanation about the "archaic" tradition of forbidding a groom to see his bride before doing the I-Dos. Maybe the woman's just glad that Reece has seen what she has to work with right now, because anything from my frazzled state will likely be an improvement. And though I should care about that too, I just don't. I'd spout all my lines here and now in the driveway if that's what it would take to keep Reece Andrew Richards looking at me like this for the rest of our days—however many fate will bless us with, considering the crazy existence she's chosen for us.

But I don't want *any* other existence. I don't want any other *man*.

I want *him*.

His energy, pure and powerful. His smile, steady and sure. And his gaze, taking me in like I really am the sun upon which his existence rises and sets.

Because he sure as hell is mine.

REECE

The sun has just disappeared beyond the ranch's lush vineyard hills—or so everyone here thinks, especially as the strains of "I Will Follow You Into the Dark" fill the air.

They all don't know what I do.

That the sun has just appeared.

Right here.

Holy God. Right here.

Walking down the small path between the capacity crowd gathered on this windswept hilltop, maybe blushing because of their admiring sighs, though I notice nothing like that—because I'm blinded by her. Drenched in the perfect, shining splendor of her. Amazed and astounded, humbled and hollowed, lost but then located again...right where I should be.

She and her father complete the journey up the aisle. I tell myself to breathe in order to stay standing. She turns her face up and blows me away with the light in her eyes. I blink with desperate force, attempting to clear the blur out of my own.

What the hell?

The blur?

Why *is* everything so blurry?

Well, fuck.

And yet, *fuck it all.*

It's my goddamned wedding day, and if there was ever a moment to find out if lightning blood mixes with a saltwater stream, this is it. I refuse to turn a drop of this shit off. Today, there are no disguises. No alter-egos. No pretending for the masses. I'm just a flesh-and-blood man promising myself to the woman of my dreams. The person who's turned my existence into a life. The human who's made *my* humanity possible.

Even so, I stuff the emotion down long enough to commit all of this to memory. Though I'm conscious of the two photographers flitting around the periphery of the ceremony—Emma and I allowed *one* magazine to record the day, in exchange for a generous donation to the Richards Reaches Out program—they can't capture all of this beauty the way my soul can. The way my heart *needs* to.

They can't see the adoring lights glittering in her eyes, like stars turned into sapphires.

They'll never capture the poetry of her hair flirting with the white roses embedded into her loose up-do or how my fingers already ache to know the ecstasy of yanking free the loose braids piled atop her head.

They'll never interpret my primal satisfaction as I gaze down her form, encased in a white dress that could probably be called Bohemian, especially with her adorable wedding Keds peeking from beneath the lacy hem. The whole thing is made out of that same relaxed lace, meaning I'm already thinking about what she's wearing—or not—underneath it.

I'm filled with even more caveman possessiveness when observing the only "bling" about the ensemble is her tanzanite engagement ring, moved to her right hand so her wedding band can go on her left, and the matching earrings that I bought her back on July fifth. We were beat that day, drained from the fallout, emotional and physical, from what we'd just endured at the hands of Faline Garand. Still, I dragged Emma to my jewelry guy in Beverly Hills, declaring we needed to commemorate her first day as a full-fledged electric mutant superheroine. But the truth was, I was just damn glad to have her alive. To be alive with her. And to prove it.

And right here and now, before we even get to the out-loud parts of all this, I stare into her stunning blues and swear to her, with every corner of my spirit and fiber of my heart, that our *alive* will always be my prime directive, my guiding light, my soul's compass, my core command. I make that promise knowing that we haven't seen the last of Faline yet—and that when the bitch does come to collect her pint of payback blood, it sure as hell won't be Emma's that gets spilled.

But today isn't for wasting a scrap of thought on that nasty bitch.

Today is the day I celebrate taking Emmalina Paisley Crist as my true mate. My soul's other side. My lifelong partner. My resplendent, incandescent bride.

My bride.

They're the only words that'll stay put in my mind, though I don't miss a single prompt from the minister and know—and *know*—that I mean every word that I speak, vow, and promise to her. But I don't need any of them plastered in my brain because they're already ingrained in my heart. Have been since the moment we confessed our love to each other.

No. Before that.

I've loved her, honored her, cherished her, and even held her for forever. Since before my soul knew who she was. Since the days, deep inside my cell at the Source, I didn't think I had—or deserved—a soul anymore. When fate proved me wrong and I had to believe in my soul because there was nothing else to cling to, she was there, as well. I didn't have her name yet, but she sure as hell was. In that darkness and torture, she was my will to survive, my perseverance to live, and my ability to face every day, even when I wasn't sure when one day ended and another began.

After I escaped, she turned into something else again. The beauty I began to notice in every sunrise and sunset. The hunger, tiny at first but growing every day, to make my freedom matter. To believe in the force of good again and the role I could play in that. And yes, she was that force inside me, still so intangible yet powerful, that made me strive to be better.

To believe I could be better.

She's the reason I keep thinking it now.

She's the reason for so much.

And yes, she's really here...the most stunning sight I've ever seen...agreeing to be mine forever. My woman. My reason. My bride.

My *more*.

And just like that...my wife.

I don't believe it.

But I've never been more ready to believe.

Even as the minister speaks the words.

Mr. and Mrs. Reece Richards.

And even as I let her grab at my jaw, pulling me down to her for the kiss that seals the deal. Even as I remind my heart to keep beating as a swell of cheers rises around us, confirming this is really happening. Even as I remind myself nothing's really changed, but everything has.

She's mine, before God and man and the whole fucking cosmos.

There's another astounding recognition that hits me along with that one. For the first time in over two years, I'm not agonizingly aware of every lightning zap in my blood and every electron jolt in my pores.

For right now, for just this moment, they've all been edged out.

By the light of pure happiness.

EMMA

I didn't believe the man could make me any happier, but the superhero-who-will-not-be-named-today *is* all about accomplishing the impossible.

And holy shit, how he looks ready to do so.

After our vows—the short, sweet version of the traditional stuff, because "using our words" this time would have resulted in more tears than what we *did* shed, as well as insulin shots for all our guests—he leads me across the grass, past the casual seating areas between the appetizer and drinks stations, through the sea of banquet tables with their fragrant centerpieces, and to the middle of the dance floor.

Every step of the way, I'm his willing follower.

Every moment of every minute, I order myself to savor every last detail.

The balmy redolence of the early evening air. The glow of the lights as they flicker to life across the party area, coming from mismatched hanging lanterns. The more romantic glow from the vintage chandelier suspended over the dance floor, its golden tones playing with the dark waves on Reece's head and the gorgeous stubble defining his jawline. The muted light becoming a perfect contrast for the silver currents in his gaze, as he turns and twirls me up against his formidable body, trapping me in the harbor of his steel arms.

And yes...I'm a willing captive, as well.

And am willing to bet I'm the envy of half the crowd here, women *and* men, eyeing my husband with the same open desire that must be plastered on my face. Like any of us can hold it back. I mean, *look* at him. Has a dove-gray tux been worn with more command by any other male? Has any pair of proud shoulders filled out the jacket better, or has any face of noble lines looked so beautiful in contrast to that regal fabric? Has any stance been so broad and confident and alluring, it's just as easy to imagine him in a knight's livery, ready to sweep his ladylove into a seductive dance in front of their whole court?

No. Not a knight.

A king.

Ready to start achieving the impossible.

And kicking off the effort with one hell of an astounding explosion.

As I watch the band take the stage—led by a figure I recognize only because I've watched his videos and purchased all his soaring, romantic music. Garrett Borns, known to the world as alt rock maestro BØRNS, is actually standing ten feet in front of my gawking face!

But Reece isn't gawking. Of course not. Even as the singer throws a friendly wave toward my husband, Reece is the epitome of confident elegance, knowing damn well what kind of an enormous surprise he's just pulled off for me. His full lips spread in a huge grin as the singer cues the band into a dreamy, slow remake of his hit "Electric Love"—and my gawk becomes full-fledged tears of joy. But before I can recover from *that* stunner, Reece scoots back by a few inches, catching his lower lip beneath his teeth, as I feel another presence behind me. I turn at the same moment that Lydia giggles, having secured a clasp at the nape of my neck. There's no need to follow any instinct in figuring out what she's done, since the bright diamond pendant at the hollow of my throat does the job just fine.

And just like that, I'm back to a gawk. And a sputter. And a gasp. And hardly daring to run my fingertips over the stunning tanzanite pendant lying against my skin, the round stone set in a dozen dazzling diamonds—fashioned into the shape of an eye-catching lightning bolt.

"R-Reece?" I finally manage as the song about louder thunder and lightning in a bottle becomes our swirling, enchanting, completely perfect song for our first dance as man and wife.

Man and wife.

It's so much. Almost too much.

Yet it's all I'll ever need.

I jerk my sights back up to my husband, needing to tell him exactly that. But while the words are so full in my heart, they swell my tongue past capacity. How on earth can I really express how he moves me, fills me, enthralls me, completes me? And how I'd be struggling to formulate the exact same words, even if this was all just us in the middle of a field, dancing to cricket song?

"What can I do for you, Mrs. Richards?" His soft query reins my musings back in. All too quickly, the teasing glints in his eyes become somber again. "Everything okay?" He dips his head to look me more fully in the eyes. "You happy, Velvet?"

I burst with a sharp, fast laugh. Can't be helped. The electric-eyed rogue already knows the answer to that one. Or does he? His gaze, growing more intense, accompanies the more serious angles of his jaw. He's actually...studying me. But is he doubting I'm anything *but* happy?

I lift a hand to firmly frame the side of his incredible face. "Happy is just the start of this, Mr. Richards," I whisper. "Just the start of *us*."

He drifts his eyes shut. Releases a long breath, once more making me wish we weren't in the middle of a dance floor with a hundred pairs of eyes and a couple of camera lenses trained on us. "I'm so damn glad to hear that, Mrs. Richards."

I rock my head back. Past the lights over the dance floor, the stars seem to dance against the darkened sky. I'm certain they're just as curious about the energy in the galaxy tonight. The fire of a love as bright as a lightning bolt thrown into the sun.

Now doesn't *that* sound like fun...

But as I linger my gaze upward another moment, preoccupied with devious notions about sneaking my husband away from our own wedding celebration before dinner even drops, my groom's dance floor game is dealt its first cut. Reece only makes our separation worse by being so damn debonair about handing me off to my father. But I can be as cool about this as he can, and I prove it by smiling at Father as the evening's permanent band takes over for BØRNS and his guys. They start a more traditional R&B song, and I'm glad for the transition. I need the few moments to get my polite smile correctly plastered on.

I love my dad. I always will. That doesn't mean I know what to say to him in a one-on-one situation, which we haven't had since my fourth-grade father-daughter dance. The theme was *Star Wars*, and we'd won the costume contest with our Leia and Obi-Wan ensembles. Even Mother and 'Dia had helped with parts of our outfits. Those had been happy times, when the money was new and we were all simply happy we didn't have to scrape by between paychecks anymore. The days before the flashy cars and the flashier country club memberships— when "family night" meant we got together and just played the "fancy" sports on the PlayStation.

I push the memories away but not fast enough so Dad doesn't catch my wistful expression.

"Guess we're a little better cleaned up than our Rebel Alliance days, eh?"

Okay, so someone was already *on* the wistfulness bandwagon—and has given me a leg up to join him.

"You tidy up nicely, Obi-Wan." I'm relieved there's real affection in the words, as well as my adjoining smile. While our relationship is never going to be the kind of stuff for a sappy sitcom and the man has pulled some douche moves over the years, he's still my dad. The place in my heart with his name and face on it hasn't, nor ever will, change. Besides, I'm speaking the truth. He's dashing tonight, fitted in a trendy navy suit with a pocket square and tie that match Mother's dress. His blond hair, edged with a little gray in front of his ears, is cut in what I call a classic Daniel Craig, with just enough of a roguish mess on top.

"Well, you've done more than clean up, little Leia." Though he adds a chuckle, the mirth dies fast. His new earnestness makes me mushy and scared at the same time, with the requisite lump in my throat. I really don't know *this* Todd Crist. Sharp Professional Todd? Got that one. Stern Homework Dictator Todd? Checked that box a *lot* of times. Newport Beach Society Party Todd? Check, check, and check. But Softy Daddy Todd?

Out with it, buster. What the hell have you done with the real guy?

"My God, Emmalina. You have just become something else." And apparently, he's become a smoker too—or has succumbed to the gruff growl of one. "No. Some*one* else." He clears his throat as a distinct sheen develops over his blue eyes. "Someone I'm so damn proud of."

"Dad." I don't withhold the soft protest from my voice. "*Daddy*. Really, it's okay. You don't have to—"

"I know that, damn it." He dances at the edge of asshole this time though issues a quick apology with the pressure of his hold. I grant it with another tight smile. He's uncomfortable but forcing himself to deal with the shit—for me. "I wish I could make this poetic for you, Lina-Bina." The tender love has returned to his face, adding to the tenderness of his sweet gift to me—the treasure of this moment. His exclusive endearment for me is better than poetry, turning on a renewed faucet behind my eyes. "But plainly put, you've just always been our little boundary buster." He laughs again, slowly shaking his head. "Your mother and I should've taken the hint from the moment you wedged both arms *and* legs between the slats on your crib, wailing until we let you out."

I dip my head, making an attempt to "cry down." Sloshing Corinne's handiwork any further might warrant the little woman striding out here to fix it. She'd never attempt such a thing with Reece in the vicinity, but he's taking a second to pose for some "guys at the reception" shots with Sawyer, Scott Eastwood, and Tom Hardy. The move also enables me to answer Dad in a halfway coherent tone. "And I thought you were going to go straight for the room remodeling story."

"Which time?" Dad counters with a snicker. "When you wanted to do a blacklight *tromp l'oeil* using Sharpie highlighters and nail polish, or when you and 'Dia thought it'd be cool to build secret tunnels to each other's room?"

"And we thought there'd be no way you and Mother would hear us pounding on the walls."

He spurts out a laugh. "At *midnight*."

I flash my teeth, grimacing apologetically. "You remember that part too?"

"Ohhh, I really didn't want to punish you two for that."

I toss a quick shrug. "You were probably wise to."

His gaze narrows. "You don't mean that for a second."

"Of course I do!"

"You didn't understand at the time. You wanted to be closer to your sister, and you couldn't understand why things like support beams and drywall should get in the way."

Self-consciously, I drag some windblown hairs out of my face. "I was a brat."

"No. You were a trailblazer." Dad nudges a finger beneath my chin. "You always were, and you always will be, Emma." A line of conviction takes over his lips. "You always *needed* to be."

A heavy breath escapes me. I lunge my gaze up into his. "You're...you're serious, aren't you?"

"As the harbor sea lions when a kid loses his chili dog in the drink." He punctuates with his devilish smirk as I giggle from his reference to the shameless Newport Beach sea lions. But he erases the grin once he continues. "You've always gone after your goals and followed the truth of your heart with everything you are, rules and expectations be damned." Despite the pride in his voice, his lips twist into a strange grimace. As I send back a quizzical gape, he explains. "Had either your mother *or* I been more like that, we probably wouldn't have ended up in a marriage defined by all that bullshit—and we wouldn't have chafed against all of it in the stupid ways that we did."

His energy seems to close in on itself, growing quietly contemplative, though his intent stare doesn't waver. Just a few feet away, my husband finishes his horseplay with the "guys" and clearly contemplates a cut back in on our dance. Still, Dad utters, "*Emma*. Listen to me." His face tightens until his jaw is a pair of framing squares embedded below his skin. "I'm not proud of a lot of things I've done...things that I know have hurt you and 'Dia. But damn it, Lina, there's *nothing* I'm *more* proud of than the stunning women you and your sister have become." His lips part just enough so I can see the adamant grit of his teeth. Their brilliance is surpassed only by the fierce gleam in his eyes. "Nothing—*nothing*—will ever change that, either. You got that, Mrs. Richards?"

I swallow hard. My throat feels packed in painful cotton, but I don't care. I may be incapable of words, but I know my eager hug tells him everything he needs to know. That I understand how rough it must have been to give me his honesty—about everything—but because of it all, I also believe him a hundred percent about his pride in me.

And yes...his love for me.

Reece has at last strode back over, bringing his strength back to my immediate atmosphere at the perfect moment. I'm positive his ability to decipher every corner of my thoughts will never stop being a miracle.

"Todd." He nods politely. "Mind if I'm a selfish bastard and cut back in?"

Dad returns the nod. "Not at all. You certainly can't be blamed." He drenches me in the warmth of one more long gaze before pulling me close and pressing a fervent kiss to my cheek. "I love you, little bean."

"I know."

And this time, I really do—to the point that the wad in my throat loosens and becomes a torrent of mush.

"Tell me those are happy tears, Velvet," my husband says in a ferocious growl disguised as a devastating smile, "or those photographers are going to get a juicy scoop on the Heir with the Hair kicking his father in-law's ass out the door of his wedding reception."

Knowing it's not the wisest reaction, I laugh. For all the man's adamancy about not letting Bolt bleed through into all this, my gorgeous ox of a husband has just given the guy a golden pass in. I only wish the result wasn't so damn sexy— and timed perfectly to the band starting a soulful rendition of Enrique Iglesias's "Hero." As the romantic melody swirls around us, I softly scratch my fingertips against Reece's jaw. "Nothing but happy tears, my love." I sigh deeply. "As a matter of fact, I might have just gotten one of the best wedding gifts of the day."

It feels good to mean every word of that—but also to know that I don't have to explain everything behind it. Reece knows and accepts the dirty family details that had fed into my dysfunctions, just as I know all of his. We see each other; we *get* each other. We might have rebelled at different times and questioned the confines of our worlds in different ways, but the paths ultimately led us to the same place.

Seeking more. Needing more.

And finally finding it in each other.

A truth we've crystallized into the completion of now.

No. Not a completion.

A commencement.

Just the beginning of our *more*...

As demonstrated by the brand-new sparks in my man's silvery stare.

And by *new*, I mean...

Wow.

It's him but it's not him, which would be freaky if *he* didn't look so stunned, as well. But his shock is more a birthday surprise look instead of a holy-shit-there's-a-monster-inside-me stare. As he yanks my body a little closer to his, with his scrutiny getting heavy and his full lips parting, I sense he's ready to enlighten us both about the whole thing.

"One of the best, hmmm?" Reece husks it so close, his heated breath fans my forehead—and the core of my body grows hotter from the proximity of his, attempting to punch through the layers of his tux and my lace. "But not *the* best."

More.

I tilt my head back to see all of his beautiful features. To bask in the full force of his laser-focused adoration. To let go as my senses ring with the intensity of him, acknowledging his presence at the powerful primordial level to which his senses have summoned mine.

At last, I smile. Drench him in the answering flow of my

unhindered adoration.

How he moves me. How he utterly, brazenly bolts me.

"No," I finally state with husky ferocity. "No...that's definitely not *the* best."

At first, Reece just gives me a savoring rumble from the middle of his chest. As I visibly shiver, he smiles like the dark wildcat that matches the sound. He presses on the small of my back to mold our bodies together with equally sinuous intent. No, the man did *sinuous* the *first* time we danced. He's moved on to other words, which look ready to dance across his lips as he dips his head lower, whisking my cheek with the barest brush of his perfect stubble...and the determined cadence of his hungry breaths.

"Want to know what *my* best gift of the day would be?"

Against my will, a tiny groan breaks free. Thank God I can muffle the sound with the bulk of his shoulder. "You mean you're not going to make me beg nicely for it?"

He chuffs out a laugh. "Not this time." And then gives me another thick breath, flowing over the bottom of my ear as he adds, "Because I want it too damn much."

The cotton's back in my throat. Twice as dense as before. No way will it allow any sound past the barrier, so I angle back enough to let Reece watch me try to gulp around it—while making my eyes cry out with my reply. *Tell me. Please, oh please. Tell me!*

He secures my stare with the iron-bright shackles of his. Captivates my attention with the meaningful, sensual slide of his lips. "The best gift of my day will be seeing you in your new wedding jewelry...and nothing else."

CHAPTER FOUR

REECE

To the day I fucking die, I'll never forget a single detail of how she answers my ballsy proposition.

That sweet, aroused flush on her high cheekbones. That wild, hard pulse at the bottom of her neck.

"I'll leave first. Wait a few minutes; make sure everyone's settled with getting dinner. Then meet me on the back porch of the main house."

And her girl balls—easily three times the size as my glowing ones.

And yeah, I'm pretty damn sure they *are* glowing by the time I get to the back porch, less than fifteen minutes after her cute little excuse about needing to fix her mascara, followed by her dash off into the house—

Landing her...*where*?

Because here I am, skulking across the back porch, behaving like a crasher at my own damn wedding—

With no bride in sight.

I jab a hand into one of my tux pockets but come up empty. "Damn it." And grumble that out as soon as I realize where I purposely left my phone: on the head table, being guarded by Foley, who needed only one glance to interpret how Emma and I plan on spending the dinner hour. He sent me on my way with a wolfish smirk before turning back toward Lydia, engrossing himself in stealing all the candied walnuts from her salad.

I've got a different kind of candy on my mind right now.

The only human on earth who can fully satiate my sweet tooth.

With the spun cream of her skin beneath my roaming tongue. With the succulent strawberries of her breasts filling my mouth. With the flood of sunshine syrup from between her thighs, pouring down my throat as she pleads my name over and over again...

Annnnd now I'm officially obsessed.

Is there any other way to be, when a woman's exposed her mighty lady balls and then all but ordered her husband to come and stroke them?

Yep. Obsessed.

Soon. Very soon.

Dear fuck, I can only hope.

I work my lips against each other, fighting the fucking need for her. For her skin, creamy as coconut. And her pussy, delicious as honey. And now, how I can even smell her out here. Her hair, full of wind. Her essence, full of sunshine.

"I'm not imagining you." I deliberately say it aloud, as if doing so will make it true. "Damn it, Emmalina. I'm not—"

"No. You're not."

Oh, thank fuck.

I sure as hell didn't imagine that, either. I just need to find the damn woman now. To get to the perfect lips belonging to that velvety voice. And preferably, the rest of what's attached to that temptress.

Temptress...

I had to go and pluck that one out of the lexicon, didn't I?

I had to seriously go and grab the perfect word for what my woman has become, as she peeks out from the draping green leaves of the weeping willow below and wiggles a quick but coy wave at me.

With her hair completely down.

With her shoulders totally naked.

With her beauty dropping my jaw. Beckoning me like a goddamned lighthouse from the sea of that tree. Its branches flow on the wind like waves, its layers rolling into and atop each other.

"Emma...lina?"

She laughs. Oh, *fuck*. Definitely a temptress.

"Come here." When I'm stuck in place, riveted to the spot like a damn virgin kid, she stamps her foot.

Stamps her *foot*.

"Oh *God*, Reece. Would you come *here* before I faint in my own sweat just from *looking* at you?"

Never, in my entire existence, have I been giddier about a female ordering me around—or about the fact that said female grabs me by the neurons in my mind as well as the veins in my balls as I step into the shadows beyond the branches, where she's standing next to a cute little swing dangling from the tree.

At the moment, that's all fine by me.

"Oh, dear fuck." The exclamation's as mindless as the rest of me, a primal reaction to the sight before me. My sun flare fairy, clad only in her sparkly Keds, necklace, and wedding ring, has moved past the realm of temptress. She's a damn angel now. A glorious, naked messenger from the stars. A miracle with the sky in her eyes and the sway of the sea in her step...

My miracle.

Mine.

Mine.

A glance to the diamond band on her left hand is a piece of glorious proof—but no sight punches the surety deeper into me than my surveillance across her face, where she's stripped away her polite bride's smile along with every stitch of her dress. Oh, she's still smiling, but this is a radiance saved just for me today...an ebullience for my eyes only.

A gift for me alone to unwrap.

"Christ."

A present I'm suddenly, stupidly, overwhelmed about accepting. That hits me so hard I crumple to my knees and drop my head. That continues to use my mind for its drumming practice, pounding incoherent rhythms, scattering my senses like grains of rice atop the drum skins. She re-centers me by moving close, and then closer still, until she's wrapped one leg against my bowed back and encircled my head with her soft, loving hands. Instantly, the energy waves pulse between us and then through us. At once, I feel the hot, surging desperation of her need for me.

Holy hell.

I'm the luckiest man alive.

And yet here I am, letting myself be crippled by that comprehension. Fucking the shit out of this incredible moment—and not in any of the right ways—by getting lost in my internal war instead of ordering the skirmish to stand down so I can fully focus on this amazing woman.

She feels my conflict too. Her loosening hold is evidence as she drenches me with the confused turquoise storms in her eyes. And then asks, in the sexy grate that flips my nerve endings inside out, "Husband? What is it?"

Husband.

As much I savor her blatant pleasure in getting to finally speak it, all I can do is drop to my knees and press my head into the soft refuge of her stomach, splaying my fingers along the smooth planes of her hips. I silently beg her to stay here. Right here. Just like this. Just for a few seconds more. To be my angel anchor until—*dear fucking God, please*—some words finally manifest for me.

"Reece?" She winds a hand deeper into my hair. "What is it? Are you...do you..." And then hauls in a wobbly breath. "Do you not like the gift after all?" The wobble becomes an awkward attempt at a laugh. "I'm sure we can find you a toaster somewhere on the gift table."

"*Fuck.*" I half laugh it myself—because despite our request for everyone to make a donation to RRO in lieu of bringing presents, the table in the ranch house's foyer is piled high with wrapped boxes. "I don't want anything—*anyone*—but you, my beautiful wife."

She huffs. "Then what..."

"My beautiful *wife*." I draw out the word to stress it even more, releasing my breath in a hot rush against her skin. At once, I know what effect it's wrought on her. Even if my nose wasn't poised a few inches above her crotch, I'd scent the heady honey of her arousal and feel the tremors moving through every corner of her womb. Her subtle physical surrender helps to finally twist free the locked parts of *me*. I turn my left hand over, trailing the curve of my wedding ring against her quivering skin. "You're mine now, Emmalina. *Completely* mine."

She sighs. Tightens her other hand in my hair. I sweep a look up her body, reveling in the sight of her erect ruby nipples reaching for the stars as she arches her head backward. "I've always been yours, Reece Richards."

"But now it's real." With whispered brushes of my lips, I retrace the shivering path I created with the sweep of the white-gold band. "You're really mine to keep happy. To keep cherished. To keep protected."

"Yes." She pulls her hands back until they're positioned on either side of my face. "Happy. Cherished. Protected. But *not* like cut crystal." She drops her head and jumps her brows, more threatening than Rainbow Johnson with a curfew-breaking kid. "And not like blown glass or freshly fallen snow or rice paper."

"Yeah. Okay. I know," I concede, really meaning it. "*I know*. But—"

"But *what*?" Her lips barely move because she seethes it so tightly. "You can't go for the whole but-you-*are*-a-mere-mortal thing anymore with me, right?"

Bullish snort. "Fine. Right."

"Or that I can be your partner in some ways but not others, right?"

"Yes," I hiss. "Right."

"So where are you going with—"

"You're my *wife*, Emmalina." I power back to my feet but keep my hands where they are, bracing her hips. All the better for keeping her locked against me as I take my turn to loom over *her* this time. I gather her close, feeling every tremor with which she reacts to my nearness...how easily she melts beneath my touch...how sweet and soft and perfect she is, enveloped by the shelter of my body. Completely safe in my arms. "You're my wife," I repeat, betraying the intensity of my longing to keep her like this...forever. "And that means caring for you, Velvet," I whisper into her hair. "And getting to take care of you, damn it."

And abruptly, my lips aren't filled with her tousled strands anymore.

I'm consumed with the soft, wet hunger of *her*.

The urgent lift of her mouth, seeking every inch of mine. The slick sensuality of her tongue, pushing up and in and across mine. The consuming ambrosia of her, lust and champagne and woman, mixing with the inescapable perfume of the fresh desire from between her legs.

Fuck. That scent...

"Then take care of me, damn it."

And that voice. Her gorgeous, sassy mockery—calling me on every drop of my misplaced nobility and yet venerating me for it too. It's like she's cutting me with my own knife but then licking the wound shut at the same time. In other circles, I'm damn sure they call this topping from the bottom—but in the bubble of her and me, it's simply the perfect, passionate spirit of the miracle I call Emmalina. The woman I now get to call wife. The lover I get to say other things to as well. Illicit things I've never bared for anyone before. My most carnal ideas. My most secret fantasies.

Secret...

And special.

Because my depraved libido has spun them up especially for her.

No time like the present to get started.

EMMA

At *last*, the man kisses me back the way I need him to—that I've all but been begging him to. And then grips my naked body like his lightning rod in a storm. And plunges his hot, commanding tongue down my mewling, moaning throat. And sears every inch of my skin with the jolting force of his touch—before taking up the space between my thighs with the straining urgency of his huge bulge.

Yes.

Dear God, yessssss.

I barely comprehend that I've also blurted it aloud, until registering the intensified storms in Reece's eyes. *Holy hell.* He's clearly taking his caretaking duties super seriously now—a realization that brings a lot of daunting pings on top of my racing thrills.

But unbelievably, my arousal has nothing to do with his blatant sexual presence, infusing our little glade more potently than a lion sniffing all over his Nala. Nor does it connect to the ferocity across his face, infusing an alpha edge to his dark male beauty. And it's not linked to the savage flares of his nostrils, along with the harsh huffs he punches onto the air—all the while keeping our bodies brutally mashed and our mouths securely fastened.

It's the fact that he simply knows I need all of it. *All of it.* He knows without even asking. Without waiting for *me* to ask. He just...knows. And he's known since the second I left him behind on the dance floor, already knowing I'd be waiting right here for him.

Nude and wet and ready for him.

Craving to be claimed by him.

Just...

Like...

This.

Yet still, so hot and frantic for him. Knowing now that I need...

So...

Much...

More.

A *more* he starts to give me, turning his kisses rougher and bolder. Descending his snarls into barbaric baritones. Tightening his hold until his fingers will surely leave bright-red dents after he's done taking me. Fucking me. Loving me.

But still not grabbing deep enough.

With barely any thought, I tell him so—and show him too. "Please," I rasp, hitching my hips up into his grip. The new pressure of my skin against his fingers is painful and primal and perfect. The slide of my uncovered pussy along his steel-hard crotch is enflaming and enrapturing. "*Reece*. My beautiful husband. *Yes. Please.*"

"Fuck." He dips his head to finish off the snarl with a brutal bite into my neck. He licks greedily at the sting, turning the pain into pleasure, while crooning into my skin, "Emmalina. *Emmalina*. My incredible, insatiable, extraordinary, exquisite wife."

I curl my head in, letting my stare go heated and hooded while watching my fingers do a sensual dance with the thick strands atop his head. Though all I'm drunk on is desire, the textures mesh in my view like I've truly had a few. Chestnut silk flows over my exploring touch. The tanzanite stone on my right hand and the diamonds on my left are racing through the lush, dark forest of strands like stars flirting with night shadows.

And still, his litany of worshipful words continues.

"My gorgeous goddess. My seductress of sunshine..."

But in return, I can't formulate a single word for him. I try and then try again, but the syllables aren't there. This refulgent man—my incredible, astounding hero—has stripped every sound out of my mind faster than he first had me agreeing to this naughty tryst. Can I be blamed for capitulating? I'm helpless against the force of his thrall, especially when he looks at me like this. Like an intense, elegant beast that's just tromped through a summer storm, bringing the savagery of his seduction along with the force of a lightning-filled sky. He's made it impossible for me to utter anything. To *do* anything. All I have the power for is returning his liquid silver stare...

And hoping to survive the tempest.

Or not.

Because maybe this survival thing is really overrated.

Especially if I'm about to be on the receiving end of the erotic promise in his eyes...and the explosive glory beneath his caveman rumble...

Ohhhh, God.

Ohhhh, yes.

Obliteration is sounding better by the second.

But first, I have to take at least one more try at getting all of this expressed in a more constructive way for us both. I have to get out the damn words.

"Reece?"

"Hmmm?"

"I—I need to know something."

"Okay. Ask away."

"I—well, I..."

His body tautens. His stare narrows. Yes, that fast. Yes, that easily. Yes, almost too intensely. I make a note to talk to him about readjusting the setting on his mind-reading thing—not that he'll really listen since he thinks the talent is simply paying attention to the woman he's crazy about—though he's got that spotlight cranked to laser strength now and is stressing himself out for no good reason. "*Hey*. What is it, Bunny?" he presses. "I'm here. *I'm here*. You can ask me anything, Emma. You know that, right?"

"Yeah, baby. I *do* know."

"Then what is it, Bunny? What do you need?"

I don't make him wait any longer—no matter how silly the question is going to sound. This really *is* a bewildering point for me.

"I need to know...is it really like this...for everyone? I mean, is every other bride in the world feeling like this today? Is every couple, with their new rings and their fancy clothes and their little private moments away from everyone, drowning in as much happiness as we are?"

For a long moment, he doesn't respond. He considers my words with an expression that turns the lightning in his gaze into a texture more like the Northern Lights, full of hypnotizing colors. A fitting comparison since the haunting ways of those glacial lights is a perfect definition for his answering tone.

"I want to tell you yes," he finally murmurs. "I really do, Velvet. But the answer is likely no." He traces across my cheek with his fingertips, which are warmed to the point of resembling light-blue gamer buttons. "You'll always get my honesty, so I'll shoot straight here as well." Another deep exhalation as he pushes his fingers back into my hair. "I've definitely thought I was in love before." His lips purse. "Wasn't a lot of times, and the circumstances were probably shit you've already read in the tabloids. Some of it's true; most of it was fabricated. The press adores nothing better than a reformed billionaire bastard."

I copy his move, pressing my hand to the plane between

his stubbled jaw and his defined cheekbone. "And the queue to be your Pepper Potts was likely a few miles long." Who the hell am I kidding? If the posts on the Bolt fan pages are any indication, the line was that long as of *yesterday*.

"At the time, it was more like the Beatrice to save my Dante." He pushes out a quiet chuff. "But lo and behold, none of them kept me from tumbling into hell anyway."

"Why?"

"Silly Bunny." He punctuates the rebuke with a kiss to the space between my eyebrows. "You already know this answer, don't you?"

I look up at him through my lashes, attempting—and likely failing—to put a coy spin on my reply. "Maybe I just want to hear you say it." And surprise, surprise—returning his honesty turns out to be the wisest move, earning me more of that warmth across his face, permeating into the grip he gains around my body before taking my lips in a long, languid kiss.

We've barely pulled apart, sharing sighs and a few more nips, before he quietly declares, "None of them were *you*, Emmalina Paisley Crist Richards." As he caresses his way between my waist and ass and back again, he continues. "None of them were you, showing me everything my world could be and everything I could be in it. With none of them did I feel like part of an *us*. Like part of *our* us. With none of them did I feel like my every breath, my every thought, my every moment didn't just matter to someone else but was shared by someone else. Seen and known and understood by that someone, as if her being was carved from the side block of cosmic stone as mine and then brought to life by the same special band of angels."

Now I'm the one who dips into silence—but unlike Reece's

contemplative version of the pause, mine doesn't consist of any linear thought. I'm nothing but raw feeling. Stunned elation. Overwhelmed love. I pray he can see the message in the teary ponds of my gaze, because my stupid lips aren't finding their way past this giant ball of emotion right now.

I get my answer, in brilliant fullness, as he plunges his hand along my scalp and then grips the curve of my waist, fitting our bodies together like the two sides of yin and yang, only with a pair of better colors than black and white. We're azure and amber. A laser blast and a sun dot. Silver and gold.

Man and woman.

Husband and wife.

A magic called *us*.

We think it together. Feel it together. And as we do, we move to consummate it together. He yanks me in tighter. I grab on to his hair with one hand and grip the bulge of his bicep with the other. Even through the layers of his coat and shirt, I feel every new ripple of his anticipation, matched to the climbing burn of mine. I breathe in and out, perfectly in sync with his labored huffs. I'm already his surrendered sunshine, ready as hell for the dark domination of his electric kiss.

And all at once, I realize that he's right.

It's not like this for everyone.

I really have been struck by lightning.

And now I'm married to him.

And I can't wait to spend the rest of my life showing him my gratitude for that. For all of this. For the bolt of him. Even for the glow worm craziness of *me*.

For the magic of us.

The task feels daunting—and I'll probably never truly, fully accomplish it—but I'll never give up, no matter how difficult it might be now or in the future. I didn't fall for Reece Richards because it was easy. I didn't say "I do" as just part of our oaths today. I don't love him because of his fast cars, his charm with my mother, or how amazing his muscled ass looks in his leathers, though all three are epic parts of the mix.

I love him because it's right. Because my heart, my soul, and my spirit can't sync to the universe without him. Because I don't thoroughly know *me* without him.

And though he's heard it from me a thousand times before, I can't wait to make it a thousand and one. As he curls in, circling his lips closer toward mine, I ready the words at the tips of my lips. What a perfect preface they'll be for the kiss that's going to turn me into the glade's new night light. *Oh, yessss...*

"Emmalina Paisley?"

Annnnd cue the needle scratching the record.

More accurately, Laurel Crist's shriek cutting through the night air.

Just as fast, I crouch against Reece and gasp frantically into his chest. "Shit. Ohhhh, shit, shit, shit!"

My husband is *not* helping matters, snickering like we've merely been outed by ravenous reporters or, say, the CIA— instead of a force much worse.

"Laurel, why on earth are you shouting into the wilderness?"

"Shit!" I repeat. "Dad is with her!"

"Dad's right." But thank God, Lydia is with them. "Let's check upstairs in the main building first. They've probably sneaked away for some alone time."

Reece's new chuckle is eclipsed by my mother's fresh shout. "Emma. Lina. Paisley. This is *not* good form, even at a wedding in the boondocks. I swear, if you're—"

"Yes, ma'am!" I finally screw up the courage to yell it back as soon as I hear her choosing the uncanny maternal instinct over Lydia's logical suggestion. "We're coming!" And offer that part while pushing away so hard, my husband stumbles back into a tree, showering us in loose leaves. As I bat Mother Nature's "presents" off my naked limbs, Reece still chortles softly. I retaliate with a glower.

Eventually, I manage to reclaim my gown off the branch over which I draped it and then jab it over my head just before we stumble out from the glade, clothes semi-wrinkled and hair beyond mussed—

To confront four pairs of we're-missing-nothing eyes.

That are attached to a matching number of instant reactions.

"Oh, dear God." Mother's blurt is first out of the gate. Imagine that.

"Pretty sure the guy was involved somehow." Lydia slides out her finest and fullest smirk of approval.

"But which one?" Sawyer wields a subtle grin of his own. "The guy ruling Olympus or Hades?"

My sister grants him a knowing wink. "Not sure it matters, Hang Man."

While I catch her eye next, mouthing *Hang Man?* with a piercing glare to underline my query, Dad turns into my hero of the whole crisis.

"Why don't we just let everyone know the cake cutting can roll as scheduled?" he suggests to Mother. Thank God for the man, who knows better than anyone that nothing mollifies the woman better than staying on schedule.

"Outstanding idea." The woman actually lets Dad scoop

up her hand and appears to obediently follow him back up the stone steps toward the ranch house's back patio. But she pivots on the top step, dropping a weighted look back to Reece and me. "The cake cutting *will* go as scheduled, yes? Attended by *all* pertinent wedding party members?"

Lydia steps back in with a gritted smile—and a matching growl. "Tell the photographers not to spaz. All four of us will be there."

"Though it looks like some of us will be having our second dessert of the day." Sawyer cleverly hides his quip behind Reece's back—or so I think, until the guy reaches over to pluck a tenacious twig dangling off Reece's ass.

"Oh, gawd." I dip my flushing cheeks into my cupped hands.

"Oh, hell *yes*." Lydia pulls the praise into her avid embrace around me, tugging to guide me toward the bridal dressing room. "But dude, you should've taken a picture first," she chastises back at Sawyer. "The Funko Wedding Bolt Pop would look bangin' with the keister twig."

"No keister twig!" I protest.

"No Wedding Funko!" Reece snarls as he and Sawyer disappear into the groom's room.

"He does know they've already got those things half done, doesn't he?" Lydia's as ready with the words as she is with a concealer stick, offering me the makeup as I plop onto the stool in front of the bride's room vanity. As I gape at my smudged mascara and kiss-stung mouth, she picks at my hair with a wide-toothed comb. It's not quite a rat's nest yet—at least I hope it won't be once she gets all the leaves and sticks yanked out. "They're just waiting for the first pictures of your outfits to be released so they can slap those together for the cute plastic bodies."

"Well, that'll be a snag." I catch my sister's gaze via the mirror, not holding back a twitch of my lips. "Because there's nothing 'cute' or 'little' about my husband's body."

Lydia frowns. "I'm not sure whether to puke or pump you for details."

"Or just skip the subject and jump to explaining what *Hang Man* is all about?"

At once, she joins me on the coy smile brigade. "You're not the only Crist wench with a man who needs an oversized Funko box. Mine just likes to take the edge off by hanging ten on some good Redondo breakers when he can." She cocks her head while stabbing a bobby pin into the end of the braid she's just reconstructed. "And then there's the better way he *hangs...*"

"Okaaaay." I cap the concealer with a defined slam and then lurch to my feet. "It's *really* time for cake."

'Dia follows me back out to the patio, giggles pouring off her lips. "You did ask!"

"And will likely regret it forever."

"Nah." She hooks her arm through mine. "It'll just be another fun memory from the happiest day of your life."

"Hmmm. Now there's where you're wrong, Dee Dee."

"Huh?"

I lay a hand across her forearm and squeeze in with tender meaning. "Every day I get to wake up next to Reece Richards is the best day of my life."

I expect a cringe-worthy side-eye from my sister. At the least, a falter in her relaxed pace along the terra cotta walkway. But neither come. Lydia's still all easy-breezy maid of honor time, even as she looks out across the valley that's now shrouded in lavender and gray shadows. But eventually, she hitches up the edges of her lips before replying, "Well, congratulations, baby girl. Your wedding cake really won't be the sickest bite of sweet I've got to endure today."

My answering laugh spews without thought. "And you're loving every morsel, baby."

"We all are, baby girl. We all are."

CHAPTER FIVE

REECE

"Well. So much for useless comparisons to the Man of Steel."

I answer Foley's wisecrack with a mocking glare by way of the long oval mirror in the corner of the ranch's groom's room. Already I discern that my stress level is several notches below his—and have some theories about that plot twist—but keep my opinions under the vest, literally and figuratively, while throwing on that garment in place of my tux coat.

Earlier, I decided to ditch the vest for the vows ceremony, a choice that's going to serve me well for the next events. The photographers will have a "relaxed look" Reece to vary up their shots on the day, and the wardrobe change justifies why Emma and I disappeared during dinner. Most importantly, it covers up my huge sweat spots. Not that I necessarily give a shit about everyone knowing what I've just been doing with my time. I'd dare any guy in the place not to think about sneaking off with a bride as stunning as mine leading the way.

On second thought, I *wouldn't* dare.

Not arguing any of my friends' integrity levels...

But Emma does look how she does today.

Like star fire in lace.

An angel brought to earth.

A piece of the sun, turning everything she touches to gold.

Every inch of my body, still zinging like an exposed wire, is *that* tangible proof.

I retuck my clothes with faster urgency. Grab up my brush and whisk it at my head, taming the goddamned whirlwind. I'm sure I'll give poor Corinne a conniption with my re-style, but I'll ply her with chocolate and charm to make up for it.

I just want to get back to my fine little Flare.

"Okay," I finally answer Foley's quip, only because it looks like the guy's expecting me to. "I'll bite. *What* comparisons to the Man of Steel?"

"Uh, Earth to Richards? Basically all of them—which, like I said, don't matter anyhow."

"Why?"

"Because of those titanium *cojones* between your legs, *oui*?"

"You're making me regret inviting you to Paris again, man." Because that's not the first time—nor will it likely be the last—for one of his dorky language mash-ups.

"Meh." He shrugs. "Worth it."

"Yeah?" I grin because even his cool-cat dismissiveness can't dig at me today. "Well, for the record, so was the little wilderness break with my bride."

He lowers his brows in response to my waggling ones. "For the record, I don't need to know any more than that."

"Whatever you say, Grumpy Cat."

"For the record, I'm going to ignore *that* one entirely."

"You got something against cats?"

"I have something against memes that grew mold three years ago."

"Nah." I toss the brush back into the mess on the marble

top of the dresser next to the mirror, figuring Corinne's mortified gasps will be outshone by Emma's hubba-hubba stares. *Sorry, expensive stylist, but my wife's carnal desires trump your trend alignment.* "I think you're just a giant ball of hard-up, Mr. Foley."

Sawyer scrapes a hand over his head, joining me in the Corinne's-going-to-kill-us corner for our hairstyles. But his crazy Samson locks have more product slicked in them, meaning only part of his clubbed-back queue breaks loose. "You would not be wrong," he finally mutters and stabs a tight look through the hock that's escaped into his eyes.

Sharp chuff. "Dude." Then another. "How were you out here for most of the afternoon and didn't take even one chance to play kinky throne room with Princess Purple Pants?" When my use of Lydia's nickname doesn't do a thing to make me forget Grumpy Cat and him in the same sentence, I'm double-taking. "Unless you *did* and that was too damn long ago?"

Foley shifts, stretching the fit of his light-gray suit across his burly shoulders. His face grows equally taut as he answers me in a shadowed growl. "We still off the record?"

I cock a brow. "Were we ever *on* it?"

The guy plummets his stare to the floor. "I haven't touched Lydia in a week."

"Excuse the hell out of me?"

"*Fuck.*" He lunges over, shoving me deeper into the room—as in, all the way back to where the glass-walled shower and king's throne of a toilet are located. "You want to play telephone through the walls with the girls on this shit?"

"And you think the plumbing won't carry the sound twice as fast?"

He chills once I lead the way back out to the bigger

part of the room. And I do mean *big*. Since this place often accommodates wedding parties that outnumber the cast of an *Avengers* movie, our two duffels and matching garment bags look like Shih Tzus on a football field. But that also means we can move easily to the middle of the room, where Foley stops with hands on his hips, as if waiting for everyone else to huddle up. Meaning me.

"All right. Dome of silence is activated," I mutter. "Or at least what we're going to get of one. *Hey*. Earth to Foley?" I almost laugh, getting to return his rib. A little under a year ago, the man was verbally prodding me in the same way, helping me through the first tentative steps of forming Team Bolt. I have no idea if I looked this uneasy but refuse to press Foley for that answer now. The guy tugs on his loose flop of hair like a goddamned nervous teenager.

Wait.

Shit.

Like a nervous teenager...in love.

Not just his Sawyer Foley, man-this-is-kind-of-cool version of the stuff.

He's got the Reece Richards, I-love-a-Crist-and-I'm-scared-as-fuck-about-it version.

But that's not adding up with the info nuke he just dropped on me.

Which makes me grit out again, "*Foley*. What the *hell* is going on?"

He whips away, lacing hands at the back of his head. "I wish to fuck I knew."

Picking up on his impending need to pace, I slide out of the way by moving back to the dresser and parking my ass against it. "You're in love with Lydia Crist."

"That's the easy part of the equation."

"And I thought that was *my* line."

"So did I."

"Meaning what?"

Yep. Here comes the pacing. And the new anguish in his composure, gritting his teeth and gripping his shoulders, as he tries not to turn every step into a restless stomp. "I wish to *fuck* I knew."

I fold my arms. "So I've heard." Then cant my head, as if the two inches of focus change is going to sharpen my Bolty senses enough to actually help him with the answer. "Just like I've pretty much known this for a couple of months now. Just like I'm sure *you've* known."

He drops his hands into twisting fists. It beats him yanking on his hair like some purple-haired MCR groupie, but not by much. "Yeah. I have."

"So what's changed in the last week?"

I'm not sure what reaction to expect, but the guy's *pssshhh* of a laugh definitely wasn't in my top ten. "Couple of people we both care for went and got married."

Okay, neither is that.

"So...what?" I go for glib because it feels the most natural. "Has 'Dia switched out chats about the offshore flow and catching up on your *Misfits* binge to real rings verses tattoos and 'let's talk a five-year plan'?"

"No." His reply is instant. And definite.

"No?"

"*I'm* the one switching up the conversation."

And I thought he'd already dropped the info nuke.

"And...it's freaking Lydia out?"

He ramps up the pacing again. "No. It's freaking *me* out."

I'm a little gaslit myself but don't let on. "Okay, man." I apologize by way of spreading my hands. "I'm not entirely following."

"You think *I* am?" With a weary whoosh, he drops onto a leather couch grouped with a couple of matching chairs next to an enclosed atrium with cowboy-style accents. The photographer had come in and taken a few shots of us out there before Lauren rushed me off to the altar. Unlike then, Foley's not such a vision of go-with-the-flow cool. "Jesus. I can't do this yet, Richards. I can't promise my whole future to a woman when there are pieces of my past still left to unravel."

I plant myself on the sturdy wood coffee table, cocking an incisive stare his way. "Pieces," I repeat. "You mean...*missing* pieces? Like suppressed memories?"

"I'm not sure." He whips up a hand before I can get in half a rebuttal. "And before you even go there, I've tried the therapy thing. *A lot* of the therapy thing. Hypnotism, regression, acupuncture—even psychics and tarot and...experimental plants. Of certain sorts."

I scrub both hands up my face, knowing better than to ask the clarification on *that* one. "And the memories have stayed locked?"

"Tighter than Pandora's Box." He braces a foot to the table and an elbow to his knee and then drops his head far enough that the errant shank of hair curtains his face again. "I don't know what they are, only that there are big chunks of my past that are missing."

"From your time in the service?" The suggestion is an educated stab based on random assumptions I've made from his equally random references over the last year as well as the long list of things he never discusses. But the guy had to have done things, seen things, and endured things that got him into the FBI at a security clearance rarely given to anyone under forty. Things that still haunt the back of his gaze, turn some of his words into cryptic allusions, and make him adamant about keeping his place on the water in Redondo despite his expansive suite back at the ridge.

But weirdly, none of that is what darkens his demeanor now. His confusion lies on a very different level, tightening his scowl as he shakes his head. "For better or for worse—pardon the expression, man—I've still got most of that right up here." He jabs a finger at his skull. "But this shit...is different. It was something I'd been resolved to just write off...until I met Lydia."

I straighten my spine. Drop my hands. "Lydia." And push out a long breath of new comprehension. "Who's been your key."

Foley doesn't move. "Who's been my key."

"And terrifies the crap out of you because of it."

He pushes out half a laugh. "Christ. If it was only terror." As he falls back, he lowers a coiled fist to his forehead. He studies the ceiling like the roof is about to break open and the sky is going to suck him into an apocalyptic vortex. "This is... more."

"More?"

"Different," he emphasizes. "Deeper. It's like being ripped open and having parts of me exposed...parts I never even knew existed. But while it's all so fucking unfamiliar, it all still feels so..."

"What?" I work at not sounding melodramatic against the backdrop of his thick pause.

"It feels..." He slides his fist around, almost turning it into a Frankenstein bolt against his temple. "It feels right." He starts twisting the bolt. "But if that's the case, why the hell have I buried all of it?"

I lean forward. Firm my chin to deliver my response, which is as certain in my mind as Arial Bold. "Because maybe you're not *unburying* it."

Foley locks me with a tighter scowl. "Excuse me?"

Arial Bold becomes Impact Caps. "Maybe you're *discovering* it." As he gives up the glower for a full gawk, I let a small smile break through. "Parts of yourself that have always been there but were lying dormant. Like muscles in your soul that have gone untrained." Seeing him understand the metaphor but visibly freak out from it, I turn my hands over as if offering to be handcuffed. "Like hiding a decent man under the billionaire douche the world chooses to see."

"Not me."

Eye roll. Because it really fits. "You binge obscure TV and shop at stores that stock their news racks with *Legumes This Week* and *The Chakra Journal.*"

"Hey. You like *The Chakra Journal.*"

"Yeah. Because they're one of four publications on the planet who didn't jump on the 'Reece the Douche' bandwagon."

"Right. And because your chakras aren't ever out of whack or anything."

"Save the New Age sarcasm for your woman, Folic Acid."

I get in the quip as we both rise, summoned by the opening guitar riff of "Uptown Funk" from the reception patio. Whether Foley's inspired by the music or my blatant affirmation of his feelings, the guy splits the biggest grin I've ever seen across his laid-back maw. He keeps up the look while giving me a gruff shoulder bump—the closest thing Foley ever comes to a hug.

"Errrr...thanks, Richards," he mumbles. "I mean it, man."

"Awwww shucks, plucky buckaroo. Anytime."

He flashes me his drollest glare. "I'm going to forget you said that." But the glint in his eyes already gives away the zinger he's got locked and loaded too—though he never gets the chance to squeeze that trigger, thanks to the arrival of my rescue squad.

At least that's what I think when Alex Trestle first appears, decked out in a suit surely pilfered from the classic James Bond vault, circa Sean Connery. At his side is Neeta Jain, my right hand for all things related to the Richards Resorts division of the company, of which she's now the Executive Vice President. But tonight, she's here in the role of happy wedding guest—or so I think before my admiration of her old-is-new-again gown gets bypassed by her stressed expression. The small twist in my gut grows when observing Trestle isn't just her match in the fashion reboot department. Tension defines every step he takes over to Foley and me.

"We don't want to intrude," he says from compressed lips, "but I'm afraid we need to."

My mind whirls through possibilities as I triage their arrival. Neither of them is blatantly bleeding or has anyone else's blood on them. The ranch's security team doesn't seem to be in tow, either. The band is still uptown funking just over the trees. There are no screams on the air or any glaring glow to denote the love of my life has accidentally dropped cover and given everyone a wedding celebration they *really* won't forget.

Which leaves one logical conclusion.

Leading me to lean over, clap Alex on the back, and reassure, "Trestle. It's fine."

"It's...what?" He gawks like my hand turned into a shark fin.

"I understand," I explain. "Lauren Crist can be daunting when she's watching the schedule, but we're fine."

"We're what? How does Lauren Crist—"

"Is Emma already back out there?" I cut in.

"Yes." Neeta confirms it, hands held in an elegant manner at her waist, as if she's standing in the Hotel Brocade's offices in one of her pinstripe skirt suits instead of here in a long, flowy green gown that brings out the gold tints in her cinnamon-colored skin. "It was when she reappeared without you that Alexander and I grew concerned."

Concerned.

It's not the first time I've heard her declare the word. The woman helps me run international resorts all over the globe, after all. It's just the first time I've heard her say it like that, with that strange edge in her voice. Like this is something a room rate change won't fix.

Like this is something having nothing to do with Lauren Crist.

I drop my hand off Alex's back. "Concerned? About what?"

"About the Hela Odinsdottir who's crashed the damn reception?"

Foley and I wheel around as soon as the growl is issued by a new arrival in the room. At once, I toss "concerned" out the window of my psyche—because as soon as Wade Tavish stalks into a room like this, with his gaze fired up and his ginger rage ramped, I know better than to stop at mild-level descriptors.

"The Hela *who*?" Foley issues the demand two seconds before I get to it.

"Odinsdottir," Neeta supplies. I almost have the feeling she's holding back a "duh" eye roll. "Goddess of the underworld.

In many texts, said to be one of the daughters of Loki; however, in the cinematic universe, she is Odin's daughter and none too happy about being banished to the land of the dead for several millennia. She is proficient at many weapons and fighting styles, but her anger and hurt often overrules her common sense, leading to her downfall."

Wade gulps and stares at her. "I think I just fell in love."

Alex shoves him. "Get in line."

"You fuckers want to *focus*?" Foley barks, spinning back to confront Neeta. "And since you're the one actually putting your brain *first*: are you telling me there's an angry hell harpy who's just magically manifested in the middle of the reception?"

Alex awkwardly bobs his head. "Manifested? Magically? I'm not sure about *that*..."

I plummet my hand to my sides but keep them curled in fists. "So what the hell *are* you sure of?"

Wade's the one who shifts forward again, though he does so with such force that he audibly skids to a stop on the polished tiles a few inches in front of Foley and me. He hardly notices because his tension is still like a physical mantel over his posture. "At the very low end of the crazy scale? We've got a mystery guest."

"And at the other end of the scale?" Foley charges. He's scowling so deeply, I'm shocked not to see miniature mountain bikers racing up and down the crevices of his face.

Just then, the band ends the happy tune in favor of a new song. It's the Muse tune, about secrets being safe and worlds that come tumbling down. *Of course.*

"Then we have a big fucking problem."

EMMA

"Bride Emma!"
"Bride Emma!"
"We're dancing with Bride Emma!"
"Dancing!"

It feels a billion kinds of wrong—and right—to be laughing like a lunatic as Tosca and Jina drag me from one end of the dance floor to the next while the band's lead singer plaintively wails through "Resistance." Normally, Muse songs are the stuff I deep clean and sob-read to, but this song is a perfect choice for commemorating a superhero love story.

The message is also perfectly timed for my heart. While I'm so impatient for the day we can let the whole world know that Team Bolt is one member stronger and more formidable than ever, my spirit listens to the lyrics soaring around me. Words that roar about love being the greatest resistance of all and keeping promises despite being broken down.

And isn't that what today's been all about? Love triumphing as our greatest power and not the shitty things we've had to go through to get here. Finally telling fear to suck it. Declaring that we're claiming each other as our ultimate power, the voltage readings on our bloodstreams be damned. In many ways, it's perfect that the recognition hits as I "dance" with this pair of giddy eight-year-olds in their frothy dresses, Tosca in pink and Jina in lavender, their rosy health reminding me of how far they've come since Reece and I pulled up in front of their house last year, making them and their older brother, Cal, the inaugural family to benefit from Richards Reaches Out. Since then, Cal has knocked out another year of college and has been able to put a down payment on a modest condo between the Brocade and UCLA, where he'll be pursuing the rest of his engineering degree while working part-time at the hotel.

At the risk of being trite—but what the hell, it's only my gray matter reflecting to itself—can I really ask for anything more right now?

We're helping others.

We're loving each other.

We have health and hope...

And now, as the band segues into "Don't Stop Believin'," we even have Journey.

Life. Made.

And given an even better sprinkle on the top of the sundae as I behold my towering, breathtaking husband across the dance floor, tie shucked and shirtsleeves hiked, and a vest accentuating his tapered physique instead of his jacket. His long legs are braced just far enough apart, making him took like a dark, wicked Zeus with his eye on a new mortal maiden.

Silly god king.

Don't you remember how you turned this *human into a goddess with the power of your passion?*

But he doesn't look convinced, even after I crook a finger at him and sing the line about everyone wanting a thrill as if he's the only one on earth who'll give me mine. Because he is. My man. My *more*. The hunk who's gradually peeling me apart all over again, even across the twenty feet separating us...

Until the adoration in his gaze is suddenly marred by a shadow. And then another. And then such a deeply troubled sobriety to his expression, I feel *my* face emulating it—though once I get to that point, only keeping time to the song's rhythm because Jina and Tosca are swinging my arms like dueling jump ropes, Reece jogs his head to the side, a silent request to meet him near the bar.

The bar.

Located *across* the dance floor from the display where an uplit fountain bubbles up from the middle of our Butter End wedding cake and where Mother has herded a couple of servers for the razzle-dazzle cutting shenanigans.

Mother *isn't* happy when I acquiesce to my husband's direction instead, but she'll have to deal. Especially because every step that takes me closer to Reece also brings awareness, prickling and potent, corresponding to the creases at the corners of his mouth. Though everyone obviously thinks he's just approaching me about some minor party detail, my nerve endings know better.

And the hairs on the back of my neck.

And the extra awareness in my senses, letting me observe the light along the top of his head.

I almost gasp at the change in his energy. He's now the color of a messy red marker instead of a goldenrod highlighter and is jacking up that flow as I watch.

"Okay," I finally rasp as he pulls me close with hands at the backs of my shoulders. "Just tell me this isn't the part where you tell me one of my friends from college is actually one of your exes."

For half a second, he gives in to what looks like befuddlement, bemusement, and enchantment at once. That's before he takes a new breath and his tension takes over again. "At the moment, we've got a different sticky." He redirects my attention with a lift of his head and a sweep of his stare. I'm still so weirded out by his energy, I don't even pause to let my heart backflip from how the gold dance floor lights reflect in his velvet grays. "Do you know that woman sitting at the table in the back corner? Long dark hair with the silver streak? Gallon of eyeliner? A red lace choker—"

"And the matching wrap dress she's hardly bothered to wrap?" My spew says it all, though I'm not shy about my relief when he looks right at her with undisguised confusion. But I'm washed in a more troubled feeling when he refuses to let his glare leave her. "Reece?" I press. "What's up? Who *is* she?"

He looks back down to me—for all of three seconds. "You're sure you don't know her? Look again."

I oblige but not without a snort of punctuation. "Doesn't look like I have to. That old perv next to her is doing the *looking* for everyone here."

One side of Reece's mouth hitches up. "Perv? Yes. But old? Think again."

I twist my lips. Hard. "Did that orgasm on the dam make you blind, my love? He's eighty if he's a—"

"He's Alex."

And now I know why he's kept me angled away from the crowd. He knew my gawk was coming. The gawk that still clamps my face as I dare a tiny backward glance. "Holy shit. I mean, the guy is always talking about cosplay and disguises, but I never knew he was *this* good at it."

"I don't think any of us did," Reece replies. "But he cobbled that getup together with Corinne's help, thank fuck."

That explains why the stylist hasn't been flitting around. I'd be running over to kiss Alex's toes for the favor, if not for being totally fascinated with how he's transformed himself into a cross between Yoda and Mr. Miyagi, with his attention fixed on the slick beauty with the impeccable skin and squinting stare—while she plays a cat-and-mouse game with her visual homage to my husband.

"Are you really sure *you* don't know her?" I mutter, glancing pointedly back at Reece.

He bristles but grits it away. My implication, hardly a mystery, is also hardly unjustified. Assuming the man has remembered every female he's "been with" is like assuming he remembers every Richards Empire employee. Impossible.

"She's not the least bit familiar to me, Emmalina. Okay?" His pause between my name and the question is the same thing as a grudging shoulder shake.

I choose to give in to the actual motion, since it shirks his relentless hold. "I believe you," I mutter, hoping it serves as a minor peace offering. Okay, so he was once a man-slut—but I fell in love with him knowing that. And while he's done some crazy shit since we've been together, sliding the Bolt Bang Missile into another woman definitely hasn't been one of them. I know that in every part of my heart and soul. *I know it.*

The man leans down, pressing a tender buss to my forehead. The contact infuses me with tiny sparks all over again, and my second tremor is more raw reaction than a purposeful shake.

"So, we have a crasher?" I ask quietly.

"Seems so."

Reece's growl is blanketed with tension. I try to ramp up my own but can't. I'm thrilled and pissed by the idea at once—but don't dare give in to the curiosity that underlines both. Giving the woman another open goggle won't just alert her that the jig is up but give her another chance to snap secret pictures—if that's what she's here for. That choker does have an amulet the size of an Infinity Stone and could easily be doing double duty as a camera lens.

"Holy shit." It spills out louder than I intended, but pure panic has a tendency to twang a girl's vocal cords beyond the norm. Screw the curiosity; now I really *am* as wound-up as my husband. "You think she might be live feeding all this?" I spit. "Have Wade and Fersh done any searches?"

Reece yanks me close again. Ensures into my hair, "As we speak. And some facial recognition programs too."

"And?" I jerk back, letting him see the anxiety spread across my face. How long has that hag been here? Has she been spying on us? Infiltrating our privacy? Broadcasting our special day without permission? Holy *crap*. Did she secretly follow us out beneath the weeping willow? Is there some awful video already up on the web, titled something hideous like "Wicked Lightning Lovers" or "Up, Up, and Away with the Richards"?

"Nothing yet," Reece admits. "But getting a clear enough image of *her* has been another challenge, which was why Alex came up with the scheme to go in as..." He trails off, scrunching his lips.

"Yoda and Mr. Miyagi's love child?"

"Yes." His affirmation is so definitive, he pulls out the *y* a little.

"Though he hasn't been able to get the same from her?"

"Not without being obvious." He grits his way into a charming smile, lifting a gentlemanly finger in Mother's direction to stall her about the cake. But the last thing I can think about right now is biting into a mound of flour, sugar, and frosting pearls. I may throw up. My stomach is tight and filled with acid. My senses are whirling and full of apprehension. It's as if that mystery witch went ahead and materialized in the middle of our bedroom.

No.

In our bedroom, with all of our friends and family watching.

Where'd she come from? What has she seen? More critically, who the hell has she already uploaded it to?

And now that my mind has taken that poker of horror in all its searing fun, I get ready to entertain myself—*ha freaking ha*—with the joyride of possible answers.

A journey for which I'll gladly return the ticket, given the better option of whirling as Wade and Fershan approach. They clearly don't have joyride tickets either, though they're both wearing that I've-got-news expression that geek guys are fond of. With these two, that could mean anything from the identity of mystery witch down to her underwear size to declaring they've invented a new internet.

Nobody understands that better than Reece, who eyes them with guarded optimism before probing, "What have you got?"

Wade jumps in first. "Either nothing or everything."

"Which means what?" My tone triples Reece's impatience. At least that earns me Fershan's haste, even though the guy looks like he'd rather be giving us the GPS coordinates for hell.

"An unidentified login to the ranch's Wi-Fi," he supplies, cringing before he's done—already observing the rising alarm in my eyes. "But only what we *think* is one," he rushes to amend. Clearly, Fershan doesn't possess Reece-level clearance into my mind, where his sweet sensibilities would be turbo-blasted by my worry about leaked sex footage. "We are not certain if what we even saw was what we saw, and there must be at least three hundred cell phones at this party—"

"Nearly all of which have been blocked from logging into

the Wi-Fi," Reece cuts in. "And also told that sending out pictures and video would amount to everything short of being socially castrated, right?"

The faces around us tauten by discernible degrees. The threat, as stupid as it sounds, isn't an empty one in Los Angeles and Hollywood, where "doing lunch" could mean sealing a multimillion-dollar deal. Or five.

"So where does that leave us?" I charge through gritted teeth. When Reece surges forward, his expression the same, at least I can get a breath in. Though his empathy doesn't sweep me with vindication, I don't feel so crazy about my frustration.

"Well, certainly not to a party-wide Wi-Fi breach," Wade assures, even if he *is* vocalizing the shittiest essence of my nightmare. "The activity we tracked wasn't usual, from a lot of standpoints."

Reece uses his free hand to pinch the bridge of his nose. "Explain."

Wade nods with matching concision. "This user was smart," he states. "Didn't fuck around. Knew exactly where he was going and how to get there. More specifically, he also knew how to cover his tracks. Extremely well."

Reece leans forward, head tipping to indicate his deeper thought. "What are you saying?"

"That we can tell you someone was using that bandwidth, but we can't prove it."

"Huh?"

"Exactly what we are saying," Fershan adds. "That—That we were both looking at it, but then we weren't."

Then maybe not.

Reece emits a long growl while grabbing my hand and squeezing—probably to give comfort to himself as much as me.

"Tavish, don't assume for one second that I'm following this."

"You think we fully do?" Wade flattens his lips. "No Easter eggs buried this time, boss. It means what it means."

"Okay. You detected a weird Wi-Fi login, but then—what—you just didn't?"

"That'd would be a wonkin' *yes.*"

"Explain." His repetition doubles the terseness of the first. And so does Wade's response.

"We agreed that it *was* weird," the guy states before wheeling around, leading the action with his dipped head. "But as soon as we investigated the logs, from our scanners as well as the ranch's backlogs, the entire address vanished."

"It is as he said," Fershan confirms. "Exactly. We saw the information across our scanner log, but then we didn't."

Wade kicks at the edge of the dance floor. "We can show you the places where we've checked, including our tracking logs and the ranch's Wi-Fi router." He stops mid-kick and straightens, pulling back his shoulders, which seem even more broad and muscular than a couple of months ago, when he volunteered to help me go after Faline Garand in the middle of the Consortium's Southern California nest. He'd been vital to helping Angelique and me break into that huge mansion in Palos Verdes—and I know he'd be an even more awesome asset now if the circumstances were different. If all this required was cracking a few gate security codes and busting into the city planner's files for this place's blueprints.

But we're not breaking open iron locks or finding a magical map.

We're trying to figure out what—or who—we're dealing with here.

A woman who, as of this moment, still has no viable identity or name.

A fact turning my bloodstream to barbed wire and fraying my nerves like rusty rebar.

Damn it.

With any luck, all we have to do is rope the wench down to whomever she's working for—and if it doesn't start with "Con" and end in "sortium," I'll mark it as a win. The ranch's security guys already know the regulars from the rinky-dink tabloids, and they promised us those twerps don't try to get in anymore, which means the mystery chica-poo has to be with a higher-paying magazine or blog.

If we're lucky.

If we're very, very lucky.

"Fuck a goddamned duck," Wade grates, though corrects himself at once with a violent head shake. "Shit. I'm sorry, Emma. You don't deserve sailor filth any more than this disruption to your day."

"He's right." Fersh jams a hand into one of his pockets, only to withdraw a paper clip that he twists like taffy. "We do not expect you to believe all this. We know logins don't disappear from logs as if a sorcerer just erased them."

While he's speaking, Reece and I exchange a knowing glance. I soak up the loving affirmation in his eyes and use it to strengthen the patience of my reply. "A being who can totally erase things off the air? Now *that*, my friend, I *do* believe."

Just like I believe that, once directly confronted, our little wedding crasher friend is going to respond exactly like Wade and Fersh do right now.

With a shit ton of astonishment.

With a little more what-the-hell surprise.

And with a *lot* more you-got-me capitulation.

Yes, even as I spin to march across the grass and through

all the dinner tables, not veering in my focused advance on the woman. When I'm a few feet away from the table, I jerk my head over at Alex, communicating my silent command to him at once.

Get up. This wench is all mine now.

He complies without hesitation—which is more than I can say for the sudden revolt from the synapses in my brain and the muscles in my legs. They all seize up as soon as I execute the swift pivot to fully face our audacious intruder—

And the world becomes an explosion.

Not literally. Okay, *not yet.* No way would I commit myself to that promise in writing right now, no more than I'd sign off on the state of my own senses, overloaded by a collision worse than a multicar pileup on the 405.

The semi truck at the front of the crash: Reece's bellow, *whomp*ing me with the same force as his electric presence at full blast. He storms into my pores and tears open my mind.

But why?

Words. He's yelling words at me.

But what?

I don't understand him.

No. I *can't* understand him.

The force of him on the air, filled with such a surge of dread and boom of fear, is like a flood of static over my ears. He's totally drowned out.

No. That's not it either.

The static is all...*me.*

My system, floundering in so much aversion and rage and disbelief, causes the ground to tilt beneath me.

If "me" is even that anymore.

I've mentally broken outside myself, ripping free from

the moorings of my body in order to save it from this clamor of insanity.

But even that might not be possible.

Because I've stomped over here to kick out an invader from my space...

Only to learn she's the bitch who's already been inside it already.

All of it.

To stand here, with the ground rocking and the air screaming and my sanity in rebellion, as the stylish piranha in front of me starts turning her face up at me...

And smiles.

Not just any friendly and serene smile.

Her expression is slow. Planned. Poised. A feline extending its claws, preparing to snag a mouse's tail. A courtesan, ready to remove her mask for her lover.

Or a Consortium bitch on high, letting that mask peel away on its own—just like I saw once before, when Tyce exposed himself to us in Paris. Only then, the unmasking was a painful experience: Reece's brother taking the massive risk of showing us his superpower. This time, the effect is wielded by a preening witch, curling her blood-red fingernails to strip away the last of the morph layer. A kitty cleaning off her cream. A Hela turned into a Maleficent. A vulture spreading her full wings.

A demoness revealing her true ugliness.

The monstress that's turning my wedding day into a nightmare.

"You."

I suddenly hate that word more than any other. I hate the serene skank it represents now, and I hate that she's made it the only word I'm capable of choking out. But worse, I hate that on the day Reece and I should be filled with celebration and love, all I can feel now is filthy hate. In every burning corner of my being. In every searing inch of my soul. In every scalding tear joining the static in my senses, dripping into the gash into which this day has just become.

"*You.*" It tumbles from me again, a pathetic sob this time. I'm the bride, damn it! Where's my badass Tarantino one-liner? For that matter, where's my fucking katana? Why don't I get to have this bitch's kidneys at my feet and her heart in my palm? Why do I have to stand here as Faline daintily slides her folded napkin to the table and then rises with matching composure, silken and sure in how she's stripped away every ounce of mine?

In how she's stripped away every good thing about this day?

In how she smiles, so clearly knowing that too, as she leans in and dares to kiss the air on either side of my seething face. "Well, *hola*, Emmalina. And so many congratulations to two of my most favorite people. Why so surprised, *amiga*? You surely did not think *I* would miss *this* occasion, did you?"

CHAPTER SIX

REECE

Come back here!

Jesus, Emmalina, come back.

That bitch isn't an ex. Or a reporter. Or a crasher.

But my silent protest is too little, too late. I see the horror crash across Emma's face even before Faline fully morphs to her true self. I see the fury flush her cheeks and the fire invade her eyes even before Faline rises to meet her for their direct glare-off.

And despite knowing my wife is capable of holding her own, I growl as dismally as a fucked newb in Pelican Bay.

Hating myself for not putting the pieces together before now. For not *knowing* the bitch would try something like this. For wanting so badly to cling to my lovesick new groom status for just a little while longer, I ignored all the signs that supplied this truth already. The high-end internet shenanigans. The slinky red dress. The over-the-top accessories. Most glaringly, the electric needles in my bloodstream that started as soon as Alex and Neeta sought me out at the ranch house, the voltage intensifying with every step we took back to the party.

I'd written off my blistering Bolty senses to an index of other causes—my post-lovemaking high, my nearly empty stomach, the security of our A-lister guests...hell, even the full moon—but nowhere in the mix had I gone near this possibility. This goddamned atrocity. The concept that Faline Garand, having already shown us her fascination with accessing the Consortium's intel for herself, would plug into the face-morphing ability for which we got a front-row seat courtesy of my brother, Tyce—also known to the Consortium as their special agent Dario.

But Tyce had ultimately paid for his power with his life. Faline is standing there next to my wife, freshly morphed from the sleek Queen of Pretend Hell into the living sovereign of the real version. And that's not the most gut-twisting part of the sight. That aspect comes courtesy of my woman, a lace-clad Ripley ready to tear the head off the alien intruder on her spaceship. And Christ help me, looking like she's ready to turn into a walking solar flare to do it.

"Cake tiiiiime!"

And Christ *really* help me, making it necessary for me to glue a plastic smile on my lips for my new mother-in-law. "Lauren, the cake is stunning. But I'm afraid we're in hold mode for just a few—"

"Uh-uh." The woman barks it so adamantly, I wonder if I'll be ordered to drop and give her fifty as penitence for my bride's disappearance. "No more 'hold modes.' This is happening *now*, and—"

"It's really not." There's no more time for tactful regret. Not when Emma shifts another step into Faline's personal space, cocking her elbows back. "You need to excuse me."

"And *you* and my daughter need to get your damn backsides across this dance floor, over to that cake table, and—oh, holy *crap*!"

As thoroughly as I've just made the woman stun herself,

with her syntax and her shriek, I'm sure I'm more shocked by the massive pulse I've just slammed into the ground beneath me, allowing me to leapfrog half the dance floor and six banquet tables, to land in a semi-crouch in the don't-fuck-with-us danger zone my bride and my nemesis have subconsciously bubbled around themselves.

"Ah! *Hola*, Mr. Richards. What a very nice surprise!"

Unlike the last time I was subjected to those words in Faline's insidious purr, she's being facetious about them now. Clearly my arrival fits right into her plan.

But what plan?

I can't shove my mind past that question mark. I'm too obsessed with watching every *physical* move the woman makes, let alone attempting a breach of her mental end game. Focus like this has a tendency to get narrowed that way once a guy finds the woman he worships within choking or stabbing distance of a harpy lunatic shrew.

"What the hell do you want, Faline?"

The woman jogs up her chin as if I've just asked if she wants to call heads or tails for a touch football game in the park. "What? No I've-missed-you kiss? Not even a hug?"

"You heard him." Emma presses forward again, bright amber light flashing from every part of her gaze. She parts her lips, baring a determined snarl. "What the *hell* do you want?"

As soon as she finishes it with a golden pulse coming from much more than her eyes, I shift over to take her hand. To all the wedding guests, it's simply a romantic gesture; Emma's sharp grunt is the only betrayal that it's more. A symbol of restraint. If I don't make her aware of how close she is to exposing herself... in ways that would be more detrimental than just falling out of her bodice...

"Oh, now look at that." Faline drops her gaze and pushes out a mocking cluck of enchantment. "Still so affectionate after all these hours. And who says love is not everlasting?"

"And hate."

I spit it while pushing in closer to Emma—needing to know that if pressed, I'll be able to grab my wife and pulse us both away from the bitch. But the factor I can't control here, just as stressful, are all the innocent souls still positioned too damn close. Alex, Neeta, Foley, and Lydia are doing their best to clear our immediate area, but I didn't help the situation by playing the Bolt version of a three-point swish. But for now, we have the harpy talking instead of acting out. It's a win for as long as it lasts.

"*Hate?*" Faline eyes me with a tilted glance and another pronounced *tsk*. "Oh, no, no, no; let us not resort to such gloomy thoughts on such a beautiful night. How does the saying go? 'Eat, drink, be merry?' *Absoluto, sí?* Who said that? The Greeks? The Romans?"

"The Bible," Emma snaps.

"Fine, then." I curl my hands into fists, knowing it does nothing for the bright-blue sparks making like snake tongues from between my tight fingers. But this way, I'll at least prevent the grass from getting singed. "To put it in non-gloomy terms, how about the ecstasy of contemplating how to snap someone's neck while making it look like they simply gagged on the ugliness of their own choker?"

Emma keeps her answering laugh contained to a tighter hand squeeze. I want to kiss her for the restraint, but every electron of my concentration stays riveted on Faline. The bitch still hasn't exposed her higher purpose. We have no idea why she's here. We don't even know *how* she's here. She's staying zealous about not providing a shred of illumination, either.

"How did I forget how amusing you are, Reece Richards?" Her regard slides across the lower half of my face, making me want to scrub it free from her oily influence. "Such a clever man, even when you're in the heights of...*explosive* torment."

Shit. Damn. Shit.

Her attempt at being sultry and subtle isn't either, evidenced by the heightened color in my wife's cheeks. I'm *not* talking about a rosy flush of fury. Emmalina's skin tone is jaundiced yellow, rapidly approaching the realm of a rich marigold. One more shove, despite all my efforts at keeping her grounded, and the woman is going to go full solar panel.

"Oh, yawn." I go for glib despite the snap-crackle-pop continuing from my palms and fingers. "This act is tired even for you, Fa-Fa-Smurfie." I delve on, incited by the burst of ire in her gaze. "You didn't go to all this trouble, wearing that secondhand rag and even raiding the rejected jewelry pile on the Fox backlot, to show up and compliment my wit and staying power. So what gives?"

I'm not sure what part of my diatribe unleashes the woman's vicious hiss, nor do I really care. Every word was designed to get her to this. Breaking her control. Demolishing her serenity. Exposing the vile hag she really is and now unleashes in full, spitting force. "What *gives, mi amigo*? What *gives*?"

"Oh, I'm not your *amigo*, Fa-Fa."

"And I'm not your *Fa-Fa!*" With a glare that's turned vampiric, the woman lurches at me. "I am the goddess who *made* you, Reece Richards. I created you. Improved you. *Elevated* you!" She whips toward Emma, letting her lips fall back to bare her full snarl and cocking her elbows up with her fists locked against her ribcage. "And you too!"

My wife's full-throated laugh causes everyone to jump back by a foot. "*That's* the story we're going with, Queen Fa-Fa? Really? Because when did you hear me ever *thanking* you for that torture?"

"Torture?"

The echo has all three of us spinning—to the source of the horrified choke, gaping at Emma with the cake cutters dangling from her limp grip.

"Emmalina?" Laurel stammers. "Wh-What are you t-t-talking about?"

"Oh, God." Emma's fingers tighten against mine. "Mother. Please. This is a private conversation."

"Here? Now? In the middle of your wedding reception?"

"Listen to your sweet mother, darling." Faline rocks back on a heel, the action doing dangerous things to the front of her dress. "It is your big day, after all." Another contemptuous *tsk*. "It would be such a shame to let anyone or anything ruin a sparkling moment of it."

Lauren strengthens her grip on the cake cutters. Actually palms one as if considering whether it slices through more than cake. "Who the hell are *you*?"

Faline glowers. "And since when do you care, Lauren Crist?"

I don't know my mother-in-law that well, but I've learned enough to determine she's a confused person in a demanding micro-verse, where likes and followers translate directly into social status and prestige. But that's the Baccarat-crystal-clear part of the question. The other part, I've never been entirely sure of.

"Since I am her *mother*, you rude cow—and it doesn't

make me 'sparkly' to hear someone's tortured her in *any* form of the word."

Until now.

Making it really goddamned tempting to rush over and throw my arms around the woman in affection and pride...

If only her daughter wasn't the new priority on my plate. In all the most alarming and demanding versions of both "priority" *and* "plate."

Because Laurel's outrage has resulted in a leap of Faline's hackles. And a fast, ferocious hiss off the woman's lips. And enough of a resulting pounce out at Laurel to spring a shit ton of latches on Emma's control.

And like a goddamned sap gawking at a slow-mo reel of the *Mission Impossible* fuse, I watch this situation instantly transform from a shit fest into a train wreck.

"Back off, Faline." Emma rips her hand away from mine and copies the woman's advance. "*Now.*"

Faline backpedals but not without leveling a withering glare. "Come now, *querida*. Is that any way for a bride to speak to one of her guests?"

"Now isn't *that* funny...*querida*." Laurel steps up next to her daughter, switching one of the cake cutters into her opposite grip so she brandishes them like a mom-tastic Valkyrie. "Because I have nearly every name on Emmalina's guest list memorized by now, and nowhere do I recall your name on it. And you'd think I'd remember something like 'Faline the Fashion Failure.'"

Before Faline can get over swallowing her tongue, my wife is on fire again. "And just to make things clear—no way, in this dimension or any other, will you ever be my *guest.*"

And again I'm caught between what my spirit yearns to do

and what my brain is ordering me to do. Spinning Emma back around and kissing her senseless because of her fine, sassy stand-up to the bitch? Or yanking her back and ditching the kiss in favor of tucking her close because she's now the shade of impending daybreak?

Pay the fuck attention to your brain, asshole.

"Beautifully done, baby." I spin her in, but she squirms against me. She's pissed as fuck and it's sexy as hell, but giving full rein to my raging libido is not a goddamned option right now. "But now you have to stand the hell down."

"Ohhhh, *pendejo*," sneers the witch who still goads with her hands on her hips and her dress gaping wider. "Why ruin all of your bride's fun? It is her party too—and now she wants to stand the hell *up!*"

I spike a glower over the top of Emma's head. "Shut the hell up, Faline."

"You will have to come and make me, Alpha Two. Right here, before your friends and family, you will need to come and *make me.*"

Emma doesn't make the moment any easier. At every new jeer from the bitch on high, she struggles against me. Her inner fire is palpable and damn near irresistible as she uses her whole body to beg me for freedom. To be cut loose to fight the monster refusing to let us live in peace. Who's stolen even this day of joy from us.

I bore my glare deeper into the woman's elegant features. Yes, her bone structure is eternally noble, with the kind of handsome nose and full mouth one would imagine a queen of old to possess—but that's where any sane person would stop their admiration. Faline's anger at the universe would have made her this haggard even if she'd aligned herself with Pixar instead of the Scorpios. Luckily for the world, Elastigirl and Nemo are safe.

"You're enjoying this," I utter between ragged breaths of new understanding. "Aren't you? Every minute of chaos. Every second of upheaval." When her only reaction is a tight but satisfied smirk, I grate, "Why, goddamnit? Just...fucking... *why*?"

As I spew the last of it, Emma feels the exhausted drain in my body and capitalizes on her chance for freedom. I choose to let her go, knowing I might need to reclaim the hold any second—but of course, with the terrific but horrific timing they always seem to possess, the two event photographers come skidding up just as Emma turns, her skin pulsating an even brighter shade of gold. At the same second, she lets out a full scream at Faline.

"*Answer him*, you bitch!"

At once, Faline laughs. When she realizes she's the sole idiot at the party who has, she snaps back into her trademark mix of sultry fury and calculated vengeance. "Why?" The woman turns her palms up, as if getting ready to wield a pair of knives.

My blood ignites because I almost believe she will.

"You *idiotas tristes*. Why the hell *not*? And because I *can*, missss-ter and missss-usss Richards." She performs an elaborate bow during her drawn-out denigration, her dark hair tumbling into her face. "Because God *forbid* I do not come and pay homage to the fucking king and queen, right? Because their day has to be perfect. Because *they're* so perfect."

Emma advances on the woman by a step. Again, I let her—until I see exactly what the photographers are capturing with their lenses. At this point, even if I electric-bounced us out of here, half her jig would officially be up. There's such a thing as saying "the bride glowed," but then there's having to reconcile that to "the bride glowed like she had gossamer skin laid over bones made of LED lights." But there's still a chance to spin this right. We can tell the photographers that she's somehow "reflecting" off of me in the afterglow of my Bolt burst from the dance floor. Yeah. That just might work...

"You done with your moment yet, Faline?" But then there's the fact that she appears more like an angel now more than ever, even in her full-blown rage. Her lacy train swishes behind her; her hair is a messy gold braid around her luminous face. I swear to God, she's never been more exasperating and stunning in the same damn moment. "Is that what you need here? The moment of glory you never got in your sorry life?"

And that's the moment I become the king of at least *one* thing tonight. Double-taking. What the living *hell* is Emma really doing—besides antagonizing Faline in ways the woman didn't anticipate? *Fuck.* That *I* didn't anticipate.

"Velvet." I warn it through gritted teeth while pushing close to her again. "This isn't shutting her down and getting her out of here."

"No shit." Emma wrenches me off, her gaze not wavering from Faline's wide-eyed glare. "But it *is* giving her the truth about herself, damn it—maybe something somebody should have done a long time ago."

Faline pulls herself up, twisting her hands inward. It looks like she's gathering a queen's robe around herself now, though I'm still not convinced the daggers-from-nowhere thing isn't a possibility. "Oh, I know my truth, *amiga*. And believe me, it is more than what you think you know after Angelique's adorable little Freud-isms about my 'childhood' and my 'troubled parents.'"

"Yeah?" Emma retorts. "Well, they have medication for that kind of shit too."

Faline raises her head. Higher. Angles it to the point where she continues to look at my wife but does it now from along the bridge of her nose. "I do not need medicine, little Emmalina Richards."

The knowing lilt of her concluding smile is like a hot poker in my woman's eyes. I have no damn idea why she's jamming more bees down Emma's figurative underwear, but the aggravation and anger on the air are like a sloppy honeycomb from those damn insects, and it's sticking to everything and everyone. If Fa-Fa doesn't get the message and quit with the imaginary robes, the regal gloat, and the cryptic verbal runaround, I'll let my temper dash an end-run around my logic and pulse her ass all the way out to the main gate.

Except—*goddamnit*—that my gorgeous, outrageous, furious wife has already decided to beat me to the punch.

No. Not decided.

Her system isn't giving her any choice.

I know because I've been there. Letting the rage take over the blood cells. Letting the rage turn into a perfect, consuming fire...

A bright, inescapable flare.

"No," she snarls, her voice already a scorch of sound—as she lifts her taut arms and spreads her beautiful fingers—with the white-hot webs already weaving their way across the tips. "You just want everything else, Faline, no matter whom you hurt to get it!"

The nets sizzle even brighter. Ignite even hotter.

A collective gasp vibrates through the whole crowd around us—family, friends, *photographers*—though none of them is as loud or freaked as Laurel Crist.

"Emmalina?" She sags, braced on one side by Lydia and the other by Todd. "Oh, holy mother of pearl. *Emmalina?*"

"Emma." My version of it is low and determined, aimed at the back of her neck beneath her right ear. She's breathing like a frantic rabbit and poised like an avenging angel. *My* angel.

Which means I have to fight for her. To get through to her, despite her psyche feeling like the tunnels of hell and her blood burning like a thousand suns—in her case, pretty damn literally. And if I can't do that, then I'll fucking be here for her.

No matter what the hell happens.

Even as she brings her hands toward each other, poising them like readying to tangle a pair of spider webs, except for one huge difference. Her webs are on fire. And she's aiming both those fires at Faline Garand's throat.

"Mother," she finally intones. "You'd better get back. You'd *all* better get back. This witch isn't getting away from me alive."

Laurel gives the dictate all the attention of a passing dust mote. "What on *earth* are you talking about?" she snaps, even rushing forward by two more steps. The woman's as boldly stubborn as her daughter, especially when goaded by a chuckle as vile as Faline's. But while Laurel finally heeds intuition and stops, Faline's clearly only getting started with her laugh. I'm not one fucking bit surprised, and I start priming my reflexes to be ready for anything...

Except for what the bitch actually does.

Swooping forward by one deliberate step—but then immediately retreating.

Only she doesn't pull back emptyhanded.

She's lunged out to secure her own wedding day gift—and has taken advantage of everyone's shock to seize it with mind-jarring speed.

A living prize.

The terror-stricken form of Laurel Crist.

"Holy shit," I snarl.

"Mom? *Mom!*" Lydia shrieks behind us.

There's not a sound from my wife, who's honed every solar-powered cell of her body into sizzling solar rays aimed at the space around Faline, to no avail. The bitch, and the sleeve of air around her and Laurel, is impenetrable. Though I funnel full-powered lightning blasts to my fingers and join them to Emma's beams, neither of us are able to put the smallest dent or crack in that goddamned force field.

Faline takes in our efforts as if watching mosquitos smash against bug lights—right before she curls another serene smile while possessively stroking the hollow of Laurel's throat.

"What was that again, *querida*?" she croons, staring Emma down. "About me not getting away?"

Protective fury wells up through me. Bursts through my palms, which crackle with heat I've never allowed to spill out before. I slam my arms hard skyward, ignoring the air I'm bending, the party lights I'm exploding, and even the dishes I'm decimating. A bellow blazes out of me, churning with a hatred too long bottled, "Fuck. *You!*"

But the witch doesn't hear me.

She doesn't hear...because she's gone.

Vanished like a wicked star. Evaporated like a lethal poison. Completely gone from the spot in which she was just standing.

And she's taken my wife's mother with her.

SURGE

PART 14

CHAPTER ONE

EMMA

I've been Mrs. Reece Richards for less than eight hours, and I've already lied to my husband.

Even worse? I'm pretty damn sure he knows it.

Reece...we're going to be okay. Reece, even this is going to be okay.

But during the ten minutes since the words left my mouth, I know I didn't mean them. *Couldn't* mean them. No matter how deep the love that pushed them up from my heart and spurted them out of my mouth. I'd whispered the lie, wanting so desperately to drive the anguish from his eyes, the torment from his posture, and the violence that had been shooting out of his fingertips. The bright-blue bolts that he'd carved into the side of a towering rock face, having already torn out a four-foot-by-twenty-foot swath of rock before I'd arrived.

I was certain Reece was set on taking out more. Enough to take *him* out.

He was ready to let half a mountain of granite, shale, silt, and Zuma Volcanics tumble down on him rather than face his own rage, guilt, and regret.

I'm sorry. I'm so sorry, Velvet.

I hadn't filled in the rest of that for him, knowing I didn't have to. Like so many times before, our minds simply know each other—despite the clenching heartache that union brings.

Faline Garand didn't just sneak into our wedding reception like a damn thief in the night. She escaped the exact same way—and took a "wedding favor" with her.

My mother.

One second, Mom was right there, turning into the champion I never knew I had in her. Fierce. Fiery. Hell, even— *gah*—funny at moments. But most of all, standing up to Faline with badass vigor that would've been eye-popping to watch even without the knowledge of the Consortium's queen bitch capabilities.

But the next moment, learning all about Faline's evil antics firsthand.

Because she was gone.

Vanished, along with her captor, from thin air.

Taken.

But where?

Nearly seven hours after that horror, we still have no clear answer. I feel it in every molecule of energy thrumming off my husband before he even reenters the sprawling ranch house at the center of the hilltop estate where we became husband and wife a few hours ago. I feel every shred of his frustration in the reverberations from his stomps as he crosses the polished wood floor, each pound a new match on the fire already fused to the inside of me. I see it affecting everything around him as he comes through the room, pulsing the intensity of the bulbs in the wall sconces and making tassels on the throw pillows stand on end. Most clearly, it's evident in the furious clenches of all his muscles—as he clearly holds himself back from a sound self-flogging.

Noble idiot.

Beautiful ox.

Beloved husband.

And yeah, the guy who blatantly reads my mind as he comes closer, his expression darkening as the full impact from my mind hits him.

I really don't think this is going to turn out okay. Or that any of this is "fine," or will be for a long time to come. Maybe not ever.

The instant I finally bonded with my mom, even for just a couple of minutes, was the second I lost her.

Because Faline had finally been a good little wedding crasher and disappeared from our sight. From the ranch grounds completely. And now, the security patrols finally tell us, from anywhere within a ten-mile radius of this place.

Damn it.

Damn *her*.

"Anything?" The request comes from Lydia, rushing in, her white-knuckled grasp locked around Sawyer Foley's hand. I peer past the messy tumble of blond waves that tease at the guy's shoulder to the TV monitor carrying a live newsfeed from the gate at the end of the ranch's main road. Not a surprise, considering the events that went down at the reception. It's one thing to ask a wedding guest to keep their cell phone politely stowed; it's another to ask the same thing when the bride is exposing herself as the world's newest electric superhero.

But I don't feel one shade of "super" right now, especially as I watch thick tears invade my sister's plea. I'm damn grateful for Sawyer, who grips 'Dia's hand a little tighter, subconsciously preparing his woman for the grim update.

"I'm sorry." Reece stops at the top of the three descending steps into the living room. Drags a hand through his thick black-brown waves while glowering at the monitor currently broadcasting a replay of me from the reception, my hands at Faline's neck. "Not a fucking thing," he adds. "These canyons are treacherous to try to search at night. The teams are doing their best. Your dad is safely home and will be in touch to tell me if they—*she*—shows up there."

But as he glances to Foley and then to me, the message underlying the statement is obvious. He's not pushing the search into the canyon. There's no point. Faline didn't simply road runner it out into Malibu freaking Canyon at night. She really did get away by disappearing in front of our eyes. If the feat was just a magic trick, then it was a damn good one— meaning she likely had someone waiting in a car out at the main road ready to take them and hide them away. Someplace *not* close, that's for certain.

And if it wasn't a magic trick?

That's a little more complicated.

And terrifying.

The possibility that Faline has a Consortium power we don't know about yet...if she actually proved that teleportation isn't just for the United Federation of Planets anymore...

Shit, shit, shit.

I can't bear to think about it—but I have to. And force myself to. Tension racks my entire form, and I tremble uncontrollably from the second Reece reaches me. I let him feel every tremor despite the stress still tangibly claiming him. His breath erupts like stuttering static into my hair as he dips his head and folds me against his big body.

And just like that, I'm home. Back in the smoky, masculine scent of him and the gripping, consuming strength of him— fortitude that couldn't be more direly needed, especially as I work to gather air and get out all the shitty words. Shitty but necessary.

"They could be anywhere, couldn't they?"

Reece doesn't relent his hold. Without words, he drops one defined nod.

"Reece."

I wait for him to drag away, obeying my behest for direct eye contact. As soon as I take in the silver tempests in his focused but turbulent stare, I stammer, "Even...Spain?"

Spain.

The Consortium's ultimate home. Where they permanently keep the hive, their most advanced and powerful lab, made up of their hexagon-shaped "experimentation chambers."

And the cells for hundreds of human test victims.

A complex we still haven't been able to find.

A secret so well hidden, even Angelique La Salle can't tell us a thing about how to get there, despite being an inside agent for the bastards for months.

The living hell Mom might be enduring this second.

Reece swallows down what looks like a wad of lead, betraying that his thoughts have followed the exact same path as mine. "I'm sorry." His grate is just as ominous, striking the center of my heart and fissuring it a thousand different directions. "I'm so sorry, Velvet."

"I know," I whisper. "Me too."

"You too?" He grabs the back of my head and gathers me tight against his chest. "What the hell for?"

"I treated Faline like she'd walked into our reception right out of the gutter—"

"Because if this place was in the center of downtown and

not the middle of Malibu Canyon, and we could've tossed her right back *into* the gutter, that would've been okay?" he growls.

"All right, so screw okay." I push closer to him, but it's still not near enough. If it was possible, I'd open up his chest and crawl right inside, if only to be right next to the strength of his thrumming heart. His hold tightens as if he's read that thought. Who the hell am I kidding? Of *course* he's read that thought.

Another long, low rumble unfurls from his center. "Yeah, okay can suck it." He twists his strong, bold fingers into what's left of my bridal braids and then spreads his legs to lock my hips between his. "I only need this, damn it."

In every one of his actions, I feel the ferocity and urgency of his gut-level protectiveness. I'm certain, without any doubt, that he needs this intense closeness to battle the terror joined with his remorse: the realization that if Faline snatched Mom that fast, she'd be able to do the same to me. My combat instincts and reaction times have gotten better but are definitely not at the level she showed off at the reception.

Now *I'm* gulping down lead.

And gritting back the need to repeat everything I just told him in the canyon—though this time, not just for his comfort.

It'll be okay. It'll be okay. It'll be okay.

But despite chanting the mantra out loud, I can't control the harsher shivers that take over my very marrow, spreading over my tendons and muscles until they dominate every inch of my frame. They worsen as I think again about all the attitude and vitriol I flung at Faline. I was so pumped on action, adrenaline, even the thrill of true love. In short, I'd become a victim of what Sawyer labels a "hero high." He claims it happens to field ops guys too: the sensation that there's nothing their power can't do or the trained agility in their body can't handle. Having to remember that they're mortal and *can* be broken becomes too much work—no matter how necessary that work *has* to be.

How vital it has to become for me right now.

As if the universe knows I need a little nudge in that direction, a pronounced sniffle erupts from a few feet away. A sound I'd know anywhere—and allow to whittle all the way into my heart—because it's been around my whole life.

Human weakness, please prepare the air bags. I'm coming in for a crash landing.

The second I lift my head from Reece's chest and gaze over at Lydia, she's already looking away—with a lot of determined purpose.

What the hell?

Is she *pissed* at me? About all of this? Is she *blaming me* for what happened to Mom?

And sure enough, the thought pisses me off too. It makes no damn sense, considering I had all my fingers pointed back this direction two minutes ago, but *she's* always the one on hand to talk me *out* of this shame game. Whether it was too many slices of pizza after the big game, too few points on the social science midterm, or too many hours keeping vigil by Reece during his induced coma, she's been there to talk me down off the ledge.

But now...

What's going on?

Does she think either Reece or I could've known this was going to happen? And if she thinks we did, does she really think we went ahead with the wedding anyway? And if she thinks that...

I can't stomach a single minute more of *that* mental spin class.

My tap-out starts with a gentle push at Reece's chest. I meet his narrowed gaze with an apologetic twist of my lips and a brief brush of my fingers through the thick stubble defining his jawline. "Just tired," I murmur, hoping it's sufficient for his concern but knowing it'll really buy me just a few minutes at best. "I'm going to go change, okay?" I'm sure my wedding gown is as exhausted as I am, having been through more adventures than what it was created for, despite being a—*gasp*—off-the-rack purchase from a chi-chi eveningwear store in the Beverly Center, where Mom and I stopped for some lunch during a day of consultations with designers. I'd been so excited and relieved to find it. Mom, of course, had been horrified.

The memory stops me in my tracks. It makes me laugh, until suddenly I'm not laughing. I'm sobbing, pouring out the fear and anxiety and dread that's thrummed near the surface of my sanity for the last seven hours. It all punches through now, bursting my control and dominating my heart, turning into racking bursts of grief in my cupped hands.

This was supposed to be the happiest day of my life.

But happiness is like the hero high.

It can be appreciated. Honored. Valued for the lessons it teaches but never trusted as the certainty that'll be there within the next minute. The next second.

"Baby girl."

I hiccup to a stop. Jerk my head up. Not that either is going to fool Lydia, who's managed to sneak up on me even in the terra cotta breezeway between the main house and the wedding party dressing rooms.

"Wh-What do you want?" I can't hold back the bitter overtones, my spirit still stung by her weird behavior inside.

"Thought you could use some help with the dress." She's

not making anything better with her own tone, threaded with nothing but sister-style tenderness.

What the hell is her deal?

I communicate as much by whirling toward her, the earthy tie-dye along my skirt swishing around my legs. "The dress?" I retort. "You mean this thing with one hook and one zipper, like the ones I was getting in and out of for myself fifteen years ago?"

It's a whip when I only meant to use a fly swatter, but I refuse to take it back—and am grateful I don't have to. What I said to Reece was partially true. I *am* really tired, and even though 'Dia's the bee under my saddle right now, it feels good to take off the kid gloves and throw a decent verbal punch, knowing we'll still love each other after this. Just doesn't mean I have to *like* her right now—especially as she scoots past me with a blithe stroll, swooping out her hand with a condescending air before drawling, "Right. Sure. The good ol' days. Jo Bros posters, lunch at Ruby's on the pier, and you dressing yourself. And oh yeah, those times when we didn't have to watch our *mother* getting 'disappeared' in front of our eyes? Remember *those*?"

"I always will."

I truly mean every syllable of the soft and sad declaration, but it only ramps our tension as we arrive at the entrance to the bridal dressing suite. There's no way either of us can ignore the messes on either side of the double French doors: heaps of potting soil and bedraggled flowers surrounded by the red dust that used to be their homes. The crimson powder *I* created when we first arrived back here from the disaster known as my wedding reception and I had no better place to direct my frustration than at those clay pots. I'd let the rage loose for a solid five minutes, turning into a human kiln—and though that episode also must be on my sister's mind again now, I turn and attempt another verbal peace offering.

"I remember it all like the times I could rely on my sister to understand that my life isn't like any other. Also, that I didn't necessarily choose any of it to happen like this, okay?"

Damn it. As trite as it sounds, tears are *not* my freaking intention right now. Still, I allow the whopping droplets to slide down my cheeks and congregate along my top lip, as I work to form more words from between my locked teeth. "I didn't just sit down and command the cosmos to give me this life, 'Dia. I didn't wake up one morning and finish off my daily devotional by gazing up at the ceiling and saying, 'Hey, God-type buddy. You know what would totally make my day? Falling in love at first sight with the world's strangest, broodiest bad boy, only to find out that he's the city's coolest, most badass superhero. Holy crap, that would just be epic. If you make that happen, I'll swear off Nutella for a year.'"

If we were having any other kind of a conversation, the two of us would be lost to giggles by now. Instead, 'Dia yanks open one of the doors and keeps her gaze fixed on one of the waist-high pots across the patio, probably grateful I've managed to clamp down the powers to a reasonable temperature.

Or so she thinks.

At the moment, I'm simply doing a better job of not showing the turmoil. But she needs to see it. She needs to *know* it as well as I do. "So...what?" I challenge, circling toward her with my arms outstretched. "What do you want me to say here, Lydia?" I scuff to an angry stop. "That all of this is 'normal' for me? That somehow, just because my mitochondria are doing the electric cha-cha, I know and understand why Faline pulled a woo-woo Matrix on us at the reception? You don't think I'm just as scared and uncertain and freaked the hell out about this as you? That I don't want to go grab my husband, bug the crap out of here, and dive under the covers at the private rental in Monterey where we're supposed to be screwing the white out of each other's eyeballs on our honeymoon right now?"

Well, holy shit.

I've done it this time.

Lydia Harlow Crist—my take-charge, smartass, one-liner-for-every-occasion sister—is actually wringing her hands. The twisty, anxious, just-thrown-into-a jail-with-a-bruiser-named-Bubba kind. "Shit. I'm sorry." She de-kinks the twist in her lips long enough to add, "I really am, baby girl."

She grabs one of my hands, pulls me across the dressing room, and then drags us both down onto the long leather sofa in front of the stone hearth. Like we've done so many times before, we turn to each other and hike up a knee along the cushion—only the movement from me is a timing catastrophe, since the bottom twelve inches of my fine lace skirts are now an interesting ombré sprinkled in clay-pot dust. At mid-calf length, the dress's pure white lace turns apple beige, then oak-bark brown, and then nearly black, a reminder of everything I've done to truly earn the Dirtiest Bride in the World award. I'm shocked that my gem-encrusted Keds show a bit of dust but nothing more. The difference between the two is like Bellatrix standing next to Umbridge. Okay, crappy metaphor—but maybe that's perfect for the moment as well.

"Ohhhh, gawd." As 'Dia moans it, she pushes the pads of her thumbs at the corners of her eyes, holding back her own tearful attack for a few seconds longer. "You know why all the superheroes' families don't get the cool storylines? Because their lives are major suckage, that's why."

Though I have sworn to myself I won't get all goopy again, I clutch her hand tighter. "I'm so sorry, my Dee Dee Doo."

"It's all right, butthead." She invokes her special nickname, reserved for the occasions when I use the unique version of hers. "I—I just don't know what to do about all this, you know?" she goes on in a watery rasp. "While I know damn well we're not firing up rocket ships or swooping down the 405 on the ends of spider web slings here, a huge part of me has perceived this all as some massive, fun adventure."

I purse my lips while giving that a quiet contemplation. "I understand," I finally tell her. "I really do. Even after Reece showed me his mask, and through so much that happened after that—the showdown with Angie in El Segundo, his public reveal at the tennis gala, you and me being kidnapped—"

"And almost killed."

"There *was* that."

"But even after that, and despite all the times Sawyer has tried telling me this isn't all just a wild 4-D ride, it just hasn't..." She uses her free hand to rub the center of her forehead. "It's just never sunk in, you know? I thought we'd all just get to unsnap our seat belts, get out of the ride pod, and go have some beers at Naja's." She stops the rubbing. Drills her hand back through her mussed curls. "But that's not going to happen, is it?"

I pull in a long breath. "Not anytime soon, honey."

"You all really are fighting some nasty-ass crazies."

"Nasty-ass," I repeat before chuffing. "Capital N and capital A."

Lydia slowly shakes her head. "This sucks."

"I know."

"That bitch took our mother. Just like that. Just because... why?"

Her last few words are struggling chokes. And once again today, I'm wrapping my arms around a person I love and then whispering into their ear with as much purpose as I can push out, "It's going to be all right. It really is."

Lydia, her face fitted into my nape, emits a loud and shameless snuffle. "Baby girl," she mutters during my answering laugh. "You're a shitty liar."

"So harsh, wench!" I protest. "I simply don't have a crystal ball." As we pull apart and clasp hands again, I give into something else inside. The boosting reassurance of hope. "But you know what? I don't need one, Dee Dee. I know, whatever's going on, that she's survived this. Faline hasn't made her pay the ultimate price."

"Not yet." 'Dia cocks her brows.

"Not *ever*," I rebut—and this time, she doesn't call me on the lie because I *know* this one to be completely true. "That's not the bitch's end game. If anything, she'll take Mom and—"

I'm not sure what stops me first: the inability to speak every horrific thing that's just drenched my mind or the screeching brakes I apply about relaying them to Lydia. Because, for all my sister's boggling physical strength and mental fortitude, she's just as drained right now as I am. She doesn't need to hear shit like *she's going to take Mom into a concrete-lined room and strap her down before blowtorching every cell of her bloodstream open. So you see, sister? Impossible to do that to a dead person, right?*

But as soon as the thoughts hit my mind, they take over my face—confirmed by 'Dia's high, harsh sob. As she lets me go and lurches unsteadily to her feet, I inwardly smack myself for the composure breach. But damn it, I'm only human. A very defeated human, sitting here in nothing but a few layers of dirty lace, a pair of sparkly Keds, and a thick wall of unshed tears. I don't have golden bracelets, titanium war sticks, or panther wrist blasters to help with the badass factor right now, and while 'Dia was chill with me venting by frying the flower pots outside, I doubt she'd feel the same if I unleashed some Flare fire in this contained space. Not in her current state of mind.

"She'll take Mom and what?" she demands into my uncomfortable silence. "And *what*, Emma? And *where*?" With fists she keeps balling and then flexing, she paces around the end of the couch, along its backside, and then around the end closest to the hearth. The depths of the fireplace, shrouded in gray and navy shadows, are just a shade darker than the glare she whips around and into me. "Do you really know, Emma? Does Reece? And if so, then why aren't—"

I cut her short because I'm on my feet again too. "We're pulling every thread we can." I grab her hand again, hoping to arrest her mind with the force of my stare. At the same time, I silently beg her not to ask for more details. It's horrible enough to fight the visions of everything Faline might be subjecting Mom to. Having to even think about relaying them to Lydia...

"Your sister's right."

Sometimes, the Bolt of LA really does have the best timing. Like this moment, appearing at the far door as he makes the declaration in the baritone that slays my senses, seizes my heart, and wins my love all over again. And a few *other* parts of me, helpless about confirming some other truths about my superhero spouse, as long as I'm at it.

One, he looks damn good in a filthy tuxedo.

Two, he makes the look even better while pledging a sincere vow to my sister.

Three, he looks absolutely the best when peering at me through the loose, dark waves that tumble around his eyes. Like he's about to order the whole world to fall away for me. Like he's going to back up the command with lightning strikes from those incredible irises of his.

With my heart answering like a thousand sparklers, practically pushing the damn organ out of my chest in its need to feel his, so vibrant and bright and bold, beating against mine once more. Honestly, if I was hooked up to any of the ridge's training monitors right now, the guy would be flashing a teasing smile, urging me to back off my pace and get in some breaths.

But I don't want to breathe right now.

I only need the assurance of him right now. *All* of him.

In all the best possible ways.

CHAPTER TWO

REECE

Before yanking open the French door, I caught enough of my reflection in a couple of the panes to know I look more like a degenerate who hiked in from his hutch in the wilderness than the tuxed-up guy who slipped a ring onto the finger of his gorgeous bride a few hours ago. Thankfully—or maybe scarily—neither of the women inside even blinks at my dishevelment. As a matter of fact, Emma's gaze gains a new glint, reconnecting me to her in a million and one perfect ways.

"Well, hey there, *brother*." Under normal conditions, Lydia would likely shoot out a giggle to punctuate that. Tonight, I at least get half a goofy smile as she tries on the new nickname. I screw together my composure, trying to copy the expression before responding.

"Hey there, bratty sister." I easily catch the pillow she hurls my way. "I always *did* wonder what it would be like to say that..."

"Well, I hope I fulfilled every one of your fantasies."

"That would be your sister's job."

"Okay, ew." She's approached close enough to take back the pillow from my grip and then use it to cushion-clobber my head. "I think that's my cue to go find Sawyer—but not before this." And just like that, she's pummeling me in a new way—

with a hug that's as harsh as it is heartfelt, nearly knocking every ounce of air from me. Not that I mind one damn bit—and, knowing she needs the return squeeze just as much, hold back nothing in giving it to her. After she greedily accepts my comfort, she declares into the meat of my shoulder, "You're still the one I'd order her to marry, you big dork."

A wry chuff tumbles from me. "And you're still the one I'd want doing the ordering, Princess Purple Pants."

She lifts her head enough to clobber the spot she'd just warmed with her tender words. "Just take care of her right, and we'll have no problems."

"That's the intention." I state it with every speck of intensity and sincerity I can muster. "Today. Forever. Always."

I don't get another drubbing for that—at least not physically. 'Dia's violent jerk back, along with her wrinkled nose, communicate damn near the same intention. "Gawd, I hope Sawyer has something for mush-talk overload. Our fantasy football grid, maybe. Or a nice Halestorm track or two."

Emma takes a second to wrinkle her nose. "Since when are you into Halestorm?"

Lydia cocks a flippant grin. "Since I found out how good they are with rope and cuffs."

Emma folds her arms. "There's this fun little expression, Dee Dee. TMI?"

"Oh, I love that one. He and I are best buds." Lydia winks at her sister. "And now you and I are even."

"For now." Emma has to shout it out since her sister is already halfway through the door.

In 'Dia's absence, Emma and I are left in a vacuum of sound—which, apparently, has sucked all my sexual suavity from the atmosphere, as well. As I set the pillow back against the couch's armrest, I'm conscious of my heartbeat taking residence in my stomach and my coordination turning in its request for instant vacation time. I'm literally so nervous, I plump the pillow five times—but on the sixth, I end up incinerating a hole in the middle of it.

"What the living hell?" I growl, answered at once by Emmaline's musical giggle. Thankfully, there's a skittish edge to her burst, as well.

"Guess we'll have the ranch add that to the bill."

Though I'm weirdly relieved by the up-and-down husks in her voice, it does nothing to soothe my jacked nerves. "Then it's a good thing I prepaid for three days, plus incidentals." I jam my hands into my pockets, rocking back and forth on my feet. "Though that's not...an incidental, yeah?" I whip one of my hands out and jab it into my hair. "Says the guy who owns a bunch of luxury hotels. *Fuck*."

The word does double duty. It's both castigation and exhilaration, marking the second I figure out I'm as dumb as a tack right now, and also the reason why. I haven't been this nervous since that first night I ever laid eyes on this woman, when she compounded the thrill of meeting her to the joy of watching her approach across my penthouse, a sweet smile on her lush lips and those wicked stilettos on her gorgeous feet. She steals my breath just as thoroughly—no; she fucking confiscates it—padding over in her adorable Keds with an adoring smile, her eyes alive with turquoise fire and a diamond band agleam on her left ring finger.

My diamond band.

Jesus H. Christ with a thousand lightning bolts.

She's really mine.

I should be celebrating that truth with elation in a bedroom ten feet off the Monterey Coast, not here, ten feet from where she demolished some poor plants in her misery and frustration. But Emma's clearly not dwelling on that—and, if the golden heat across her face is any indication, she's set a mission to make sure I'm not either. She flows her body next to mine with a satisfied sigh, and I answer her with a guttural groan even as I encircle my arms all the way around her graceful curves.

I breathe her in, so much sunshine and honey and heat.

I soak her up, so much energy and need and connection.

I rejoice because of her here, close and tight and safe.

But for how much longer?

And *that*, shitty as it is, wins the prize for the only thought I *am* certain of today. The sole surety that thrums through the head I lower to nuzzle her neck, using every tool in my primal arsenal to keep her settled right here, feeling so good and smelling so good and being simply right. Being my *more*.

I let out a breath nearly in tandem with hers, which emerges as a happy-sounding sigh. Thank fuck she feels it too: that we need just one second to remember we're supposed to be totally giddy and climbing all over each other by this point of the day, not counting every minute that stretches by without even a signal flare from Faline.

And that officially marks too many damn times the woman's name has invaded my mind in the last twenty-four hours. Hell, in the last *four* hours. I part my lips, murmuring the only name I should even be thinking of chanting right now. The name that should have been there already.

"Emmalina. *Emmalina Paisley Richards.*"

She lets me rock her head back so I can suckle at the front

of her throat as well. "Hmmmm." There's a dreamy mist in her voice and graceful adoration in her fingers, which she uses to grip my biceps. "I don't think that'll ever get tired, Mr. Reece Andrew Richards."

"Well, you'll need to let me know if it does." I nip into the small valley at the other side of her neck, savoring how her breath snags as soon as I get to the sensitive skin just below her ear. "Your satisfaction is our goal at Richards Resorts."

She trickles out a laugh while pulling herself up by a few inches—just enough to wrap one hand against the back of my head. "My *complete* satisfaction?"

At first, all I do is groan. Along with the hand at my scalp, she anchors one of my ass cheeks with her ankle. Finally I'm able to growl, "Yes, ma'am. *Completely* complete."

"Even if that entails me getting to fuck the boss?"

And just like that, the control I've been dictating to my cock is history.

"Completely complete." I echo it because I don't have to think about anything else. Because I *can't* think about anything else.

"Well, Mr. Richards." Her tone is as sultry as her touch, as she travels her hand into the crevice between my neck and shirt collar—and then tugs up her knee, urging the center of my body to fit tighter with hers. "I may have to do some market testing on this...guarantee of yours."

She finishes on a gasp as my crotch tightens and grows, pulsing inexorably at the center of hers. Her all-over shiver brings on the sensation I'm holding a masterpiece in the making, a stunning sculpture still captured in clay. But as deeply as I crave to mold her, I know she's dictating my evolution too—and I'm beyond welcoming of it.

We both need this. We both *are* this.

Clay and creator. Paint and artist. Servant and master. Surrender and desire.

The exchange that makes us whole.

The connection that makes us strong.

That will make us even stronger, even if we selfishly indulge this consummation. Yes, even in the midst of the chaos Faline has rained on us. No. *Because* of it.

I'm so drenched by that truth, I drag up so Emma can see it in the burning boldness of my gaze, fed by the certainty of my soul. At once, I'm glad I've made the move. Her face is nothing short of captivating. Her high, creamy cheeks are teased by a thousand white-gold strands fallen free from her braids, and enough of her sparkly, rose-colored makeup is still left to lend her the glamour of a sexy woodland fairy, especially with the hem of her gown now dipped in forest shades.

Her dress.

As much I love the thing, I direct a pointed glower down at it. "What happened to you getting out of this thing?"

She colors enough that her cheeks match her pretty eye shadow—before she swings her chin up again. "Maybe part of my satisfaction package is Reece Richards taking it off me."

I'm damn glad I put an inch of extra room between us. As soon as the words leave her mouth, my cock pulses and takes up the space—and then even more, as soon as my fly taps at the filmy layers of her dress. "Ahhh," I murmur. "I see. Well, my apologies, Mrs. Richards. I guess I didn't read the fine print of your package...details."

My purposeful pause between the last two words, along with my lingering gaze over her mouth, renders the exact effect I've intended. With her pupils dilating and her chest pumping, the woman presses back toward me with the urgency of a tide to its shore. Just as quickly, I shift away, but she has her own hidden weapon in this game.

Her fingers.

Those tapered, talented, beautiful, incredible digits...

Closing around my crotch with an exquisite mix of pressure and softness...

"Jesus *fuck*." I spill it on a groan, weathering the mixture of elation and aggravation from the depths of my balls, grabbed like pouches of fine diamonds. It's agony. It's ecstasy. She's captured the very core of me. Okay, in more ways than one, that goes without saying—but at this second, the one that dominates my attention the most is the pressurized zone beneath those knowing, feeling fingers...

"As you can tell, Mr. Richards, I'm *all* about the package."

I drag my stare from her mouth to her eyes—as I let my head answer the pull of her entrancing beauty. "Well, then. I'll have to be more attentive about the details."

Details I'm all too happy to catalogue as I sweep my mouth atop hers in a crushing, consuming connection.

The succulent fruit of her lips, spreading at once beneath my commanding stab.

The addicting grotto of her mouth, as her tongue welcomes mine in a torrid tangle.

The spellbinding pliability of her body, absorbing my passion without question or hesitation or resistance.

And yes, even after I pull my lips back: the complete spell of her gorgeous face, flooded but afire at the same time, her blinks slow but her breaths fast...

Waiting.

Waiting for *me*.

Ready for me.

And holy fuck, am I ready for *her*.

"Turn around," I husk, using my hands at her hips to help her. As soon as I have her body spun, with her proud shoulders and lithe back and entrancing heart of an ass facing me, I twist the tiny hook at the center of her nape, leaning in to lick at even that tiny piece of newly exposed skin. She hums in new arousal. I growl in fresh desire.

"Oh!" she rasps the second I tug at the zipper that'll guide my hand down to the middle of her delectable ass.

"You're delicious," I grate into her skin, continuing to taste and bite along her spine, savoring the tropical blends of her unique taste mingled with the tart tang of her perspiration. Yeah, even that flavor is pure ambrosia on my tongue. The perfect blend of spicy and sweet, so satisfying and yet whetting my hunger for more.

So much more...

"Oh..."

The word tumbles from Emma as five syllables instead of one, each interspersed with a new tremble of her whole form as I push the zipper lower...and keep following with the tip of my tongue and the edges of my teeth...

"Oh!"

Only one syllable this time, scissoring the air with sharp shock and new lust, as the dress drops into a puddle at her feet and I dip down to bite firmly into the tops of her buttocks. This flesh is even more mouthwatering than what I've already feasted on, and I tell her so with an extended moan as I follow the direction of her gown and land on my knees with a thud on the thick area carpet between the couch and fireplace.

"Fuck me to hell and back." The snarl feels damn good to

indulge as I grip harder into her perfect, rounded flesh—and then lower a greedy bite into that perfect cream. "And everyone says bunnies taste gamey."

It makes her spurt an adorable laugh, meaning other parts are surely gushing as well. I inhale deeply, confirming that. The air is potent with the heady perfume of her soaring sensuality, causing me to suck in another long breath. I'm not even close to being a satisfied diner tonight.

"Reece," she begs atop a gasp as I bend in and lap my way to the crease between her crotch and thigh.

With a brief growl of frustration, I stop for just a second to jerk down her lace panties. They plummet atop of her gown, and I nod briefly in caveman satisfaction.

"Oh, Reece," she exclaims as I stroke up the insides of her thighs with lusty languor. Finally, I arrive at the triangle between them. I focus in, my world becoming her exposed pussy: the world made for me to be lost in. The beautiful scent of her. The rich colors of her. The silken grip of her, folding in around my delving fingers... "Oh, *God*!"

I caress in again, stretching my middle fingers until they find her tight, luscious opening, surrounded by the fragrant fruit of her sex. The peachy flesh is already drenched for me, and her intimate walls pulse with steady rhythm, begging for my deeper invasion.

"Get up here." I release one hand long enough to smack the couch's leather seat. "Both knees on the cushions, Bunny. Then rest your head against the back and show me all the pulp of your pretty fruit."

With aching little whimpers, she complies. I've never seen anything so damn sexy in my life. Fleetingly, I think about getting up to lock the door, but my libido screams its denial of the request. Could have something to do with my crappy-but-flawless timing. As soon as I worry about the door, Emma stretches her legs apart to gain more of her balance—resulting in the perfect lift and sway of her ass and the further unfolding of her fucking gorgeous flower.

So yeah: crappy.

But *hell* yeah: flawless.

Especially as she adjusts her balance by just one more inch...

Enough to spread herself even more for me...

"Dear *fuck*." For long seconds, it's the only thing I'm capable of spouting. Or thinking. And sure as hell am obsessed with *doing*. My instinct screams with it. My balls, still throbbing from her sexy fondling, are aching for it. My dick has all but become an actual lightsaber, threatening to slice right through my pants to have it. To have *her*. Stretch her. Consume her. To be totally, rapturously, surrounded by her...

But only after I've had my mouth on her.

Have tasted every layer of her pink and red dessert. Have made her tremor beneath my tongue and felt her quiver to the depths of her core. Have grabbed her hips even tighter to keep her locked as I ravish her some more...

Just like I dip in and begin doing now.

And groan as she bucks against me, all of her tissues pulsing at my eager, hungry lips.

And growl as her juices become a tangy river flooding along the length of my tongue.

And hum in complete command, finally flicking aside her soaked hood and taunting the erect button below until she's panting and sobbing and twisting at the back of the couch so hard, the leather squeaks beneath her grip.

"Reece. *Reece.* Goddamnit!"

I remove my mouth from her by barely an inch, releasing a hum of feigned disapproval. "Now, is that any way to address someone dedicated to the quality of your 'package,' Mrs. Richards?"

She laughs again, though the sound is a wobbly string of oh-hell-he-really-did-*not*. But as soon as she recognizes that hell yes, I certainly *did*, she blurts, "Mr.—Mr. Richards. P-P-Please. Oh, *please.* I-I need—"

"You need..." I draw out the verb, blatantly goading her—all the while continuing to simply tap at her clit every few seconds, reveling in the resultant vibrations throughout her body, strung as taut as an electric line across a lake. And holy shit, how I love being her lake.

"I-I need..."

"Tell me, Mrs. Richards." One more tongue tap on her erect little nub. "I'm here to serve. I want to know exactly what you need. Exactly what I can do to make this beautiful bloom of a cunt become a happy, orgasmic little flower."

"Oh, God."

"No. 'Mr. Richards' is just fine." One of the hottest goddamn things she's said to me from the start—and that'll never get old, even as we do.

If we get the damn chance to grow old.

If we get the damn chance to see next *week*...

Thoughts that are banished at once with my obstinate grunt. That doomsday isn't permitted in this reality. That poisoned needle gets nowhere near the shining bubble of our bliss.

You can't take this away from me, I silently snarl at fate. *Not time to pop the bubble, you bastard.*

"It's...it's so good. Just...just please...I need..."

"Uh-uh." I enforce it by shifting my mouth by an inch, sliding the flat of my tongue along the succulent cushions of her labia. "Ask *nicely*, like a good little bunny." And then nibble into her inner thigh, loving how her firm flesh pebbles beneath my mouth. "'Mr. Richards, will you please give me...'"

"Mr. Richards," she rasps at once but makes the mistake of celebrating with a deep breath. That's my cue to trail my lips back in, exploring even more of her soft and quivering flesh... and turning her voice into a matching cadence. "W-W-Will you p-p-please...give me...*oh!*"

She cries out as I circle her glistening entrance with the tip of my tongue. I pull back just enough to stare, enraptured, as her muscles knead the air in their quest for fulfillment. I go back in, using a fingertip this time. Tease at her, working the penetration at different angles, studying what movements make her gasp the hardest, tremble the most, flow with the most fresh arousal. I'm so captivated, I could seriously do this for the next few hours. Hours we don't have, damn it.

How the hell have I bedded so many women and not taken the time to study the beauty of an aroused pussy? And *there's* an all too easy and instant answer. None of those blooms belonged to *this* woman. This creature I want to know everything about, from top to bottom, from outside to in...

Which is why I twist my wrist with slow purpose, penetrating her deeper with my thrusting, pulsing finger.

And, once again, look on in fascination as she welcomes me into the tight, hot clutch of her most intimate core.

And join my groan to her gasp as I flow more electricity into my digit, zapping her walls with a bright-blue burst of sexual energy.

And then smile as her flesh answers mine with an equally brilliant glow.

We're connected. Cobalt and gold. Steel and satin. A Bolt and his Flare. Energies climbing. Passions rolling. Arousals reaching...

"Oh!" Emma erupts again, shredding the word inside her clutching throat. "Oh, dear *hell*. I'm...I'm not sure I can..."

"Of course you can." I'm purposeful with the words but not my self-control. Knowing it's a damn mistake to do so, I join another finger to my first. But I need—I *need*—to watch her wet tissues welcome me, stretch for me, clench around me. My cock beats harder at my fly, beyond craving that tight tunnel to heaven for itself.

So close now...

Not close enough.

But how can I ask her to focus on keeping her desire tethered if I can't force the same deference on my own dick? *She's worth it. So fucking worth it.* The mantra becomes my dogma as I manipulate my hand with more determined twists, beginning a steady, taunting fuck into her dark, soaking depths. Soon, every push elicits a matching pant from Emma, as rough and primal and urgent as my treatment of her incredible cunt. For a long moment, I close my eyes, committing the sound to memory. This erotic rhythm will be the soundtrack of my most illicit fantasies for years—decades—to come.

If fate allows me to see those years.

Another attack of doom on the bubble. This time, I fight back by focusing on more comfortable things—like the incessant beat of my cock at my fly. The strain of my flesh and the growl of my veins are channeled at once to my voice, as I drive my digits deeper into her and instruct, "You can do this, baby. And you *will* do this. Just tighten everything, like I've taught you in training. Focus the effort into all the muscles around here." With my free hand, I fan a possessive touch across the flat plane over her womb. "Rein it in. Hold it back. You can do this. Just like in training."

She grips harder at the couch. Never in my life have I ever thought squeaking leather could be such a lust-worthy sound. Even her protesting growl adds to the perfect aesthetic of the moment. "In training, I'm not nearly naked and being turned to mush by a certain bastard's magic finger wands."

Before I can help myself, a chuckle spills out. "Says the enchantress with the pussy that could tame every ogre in the kingdom?"

Her giggle is like music. "*Every* ogre?" And her gasp, more perfect than the night wind that buffets the windows.

"Don't get any fucking ideas." I reinforce the dictate by withdrawing my fingers, instead sliding them around the erect red ridge at her center and closing them around it in a brutal pinch. "This talisman belongs to the king alone," I growl in tandem with her sharp scream. "And the king refuses to share."

"Well." She stops to indulge another whispering tremble as I give in to an extra pinch of her pretty clit. "That sounds like a problem for the queen."

"That so?" Our little break for levity presents a perfect chance to shift my ass—and the rest of me—into a decent gear. "Now how exactly do you figure that, m'lady?"

"Well, if the king's got a thing for the enchantress with the talisman..."

"Ah. But what if the king is a wise man and ordered the enchantress to become his queen?"

"Forced wedlock?"

"Oh, never." I emphasize with a pair of adoring kisses to the indents at the small of her back. "But a little tenacious seduction never hurt anyone..."

"Of course not." Her hips quiver in time to her unsteady sigh. "Though a little screaming can always be so much fun."

And that fucking does it.

So much for his majesty the urbane king, who's reached for the fastenings on his pants with the refinement of an underwear model. I'm yanking and tugging and wrenching, only to encounter frustration with every move. "For fuck's *sake." Seriously,* fuckers? So I'm not a goddamned model, but that doesn't mean I haven't been offered contracts. So when did this shit get so damn difficult? Another easy answer. *Since you decided to play with your wife's pussy until she creamed all over your fingers and turned your cock into a caged beast.*

If that beast could chomp off my hand, I'm damn certain it would. But thank fuck for metaphors that only sound good on paper, because that bastard really fucking needs my hand right now. To stroke and squeeze, ensuring every screaming vein beneath the stretched skin feels acknowledged and appreciated. To tell them all it's okay; everyone's welcome to come out and play. And as soon as the blue-silver drops appear in the slit at the top, guiding their trajectory into the crevice that'll bring on the best pleasure for my gorgeous, sparkling girl.

Between the perfect globes of her upturned ass.

As soon as my precome drips into her sensitive valley and she reacts with the most erotically charged shriek I've ever heard, I realize that "sparkling" was just the woman's opening show.

"Sweet Christ," I grate as soon as her freshly amped

cells send their aroused signal to the pores of her skin. She's a thousand prisms flooded with dawn's light. A million stars blown apart by an astral explosion. A flowing fabric of living threads, surely woven by the angels themselves. And when I reach out, flowing a hand down the graceful slope of her back, she feels just as magical.

She feels like my miracle.

With every breath I pull in while leaning back over her, acknowledging every one of her vertebrae with a savoring suckle along the way, I connect even more of my circuitry to that certainty. Knot even more of my spirit into the brilliance of hers. Lose myself in the gilded splendor of her body, the siren call of her soul.

I'm a ship in the night, helpless to resist.

I'm an aimless rudder, craving her guidance.

I'm a mast struck by lightning, needing her light to wrap around me. To repair me. To be one with me so that we can stand strong together in this storm we're still attempting to call a life.

And with my sole, urgent thrust, she is.

And we're groaning together as she surrounds me completely with her light.

And we're moving together as I fuck into her with mine.

And we're filling the room with craving, aching, burning, lusting, loving—not just because it's crashing through our blood, swelling through our hearts, and exploding through our senses.

Because it's taking flight throughout the room itself.

Glowing from the place where my fingers mash atop hers, neon blue against gold-glitter skin, writhing tighter and tighter as I penetrate deeper and deeper.

Bursting from the union of our bodies, the same mix of light splashing into the air every time I drive in, filling her with more of my cock each and every time.

Reflecting off the vanity mirrors along the wall, each glass sheet accepting the light and then casting it out, turning our passion into dueling auroras along the ceiling over us, their rhythms growing and swelling and intensifying as we move and grind and fly together.

Higher...

Higher...

Until there's no more blue, no more gold, and no more striations of either.

There's only blinding, searing white. A place where we're no longer lightning and sun, or he and she, or even man and woman.

We're a nucleus.

A creation.

An explosion.

A fusion.

Her fire is my fire. Her pinnacle is my pinnacle. Her climax is my climax.

In her, I finally find my wholeness. My power.

Myself.

As the truth of it resonates in my soul, my senses finally reconnect with my body. I rest my lips against her ear as I let out a rumbling caveman grunt, acknowledging that even though my cock's just rocketed to the sexual version of outer space and back, it still feels damn good to expel the last of my seed on the mortal plane.

"*Oh.*" Emma's exclamation is full of soft wonder as her head dips beneath the weight of mine. "Oh, *damn.*"

I jerk my head back. "What? Did I hurt you?"

"No. *No.* Don't move. I think I'm going to...oh, I *am*..."

And I twine my fingers into hers again, doing my best to give her every drop of my essence as her cavern quakes around my cock once more. Her high, heated sighs are a perfect symphony in the air, and the scent of our lust gives me a contact high of primal joy.

That same primordial drive pushes my head back down to where I eagerly teethe her neck. With my thick stubble helping the abrasions, the woman will likely look like she got mauled by a mountain lion tomorrow, but the conclusion only spurs me to go harder. She actually lets me, at least for the better part of another minute, until she ducks away with a weary giggle. "My savage Zeus."

I scoop in, biting the edge of her ear. "My erotic enchantress."

She tilts her head back, offering her lips. "My beloved husband," she whispers when we're finished with our wet, gentle tongue tangle. The words sluice straight to the center of my chest, growing and billowing in my heart like a cloud filling with spring rain, only the drops consist of nothing but fulfilled joy...overflowing gratitude. I'm thrumming from its radiance. Dizzy. Vanquished. Demolished. Damn near speechless—except that the answering words I have for her are too damn perfect to ignore.

So, summoning up strength from God knows where in my depleted body, I scoop the hair away from her neck, lower a worshipful kiss into its soft sheen, and murmur, "My beautiful, beloved queen."

Her sigh, emanating from such a huge breath that her whole body rises and falls from it, is all the answer I need. After we fall into several minutes of a reflective silence, I finally and reluctantly pull away from her—but only long enough to pivot around until I can sit down, never letting my touch stray from at least some part of her skin, still as vibrant and sleek as gold satin. I continue to openly admire it while tugging her over to sit on my lap, transfixed by how the tracks of my reverent strokes are marked by a lighter shade of yellow for a few seconds. But when she shivers as well, I crunch a curious frown.

"Everything okay, baby?"

"Says the guy who just gave me a double dose of wedding night fireworks?"

Her tinkling laugh is pure music in my blood. I greedily soak it in before cuddling her closer. "Says the guy who also knows this wasn't the wedding night you've dreamed of."

Emma reaches up, clutches the side of my face, and doesn't stop tugging until I look directly into her eyes again. More golden magic greets my stare, like flecks of the real stuff in a clear Sierras stream. "All my best dreams only have one thing in common, mister." She gently turns up the edges of her mouth. "*You.*"

I pull in a resigned breath. "And a world in which you actually know where your mother is?"

The smile fades from her lips, but the flecks still gleam in her eyes. "My mom...can be a piece of work sometimes. She'll spend three hours picking out shoes, three days on menu selections for the Charity League's fundraiser, and then three *weeks* finalizing the right theme for that party. So yes, she's loony and trivial and even much too materialistic." She tilts her head, resting her cheek on the ball of my shoulder and her hand on the center of my chest. "But one thing she's *not* is weak—and another thing she's not is dead. I'm as sure of it as my own heartbeat," she insists. "I just *know* it, you know? If she were truly gone, I'd feel it. She's my *mom*. I know that sounds crazy, but..."

"No." I run the pad of my thumb along the crest of her cheek. "It doesn't. At all." My next inhalation brings a pronounced ache. "As soon as Tyce was gone, I truly felt it. There was a...void...in my bones." I shrug. "That's still not right, but the closest I can come to describing it. I just felt this discernible absence...like someone had yanked the chain on a light in my psyche."

She draws up again. Stares at me with unblinking turquoise intensity. "And with your father too?"

I circle my thumb back into her hairline. "I'm not sure," I mutter. "I mean, the memories from that moment are jumbled." That's the fucking understatement of the year. My retention of that entire night in Paris, including the party-that-never-was at the Virage and then the insanity in the caverns below, is a massive mix-up. Streams of my mental clarity are hole-punched by black voids, misty images, and gut-deep roadblocks. "I was still struggling with the shock about what Tyce had done—and the rage at my father for being responsible for it." I grit my teeth, struggling to mitigate the sting behind my eyes because of the recall.

Then again, there's the easier option. To surrender to the healing warmth of my wife's silken touch. "That makes sense." And the haven of her confident voice.

"Sense." I repeat her word on a short chuff. "Not a word we can often lay claim to these days."

She takes a second to render her response, tossing in a quiet huff of her own. "If I wanted a world with nothing but 'sense,' Mr. Richards, I'd have stayed in Orange County and married a banker."

She's making an effort at the cheer-up thing—that much is glaringly clear—but I can't help uttering, "And the place would be better for it, Velvet."

"And that is the *last* time you'll say something like *that* to me," she spits, resettling against my chest as her figurative hackles settle again. "I want to be *nowhere* but *here*, mister." She tucks her hand inside my shirt, rubbing until finding my nipple and then twisting with grinning determination. As I hiss and narrow a mock glare, she elaborates. "*Right here*—on the lap of the sole man on earth who can turn the pants-around-the-ankles couch-surfer look into the sexiest thing I've ever seen."

I laugh. "So I could've been bingeing the CW with a tub of cookie dough between my thighs for the last year?"

"I highly prefer what you just did with your thighs."

"Me too, Bunny." I lower my head to tenderly take her lips—though at once, I know that won't be enough. I dip in again, intending to rectify the mistake with a scorching crush—

Except that another mistake is now back to haunt me. The one where I let my libido talk my body out of getting up to lock the damn door.

Oh yeah, that portal is swinging open wide and fast now—and for a second, I wonder if the wind has simply kicked up that violently—until my sister-in-law's face and form appear, defined by panic I've not seen on anyone beyond the scumbags I've cornered in dark alleys. Thank God she's still in her gown and heels, slowing her normal dervish whirl of movement enough for me to sweep Emma's gown off the floor and drape it across both our nastiest bits.

"Baby girl!" She bursts it rushing across the room before realizing the state in which she's just found us. "You need to come—oh, holy *shit*."

"She's beat you to the punch, sister."

I mutter it as 'Dia spins around, dropping her face into her braced forefingers—but the commiserating giggle never comes from Emma. Instead, she's scrambling to sit up while not turning me into the dick flasher of Malibu Canyon. "Dee Dee?" she charges. "What is it? What's going on?"

Lydia groans while pivoting her head, gawking at us through her parted fingers. "Dear gawd." She spins back around. "Get yourself decent and then back up to the main house. And make it fast."

"Why? What is it?" Emma demands. "Have they found Mom?"

She's too busy readjusting her dress to catch the defined slump of 'Dia's shoulders. "It's more like *she* found *us*."

Emma emits a tearful cry. "Oh, thank God!"

Lydia drags a hand through her hair. "I wouldn't be doing that just yet, baby girl."

"Why?"

Lydia tightens her lips. "Because you might need to be sending up prayers for other reasons first."

CHAPTER THREE

EMMA

I burst into the ranch's main building in bare feet and with my dress half zipped, unable to think about anything beyond basic propriety after shoving myself back into the thing. Tears run unchecked down my face, already prey to the thousand horror scenes I've steeled myself for. Between the dressing suite and here, my imagination has covered everything from *Carrie*-level buckets of blood to finding Mom catatonic and curled in a corner.

I finally make it into the living room...

And skid to such a hard stop, the balls of my feet chirp against the wood floor.

A thousand scenarios, from the gruesome to the anguished to the soul-splitting. But none of them have come close to covering this.

Mom is seated in the center of a horseshoe-shaped sofa, holding hands with Dad, who clutches her as if expecting her to disappear again any second but gapes as if she already has. Lydia stands off to the side, staring in the same way but with Sawyer as her physical anchor. Alex and Neeta are still here, though Reece sent Wade and Fershan back to the ridge to conduct the search for Laurel with their advanced machines and scanners. As a whole, I'd describe everyone in the room as past the point of tense.

Everyone except Mom.

Who looks like she's been treated to pot brownies and Doritos for the last few hours. On a unicorn ride. With Chris Hemsworth.

Okay, maybe not the Hemsworth part.

I step down into the room, peering at her more closely. "M-Mom?"

Her whole body bounces a little. "Oh, Emmalina!" She smacks her hands together but keeps applauding with just the tips. "Oh, yes! *Here* you are, honey!"

Sooooo, maybe Hemsworth after all.

"Ummm. Yeah." I almost issue it as a question but manage to funnel the curiosity into the looks I scoop around to everyone else, even Dad. But clearly, they're all as stunned as me. This isn't Laurel Crist. The woman I know as my mother was never this walking smile emoji. Of course, nobody would ever label her as *gloomy*, but she's always been careful about her happiness, as if the universe has only allotted her so much each day and she has to select where to dole out each ration. But the woman sitting in front of me now is practically radiating the stuff, her eyes agleam and her smile open and even her backside getting into the action, bopping on the cushion in time to some song only she can hear. The song is definitely either EDM or the *My Little Pony* theme song. Or both. Like it matters. Clearly not to Mom.

Or *is* this Mom?

I inch closer to the woman, as if that tiny distance will give me clarity—and dealing with the frantic throb of my heartbeat when it doesn't. Suddenly my mind flings me back into the bunker back at the ridge, where 'Dia and I stood a few months ago, gripping hands and fearfully wondering if there was anything left of Kane Alighieri in the grimacing hulk that was facing off against Reece atop a downtown skyscraper. We were so convinced Faline had done something to electronically possess him, though it turned out she was simply nearby, remote controlling him.

But he'd been in agony because of it.

Had begged Reece to set him free from it—by killing him.

Mom does *not* look ready to plead with anyone for anything.

I've actually never seen her look happier with everything that's right in front of her.

"What. The. Hell?" I push it out at Lydia through tight teeth and compressed lips, not lifting the volume above a mutter.

She leans in, matching my grate with her own. "Told you to gird your loins."

"Loins?" I spew. "Kind of the wrong end, sister."

During our exchange, Angelique steps over. Like 'Dia, she's still dressed in her wedding attire. For her, that's a striking silk pantsuit in a luxurious shade of rust. Her long blond hair—well, the high-quality wig that covers the Consortium-inflicted burns across her skull—is pulled into a long braid that drapes around from her back. Her aquiline features are ready with the smile she already knows I need. And she's clearly prepared for the challenge I'm going to issue.

"Talk to us, Angie." But Reece beats me to the punch, maneuvering to block Mom's sightline to me. "What do you feel?"

He dips into a discernible stillness after that, implying the adjunct he doesn't dare vocalize.

And who *do you feel?*

Angelique acknowledges his subtext right away, giving a brief but terse nod. Just as fast, I interpret her action with all the worst implications. I talk myself off the ledge with a firm dose of logic. Do any of us even know if her Bolty-sonic psychic thing even works from beneath a wig?

So much for getting off the ledge. I have my answer as soon the woman's forehead develops more crimps than a normal headache deserves. Oh, she's felt something, all right. More than that, she's likely felt some*one*—and not a fly-by from the tooth fairy.

"It's all right, Angie." I step over and take one of her hands, hoping it helps to smooth at least a little of the stress across her face. Despite all those taut lines, she's still one of the most visually stunning women I've ever seen. I thought it the first night I ever met her, and it's still the truth—though unlike then, I'm no longer intimidated by her outward splendor. She's striking to me now, even on the rare occasions when she sheds her wigs and exposes the mottled dome of her head, because of what she's decided to do on the inside: continuing her commitment to our cause even when she has every reason to hide from the Consortium forever.

That's why I reassure her again. "It's all right. Don't force it. If you don't sense anything, then just tell us that too."

"She was here. Faline. Her energy signature is everywhere in this room."

"Goddamnit." Reece growls it nearly beneath his breath before turning and facing the huge window that overlooks the ranch's acreage. At this moment, it's become a large black mirror, illuminating the long A-frame of his legs and the massive right angles of his arms, with his hands jammed at his waist. *The power pose.* That's what his stance is called by motivational gurus. But at the moment, it's more like the frustrated-as-fuck pose.

As he adds a daunting exhalation to the whole aura, Angie pivots and approaches him, transforming my admiration for her into outright props. Ah, the *mademoiselle* has guts. Though Reece isn't outwardly sparking or glowing, he's in full Bolt intimidation mode in every other way. I don't know a lot of men who'd dare approach him in this state, let alone women. But here's Angelique La Salle, holding up just a couple of steps from him, keeping her chin hoisted, her spine straight, and her purpose intact.

"Reece." Though as she states it, she swings her head around, including me in the address as well. "You need to know—both of you—she left more than the psychic energy."

I give her an open frown. "More?"

"Oh, whee," Reece deadpans. "Easter eggs from the bitch, eh? Give them over. They'll be good and rotten by the time I shove them down her throat."

Angie pulls in and then releases a weighted sigh. I watch her carefully, wondering why I'm suddenly imagining her as the camp counselor who has to warn the kids about the psychopath in the woods. "She left...a message."

Reece pivots away from the window. He lowers his thick brows past the fringe of messy bangs. "For who?"

"Not clear." Angie folds her arms. "Perhaps for us all." She slowly shakes her head. "But the syntax itself...*very* clear." She peels one hand away, raising it to brace her dropping head. "The words, they are like a loop...over and over and over in my head..."

I'm compelled forward as soon as she says that, her voice

going scratchy and stressed. Part of me wants to comfort her more than just clasping her hand and soothing her forearm, but no matter how much I admire Angelique, there's the section inside that knows we'll never be completely tight. I'm glad to see her and Wade getting closer, especially since the three of us infiltrated the Consortium's complex in Marina del Rey. If those two are forging something good, maybe I don't have to keep thinking of that night as a complete disaster.

After all, it's not going to hold a candle to *this* night.

Especially with yet another "fun" addition to the timeline.

The missive I don't want to hear from the bitch I hope I never see again.

"What's in the loop, Angie?" I urge, staying as polite and considerate as I can. Dealing with her powers isn't as easy for Angie, who can't hit the training center to work it out or go on field trips to the canyons for real-life target practice. "What party favor did the shrew leave behind?" Besides my mother—and what seems like half of her mind.

Angelique squares her shoulders, taking in Reece and me with her steady gaze, before stating, "'Who is next?'"

Reece cocks his head. "Okay." Draws that out to underline his bafflement. "Who is next...for what?"

"Wait," I cut in, tilting my own stare at Angie as comprehension slams in. "*That's* the message." Angie's half smile gives me more than enough affirmation. "That *is* it," I assert. "'Who is next?' That's what's on loop."

"*That's* Faline's message?" Reece elucidates.

I bite the inside of my lip and grimace. "But do we want to know what it really means?"

Reece's glower is tauter. "I don't think we have a choice."

On the couch, Mom has stopped bouncing. Clearly,

her internal playlist hasn't been restarted. Her bopping has become fidgeting. Finally, she pops to her feet. "Now, what are my sweet girls and their swains all whispery about over here?" Fortunately, she's too busy linking her arm under Sawyer's elbow to notice the gawk Lydia flashes my way while mouthing out *swains*? "Weddings are such a fab excuse to talk about other things, aren't they?" Mom throws an eager look up at Sawyer. "Like *other* weddings?"

Reece's glare turns into a gape. My confusion sputters into a laugh. Lydia's tension escalates into a horrified groan. "*Mother.*"

Laurel pouts. "*What?*"

The only calm one still left around here is Sawyer. Holy shit, he's even wearing a new smirk—and that's before he tilts his twinkling greens down toward Mom. "I'm not exactly opposed to the idea."

Lydia flips back to gawking. "*Sawyer?*"

My heart does a double cartwheel on behalf of my sister, and I watch with tears as they share a look of meaningful intent. But just as I cue a romantic Andrew Lloyd Webber swell from my own internal playlist, everyone's attention is yanked toward the sound of thunderous bootsteps resonating in the foyer. A couple of seconds later, there's a shitload of khaki and green in the portal, courtesy of the ranch's security supervisor and the reps from every law enforcement department called in on the hunt for Mom.

Zack, the Ryan Gosling look-alike who's been stressed about keeping his security supervisor job since the debacle at the reception, looks more relieved than all of us put together when he lays eyes on Mom's happy, healthy form. "Mrs. Crist." He rushes over, and I wouldn't be surprised if he dropped at Mom's feet and kissed the pristine toes of her pumps, but he holds it together and simply offers his hand. "Ma'am, I'm pretty sure I've never been happier to see such a lovely lady brightening this room."

"Oh, fiddle dee dee, Mr. Wilkes. How you do flatter a girl." Despite Mom's completely dorky Scarlett O'Hara, the line actually fits. His name badge is inscribed in bold black with his last name. *Wilkes.*

A burly Highway Patrol officer steps up next to Zack. "We're *all* celebrating your safety, Mrs. Crist," he offers in an eerily great Soldier 76 impression. "But most of us are doing it down by the highway, where we've had a command center set up since you vanished." He eyes her, openly wary. "How the hell did you get past us?"

I'm not going to get a better opening to connect the circuits on my own curiosity, despite having a scary—and strange—answer for that query already. But I need to hear the explanation myself. I need to know what my gut is telling me is real. Is *possible.*

"Mom." I tug on her hand, leading her farther into the room. She follows without a peep of protest, which almost makes *me* go wide-eyed with wonderment. "Why don't you come back and sit down next to Dad? You've been through..." I have to stop, questioning my next words, but suck it up and say them anyway. "Quite an ordeal."

"An ordeal?" As soon as Mom blurts the echo with shock she usually reserves for things like Whole Foods running out of soy milk, I know my instinct is right. Whatever Faline did with her or to her, it seems to seriously be on the plane with a few rocking orgasms.

And *there's* a mental image I never need again.

Though with uncanny timing, the woman seems hell-bent on ensuring I never forget.

As soon as Mom's parked all the way on the couch again, she twists toward Dad—but doesn't stay that way for long. She clamors all the way over, cuddling into his lap. Inside two seconds, she's got her hand tunneled in his hair and her tongue rammed into his mouth.

At once, I go for a moment of commiseration with my sister. 'Dia's no damn help, looking like someone's just told her the end of *Infinity War*.

"I missed you," she whispers to Dad after they break apart with an obnoxious pop. "Oh, Todd. I missed you so damn much..."

"*Mom.*" But I'm not fast enough. She hauls my dazed-but-grinning father down for another round of the Crist Passion Fest. "*Mother!*"

"Hmmm?" Her sigh is dreamy—and disturbing. Not just for the obvious reasons. While it's kind of cool to see the woman yearning to climb Dad like a monkey, instead of her tennis instructor or the sommelier at Le Chat Bleu, it's one more chunk of strangeness on top of the mounting stack of what-the-hell-just-happened. "Oh, all right, dear," she finally grumbles, returning to her proper place on the cushion though keeping her fingers laced with Dad's. "I suppose you have a point. And besides, these gallant gentlemen would probably like to go home now." She stretches her neck and gazes around the room. "What time is it?"

"Three a.m." Sawyer beats us all to the punch on it after turning his wrist up to check what 'Dia calls his *Mission Impossible* watch. The thing does everything except go to the bathroom for the guy.

"On what day?" Mom returns.

Sawyer frowns but responds. "Sunday."

Her head rocks back like he's just punched her. "That's all?"

"Mother." I step in, perching on the coffee table in front of the couch. She'll likely give me hell for sitting on furniture not meant for my butt, but I opt for the risk. Angelique's taken the chance to move into a nonthreatening position behind the couch, where she's started to direct her psychic spidey senses at the back of Mom's head, and my new location gives me a direct trajectory on both of them. "You were gone for almost eight hours."

"That's *all*?" She spurts with an incredulous laugh before I can reach to check her for fevered delirium, gazing around as if *we're* all the ones who need the loony bin. "It felt like...longer. It *was* longer." But when her stare settles again on Dad, she stills it. Focuses it. Pleads him with it—as if he's the only one on earth who will understand what she's saying. The moment tugs at a million places in my heart, though the resulting holes are drenched with confusion.

"What was, Mom?" Lydia takes the words out of my mind and mouth, pushing to sit next to me on the table. Shockingly, I almost bite at her not to sit on the non-butt furniture but am saved from myself by the rugged giant of a county officer, who steps up with a stylus poised over his smart pad.

"Perhaps we can start at the beginning, Mrs. Crist," he says with an amiable drawl. "How far back do you remember anything? Do you recognize *this* place?"

Mom *humphs*. "Of course I do. This is where my daughter got married." Her expression mists over, and she glances up again at Sawyer. "But really only last night? Are you sure?"

Lydia leans forward. "He's sure," she says gently. "But why are *you* so sure you were gone longer? What the hell happened, Mom?"

"One step at a time," the officer insists. "Do you recall anything about the circumstances of your disappearance, Mrs. Crist? Any reason why Ms. Garand would want to abduct you?"

Mom's puzzlement becomes a full glare. She wastes no time stabbing it up at the officer—and clearly, if she had her way, would impale him with it too. "*Abduct* me?" she finally snaps. "Who said anything about her abducting me?"

'Dia forms a hand around one of Mom's knees. "She snatched you. Do you remember that part? How she clutched you in like a puppy and then—"

"Maybe we should let her tell it." Though my interruption earns me 'Dia's fresh glower, I make up for it with an apologetic glance. "She was there, Dee Dee."

"I certainly *was*." Mom's all-in with her irritation at this point. "But I certainly wasn't 'abducted.'"

Fortunately, Lydia senses the right second to slow her roll. She straightens and pulls in her hands, resting them in a taut ball in the middle of her lap. "All right...so what *did* happen?"

Though Mother purses her lips, the happy sheen in her gaze returns. "I was...well, I guess you could say I was flown."

"Flown?" The officer quickly scribbles that on the smart pad. "In what, ma'am? A private plane? Helicopter? Do you remember any markings on the aircraft?" Though he scowls at the words as soon as he rechecks them, clearly knowing what we already do. The manhunt for Mom was so intense all night, even the birds were likely banned from the airspace over the canyon.

"Oh, *pish*." Mom waves a hand. "Of course not." Lydia and I trade another is-this-our-life look. *Pish?* "She flew me on wings of dreams," she goes on, her gaze getting that bizarre sheen once more. "Beyond the clouds. Beyond the stars. Beyond all of...this."

As she sweeps her hand out again, going wider to encompass the whole room in her incrimination, I look again to Lydia. It's no secret glimpse anymore, with new guests invited to the what-the-hell party. Reece, Sawyer, Alex, Neeta, and even Dad are in on the worry this time.

Is this our life?

Screw that.

Is this our mother?

Thank God for the officer and his patience. Besides looking like he's heard the whole "I flew beyond the clouds and stars" thing at least three other times since Friday, he's dutifully noting every word nonetheless. "Okay, so no aircraft markings to speak of," he states. "What about what *she* said? This Faline Garand..."

"Yes!" Mom straightens like he's offered a cookie and stripped it of all calories. "Faline. My angel."

"Your—" I'm the one jolting to my feet now. "Your... *angel?*"

"Oh, dear." Mom nervously flutters her fingers across the back of Dad's hand. "I botched the dickens out of that one, eh? I simply knew you'd start pitching a fit, Emmalina."

"Me?" I spin away, sweeping my hands out like there are spider webs in my way—and maybe there are. My limbs feel stiff and draggy. *Shit.* Has Faline returned? Has she added invisibility to her never-ending bag of tricks and is standing in the corner this very second, as delighted as a cat playing with her mice before she pounces for the final blow? Though I'm stunned to be standing after that last hit. *Faline. My angel.* "*Me*, Mother?" And yes, it's "Mother" again. If I think her as "Mom" in this second, my heart will go nuclear inside my chest. "Pitching a fit?" She's got to be kidding me. "Where are your hidden cameras, Laurel?" Oh, yes; "Laurel" feels even better. "Because this isn't real. You are *not* real about this."

The woman actually sways as if I've wounded her. "You don't know anything about what's real, Emmalina Paisley."

"I know that Faline Garand is the queen bee sadist of the Consortium's hive!" I'm fully shouting now, and it feels so damn good. "That she was the bitch who ordered Reece's kidnapping in the first place and then supervised his torture for six months. She was also the reason downtown LA was destroyed—by using one of Reece's friends to lure him in so she could infect Reece with a virus and regain control over him." I readily borrow Reece's power pose, knowing it probably makes me look more like an enraged fairy after making mud pies than a grown woman consumed by hurt and shock, but my composure needs all the help it can get right now. If I let my rage ramble my tongue much longer, I'll be spewing about how we stole Reece's mind back from Faline by inducing him into a coma, before Alex and Fershan figured out that regular solar power "bumps" to Reece's blood would keep her mind control worm away forever.

But the bitch will never know that.

Must *not* ever know that.

Ever.

No matter how many times she takes my mother on joyrides "beyond the stars"—whatever the hell that eventually means—employing the superpower wine-and-dine as an angle for information...

And God knows what else.

Recruitment?

Financial aid?

Cult-level worship?

All of the above?

But how the hell do I make Mother aware of that when she won't even look at me anymore? When she won't give me the one *second* I need to show her, with the anguish on my face and the plea in my eyes, what kind of a demon her "angel" really is?

Or will even that be enough?

What the *hell* kind of mind trip has Faline worked on my mother? And more crucially, is it all permanent? And if it is, what's Fa-Fa's ultimate end game? And why does even thinking of *that* answer make me drip with sweat and struggle to control the flames of fear and fury that hit with the intensity of the sun?

But why?

Why control it?

The whole world knows now. The leaked videos have probably been replayed to both arctic ice caps and back. If Mother really sees what all of Faline's treachery looks like, on her own daughter...

The heated flare comes faster than I anticipate, making me sway like I've guzzled a bottle of Patrón. *Mui bueno* on the parallel, since that's exactly how I feel. Reece rushes to steady me, wrapping a strong and protective grip around me. "Velvet," he growls at the same moment I whimper, remembering there's a damn good reason why I try to avoid cranking on the sunshine spigot all at once. It hurts. Oh *God*, it seriously hurts. "What the fuck are you—"

"Showing her," I spit, swinging my sights toward the

couch again. "Showing *you*, Mother—what Faline Garand is responsible for causing in your own d-d-daughter." I can't help the tormented stammer. Every inch of my skin feels like a third-degree sunburn. My nerve endings are a pack of a million ignited matches. Even my eye sockets are scalding, though I don't surrender my furious scrutiny toward the couch.

At once, I wonder if the gamble paid off. Dad's clearly enthralled and appalled at once. I'm like a walking ooze of golden lava. Hypnotizing to watch but horrifying to think of even touching. It's evident across every inch of his face, and it makes me attempt a remorseful wince his way.

But when I look back at Mother...

Still nothing but the I've-chugged-the-Kool-Aid smile.

"Oh, darling." She breaks the searing silence with a rasp I can't interpret. "*Look* at you." And still no clarity, except for a husk of emotion that could be anything. "Emmalina. You're *beautiful*."

Well, *there's* something to clarify—despite how it tears at my fibers to drum up the strength and feels like summoning fire more than words to my throat. "And I'm also in agony, damn it!" Still, I chalk up the win for keeping every syllable halfway civilized. How I haven't given voice to the vicious screams in my spirit is reason enough to ask for the entire bottle of that tequila—except that I recognize, deep down, there's really no victory here.

Faline hasn't just wooed my mother. It's been a complete brainwash. The truth glares even stronger as Mom bounces to her feet again, whipping around the coffee table before striding to me with an ebullient smile.

"Oh, my sweet and incredible girl." She jerks me away from Reece, stroking a hand over the back of my head. I want to fight her off, but I'm too muddled for anything but silent surrender. Eight hours ago, she was the woman who could barely embrace me before I walked down the aisle to Reece, citing how one wrong swipe of her makeup would ruin Corinne's cosmetic handiwork. Now she's grasping me like a freaking life ring and cooing in my ear, "You can do this, daughter. Pain is weakness leaving the body. Evolution cannot happen without a crucible."

Okay, screw muddled. I grit my teeth and shove away from her. "What the *hell*?"

By the time I'm done, Mother's all Snow White bright and happy ga-ga once more. She even clasps her hands together like Prince Charming delivered the glass slipper, the enchanted rose, *and* the sparkling locket at once, presented on a leaf made of fairy tears. "You *are* breathtaking, Emmalina. One of the most beautiful beings I've ever seen. You're enhanced now. Enlightened. Evolved. A magnificent miracle."

I stumble back by two more steps. Take no measures to hide my open repulsion. "But not for that bitch's glory," I spit. "*Never* for her."

Mother slowly shakes her head. Her face, so innocent now that Corinne's airbrush mastery has faded off, is painted with different pigments. The darkness of pure derangement.

Which, disgustingly, makes her the perfect candidate to hurl the most disturbing iceberg into the chilling journey our wedding night has become.

"We are *all* evolving creatures, daughter. So why is it so hard to believe that someone has discovered the key for accelerating the process?"

The person I formerly knew as my mother is rocking with the words she nearly sings out—but despite all the affectation, one look tells me that she's not being remotely fed the words or controlled in any way. Angie confirms the supposition with a tight nod; Faline still hasn't come back to lurk or manipulate—making all of this shit from Mom even more unsettling to watch.

"*Emmalina Paisley*," she croons. "Just look at you! *Both* of you!" She gestures toward Reece, as well. "You are living, stunning proof of the new and rising world. Of our brave and beautiful future!" She lifts that hand, higher and then higher, and joins the other arm to the movement in a bid to be a rising phoenix—

Or a demon-possessed lunatic.

"It's perfect! It's wonderful, my daughter! Now, we all must answer the purpose by heeding the call."

Reece steps forward—at the ready with one hand fisted in front of him, blue escaping out both sides as if he's wrestled down a whole lightning bolt. I've never been more relieved to see him sparking up this early. "The call...for what?" he charges in a low growl.

Mother just sends back the serene cult-girl smile. "Oh, you know that already, my son." And her gaze gleams like ice cubes tossed into bright-blue Kool-Aid. "Who is next?"

CHAPTER FOUR

REECE

The night the Consortium changed my life, I'd thought about taking a cruise. Two quarts of Spanish brandy were sloshing in my veins and Angelique La Salle was eyeing my crotch like I'd stuffed Aladdin's Lamp and its wishes there, but the limo in which we traveled had suddenly become a glaring symbol for the "cage" of my life. I'd yearned for the serenity of the sea, a place to get truly lost.

I couldn't have been more messed up.

I was about to find out what a cage really was. And what "getting lost" really felt like. In all the worst senses of the phrases.

In those months, I felt a lot like I do right now.

I'm not locked in an eight-by-eight cell. Or strapped down on a gurney, being told that no one in the world even knows I'm missing. Or being shot up with raw electricity, my screams absorbed by padded walls.

But one element is still the same.

Maybe the most vital one.

That voice. *Her* voice. The accented purr that belonged only to the darkness of my memories, until that night nearly a year ago in the hangar at Teterboro, where the soundtrack of my hell was no longer nameless or faceless.

Faline Garand.

Her satiny murmur is the same it's ever been, buckling me down no matter how physically free I am on this beach. Trapping my mind despite the whoosh and release of the Pacific, sloshing over my ankles and foaming between my toes. The feral intensity of her black gaze is nearly all I see, a shadow beneath the dark-blue and green eddies along the sand and the pale moon setting on the horizon.

Faline *fucking* Garand.

Even taunting me throughout every moment of my mental replay from a few hours ago, when she wasn't anywhere near that room at the ranch—but might as well have been. She was there in every keen gleam of Laurel Crist's gaze, slashing out at me with possessive glee. She was alive in every demented word the woman spoke, a message I've heard since the first night of my captivity...a cabal of crazy backed by the Scorpio cartel's riches.

We are making history, and you are now a part of it, ma chere. *One of the most important parts...*

I enhanced you, Reece Richards. I improved you...

Evolution cannot happen without a crucible. You are a part of the new and rising world...

"Fuck!" I punctuate it with a sharp kick at the water, watching my electric fury flow out and then back up, spreading across the approaching waves. It's too early in the day for any surfers or fishing boats, thank God, but I grit my teeth harder, wishing more than anything for a good, obstinate granite cliff—or five—to spar with.

I need to destroy something. No. More than that. I need to see the evidence of what I'd rather be doing to myself.

Of what I *can't* do to myself. Not willingly, at least.

Like it or not, I need every ability this body is capable of. Every power I can wring from it. Every volt in its bloodstream, electron in its muscles, energy in its pores...

But most of all, every ounce of conviction in its soul.

The soul that's telling me this decision is right. So fucking right, I can't talk myself out of it even after two hours of pacing up and down this beach. But no matter how tight my heart has clenched, literally forcing my hand atop it in a pounding protest for the pain to stop, my conscience has wielded a bigger megaphone.

But also a softer one.

The one I've been paying more and more attention to. Not that I've wanted to, damn it—especially after recognizing exactly who belongs to that provoking murmur. A voice I thought I'd banished from my mind. Permanently.

The asshole who donated his sperm to my creation.

I can't even call him *Father* anymore. And forget the fuck about *Dad*.

Fathers don't sell their sons to an international crime cartel that funds a band of insane fringe scientists. Dads don't sleep with bitches on high who run cartels, even in the name of saving the family empire.

Screw the family empire.

"And screw you too," I spew at the memories of the man, unceasing and unrelenting, that have been like persistent ghosts in my senses since I came out here to mull all this shit over.

Which has been feeling a lot less like mulling and a lot more like internal skirmishes. Which have weakened my mental armor all the way around...

Weaknesses the memories have been more than happy to take advantage of.

"But damn it, I don't want to go to Tyce's stupid lacrosse game!"

"I understand your frustration, Reece Andrew. But you do know this is the semifinal game and that he'd really like you there...yes?"

"Tyce doesn't care what I do."

"I think Tyce might disagree with you about that."

"If I disappeared off the face of the earth, he'd never notice."

"Again, I think Tyce might disagree with you about that."

"Which means you're going to make me go to the game."

"You're thirteen years old now. I'm going to let you make your own choice about it. But just remember that doing the right thing often doesn't mean doing the easy thing."

The replay accompanies me up the ladder of the lifeguard station, a dark refuge in the middle of the Redondo Beach sand. By the time I get to the platform at the top, I've replayed all of the lacrosse match I finally did attend—and the fact that Tyce truly couldn't have cared less if I'd sent a cardboard cutout in my place.

Or so my memory first tells me.

As I park my ass down on the landing, different details of that day start to come back to me. Minutiae I've never clearly recalled before...but now, perhaps enhanced by electronic insight, I do. As if I'm moping through that entire afternoon again, I see different things. *New things.*

I see Tyce scoring the first goal of the game and pumping his stick in Dad's direction—except he's actually *looking* at me.

I see him taking a break at halftime and sneaking me a chocolate chip protein bar from the team's nutrition wagon.

I also see me, answering his offer with the biggest eat-shit-and-die glower probably ever stabbed at a big brother in the history of brothers.

Despite that, I also see him after the game, telling his buddies he won't go for this celebratory trip to Power Pizza unless I'm invited too.

I see him doing the right thing.

Not the easy thing.

"Christ." I mutter it to nobody or nothing but the sun-faded boards under my upright knees. "Why didn't I see it all sooner, you asshole?" *Hiding your loyalty behind all that sarcasm. Giving me all that shit, all that time...*

"Because you loved me." I shift the weight of my elbows on my knees, lifting my hands to jam their heels against my eyes. It helps the stupid sting there, but not enough. "Ah, damn it." I'm going to lose it. Right here. Right now. Well, at least I'm alone out here, and that means—

"Hey."

Shit.

I force the tears back with a rough cough before rolling to my feet and holding out my hand to Emma, helping her up the last few rungs of the ladder. As soon as she's all the way up, I draw her in close and tight. Fuuuuck, yes. Best melancholy killer on the planet. Probably the best-smelling one too. Her hair is a mixture of sea spray and coconuts. When I curl my head down, going at once for her upturned lips with mine, a hint of something sugary joins the mix. After a second, I recognize it as maple syrup.

"Well, hey yourself," I greet softly, raining a few more kisses up the bridge of her nose. "How are you?"

"Hey. That's *my* line, buddy." She takes a few affectionate pecks at my chin. "And I have more validation for it too. You've been out here for hours."

I give in to a small smirk as soon as she concludes that by

running a hand down my bare chest. She's on the brink of asking why I'm not cold, since she's in sweats and a thick Henley along with a borrowed sweatshirt from Lydia, but she knows better. After the last twenty-four hours, with my stress running high and getting to screw her like the newlywed husband that, *yes*, I am, my core body temperature has been simmering steadily at what most would consider a lethal fever.

Regrettably, as we've learned over the last ten weeks, my poor woman runs the exact opposite: while her powers are as intense as concentrated solar panels, they "go down" like the sun too. I think there might be a commemorative Emmalina plaque on the wall of Fuzzball Socks' corporate offices, since the woman bought out their entire inventory in the middle of August.

I'm not a damn bit surprised when my adoring perusal of her form turns up a peek at her favorite Fuzzballs, scrunched between her thickest polar boots and her bunched-up sweats. The pattern, called "Bolt-a-licious," has little blue bolts and wine bottles against a neon-blue background. Emma's often joked that someone finally gathered enough booze in one place for the occasions when she *is* tempted to drink.

Which might just be around the corner.

Who the hell am I kidding?

I'm so sorry about this, baby. You'd better start popping those corks now.

"Sawyer and 'Dia are making French toast." She rests her head against my shoulder, filling my nostrils again with her warm, fresh smell. That explains the maple syrup. I turn my head and close my eyes, working to commit the scent to memory, as she offers with that same gentle coaxing, "And there's strawberries, blueberries, and whipped cream. *And* the most decadent organic coffee I've ever had." She turns, huddling into me as daybreak brings a stronger wind across the empty beach. "Hmmm, I think I like sleepovers at Sawyer and 'Dia's—even if it's just because they're closer to Mom and Dad."

I chuff. "And even if we didn't exactly sleep?"

"We can rectify that between breakfast and leaving for Newport. I just got off the line with Dad, and he says Mom is finally sleeping peacefully, so he wants to give her a few hours before we check on her. So that gives *us* some time to do the same."

As she talks, there's another chilly gust. I drape an arm around her, bringing her closer. *Not close enough.* Will it ever fucking be? And yet here I am, getting ready to say...

The shitty thing I'm about to say.

"I'll probably sleep...on the plane."

Yep. Shitty. To the crappy degree that I thought it would be. But that's where my expectations and the reality part ways. I'd narrowed down Emma's reaction to just a pair of viable choices: seething fury or heartbroken tears. But for one long moment, then the second and third after that, she erupts with neither.

And when she doesn't erupt at all...

My unease switches into straight-up unnerved.

At last, thank fuck, she breaks her stillness with a pronounced inhalation. That breath tells me everything and nothing. Rage and bereavement are off the table, but I have a feeling the words she's preparing will cut just as deep.

"On the plane," she echoes, her murmur almost as invisible as the wind. "Because you're going to Spain." She swallows hard. "To try to find Faline."

I clutch her in a little closer. "I have to, Velvet."

"I know."

"I mean, what if your mom wasn't her first 'recruit' for this stunt? What if she's been beta testing it on others, ironing out the kinks in the process? Or worse, what if it's been successful from the start and *this* is how she's been spending the last two months? What if she's been busy building a whole army of goddamned minions?" Every query that's been swooping through my mind for the last two hours turns into a tumbling rush that won't stop, an avalanche finally set free. "And what if she doesn't stop at just an army? The woman is insane—"

"*Reece.*" She emphasizes it by swinging over and straddling me, her hands on my cheeks and her hair whipping down, encasing us both in its curtain of white-gold brilliance. "I said I know, husband—and I meant it."

Her new position immediately affects opposing parts of my body. My mind instantly calms, accepting what she's saying with a massive rush of relief. But the perfect cushion of her thighs around mine, joined with the snug slide of her crotch, means my cock already has bigger, better ideas than the "talk" we need to have right now.

Much.

Better.

Ideas.

"Holy God, I love you." I croak it against her lips and into all the soft, perfect curves of her chin, her cheeks, and even across her eyelids and brows.

"Hmmm," she murmurs, raining the same adoring affection across my face—between her aroused little sighs. I'm not the only one aware that she's poked at the lightning. "So you enjoy showing me."

"That an invitation, Mrs. Richards?"

As I trail my touch beneath her sweats, lightly fingering the sensitive spot at the top of her ass, she unfurls a sweet mewl against my neck. "Well, as long as we're talking about women going insane today..."

"Hmmm, yes." I dip my other hand around, adding the abrasion of my fingernails to my fuller, deeper caresses on her soft globes. "That does seem to be the popular theme..."

"Maybe you should alert marketing." She adds the edges of her teeth to her nuzzles, angling a little higher to hit the curve of my ear. My groan breaks free as she lingers over the top, knowing exactly what spots send the most electricity through my system. I'm crackling with arousal and energy, my face filled with biting wind and white-blond hair, my veins alive with lightning-bright fire.

"Maybe I should throw you over my lap and spank you for damn near turning me into a neon sign in the middle of the beach."

She ceases the blow job to my ear. "Ohhhh." But compensates with a worse torment—straight along my cock. "Yes, please."

Jesus *fuck*. Where the *hell* has the woman learned how to roll her hips over me like this? Knowing just where to push in, slide along, and bear down until I feel like nothing but one massive, exposed nerve, waiting with bated breath for another stroke of her exquisite crotch? And how the hell have I gotten so lucky to capture the passionate heart that goes along with this talented pussy...the wondrous woman who feeds the fires of this astonishing sensuality?

"Emmalina." I croak her name, knowing I shouldn't—and won't—even try to answer those queries either. "Dear *God*."

She lifts up just a little, wiggling her head to let the wind yank her hair out of both our faces. Once the path is clear from her lips to mine again, she leans in but doesn't touch down. Hovering those lush pads just a breath above mine, she whispers, "Still want me to bend over for that spanking, sir? Or should I just—*oh!*"

The little minx stops her purposeful undulations along my dick as soon as I raise a hand, push it against her sweats, and then slap her right ass cheek with a noticeable *smack*. "Who said anything about you moving, little Bunny?"

"*Oh!*" she cries again as I repeat my incentive to her left cheek. "Certainly not me, Mr. Richards." She drops her forehead to my sternum, turning into a puddle of sighs and whimpers as I deliver a couple more strikes to her firm, full backside.

"Holy fuck." My voice is as husky as hers. "Now I *do* want to bend you over, woman." I massage away the minor pain I've doled, transforming the stings into tingles along her ass and thighs. At least that's what her gorgeous little sighs tell me. "And then slicken this sweet little back hole, preparing you for the pleasure of my cock..."

A long, high hum flows out of her. "I'll just have to make sure we have some lube loaded into a TSA-approved receptacle, then."

This time, I'm the one coming to an abrupt stop. Tends to happen when dawning comprehension turns into a holy-shit moment at the speed of light. Nevertheless, I manage to utter, "A TSA...what?"

Emma's brows knit, though the rest of her face is still filled with sultry inquisition. "Oh. Maybe we don't have to worry about them, if you've booked a private charter?"

I plan on doing exactly that but quickly decide that's not a detail she needs to know—not when it's clear we haven't gotten to the bigger point here. *Fuck*. Wedding ring's on my finger and I'm off the bad-boy billionaire list for the rest of my life, but my cock is still getting in the way of this Reece Richards adulting bullshit.

But I still have to find my balls—the right-choice-over-easy-choice kind, not the ones beating at my track pants like lightning trapped in golf balls—and use them to stomp all over her verve in ways that are *not* going to feel good.

"Uh...yeah..." Definitely not good. Not even two syllables in. "About that charter, baby."

"It *is* a charter?" She bites her bottom lip and waggles her brows, unwittingly twisting the emotional knife.

I'm tempted to jab a fist toward the sky where a few stars still linger. *Got the point, Big Guy. Loud and clear. Thinking with the nuts means winding up as the putz. Yeah, okay. I know, I know.*

"Did you get one with one of those cool bedrooms too?" Her eyes dance with such provocative promise, I'm on the brink of reneging on the promise I've made to my own heart for the sake of keeping hers this glaringly happy.

"Probably no bedroom this time, baby."

"Well, fiddlesticks." She pushes out one of the cutest pouts God ever fashioned for a woman. "That's all right." Then hovers it close to my lips while molding those perfect breasts of hers even tighter against my chest. "We'll make do, no matter who's on board. We've done it before..."

I clamp back a moan but only by grinding down a layer of tooth enamel. She had to go and get heavy-lidded on me, betraying exactly what images are filling her heated thoughts.

An empty first-class cabin. Clouds outside the windows, and our steamy stares inside. Champagne bubbles on our lips. Macaron frosting across her pussy...

Shit, shit, *shit.*

Do it. Talk to her. Tell her.

"Velvet—"

"Hmmm?"

"Only Alex will be on the flight with me."

Shit, shit, *double* shit.

Her lip slips free from her teeth. She jerks up—okay, shoves away—from me with rigid shoulders and a stiff spine. The only characteristic she keeps? The bright-blue glints in her eyes—the same and yet as different as a forest fire from a hearth. As pure ire from gathering lust.

As a graveyard stillness in the middle of such a dazzling dawn.

And when she does finally speak, leading to an accusation straight out of a Poe poem. "Because you're only taking Alex on the mission."

I drag in a long, hard breath. Expel it so heavily, I'm stunned the seagulls riding the sea wind really haven't turned into ravens by this point. "Because it's not just a damn 'mission,' okay?" I reach for her. She shirks away. But despite her hair whipping back into her face, hiding her tightening features, I spit out, "Can you please, just for a second, try to understand that, Emmalina? I could barely think straight in Paris knowing what kind of danger I was exposing you to, and everything—*everything*—we'll be facing in Barcelona is going to be a hundred times worse than any of that game. We'll be at the hellmouth, baby. This isn't my father's cat-and-mouse game. It's *Faline's.* Remember her? The one who's joined the 'Superpower of the Week' club and is now going for the commemorative collectibles option as well? Can you wrap your mind around even *part* of what I'm saying with that?"

She swings her head back around. *Damn it.* There are a billion gold blades now forged in her stare, and when she twists her lips, tiny sparks rupture from their enticing corners. I'm damn glad I got my Paragon of Protectiveness speech out, because I'm damn sure I'm an inch away from hauling her back for a fierce kiss, a frantic apology, and a complete stance flip on the decision I've made about her and the hellmouth trip.

Never have I been more grateful for one of the woman's now-you've-*really*-pissed-me-off modes. "I'd ask if you're even kidding, but I already know the answer." Her impudence kills the lip sparks, and I attempt, unsuccessfully, to be grateful. "You're not kidding, because you're really that stupid, aren't you?" And as she jerks to her feet, the rest of my morning wood becomes as flimsy as the boards of this lifeguard stand. "But I'm going to humor you by answering your ridiculous question. *Yes*, I can wrap my mind around what you're saying. Not *part* of it; *all* of it—because *yes*, I remember exactly who we're dealing with here. I was there when she almost shredded 'Dia and me in a jet turbine. I was also there for the trap she had your dad set up at the Virage, and I watched the city I love be laid to waste because of her lust to get that damn virus into your head. But most of all, I was there when she strapped me down and turned my blood into funnel cake—only to throw away my chance of eradicating that sadistic witch when I had the chance." She stops, pulling in air in heaving spurts, as if all her fury has wiped breathing off of her body's to-do list. The morning light washes over her grief-stricken face, highlighting the thick aqua tears in her eyes. "So don't tell me I don't know what hellmouths look like yet, mister. I think I've got that part *more* than covered."

"Agreed." I'm able to give up that part without second thought—but take a turn at sucking down some massive breaths before going on. "Which is why you can't, and you aren't, coming to the one in Spain with me."

She doesn't release a single sound. This time, her wrath gets plated in gold: the sun-colored stuff that radiates out of her palms and across the sand, detonating a hunk of the berm into a flume at least fifteen feet high...

Until it heats into a towering flume of flared glass.

Locking me into yet another conflict of reactions.

At once, the mushy poetic parts of me are nearly moved to fucking tears of my own. Though her rage constructed the sculpture, her love birthed it—and her heartache is evident in every swooping, shimmering inch of it. But it's also the monument to her inexperience—an ignorance that could have deadly implications, if exploited by the wrong circumstances—or the most heartless opponent.

In this case, that might not even mean Faline.

For all we know, that bitch could be just the gatekeeper for worse monsters.

As if my churning gut needs one more tap toward full nausea, there's a blast of strong wind across the shore, instantly turning the sculpture into a pile of shattered shards on the sand. I bite my tongue, holding back the obvious commentary. I married one of the smartest women on the planet. She already gets the symbolism.

Still doesn't mean she's approving of it.

"Damn it." She sobs out the growl, bracing her hands on the railing and dropping her head between her slumping shoulders. The damp wood smolders beneath her bitter grip. "I'm your wife," she spits. "I'm your *wife*."

"A fact I haven't forgotten, Velvet." I rise as well but stand well clear of the invisible force field of tension she's thrown up around herself. "And haven't stopped being grateful for."

"Of course," she counters. "So grateful, you're jetting off to Spain less than twenty-four hours after our vows."

Since I'm clearly going to owe somebody for a new lifeguard stand, I let my sparks fly, carving a couple of baseball-sized holes into the boards next to my feet. "Because you're not just my wife, damn it." I let the seethe of that sink in for a couple of long seconds. "You're the center of my soul. The compass of my integrity. The love of my fucking existence."

The wood beneath her hands starts to char. "Oh, *damn it*, Reece," she softly moans.

"So you know what that also makes you, right?"

She shoves out a sound as jagged and violent as her falling sculpture—though this time, I'm sure parts of me have been sliced open from the fallout. I'm about to break my pledge about giving her space, when she whirls and covers the distance between us in a single lunge. At once I wrap her close and tight, uncaring that I can't control my laser fingers in time. I can buy Lydia a new sweatshirt. I *can't* recover the trapped sweetness of this moment, engulfed by the wind and the sunrise and the silent sanctity of our pressed hearts.

And the truth they must now accept.

With slow reluctance, Emma finally slips one hand free from my neck. Slides it down to the plane of my pectoral, where she rubs her fingertips in a soft, cherishing circle.

"Will there ever be a day when I'm *not* your liability?" she rasps.

I pulse a quick laugh into her hair. "In the truest sense of the form?" I return. "Good fuck, I hope not." I clench my pecs, already anticipating the *whap* that earns me. And then continue the tension into the coil of my grip, also already knowing how she'll try to step away. "But in the sense that you'll have your skills trained and your instincts honed so I don't have to split my mind worrying about you in a battle or fight?" Since that stills her, I shift my hold up the backs of her shoulders and start a few worshipful caresses of my own. "You'll get there, Emmalina—faster than you probably think. You're just not there yet, and that's no reflection on *anything* other than the fact that you're still piecing your bloodstream back together and learning what it can do." When she attempts a new huff, I dig my massages in with new intent. The disciplinary kind. "You remember what happened just yesterday? With the cloak of invisibility on the obstacle course cutout?"

She rolls her eyes. "I was kind of *there*."

"But what if you'd gone wide with that pulse and made it so *I* wasn't?"

Well, *there's* my definitive eye-roll killer. "I-I wouldn't have let it get *that* out of control," she defends. "Besides, the cutout wasn't *gone*. I just made it invisible."

"But how do you know it'd have the same effect on a carbon-based life form, like a man?" I rebut. "What happens when you 'erase' something that breathes and moves? And for that matter, what *if* that organism shifts? What's the danger to them? To *you*? And if you learn to control the beam, what's the range you have on it? How effective is the power at a bigger distance? And for how long?"

"All right, all right!" She doesn't move away but shoves at my chest as if that option's not off her table. Her bottom lip pushing out in a defined pout, she mutters, "All I want to do is *help*."

"And you do." I dig fingers into her spine and pull in so hard she has no choice but to obey, wrapping her arms around my neck once more. "My incredible, brave woman...don't you get it? You help more than anyone on the team. More than anyone can ever *hope* to."

"That's not what I mean, and you know it."

I prevent her from being subjected to my laugh, likely as unwelcome as my schmaltz despite its loving intention, by taking her lips firmly but tenderly. "Well, right now, you're going to be the biggest help by—"

"I know, I know," she grumbles. "By sweeping the porch, keeping my apron clean, and making sure there's no troublesome smoke on the horizon."

"Huh?"

So much for thinking her eye rolls are over. "I'll keep the homestead safe, Pa. Don't you worry none about your womenfolk," she cracks—making me kiss her to save her from my laughter again.

"My wo*man*folk," I correct. "Just you, my Velvet Bunny. *Only* you. Always." One more long, languorous kiss later, I growl, "And the only 'broom' I want to hear about in your hand is the one you use to sweep up the remains of Foley's ass after you've kicked it into the training mat a bunch of times."

She punches out another sound of feral frustration— though the chest smack she joins to it is a flimsy stand-in for the same attitude. "You're making it damn hard to hate you right now, Reece Richards."

I lean in, smooshing my lips to her temple in a passionate figure-eight. "Same way you make it damn easy to worship you, my goddess."

"Sweet talk isn't going to help you."

"Then what will?"

⚡

Three weeks and too many conscious hours later, I keep my mind engaged—along with my cock—by remembering exactly what her answer was to that. By the time we finished, having broken into the shack on the lifeguard stand to do so, we'd missed Sawyer and 'Dia's French toast and I was transferring a hefty payment to the Redondo Beach city works department.

Worth. Every. Cent.

Alex returns to our tiny table at the *Granja Viader* café, though I almost haul back and deck him as he does. Though I brought the guy along because his mind runs like a Bugatti, his crisis composure is steady as a Humvee, and he's a theater geek who can turn a bull rider into Marilyn Monroe using a mop, a bed sheet, and some lipstick, it still takes me a second to remember he's pulled off close to the same miracle for both of us. For the last few weeks, he's been a swishy cross of Freddie Mercury and Fabio, and I've been a half-bald estate accountant with a thing for downing one coffee after the next.

Upside? The habit has helped with staying awake for the nonstop pace we've kept since getting here. Downside? After three hundred coffees in twenty-one days, "jittery" has officially become a mix of high and paranoid.

"Is that them?" I jerk my head toward the screen of Alex's burner phone, not needing to elaborate any further than that.

"Wrong burner," Alex mutters. "This is my connecting line back to Wade and Fersh. I'm telling them that everything we thought was true."

Fast scowl. "About what?"

"About you on caffeine."

Darker scowl. "So my little 'character quirk' was all a science experiment?"

"Pretty much." He smirks. I think. It's either that or the fake caterpillar draped across his upper lip has constipation. "Controlled environment plus situational necessity. Seemed a natural fit to answer our collective curiosities."

I give up on the scowling, mostly because it makes my head itch. Emma pleaded that I not get my typical hair trim before the wedding, stating my "Edward Cullen side" is a definite turn-on. I'd obliged without thinking, anticipating a solid week of plunging it between her thighs during our time in Monterey. Now nearly all of it is stuffed under a latex dome stretched between my ears—and I do my best to distract myself from that weirdness by snapping, "If my caffeine sensitivity is really on your curiosities list, I'm worried."

This time, the heavy fuzz over Alex's eyes dips low. "Why wouldn't it be?" He flips his long black wig. "By figuring out your triggers for the fingertip fireworks, the team can work toward developing serums that'll help you access or inhibit them better based on the need of your situations."

Narrowed gaze. "My...situations?"

He nods, overflowing with too much sagacity for the getup. I'm not sure whether to be intrigued or creeped out. "It'd be like the difference between hauling around a lamp with frayed wires or one with a secured cord. You get to plug in and turn on when *you* want to and adjust the brightness for the purpose *you* need."

Now I'm neither intrigued *or* freaked. I'm damn sure I'm simply entertained. "Trestle, did you just compare me to a floor model at Lamps Plus?"

"Of course not." He takes a swig of his *Cacaolat* without breaking eye contact. "You're way more Neon City."

I laugh. I don't want to, but I do. Leaning over with both elbows on the table, I return his easygoing scrutiny. "That's really the secret hypothesis behind why *I* got to be Grandpa Joe-meets-Quackmore Duck?"

"More or less." He shrugs while sneaking a glance around the room. "Well, that and the fact that we're all enjoying the poetic justice for a few weeks."

Intrigue pops back onto my mental plate. "Poetic *huh*? Or do I even want to know?"

"Do you even have to ask?" He gestures at my head. "I had the chance to turn the Heir with the Hair into Chrome Dome Dexter for a little while. Can anyone say hell to the yes, please?"

"Fuck." I dip in toward my fifty-first coffee, glad for the distraction from my itchy scalp *and* the lingering memories from the lifeguard stand, joining Alex to take in the atmosphere of the iconic Barcelona *granja*. Stepping into the historic café is like diving inside a churro, the air sugary and warm and fragrant, with conversation flying around us in the city's musical mix of Castilian Spanish and the Catalan dialect. Patrons bustle in and out, many of them opting to take their drinks and baked specialties out into the late-summer sunshine. The rest of the café's customers, either standing in line to be served or gathered at one of the small tables surrounded by framed vintage photos and war medals, have kept their dark sunglasses on.

Which, of course, makes our casual-but-not-casual surveillance an even more difficult challenge.

Anyone in here could be the contact we've arrived to meet.

The man who's promised he can get us inside the Scorpio cartel—and one step closer to discovering exactly where those bastards are hiding the Consortium's hive of torture.

Not that we couldn't accomplish the exact same thing if we'd quietly spread the word that Reece Richards and one of his team members were in town and looking for an audience with anyone bearing a distinctive scorpion tattoo. But our friend Kane, former Spec Ops stud and a walking testimony to calm and careful, came here four months ago with the exact same game plan. Back home on the ridge, there's now a memorial marker bearing his name.

I've come to accept the fact that my eventual fate may be the same—and I know Alex shares that grim credence—but if I can help it, I don't plan on making my wife into a widow before we've even enjoyed our honeymoon.

So onward with the itchy head, the nonstop coffee, and sneaking fast glances around the café.

After my third perusal of still not spying anyone even remotely resembling a guy named "Saber," I look back over to Alex. "You sure he said his name is *Saber*?"

Alex ticks out a fast nod. "Confirmed it myself. Twice. He even said it's the name his *madre* gave him. When I asked him if it fit, he just said I'd find out for myself. He also said we'd definitely know him when we saw him." He narrows an irked glare back down to his drink. "What he *didn't* say is that he'd be over thirty minutes late, unless 'Saber' is Catalan for 'toothless old lady flirting with the dude in the café corner.'"

I chuff. "She likes the way you're handling all that hair, man." I pick up the spoon from my plate and pretend the molasses-texture stuff in my cup needs to be stirred. "Makes her think you know what you're doing with the 'stache, as well. Or what *she* wants you to do with it."

"Fuck you," Alex grumbles.

"Not interested," I counter—and am appreciative of how he drops the bravado for a few seconds of authentic sympathy.

"Hey, I know it doesn't help now, but what that bitch did to you and Emma, on your *wedding day...*"

"Yeah." I stir some more, though it's really not helping the dregs in my cup. "Thanks."

"And the fuckery with your mother-in-law too?" He shakes his head and throws a frown across the room, only to regret it when the hair and the mustache get a new perusal from the sassy senior in the corner. "That was some weird-as-hell shit."

"Says the guy still being visually felt up by Hot Mama Barcelona?"

Annnnd there's a fine, fine example of a classic humor-as-deflection move, kids—except that my gut won't let the escape stick. All too quickly, it's back to reminding me of the crap oozing inside, as thick and dense and bitter as the coffee slag in my cup. But guilt and fury never earned their reputation from being as pretty as latte foam. *Soon*, I tell myself. *It'll be better soon.*

The second I can get my hands on Faline Garand again. And ensure she's completely stopped from recruiting anyone else into her "Faline's Angels" army.

"*Unnppff.*" Alex's rough grunt is actually a welcome slice into my brood. "I might have to go ask Mama what she has in mind for fun if this Saber fucker doesn't show soon."

I take in the full scope of Trestle's glowering profile. Other than the wig and added facial hair, his disguise is limited to long-wearing tanning pigments, meaning the strength of his actual features isn't diminished. And they *are* formidable, with a broad forehead and bold nose balanced by a full mouth that likely got him called back for lots of roles like "Hot Hunk Number Three" during his stage career. But with an obscene intellect like Alex Trestle's, I'm not shocked he got recruited for whatever uber-secret spy shit the government had him carrying out at Foley's side. He's a damn good asset to the team, and I feel fortunate to have him.

"Nah," I finally say. "I think you should hold out; wait for the *really* fine grandmas who come in around sundown."

"Yeah?" Alex slides into the deadpan without a flinch. "They're cuter later on, eh? Even more captivating than my sweet girl in the corner? Look, she's even showing me her gums."

"And what fine gums they are; however—"

"You're not even looking."

"You're right. But trust me, the best things are worth waiting for."

Except, it seems, our friend Saber.

Fuck.

I push away my cup, saucer, and spoon, considering a trip up to the counter for a second serving. God knows I don't need a single drop more of caffeine, but damn it, despite our witty revelry, Alex is nearly fed up with waiting for our tardy friend— and I'll have no valid argument for sticking around other than my own stubbornness. Waiting around for another contact like Saber to appear will take more effort, money, and time. I'm willing to part with plenty of the first two—but the latter, when every second away from my wife feels like another gouge in my sanity?

But Alex's impatience gains more justification by the second. By now, with tautening nerves, I'm starting to commiserate. Thirty minutes is a stretch even by the relaxed standards of the region. *Shit.* Saber is a no-show, which means we're back at square one. Maybe farther back than that.

But the last laugh on this one belongs to fate.

As a guy strolls in as if he just tumbled out of a club in nearby *Poble-Sec*, looking like he literally just partied the night away—but locking his lazy regard on to us after he's one step inside the door. But that's not what gives him away as Saber. Credit for *that* part goes to his animal-print jeans, Punisher T-shirt, leather arm gauntlets, and the mix of orange and yellow throughout a haircut clearly honoring Elvis Presley.

Alex emits his trademark snort again. "Guess they're serious about *fashionably late* around here."

"And keeping the vintage stores in business," I add, though I don't get time to crack my "Elvis and a nun walked into a bar" joke, since Saber makes it over to our table with shocking speed for a guy with such a lazy gait.

"Wait five minutes and then leave separately." His gritted instruction has me nearly double-taking. The guy is British, his accent cultured. I admit it, I was expecting street-smart Catalan or even a Jersey drawl—but I should know more than most that what one sees is not always what they get, especially with a worldwide cartel like the Scorpios involved. There's more of the clipped London tone as he adds, "Take a right out the door and then left on Pintor Fortuny. In the Museo de las Ilusiones, find me at the roaring lion."

"The roaring lion," Alex mutters as soon as the guy seems to disappear through the back of the café. "Of course. Why not?"

I push to my feet, already antsy about getting the fuck out of here. "I'm taking it as a good sign. If the guy's making us jump through hoops already, he's likely got the intel."

Though good sign or not, the next five minutes will be some of the longest of my life. It feels like centuries since I was last holding Emmalina on that beach, raining goodbye kisses all over her breathtaking face. I'd demanded those moments be our official farewell, knowing that if she came with me to the airport, I'd have likely caved to every selfish desire in my being and hauled her onto the jet with me.

I wish she'd come to the airport with me.

The Museo is just a couple of blocks away from the *granja*, about a five-minute walk under normal circumstances. My trip takes me about double that, due to making sure I don't get near Alex, as well as making a few stops to scan for possible tails. When it's clear nobody on this boulevard cares about the Heir with Little Hair and his nifty pocket protector, I enter the place and plunk down the modest fee to get in.

Walking around, I'm a little perplexed as to why nobody in America has riffed off this concept yet. The space is a vast and quirky collection of wall paintings for Instagram addicts, from the silly to the fantastical to the strange. On my way to find Alex, I pass a group of teenagers pretending to swim away from a great white shark, a couple smooching at each other as hearts "fly" between them, and a geek boy dressed as Luke Skywalker, wielding a lightsaber against a looming Darth Vader.

I find Alex in front of a wall adorned with giant white and silver wings, attempting to selfie himself with the things sprouting out of his back. His dorky expression doesn't make me feel so weird about being Chrome Dome Dexter anymore;

nevertheless, I murmur, "Just keeping up pretenses, Trestle, or is there a purpose for that?"

Thank God I didn't blink, or I'd have missed the guy's furious blush. "Killing time," he rushes out. "But the wings reminded me of Neeta."

So *now* I blink. Between the graduated widening of my stare. "*Neeta?*"

The guy kicks at the floor. "She mentioned being into this writer, Angel something. The wings are a thing with the woman's readers—who are all pretty damn cute, I might add, though—"

"Not as cute as Neeta?" Unbelievably, I keep the tone from being smarmy. Not so much luck with my smirk, which brings three seconds' worth of a great distraction, considering the tense circumstances. "You going to hashtag it too? How about hashtag-Neeta-my-Angel? Better yet, hashtag-Neeta-Angelita?"

"Fuck off." Alex stuffs his device into his back pocket and turns away. "Where's that goddamned lion?"

It's too much fun to pepper my snicker in his wake. "Now *that's* what Chrome Dome calls a proper piece of comic relief."

"And if you're done, maybe we can go over a few contingency plans?" he snaps.

I jam my hands into my Dockers pockets and pretend he's said something extraordinarily interesting about the faux castle bridge we've just passed. "Just in case this really is a trap, an ambush, or just a schmuck nicknamed Saber ready to take twenty-five thousand off my hands without even offering to blow me?"

"Something like that." He stops to tie his bootlace. "Only I wouldn't let that dude's mouth near my johnson if we were the last two people left on earth."

"Decent point." Because for all his trendy touches, nothing's a stronger ode to Saber's tag than the guy's teeth, filed into weapon-like triangles.

As if the universe knows we're talking about the guy like a couple of reality TV gossips, we round the next corner and nearly run Saber down. But if he's unnerved, he doesn't show it. With his same I'm-bored-but-not-really mien, he shifts his weight and swipes the Candy Crush off his cell's screen. In its place is a more official image, resembling the login screen for something like a bank. I'd bet my right testicle that's exactly what it is, especially when he flashes a full and jagged grin our way.

"You found it. 'Grats," he says, nudging his chin out at both of us. "You having fun? Want to look around a little more? We're all settled up"—he toggles his phone against the air—"so right now, my time is yours, mates."

I draw in a deep enough breath to reasonably feign some calm. "Thanks, but I can find plenty of this back at home." But take advantage of the Dexter façade to let my fingers drum against my thighs. As long as I yank back any telltale sparks from the tips, everything's good. Needless to say, I might be an Oscar contender by the time this afternoon is through.

Alex sidles a little closer. "I think what Mr. Dobster is trying to say"—because the bastard couldn't give Dexter anything *normal* for a last name—"is that we're anxious to move on with things."

"We have clients waiting." My addition feeds our cover story about representing a tech firm wanting to get hard-drive components—and a few other illegal "parts"—on the cheap.

"Well then..." Another shark-toothed grin. "Today's your lucky day."

I know better than to look directly at Alex but catch the curious tick of his head in my periphery. "What do you mean?" he presses.

"I mean that what I said in our first conversation is true," Saber drawls. "You pay and I deliver, mate."

"Here and now?"

I pivot, rephrasing Alex in even clearer verbiage. "Are you telling us the contact is ready to meet immediately?"

"Ready as a lion ready for new blood." Blatantly pleased with himself for the theming, Saber adds a small flourish of his hand before pushing it at the painted wildcat's muzzle. At once, one edge of the wall slides away into a hidden recess, revealing the warm light of a separate room beyond. Another hand swoop later, Saber's missing everything but a top hat and one of those little lion tamer chairs—and sure enough proclaims, "Step right up, folks. Your adventure has begun."

Though even to a guy like "Dexter Dobster," comparing this plain back office to an "adventure" is a mighty strained stretch. Not that we're here for the décor, which consists of a utilitarian desk, three office chairs with worn cushions, a filing cabinet, and a multi-armed floor lamp that was last popular when John Hughes films were. If I'd known, I would've ordered Alex to let me be one of those cool guys from one of those movies, with a loose pastel tie, a Members Only jacket, and badass shades.

But now's not the time for what-ifs.

As the wall slides shut behind me, I'm focused only on the things that *should* matter. Detecting any hidden security cameras. Or unusual movements from the room's edges. Or *other* walls that start moving unexpectedly.

Though that's not really necessary, since there's actually a visible door located behind the desk, at which Alex and I direct most of our attention after ruling out that the shadows aren't moving or watching us. Reason dictates that our mystery insider will be making their grand entrance through the stained and worn portal...

And reason doesn't let me down.

At least for another couple of seconds.

Until the meeting for which I've paid a shit ton of pennies begins...

And becomes an immediate shit *storm*.

No.

This isn't a "storm." It's a goddamned typhoon, raining sheets of freezing shock and blasting winds of breath-stealing rage. But neither of those are why I force myself to move, even if only by one scuffling step, and lift a trembling hand, flexing my fingers and even igniting the tips with dim blue blasts.

I need to know this is all still real.

Some vague part of me wants to laugh about that. Ironic, right? I'm firing up the electricity in my hands as a validation of *reality*. It's fucked up. It's insane. But it's true. I need to confirm that I didn't just walk past that wall and into another dimension where right has suddenly flipped into wrong and death has become the new life.

Because that would explain everything, wouldn't it?

But I don't want everything explained.

I sure as *fuck* don't want *this* explained.

The atrocity more bizarre than me. The reality stranger than the shit running wild through my blood. The insanity I force myself to face, and to voice, past the shock-shrunken tube of my throat.

"Dad?"

CHAPTER FIVE

EMMA

"Call me Daddy."

As I expect, my dictate is met by nothing but a bunch of grunts from Sawyer—who still hasn't accepted the fact that my knee is parked in the middle of his spine and I've got his arm bent so far back, I could break it. Okay, so he knows I won't—and my head agrees with the assessment—but at the moment, I'm not exactly thinking with my head.

I'm not totally sure *what* I'm thinking with.

And it's freaking me the hell out.

Simply put, Flare wants to come out and play today. As in, Emma can just go book herself for a mani-pedi and let electric supergirl do alllll the work—only the mutant's also out to completely redefine "work" while she's at it. Flare doesn't just want to be Team Bolt's lead blonde today. She's not settling for simply being the flame in my blood. She wants it all. The power in my muscles. The revs in my nerve endings. And yes, even the motivation in my mind.

Which scares me the most of all.

Who the hell am I kidding? There's not a lot that *isn't* scaring me in some way, shape, or form these days. Okay, fine; really only twenty-one—but when they just happen to be the first three weeks after a girl's wedding day, she gets a drastic discount on the overly emotional express.

Even if the ride takes her down to the training-room mat, parking her knee in the middle of her husband's best friend's back, ordering him to say stuff he probably hasn't even muttered for his girlfriend.

His girlfriend—as in my sister.

As in the figure barging into the training center with vexation to match her light-red mane, huffing in furious time to her resonant stomps. "Baby girl, if you let any more of the sunshine in, I'm going to align your Jupiter, your Mars, and steer your stars into the cooler!"

But not even 'Dia's threat about tossing me into the lead-lined closet, installed into the ridge's training center as a safety precaution at Reece's order, makes me relent the pressure on Sawyer. "Daddy," I rasp with gritted glee, leaning farther over him. "Say it, Folic Acid. Call me *Daddy*."

My use of his military call sign has the guy growling and then lurching, but that's it. My hold, informed by his diligent training and enforced by my fired-up strength, has been executed perfectly—a certitude I feel in the guy's convulsing muscles, with the instincts one only gets from doing this stuff day in and day out for nearly four months—but I also want to hear *him* admit now.

So maybe I don't just *want* it.

Maybe, just maybe, I've freaking *earned* this. *Deserve* this.

"Emma! For fuck's sake." Not that Lydia understands any of that. Yes, my sister is a trained athlete. Yes, she's spent years honing her physical skills as opposed to the few weeks I've spent at it, but preparing for tennis matches is a hell of a lot different than readying for *battle*. With *electric mutants*. And possibly even their leader, who clearly has a handle on her numerous powers better than I do, not to mention the army of brainwashed mortals she's now amassing. Which likely includes our own mother...

So, yeah. Nothing like a little insecurity and fear to amp the voltage count in a girl's senses.

"Em. *Damn it.* You've proved the point. You won the round. Now stand the hell down. Or roll the hell off. Or...whatever!"

And make it really freaking simple to ignore her screaming sister.

"Hey! Are you listening to me? What the hell has gotten into you?"

Hearing her shriek the words makes them reverberate inside my own skull. Whoa. What the hell *is* wrong with me? I'm used to the mitochondrial mayhem that spirals in time to my emotions, and I've learned to reload that shit onto a separate emotional hard drive in order to keep it in check—but right now, it's not working. My system has hacked both drives, smashed them together, and then used my pent-up frustrations and impatience to set them aflame. Everywhere I look inside, there's only white-gold fire laced with brilliant blue intensity.

And it's beautiful.

Sunbeams through a storm. Luminescence and lighting.

And I never want to let it go...

"Emma." Lydia is closer now. Much closer. Practically looming over me as I keep Sawyer pinned. "Rein it back *now*, sister, or I'll do it for you!"

At once, I jerk my head up. Blaze a glare into her that's as fierce as the fires exploding from my pores. I know this. I *see* this, reflected in the flares of her eyes and even in the places where she's nervously wetted her lips, the shine looking like rain puddles in a new dawn.

And isn't *that* my perfect segue.

A new dawn...

"Rein it back." At once, my brain registers the strangeness of my echo, despite not being able to stop it. Still, holy freaking shit. I haven't sounded like this much of a mouthy teenager since I *was* a teenager. And I haven't sounded like this much of an arrogant bitch since...

Never.

"Well, all right, sister of mine." But there's more of my mouth, taken complete hostage by an irritation I can't control any more than a three-year-old without a nap. "If you insist."

I actually shock myself by complying with her command, pushing backward and rolling easily to my feet. The action frees Sawyer, who's all too eager to spring to his own full stance...

Or does he?

It's nearly impossible to tell.

Because he's nearly impossible to *see*.

"Sweet Jesus kissed Houdini," Lydia gasps.

"Mother of holy fuck," Sawyer snarls at the same time.

"Errrmmm..." I manage softly. "Abracadabra?"

The air stills and thickens—not that the palpable soup helps the situation. There's still nothing left to see of Sawyer, beyond his upright head and braced boots—the only visible parts of him, in the aftermath of the energy still sizzling from my spread fingers.

The explanation for the shocker is easy to deduce. Just like what happened out on Rindge Dam before the wedding, I was concentrating on heeding my sister's decree, yanking my powers back *in* and not *out*—only this time, Sawyer was in my way instead of a particle board cutout. Consequently, I sucked the waves of his visibility right off the air, as well.

My sister whips her stare back toward me. "What the living *hell* did you do?"

"And how long have you been able to do it?" Sawyer jumps in at once—prompting her to spin back at him.

"Are you *serious*?" she charges.

"As serious as I am invisible," he returns.

"And now you're giving me *jokes*?"

He shrugs. At least I think he does. "I held back the one about asking if you could get the Twix out of my pocket."

I compress my lips. Fast. Sawyer isn't so ready with his own composure, already surrendering to a string of chuckles.

Lydia remains in fuming mode, looking ready to spit tacks at us both—until her guy's head starts "floating" on the air in her direction. His booted feet are right beneath him—and help him to rush over as 'Dia scurries backward, gasping in horror.

"*Hey.*" His bark stops her retreat but not her gape. "Sparky, come on. It's still me. I'm still here."

"The hell you are." Lydia snaps her glare back to me. "Bring him back. *Now.*"

I want to laugh again but can't. I'm not even feeling bratty, rebellious, or gloriously mighty anymore, either.

Actually, I'm not feeling anything except a lot of nauseous.

Still, I mumble, at least loud enough for the two of them to hear, "Ahhh, shit."

"'Ahhh shit' *what*?" Lydia insists. "You—You know how to *reverse* that, right?"

I'm also the one now swiping my lips with one hell of a nervous tongue. "I—well, we—Reece and I—just found out about it before the wedding, during field training out at the dam."

Sawyer's disembodied face warms with a smile. "Where

Reece pushed you in some new ways—making the new power manifest itself. *Nice.*"

"Okay, *why* are you being such an adolescent about this?" 'Dia seethes out a growl as punctuation. "This isn't some new game for your DS, Sawyer. This is *your*—what the hell?"

I almost echo her when following the trajectory of her rolling eyes—to the spot where Sawyer is supposed to be.

Where even his face and feet have disappeared.

"What did you do with him *now*?" 'Dia yells at me.

"I—nothing! Lydia, I swear! I—"

Am suddenly, unequivocally proven true on my assertion— as my feet are swept out from under me and I fall back onto the mat with a *wham* that sounds worse than it is. That doesn't stop Lydia from screaming as if I've been taken down by a ninja on crack, flipping my instincts back to their original mode. Inside two seconds, *rein in* becomes *strike back* once more. The flares fly in my blood, stripping my control of the atmosphere around Sawyer. He's back again, fully visible—including the wicked grin he flashes as I redirect the momentum of his attack, making him fly over my head into what should be an ass-over-elbows tumble. But he's Sawyer freaking Foley, and he knows better. He ducks, rolls, and recovers during the time it takes me to regain my footing and spin around to face him.

"Ohhhh, shit, shit, shit!" Lydia's wrong-place-at-the-wrong-time mumble accompanies her flight off the mat as Folic Acid and I circle each other. We pace and toss mocking snarls, savoring our standoff with sneering joy.

Sure enough, as soon as Sawyer catches enough of his breath, he jogs his jaw as preface for his deceivingly friendly drawl. "So. Nifty little trick you got there, missie."

"But it needs work," I return. "That was what you were

going to say, right?"

His gaze narrows, but the centers still sparkle. "Hey, finishing my thoughts is *her* job." Then turns those minty greens toward Lydia for a fast wink.

"Damn straight it is," she replies, twirling a strawberry curl and eyeing him like a kitten staring down a six-and-a-half-foot ball of yarn.

Someone's decided to jettison the anger and reclaim her mojo.

But I can't share the light moment. I try—dear *God*, I do—but just like that, I'm reduced to an emotional puddle, once more edgy and bitchy and violent. I look away, ashamed of my yearning to visually erase Sawyer again. Or stab my hands up at the skylights and melt all the panes to sand. Or march the hell out of here, retreat to my upstairs patio with three tubs of Ben & Jerry's Half Baked, and cue up every Spotify angst mix for my headphones.

And barely silence my scream of outrage.

None of this is close to fair. Three weeks after my wedding, my sister gets to moon with her boyfriend like some saucy streaming romance scene while I'm not even able to track my husband's phone to where he really is in Spain.

My husband.

Who hasn't even spent one night with me *as* my husband.

Whom I miss with a need that burns in my blood more intensely than the solar power infused into it.

Not. Freaking. Fair.

A realization that's as unsettling, unnerving, and uncontrollable as it is utterly unavoidable.

And there it is. Yet another new reason to scream the roof down.

I'm desperately, achingly in love with the man who pulsed his way into my senses fifteen months ago. But I've also prided myself on avoiding the Class-One Clinger game—not nearly as easy as it looks when Reece Richards is the man in the equation. It's taken determination, discipline, and conscious personal decision to be a separate entity from the god I feel wired into, all the damn time.

Even now.

When the wires are stretched across borders, oceans, time zones, miles, hours...

Days.

Okay, screw the ode to bitchy and pouty. Why not move on to pissed and lippy while I'm feeling so inspired? "Actually, I'm relaying my *husband's* thoughts," I snip. "As he communicated them to me within twenty-four hours of our wedding—informing me that instead of enjoying my honeymoon with *him*, I'd be getting tossed around on mats by *you* and stress baking my way into diabetes. So can we maybe just waive the 'new powers' processing fee, get the paperwork filled out, and get down to business?"

By the time I'm done letting all of that jettison out, my chest is pumping, my blood is burning, and the fringes of my gaze are bright gold—only making it harder to take the quantum-level Zen of Sawyer's calm reply. "Let's have at it, baby girl."

"Oh, dear hell." Lydia flashes a glower I've never seen off a tennis court. "Did you really just bait her like that? *Really?*"

Sawyer swings his brilliant gaze to her. "Just some playground trash talk, Sparky." Then leans down and in, smushing his lips to one and then the other of her cheeks. "Don't you worry none, Ma. I'll be careful with my Red Ryder carbine-action two-hundred-shot range model BB gun."

I snort and cross my arms. "You'll shoot your eye out. But please do *not* let that stop you."

Lydia glowers. "It's not *his* firepower I'm worried about."

"Gee, thanks." I use the snark to camouflage the true pangs that take over—though my effort's a wasted one and I know it from the second the door opens and the air is tinged by expensive French perfume. While the scent gives Angelique away as the newest arrival from the patio between the training center and the ridge's pool deck, I also already know who's not far behind. Sure enough, she's hand-in-hand with Wade now. The writing's been on the wall about the two of them since before they teamed up with me on that mission of insanity to Palos Verdes—if I can get away with even calling it a mission anymore—yet sometimes, nothing but seeing is believing. And sure enough, our head tech geek and supercharged empath give us plenty to see.

And even more to believe.

Damn it.

Because that little part about Angie and her superpowered intuition? It's all true—and proved completely as much—as her stare lands on me.

Remains on me.

Unswerving. Unrelenting. Unnerving. No; worse. She's unhinging me. Literally pulling the lid of my composure off its hinges and seeing right into every detail of me. Despite my answering glare—and my silent order at her to get out of my psyche—she just keeps staring and feeling and *knowing* all this ugly crap that's going on in my head and my heart. Worse, I'm not sure what to do with how she reacts to it all. Her expression seems like a cross of bewilderment and wonderment, which I have to accept as better than sappy sympathy but still hits me with matching confusion—which does *not* help me in the effort to regain control over all of this angsty garbage.

Sawyer's hefty whomp, resounding through the barren room like he's just broken boards instead of smacking his palms, orders me back to full attention. "Mr. Tavish," he declares, nodding toward Wade. "Just the right arrival to the party, at just the right time. No offense, Angie." He bows toward Angelique, who mirrors him with a serene dip of her wigless head. "We just happen to have a new development in the team's powers roster, and some logistics team interpretation would be welcome at the moment."

Wade jumps his tawny brows. "A new development? In what way?"

Sawyer swings half a grin back my way. "Think you can recharge for another round, Mrs. R?"

Before he's done, I'm brandishing a full smile along with palms that glow like miniature suns. While this isn't my complete happy place, because that can only happen if I'm at my husband's side, I embrace this as the next best thing. Preparing myself to be better, bolder, stronger, faster—so that when I *am* beside Reece, I'm not just "Mrs. R."

I'm Flare.

In all her blazing, brilliant, badass glory.

Channeling the heat of her power into every crevice of her being and every cell of her blood...

As I do right now.

Remembering the truth that guides her from the inside as well the skills that grant her confidence on the outside...

As I do now.

Twining the force of her physical might with the will of

her spiritual guidance, to make her a being worthy of standing at the side of Bolt.

As I *hope* I do now.

Crouching low. Bracing my feet. Readying my arms. Homing my focus. Yes, even freeing my mind from any more thoughts of Reece.

All right, *trying* to.

And realizing, as Sawyer prepares his own stance for our next spar, that banishing Reece Richards to even the back of my mind is like ordering the tide to back off the shore or assuming leg warmers will never be a trend again.

Or telling thunder to stop stalking the lightning.

Yep. I've officially become thunder.

A new kind.

My storm front is white instead of black. My power isn't sound but light. I'm a burning billow of magnificence and radiance, filled with strength and ready to rock this challenge...

Until suddenly, I'm not.

"Wh-Whaaaa?" The stammer belongs to me, but it's been surrendered to a muted, cotton-thick fog. My arms and legs feel swaddled in the same strange stuff. "Wh-What the h-h-hell?" I don't think I've meant the words more. One second, I was hunkered low and battle-ready. Then the next...

Flat on my back, gaping up at lights and walls and a ceiling that won't stop madly spinning—at least when I can glimpse them through the press of faces directly over me.

"Fuck," Sawyer mutters.

"You want my feedback on *this*?" Wade injects.

"You seriously asking that?" Sawyer spits.

"Shut. Up." Only when Lydia seethes at both of them do I start to get really scared. Dee Dee doesn't sound like that unless *she's* scared. To add weirdness on top of freakishness, Angelique leans over, fully in my view again. Her face is set with even more befuddling lines than before.

"*What* is going on?"

Just like that, I'm back to giving my karmic screen test for the moody bitch in the room—and I already can't stand myself by worse degrees than before. But for some reason, despite the self-loathing backlash, I can't seem to help it. My query takes on a second meaning. What the hell *is* happening? Did Faline somehow implant *me* with a remote-control device and is only now activating it? But if that's the case, why can't I hear her inside my senses like Reece did? And if not, then why do I still feel like some crazy alien being has plunked down roots inside me and is slowly taking over?

"Okay, does *anyone* want to remember we're in Southern California and not somewhere between Gotham and Riverdale right now? Juggie? Betty? Batman?"

I'm ready to keep going, but Angelique's heavy sigh takes over the air. Still, 'Dia's the one who takes hold of my hand and gently pulls me upright while explaining, "You're the one who can probably answer that question better than us, baby girl. You just went from super solar girl to the pass-out queen inside of three seconds."

A flick of a side-eye. "I did *what* now?"

Followed by even less of her snark and even more of her fear. And yes, I wish I could write off the vibe as something else, but I know my sister as well as I know myself. It's *fear*. "You don't remember?" she asks quietly. "Not anything about what you were thinking or feeling...right before you went down?"

"I remember plenty," I return. "But nothing different from what I've been feeling in the last three weeks, if that's what you mean."

"Which is what?" The question comes from Angie this time, as she kneels next to 'Dia and sends out more of that *Helter Skelter* meets Madame Morrible vibe with her gaze— and the emotional probes that now feel like she's taking a melon scoop to my guts.

"Well, what do *you* think?" I sound a lot like Morrible myself, but damn it, I'm allowed. "I feel like crap, if you really need to know. Every morning, I want to throw up. Every night, I'm in bed by eight but can't fall asleep for another two hours. In between, I swing between feeling like I can conquer the world and feeling like it's already conquered me."

Whomped by a wave of the latter, I turn and sag back into Lydia's lap, using one hand to swipe down my face. It does nothing to fade the stupid sting from behind my eyes and everything to emphasize how my equilibrium is still pretty damn shot. "All in all, like a woman who's missing the crap out of her husband right now," I wearily snap. "So how's all *that* sound?" But I force myself to sling a diplomatic glance at Angie. "Pretty much right on the money?"

Lydia tucks me close in a comforting hold. "That sounds like you broke the whole bank, baby girl." But her soothing tone is contradicted by her trenchant glare, speared straight up at Sawyer. "And an even better reason for you guys to quit while you're ahead today."

"Oh, hell to the *no*." I rush it all out before Sawyer's done with even half his nod of agreement. "Are you even kidding me?" I erupt at him while scrambling away from her. "Whose side are you freaking on, Foley?"

He jerks his jaw fast and violently, knocking some of his hair loose. The stuff's gotten longer and darker in the last few months, a visual representation of how much time he's spent away from the waves—mostly to help Reece with my training. A lot of those sessions have meant pushing me far beyond my physical and mental limits, even when I've pleaded to quit and stop. But he picks *today* of all days to flip those tables?

"You damn well know that's a rhetorical question, missie," he replies in a calm but growly murmur.

"No," I retort. "It's a legitimate one. You've been the Grand Poobah of Tough Love for eight damn weeks. You've done everything from three a.m. call times to calisthenics in the walk-in cooler to memory games using ground squirrels on the hill." I would still swear in a court of law that all the ground squirrels in this canyon are genetically matched clones, but that's beside the point at the moment. "But now, I take one tiny stumble, and you want to pull the damn pl—"

I stop at the first pierce from the guy's glass-sharp glare. "You *fainted*, Emma. In nobody's book is that a 'tiny stumble.' As a matter of fact, I think we should have Fersh run a blood panel on you just to make sure everything's still playing nicely in your hemoglobin."

I grit my teeth—well aware of the I-just-saw-a-UFO look that Angie's still giving along with the OMG-my-sister's-going-to-become-an-alien-too gawk from Lydia. Emotions rush in again, accompanied by that urge to punch out and break something—but I wonder if that's just natural when one is plunked inside a figurative fish bowl. Just damn it, I wish that fish bowls weren't so dizzying either, as I learn all too quickly when pushing completely from Lydia and attempting to stand.

Operative word here: *attempting*.

"Ohhh kay there, Twilight Sparkle." Lydia's face is wobbly underneath her stab at humor while she helps me land safely back on the floor, directly on my backside. "That's enough of trying to go gallop off to the Delta Quadrant."

I nail her with a glower. "I'm going to forget you just mixed two universes that should *never* be even *close* to each other." And tell myself that the scrutiny is about setting her straight on that, not fighting for a focal point to stop the room from spinning.

"Same way we'll forget you tried to buck my call about the blood work." Sawyer has the nerve to tack a chummy smile on to that.

"Tried?" I volley. "Who says I've given up?"

"*Emma.*" Lydia's full-throttle growl has gotten daunting in the months she's been with Sawyer. "For the love of fuck."

Angelique, who's been verbally silent but communicating *a lot* with the UFO spotter stare, leans forward again. She works her hand beneath mine, fitting our palms together. "I think the bloodwork is a wise idea, Emmalina." She closes her grip in a little more. "As well as giving some thought to your training plan."

I turn more fully to her. Regard her carefully. "My training *plan*?" I get out a brief chuff. "We're just taking the rest of today off, Angie. There's no need to restructure the entire plan."

The woman compresses her lips tighter than I've ever seen. She maintains the vibe while tossing her gaze toward the far wall. Her evasion is so deliberate and weird, even Lydia finally notices.

"But you think there *is* a reason," my sister declares. "Don't you?" She twists, grabbing the ball of Angie's shoulder before urging, "What are you feeling, Angie?"

"No." I yank on 'Dia's elbow, making her relent the hold. "It's not what she feels. It's what she hears."

"Then what the hell are you hearing?" Lydia revises.

"Because it's not just nothing." She zips her gaze from Angie down to me and back again. "Is it?"

I wish I could tether back her interrogation again, but I can't. Angie's entire mien gives away her knowledge of *something*...a ping on her extrasensory radar that's new and obvious but startling—and definitely perplexing.

"Angie." My prompt is more stressed than strict, but nobody's going to blame me for it. The woman's gaze alone, buzzing the room like a police searchlight trying to follow a bumblebee, is clearly amping everyone's skittishness by the second. "What's going on?" I urge. "What do you hear?"

She gives the bumblebee tracker one more try before clamping her stare back down on me.

She stiffens her posture. Resets her jaw.

But for all the mess of the prelude, her final reply is completely certain. Utterly unhesitant. "Heartbeats."

"Huh?" Lydia's faster about the rebuttal than I am.

"That is what I hear," Angie explains.

"Heartbeats?"

"Heartbeats."

I have to consciously tell my answering laughter to stand down. "Well, I guess we're all good, then." And to refrain from any comments about the most underwhelming moment since teeth nails and their three seconds of fame. "Let's hear it for beating hearts. Hey, I'm alive, everyone! Celebratory margaritas by the pool after I go for the mandated bloodwork?"

"No!" For the first time since she walked in, Angelique isn't one shade hesitant about her reaction. Practically shoving Lydia aside to do so, she reaches and snatches one of my hands. "Not...*margaritas.*"

"Why not?" But as I blurt it, not hiding my bafflement, a

lightbulb seems to click on for Lydia. It's either that or she has a sudden leg cramp, but I've seen plenty of the latter to know when those overtakes her. What's she getting that I'm not? That has her mouth falling into a full *O* and her eyes bugging as if *both* her legs have cramped up now? "'Dia?" I demand. "What the hell is—"

"Heartbeats." Her interruption is so hoarse, it almost turns the word into "harpy." Or "Arby's." I can't figure out which—though I suddenly crave a roast beef sandwich more than my next breath. "Holy *crap*. Heartbeats."

"Okay, we've established that part." I eke out a smile. "Remember?"

"No." She leans over, wrapping her hand around mine and Angie's at the same time and then squeezing in. Hard. Her ferocity only starts there. As soon as I look back up to her face, it's to stare in a new state of stunned as pools of royal-blue tears thicken in her eyes. "*No*, Emmalina."

"No...what?" Though now, I wonder if I really want to know. Holy *shit*. Lydia didn't look this simpery and smushy even during the wedding—and as she continues gazing at me like a gold-plated roast beef sandwich, I vacillate between wanting to dig in my heels and scramble away or really parking my backside and hauling her in for a closer hug.

"Heartbeats." Her echo is raspier than before—tempting me to go for the escape option, despite the smile that wiggles along her lips—until she pulls in a *lot* of breath in preparation for what she levels next. "Heart*beats*, Emma," she emphasizes. "Not as in multiple beats." She darts a glimpse toward Angie, who dips an encouraging nod. "As in...multiple *organs*."

Ironically—or maybe not—my pulmonary system shuts down for a long second. At once, I sense the reason. It already senses the deeper truth of what my sister is trying to say. Senses it...*knows* it...

But still battles the full acknowledgment of it.

Which is why, when my heart finally starts the biological service once more, I whoosh out a breath of skeptical resistance. And then blurt, "I still have no damn idea what you're talking about."

Because officially, I really don't.

Because technically, this isn't supposed to be happening.

I'm not supposed to be...

We're not supposed to be...

It's not physically possible for Reece and me to have...

But all of that was before.

Before Faline turned my DNA into electronic soup. Before I let Wade and Alex finish the job by wiring me up to the voltage of the sun. Before every molecule in my body was changed...

As well as how it could receive the life from Reece's body.

Holy shit.

My sensitive body. My swinging moods.

Holy shit.

My missed period, which I wrote off to wedding and fresh superhero stress.

Holy shit.

A cavalcade of so many thoughts and feelings and realizations and stupefactions, all affirmed by my sister's declaration, delivered with a wider split of her joyous grin and thicker tears in her shining sapphire eyes.

"Emma...*baby girl*...you're pregnant."

CHAPTER SIX

REECE

"Reece. *Reece*. You can't do this, man. Listen to me! You can't—"

"The hell I can't."

My growl, cutting into Alex's caution, doesn't feel like me. It comes from a separate animal, so violent I don't recognize the fucker, burning with such hot fury even the electric connections in my blood are trying to strike but hitting major misfires. I snarl at the pathetic blue light fizzling from my fingertips instead of the slicing blue lightning I'm looking for. I'm *fighting* for. But nothing is working, meaning my fungus of a DNA donor remains a writhing, worthless waste of air sprawled across the desk, beneath my knee in his lower abdomen and my hands in the center of his neck.

Seriously, man? Superpower ED, at a fucking time like this?

At least my growing frustration means my hold won't wane on the bastard—though I'm damn sure if he were dangling off the side of the desk by sewing thread, I'd find a way to hold on to him.

And then haul back an arm, coil my hand into a fist, and drive it down into his face.

Like this.

Then again.

And again.

"God*damn*it." Alex's snarl comes with something new. His grip. For a lanky theater geek, the dude's got some impressive torque behind his build. It requires him to put both arms into the effort, but he's able to keep me in check long enough to get in, "You can't do this to him, Richards! Not right here and not right now!"

"I paid fifty thousand dollars to walk into this room." The reminder brings a worthy benefit, shooting enough force up my arm to break free from his hold. "You bet your *ass* I can do this here and now." And likely a hell of a lot more if I want to. And oh fuck, do I want to. *Need* to. In the name of my brother. And Mitch. And God only fucking knows how many others have suffered, and are *still* suffering, because of what Lawson Richards has done.

Because of what *my father* has done.

My father.

Part of me still doesn't believe it. *Can't* believe he's still alive and right here, in my grip. Of course, now he's a shade of red going on purple, but if my wrath has anything to say about that, the purple will soon be a perfect shade of blue. Yeah, the cool new one in the Crayola box, called "Revenge Blue." Fuck, yes. So much better than "Bolt Blue."

Which has me reconsidering the whole superpower shutdown catastrophe.

Maybe, as Emmalina has said—and proved—to me so many times before, the shit twist has become an epic twist.

And maybe this is going down exactly as it should be.

Because strangling this asshole with my raw human strength is a hell of a lot more satisfying than just letting some baby lightning bolts do the job for me. It's grittier. Cruder. More raw and real and savage than I ever imagined—and yeah, I've imagined this a lot. Wondered what I'd do if I was ever given just one more chance to be face-to-face with this fucker.

I've always prayed I'd do exactly this.

I've always wondered whether I could.

I've always been curious whether it would be as easy and as fulfilling as the details in my fantasies.

I'm damn ecstatic to learn that it is.

Except for the fact that I'm *still* getting interrupted. That damn Alex is like a dog with a bone, and it's *not* fun to be the bone. But he's not letting go, no matter how many times I try telling him the bone isn't worth it. More importantly that the bone is committed to a much higher purpose right now.

Red to purple.

Purple to blue.

Die, motherfucker.

I push my thumbs in tighter against his windpipe. Feel him struggling to take in air around the compressed tunnel. I think about all the times I felt stripped of the air in my body too. The first time I was strapped down to a Consortium lab gurney. My first night locked in that cell in the hive, alone and shivering and terrified. The first few hours after I got out, stumbling down empty streets and through a warren of alleys, lost and disoriented and ashamed—not knowing I had been turned into a full freak to be feared.

A freak.

A freak.

I say it one more time, out loud this time, spitting it right into my father's face. "That's what I am now, you know. *Right*, you bastard? That's what I am to this world, because of you!"

Dad croaks and rasps, battling for every molecule of new air. Despite that struggle, he manages to grit, "I...I know."

It's the strangest olive branch I've ever encountered—meaning despite my instincts, it's probably not real. I grind my knee in harder. Close my fingers around his extended trachea.

Which is why the asshole's gaze continues to freak me the hell out.

No matter how valiantly he squirms from the neck down, the man is still staring at me with a warmth I haven't witnessed from him in well over fifteen years—and, from deeper in his eyes, with a light I'm not sure I've *ever* seen. Something admiring. Affirming.

What the living hell?

I'm damn near kneeing the man in the groin and clearly intent on beating or strangling him to death—perhaps both—and he's lying there giving me a visual *atta boy*?

The anomaly is so jarring, I relent my pressure. Just for a second. Only to scrutinize him under better conditions.

To be completely jarred by what I see.

More accurately, by what I *don't* see.

That his weird attention doesn't seem to be electrically enhanced in any way.

"Fuck," I mutter—before pulling my knee back in and shifting my hands from his neck to his shoulders. But I don't surrender my overall angle, making sure the bastard can still see the rage across my face and feel the fury beneath my grip. He's poked my curiosity; that doesn't mean he's escaped my wrath.

All right, maybe he's more than poked at things.

If the Consortium hasn't fucked with him, then how is he even here? *Why* is he even here?

They're the gateway questions to a shit ton more, but somehow, Dad—*Lawson*—seems to sense that too. My mind wraps less around the idea of calling him *Dad* again than him surviving the insane incidents that went down in Paris. Literally, *down.*

Dad jerks my attention back from a thousand miles away with his new chokes, courtesy of my new pressure on the middle of his lungs. Despite the satisfaction of watching him struggle, I let up enough for him to drag in new air.

At last, he gurgles out, "S-S-Son."

"*Don't* call me that."

He nods with calm understanding. Too *much* goddamned understanding. My blood seethes even hotter. *Fuck this.* The bastard can't swoop back in from the dead and think we're going to suddenly do the father-son kumbaya. It doesn't work like that, even in the altered version of reality in which I constantly live.

"I-I know this is a lot to take in..."

"To take in?" I bark out a laugh. "I'm not *taking in* a goddamned thing here, Mr. Richards—least of all, whatever you're pulling with this bullshit." My grimace pulls at the edges of my fake chrome dome, and I'm tempted to scratch at it like a dog with a stubborn flea, until I realize I don't have to. Off comes the dreaded thing with my furious tear, and I admit that hurling it against the wall helps take my tension down by a notch. "Pulling a Jesus doesn't make you my savior. Bring Tyce and Mitch and Kane back, and *then* maybe we'll talk."

During the long seconds consumed by my raging locomotive chuffs, the man has the decency to add a remorseful scowl to his performance—or whatever the hell this is. "I can't change what happened to either of your friends." He drops his head, stabbing his thumb and forefinger into his watering eye sockets. "Or Tyce." He coughs hard, and his shoulders shake from his heavy inhalation. "My boy. Oh, God. *Tyce.*"

I shove away, suddenly unable to stand being in the same vicinity as the stinking choad. "And Christ wept in the fucking dumpster," I mutter, swallowing against a surge of bile. "Save it for someone who'll believe it, Lawson, because I'm not that quinoa brain anymore." I pace the length of the room like a tiger in a cage, feeling every inch the role. "I'm the guy who watched my brother take you and your cute little EMP down and sacrifice himself in the process. *Fuck.*" Saying it out loud is the nightmarish necessity, bringing on the assault of images not only from that night but that moment. Once again I'm in that cavern underneath Paris, watching Tyce launch himself at our own father, knowing damn well what he was risking—and eventually gave—in doing so. His own life.

There's a rustling off to my right, and I'm glad for the minor distraction of watching Alex tug away his own disguise. But he performs every action with a careful eye on my father, his stare full of assessment. Since he was part of the support team back at the ridge when we went through the shit storm in Paris, this is officially his first face-to-face with Lawson Richards—a man he knows nothing about because the asshole *should* be dead by three and a half months.

But fortunately, that incongruity isn't messing with such a huge chunk of Alex's psyche. He's able to sift faster through the post-bombshell rubble than me and move this shit forward with the assumption that needs to be voiced. "So clearly, you were wearing some heavy-duty protective gear down in those tunnels and survived the skirmish that took out your son."

With a cautious glance my way, Dad eases his way back to

a sitting position. Wisely, he doesn't so much as sniff at moving beyond the top of the desk. I'm not even sure I trust him at *this* point, but the upright posture allows a better sightline to his face—and a faster assessment of the degrees to which he's lying. I still don't know his angle here, and my nerves have become unstable storms because of it.

He tilts his head back toward Alex before stating, "Early on in the Consortium's research efforts, they developed fabric made from thread woven out of lead. It became clear that control staff would need protection should experiments or subjects get out of hand."

I slam back against a wall, my impact matching the bellow of my laugh. "Subjects... So *that's* what you all liked calling us back in the break room. Guess that was fun, eh? Joking around about what shenanigans the 'subjects' were up to while you enjoyed the weekly potluck and chugged down your Red Bull?" The acid burns hotter in my belly as I laugh again, not so loud and not so heartily. "'Sorry, guys. Wish I could stick around and scroll through a few more memes with you all, but I gotta get back to my *subjects*. I'm behind on tortures, you know. Alpha eighty-nine decided to puke when I upped his voltage. Sonofabitch threw off my whole day, damn it.'"

Once more, my father has the sense to give up all the outward signs of a mortified reaction. With a crestfallen face and sagging shoulders, he dips his head and then slowly shakes it. "You have every right to your bitterness, son."

"I also have every right to hurl a lightning bolt through your chest if you call me son again."

Dutifully, he falls into silence. A similar silence falls over Alex, who discards his former hair, mustache, and brows onto the desktop. With his hip parked against the edge, he quietly taps out the opening drum riff of *Hamilton* with four fingers—until Dad cuts into the air again with his aching growl.

"Christ." He braces his head with both hands. "It was never supposed to get to this."

I don't flinch a single muscle. "If you think we care, let me introduce you to a little concept called *delusional*." But maybe I'm the one who needs to head the line for that T-shirt, because my lie would trip a four-year-old's bullshit meter. While I can barely stand the sight of my father, who's paler and thinner than the day he "died," my rage hasn't blinded me to the importance of his resurrection—and the opportunity of all the answers it represents.

"I'm already intimate with *delusional*." Dad's reply is gritty. "The bastard was salivating over my shoulder the entire time I signed on the dotted line with the Scorpios."

I cock one brow. "And when you jumped into bed with Faline Garand?"

He regains his feet. "One had nothing to do with the other."

A barked laugh. "You *sure* you know what *delusional* means?"

His spine turns into a steel girder; his features harden like poured concrete. "I turned to the Scorpios for financial help only."

A new bark, from Alex this time. "No one keeps things strictly financial with the Scorpios."

Dad pulls in a sharp inhalation through his nose. "They stood to gain as much from the deal as Richards Resorts, without attempting anything illegal. That was part of the deal's allure for them. Clean money. Legitimate millions."

"The millions they turned around and offered you for your sons," I growl.

"Buy two, get three?" Alex adds, narrowing his glare. "Because, after all, they'd already snagged one on their own."

A thunderous pound through the room becomes the punctuation to his accusation. While the sound is startling, it's hardly shocking—especially when the two of us look to where my father has made everything on the desk jump from the descent of his closed fist. "Do you think I made that deal *willingly*?" he snarls. "That *any* of that was my real motivation or desire?"

Alex folds his arms, cocks his head, and channels his full Jack Ryan for his wry response. "Do *you* think we'd buy the line that you *didn't* know your own son had been targeted, tracked, and then abducted by those monsters?"

Dad's shoulders drop again. "Not until they'd actually done it." His confession is so rickety and rough, it really is nearly believable. *Nearly*. I refuse to push my mind over that final line of change. Believing him will mean letting go of my fury for him—and right now, just as it was for so many months inside the hive, the anger is the core of my strength, the reason I'm persevering through this surreal shit. "Whether you believe it or not is inconsequential," he goes on, pushing upright again. "It's the truth." With steps like a jerking automaton, he starts to cross the dingy room—in the opposite direction from me, thank fuck. "We'd been enjoying huge success, expanding the existing resorts and starting to conceptualize new properties. The Scorpios were so pleased with the dividends on their investments, they wanted me to consider bringing other ventures under the Richards name for legitimate development."

"And one of those concepts was the crackpot plan of the Consortium?" Alex supplies.

"It didn't sound so insane at first," Dad defends. He's reached the other side of the room and lowers onto the arm of the couch. "When I first took a meeting with Faline and Dr. Verriere, the originating scientist behind the project, they were impassioned but rational—and very clear about the ultimate good of their purpose. Verriere explained that while Frankenstein's fictional tactics had been the nucleus of *his* project, it wasn't his intention to become a screaming lunatic with an army of lumbering giants at his disposal." He pauses, his gaze gaining the mist of remembering far-gone times. "Verriere was driven by more than simple scientific curiosity. Genetic deficiencies severely stunted the growth in his legs and one of his arms. He was so convinced that the bio-electric process would work, he was willing to be the Consortium's first human test subject."

I step closer before even realizing I'm doing so. After catching myself and scuffing to a stop, I press, "And what happened?"

Darkness takes over Dad's face. "It was a raving success— for all of eight hours."

"And then?"

"The power surge backfired on Verriere. His system couldn't process all the extra voltage." The storm across his features vanishes behind an emotionless wall. And *there's* an expression with which I'm *more* than familiar. "His blood exploded from the inside out. He was gone inside another hour."

Alex and I exchange a significant glance. Once more, we're nonplussed but not staggered. But I also sense that, like me, he's also intensely curious. None of this adds up to how things eventually shook out. To how *I* turned out.

"Seems like that should've been your writing on the wall," Alex finally tosses out, again borrowing a chunk of Jack Ryan sarcasm.

"Writing?" Dad returns. "Think more along the lines of a ten-foot-high billboard."

"But something changed your mind."

"Not something." I move forward, working my knuckles against the top of the desk like a curved pizza cutter. "Some*one*." As soon as Dad's stare locks on me, I elaborate. "When Faline Garand wants her way, she won't stop until she gets it. Take it from the guy who spent six months in her shackles."

Dad compresses his lips. "Or from the idiot who made the mistake of spending one night between her legs."

Alex groans. "So you *did* go there."

"After five martinis and watching Verriere die before my eyes"—really fucking wisely, he casts his gaze anywhere in the room but at me—"yes." By now, he's back on his feet and pacing back and forth in front of the couch. "Christ, *yes*. And let me tell you, the wind-up was much better than the pitch."

"And let me tell *you* that if I hear any more stats like that, I'll line-drive a lightning bolt through your cheating *dick*."

I back the vow up with ballpark-worthy fireworks of my own, tagging the top of the desk with a row of bright-blue laser dots. I never thought I'd ever openly admit it, but the return of my full power is actually reassuring—especially if it means I'll really get to follow through on this promise. But Dad acknowledges my message with a succinct nod and pivots to continue with his steady pacing as well as his astounding—but bizarrely believable—explanation.

"I love your mother, Reece. I always will. What I did that night with Faline...well, it wasn't a usual practice. Nor a repeated one."

Shit. I even believe that part. Not that I'm going to give the bastard even that morsel of assurance.

"A one and done," Alex murmurs. "Though I doubt the bitch let you ever forget the 'done' part."

"Bingo," Dad states. "To the tune of video footage and photographs that were instantly turned into blackmail material—forcing me to stay quiet about what had happened to Verriere, even after the Consortium obtained alternate funding and continued building the Source, vowing to continue what Verriere had started, except using young, fit subjects who could withstand the violence of what was being done to their bloodstream."

I push away from the desk, advancing toward him. "Alternate funding from where?"

"I still have no idea." Dad doesn't back away, even when I come closer with lightning crackling from my fists and in my gaze. He almost seems to *welcome* my violence, as if I'm expressing what he can't. "Though it was why I eventually played along with every step of their happy bullshit." He still doesn't waver, giving me full access to the sincerity in his gaze and the undaunted set of his stance. If this is all another lie, he's become a fucking expert at the skill. "I convinced Faline that her extortion game had enlightened me about her passion for the project and made me see their cause in a whole new light. I worked at getting closer to her, in the hopes of tracing back the money and then taking down their sources along with all of the 'research' facilities."

"But...?" Alex jabs out the prompt, obeying an instinct that's clearly sharper than mine. Only now do I hear the implied doubt in Dad's statement, though the lapse is understandable. Until ten minutes ago, I'd assumed my father was still a pile of rotting parts in the *Morgue de La PP*, along with the secrets he took to that inauspicious grave with him. Now, he's not only filling out the mystery but apparently on his way to making shit right by it, as well. Well, as right as he possibly can, given the insane circumstances.

"But then she started keeping me at a stiff arm's length," Dad continues. "At first, I thought she'd gotten wise because of the lack of sex, though that never seemed to be a problem once I'd softened her with trinkets and satisfied her with toys." He has the grace to color, as well as avoiding eye contact with me once more. "But she was really different. Decidedly distant. A couple of weeks after that, Tyce went to Richards Hall for an unannounced visit. He was talking about things that made no sense to your mother but connected the most terrifying dots for me. Sure enough, asking questions in the right way to the right people, I learned that you'd landed in that bitch's test lab and had been there for weeks." He stops, bracing hands to the armrest. A second later, he drops his head over as if preparing to hurl. He sounds like it too, while continuing in a low grate, "It was like I'd stepped into a nightmare—only it had no foreseeable end."

I'm motionless. And in so many ways, emotionless too. Both statuses are on purpose. If I move, that might mean having to feel again. And if I feel, that means...

Confronting the storm that wallops me anyway.

The fresh rage. The old sorrow. The ongoing confusion that's bound the two feelings since the first moment I was ever bound to a Consortium gurney. Fuck. It was so long ago, but it seems like only yesterday.

"But you could have brought it to an end." I seethe the words as the whole scope of "it" plays out in my mind. The torture of my captivity. The terror of my escape. And finally, the confusion of my freedom. Of being "banished" to the West Coast for a partying "bender" I never went on. That this bastard *knew* I never went on. "You could've gotten me out of that hell, Lawson."

As wrath rekindles every cell in my bloodstream, I break out of my statue state—and become a focused rocket of revenge once again.

"You could've *saved me*."

And within seconds, am right where I want to be. Pouncing down on the man I've just spun around with one electric pulse.

"Instead, you shunned me."

Glaring down into his face.

"While you knew—you *knew*—what had really happened to me."

Crushing down onto his windpipe.

"To *Tyce* and me."

Tighter. Harder.

"Your own sons, sacrificed by you. And then resold by you. And then paralyzed and punished *again*, in that cavern, because of you."

Rejoicing in his chokes. Savoring his strangled gasps.

"And then killed. *Killed*, because of you."

Ignoring the tears that spill from the corners of his eyes. The orbs, so much like mine, pleading for clemency and compassion.

So much like mine...

No. *No*, goddamnit. Not a fucking thing like mine. Or like *me* at all.

"He's dead," I spew from numb, tear-soaked lips. "My brother is gone, and I'm naming you as his murderer, Lawson Richards."

And *here* is the moment I need. Have prayed for. Have all but dreamed about getting, from the moment I had to lower Tyce's ashes into his memorial up on the ridge at home. The juncture of providence and payback, of fate being balanced, of wrong finally becoming right...

But it's not.

Fuck me, it's *not*.

If I close in and crush down, all I'm getting from my father is air and silence. All I'm giving back to the world is what it already has. In its eyes, the man has been buried once. Eliminating him *this* time will serve no fucking purpose except my three seconds of satisfaction. Not even that. I've been through these moves before, crossing that line between deciding a person's life and death—and even though Kane begged me to end him, there was no life-changing ray of light that appeared after I did. No magical alteration of the time continuum or manifestation of knowledge that encompassed all the cosmos.

There was, simply, nothing.

An emptiness I can't return to right now.

A breach I refuse to dive into—even because of him.

Doesn't mean I have to like myself for the decision. Or to be suave and serene about it.

I'm allowed to let out this tormented roar as I let my father drop to the couch like a used gym towel.

I'm allowed to turn and stalk back across the room, yanking at my hair until strands come out between my fingers.

And yeah, I'm *really* allowed to let that bastard sit there with my last words echoing in his head, because I still mean all of them. Because he's still Tyce's murderer. Because he should still be goddamned grateful I've decided "eye for an eye" is just a stupid colloquialism. Because, no matter how violently I'm beating myself up for letting him live, he'd better damn well realize that I didn't do it for nothing. That in exchange for his damn breath, he'd better start giving up details besides how tormenting it was to know his son—his *son!*—was being held prisoner by the harpy lunatic scientist he'd fucked and then allowed to blackmail him.

"Reece." He sounds like an asphyxiated toad, and that's just fine by me. Moves like one too, struggling to sit upright on the couch, crunching the leather under his worthless ass like a rubber lily pad. "You have to understand—"

"Shut up," I growl from locked teeth, letting my sparking fists fall wearily to my sides. "I already *understand* more than I want or need to."

"No," he croaks. "You really don't. Not how you think you do. Not to the extent that you must."

"And what the fuck does *that* mean?" As I bellow it, I whirl again. Shoot out my arms, capturing the entire desk in my electric grip. Whoosh everything violently left, the whole heavy wood piece sliding like I'm rearranging doll furniture—except for the electric cords that pop away from the wall sockets, dragging minor sparks in their wake. "Tell me, asshole!" And by now, I've made it clear he has no choice. He's pinned beneath the toppled desk, his back against the couch and his legs dangling from the center, his gaze popping wide as I approach through the leftover flickers of once was the desktop lamp. "You going to tell me they threatened to *kill* me—and then Tyce too?" I shake out my fingers, flipping everything left on the desk into his face. He flings up his free hand, warding off the flying papers, paperclips, pens, and calculator. A small foam smiley face bounces off his head, with its motion-activated motivator stuck on repeat. My father and I continue glaring at each other beneath a barrage of one word in high-pitched Spanish. "*Maravilloso! Maravilloso!*"

"They...they didn't threaten to kill you," he finally admits, getting a hand on the smiley and flinging it to the corner.

"That so?" I spit. "Well, maybe they should have." There were plenty of days when I'd wished they had.

"*Maravilloso!*"

"The bastards were smart." Dad breaks up his croak with a violent cough. "If they'd offered, they knew I might have taken them up on it."

It's a damn good thing Alex is here. I would've doubted what my ears really heard if not for the shocked gape with which he leans back in. "An offer to kill your own sons?"

"*Maravilloso!*"

Dad whooshes all the dark smoke of his glare back toward Alex. "Why do you think I 'killed off' *myself* just to get away from them?" he rebuts and ticks his head around so I'm included once more in his tight-lipped explanation. "In the end, death is going to be better for *all* of us, boys. So much, *much* better than what those moon pickles are planning."

His voice has descended so low, I almost spurt out a laugh. There's ominous and then there's melodrama, and my father's mien is teetering on the latter—except for one detail that I really can't ignore.

That I've never seen him venture anywhere near shit like this before.

And so, I do what any rational kid would do in this case. Attempt to call Daddy Dearest out on his bullshit.

"Errrmmm...moon pickles?"

My father only tightens his lips and squares his jaw. "You

prefer scientific psychopaths? Or whack jobs on a mission to wipe out humanity?"

Well, shit.

As Alex actually sputters that out loud, I'm both comforted and unnerved. Once more, having him here serves as confirmation that I'm really not losing my mind—that my father's weirdness is really a thing and not just my imagination—but on the other hand, maybe I wish it *were* my imagination. What Lawson is rambling about...it's the shit of a Michael Bay or Kevin Feige film. Nothing comes close to reality. Yeah, even the version *I'm* living in. Next thing we know, he'll start spouting about apocalyptic horsemen, cryptic prophecies, and Faline's new "army" having sudden cravings for brains and spleens—or worse.

But up until two years ago, I'd also tossed fringe scientists, DNA manipulation, and electronic superheroes into those bins too.

"Maravi...llo...sssss..."

The dying smiley is ideally timed to the weirdness going on in my psyche. I've never spent fifty K on something that felt like more of a winner and loser after the same toss of the dice. We got our straight ride into the heart of the Consortium, all right—only to be told our freight car has already jumped the tracks. My money's basically bought me two tangible facts to walk away with. Number one? My father faked his death as much to the Consortium as to the rest of the world. His threadbare clothes, hanging like potato sacks on his gaunter frame, are testament to the strictly underground existence he's been living since the Paris catastrophe, as well as Saber's insistence that the fifty thousand be in unmarked cash. Number two? Despite the invisible existence, he's obviously been maintaining tabs on me—and not just a few casual Google searches, either. At least that satisfies the curiosity Alex and I were harboring about the speed with which Saber contacted us after we hit the city.

But dealing with the underbelly of society has taught me a few truths about curiosity beyond the cat-killing shit—most importantly, that satisfying one often germinates five more. I have no compunction about giving voice to my not-so-little seedlings now—directly to the bastard who spawned me *and* them.

"All right." I level it while reaching out, palms up, and easing the desk off the center of Dad's chest. "What the hell; you've got my bite. Exactly what's up the moon pickles' collective sleeves?"

"Aside from the plot you already have evidence of?" Dad returns while rubbing out the edges of the pain across his sternum. "And before you even ask: *yes*, I know exactly what Faline was up to with that stunt at your wedding reception. She's been obsessed with the teleportation power forever. I've watched her burn through quite a few 'volunteers' in the Source to iron out the glitches in getting it right."

"Fuck." I dip my head and drop my arms at the same time. "So much blood on that bitch's hands."

"Oh, I didn't say they died." As soon as he halts his hand, he coils it so tightly that the bones in his wrist are stark knobs against his skin. Our gazes lock again, and his jaw clenches just as hard before he grits, "As I said before, son, I would have begged for your death if I could have."

I'm silent—and too damn horrified to correct him about the label. The implications of what he's saying... I inhale furiously to hide my head-to-toe shudder. Unbelievably, I'm suddenly grateful that I only had to lie on a steel slab and watch my monitors fluctuate with the voltage in my veins.

"And she continues to keep hundreds in captivity at that complex." Alex's voice is dipped in a bed of glass too—and my father winces as if his face has been shoved into that bunker.

"Facing hundreds of fates worse than death," he grates before letting his head drop back against the couch's worn cushion. "Which is why I had to emerge *from* death and run the risk of finally contacting you." He scrubs a hand down his face. "The circumstances still aren't ideal, but I knew I might not ever get a chance like this again." A hint of snark pulls at the corner of his mouth. "Unless Emmalina refuses to go anywhere but Barcelona for a honeymoon? Which reminds me. Congratulations, my boy. That woman of yours is solid gold."

"As the sun," I fill in. "Which, regrettably, the entire world knows now."

He looks dunked into that pool of glass again, though maybe only up to his nose this time. "You've got her in a secure location, yes? Under an electronically scrambled security system?"

"Yes, sir. And being trained every day by my right-hand lieutenant and kept busy every night by her sister and Angelique."

"Not your mother?"

I hoist the wall on my composure a little higher. With a blank expression to match, I offer, "She makes it to California when she can."

With the scowl I've expected, he murmurs, "She's staying busy, then? Your mother?"

The walls stay up, but I make sure he sees me stiffen. "You

don't get to have access to that information, Lawson," I rebut. "Especially because I'm still not clear as to why you've chosen to let her go on being a widow."

"Fair enough." He holds up both hands. "And an ideal segue back to the theme, at that."

"Which would be what?" I counter.

"That often, death really is the best answer." As he lets the statement sink in, he pushes his hands to his knees and uses the momentum to swoop back to his feet. "And in that cavern in Paris, it became my *only* answer." Though the assertion's nothing but a tight mutter, it resounds on the air like a boom of thunder—the same way each of his steps on the creaky boards is like a fingernail scratch on a chalkboard. "The only way to get away from being that woman's puppet and acting the part of a mixed-up asshole who'd really bought into their illusion of a designer master race was to kill that man off for good."

"Acting...the part." Though I've comprehended everything he's said, I fixate on the phrase I still don't *understand*. "Okay, hold up the goddamned turnip truck. I was *awake* that night, Lawson. My limbs were paralyzed and my voice was strangled, but my ears and my brain still fucking worked. I remember every word you fucking said."

"I know," he utters. "So do I."

"You compared Tyce and me to Dobermans. You called Chase your Shepherd, 'loyal to a fault.'"

"I know."

"You said we were alive to serve the family's purpose." Every one of my syllables is a vicious spit, and they feel damn good. "To serve *your* purpose."

"I know."

"And you knew then, as well." I clear the three steps back

to his side and twist a fist into the front of his shirt, uncaring that my rage burns through his thin garment in less than a second. I simply slice down until closing my grip over his belt, using that centralized leverage to slam him back down into the mess across the desk. "You *knew*, goddamnit. You were conscious and clear about every vile syllable that sprung off your lips. Nobody had a gun to your head, control chip in your brain, or needle in your arm." I lock my teeth so hard they hurt—and let him see the tension of that grit. "And now you're telling me it was all some kind of *act*?"

My father swallows hard but doesn't flinch his stare by an eyelash. "An act I abhorred," he rasps. "Through every hideous, horrific second." A breath escapes him in broken sections of air. "As that lift carried us down to the caves, I swallowed my own bile. Reece...son..."

"*Don't.*"

"I hated myself for what I did to you." He may not be faltering in the gaze, but he's also not pulling any punches with it. His eyes shimmer with thick liquid. His nostrils flare hard, in and out, harsh bellows of brimming emotion. "All of you." He wrestles beneath me, though not in the brutal struggles of attempting an escape. He's really wriggling only one part. His left hand.

In which a thumb drive suddenly appears, apparently yanked from his pocket. The lining of his pocket still hangs free, like a demented white flag of surrender, as Alex and I gawk at the two-inch stick peg like it's the key to the national nuclear launch codes.

At last, Dad draws a deep breath and mutters, "I did all of it. I'm not fucking proud of it. But I came out of all of it...with this."

Alex leans in and pulls the USB away. "Which is what, exactly?" he demands.

"Just about everything you need to know about getting into the Source and taking down those batshit bastards for good."

Alex cocks a brow. "*Just about?*"

"I was working on making it everything," Dad offers. "But dying took a bite out of my process."

Alex purses his lips. "Yeah, that has a tendency to hinder things."

"But there are, as you've said, hundreds of people who can't wait on our 'process' any longer." Dad's focus is shockingly steady for a man dangling six inches off the floor, being wedgied by his own son. His concentration earns him a few more of my reluctant props, but not enough to drop him yet. "Once Saber relayed the news that you were definitely coming to Barcelona again, on the hunt for any information about Faline or those lunatics, I knew I couldn't wait any longer." He dips a nod toward Alex's hand. "What I have isn't everything, but it's enough." And then shoots his unblinking regard back up to me. "And I died to keep it safe for you, Reece."

Yeah, so he's not blinking—but *I* am. Just enough times to convey my abject confusion. "Safe for *me*," I echo. "But why not use it yourself?"

Alex, with the instinct of a truly fine wingman, steps back over to elaborate. "You've stayed dead enough for anonymity, but you clearly have underground connections to get shit done—and likely not just here in Barcelona. Why give this intel to us and not use it to organize your own army against the Consortium? Or for your own purposes, period?"

Dad huffs out a laugh. Well, as much of one as he can, given how his pants are likely bisecting his ball sack. "You mean, why didn't I sell it to the numerous black-market buyers who'd love to get their hands on this kind of intel about the organization?" When he grimaces, I'm given my confirmation. Ball sack bisected. *Mission accomplished.* Part of it, anyway. "Isn't the answer to that clear by now?"

Alex joins me in contemplating those words for a long, tense moment. At last, my wingman growls the conclusion we have no choice but to come to. "Well, shit," he grumbles. "You really do want to take out those cocksuckers as badly as we do."

Dad blows out a breath of blatant relief. "But I don't have any of the raw resources to do so." And then releases a bigger *whoosh* as I ease his feet back to the floor. "Mounting this huge of an effort is going to take everything I don't have"—he jabs a couple of fingers into the top of my chest—"and that *you* do, my good Mr. Bolt."

Somewhere inside me, there's a jibe clamoring to get out at him for that—but damn it if my old man doesn't manage to shine up the archaic words like only an experienced hipster could. "All right, all right, Jeff Goldblum," I spit. "You want to fill us in on exactly where to start on that everything?"

Dad discreetly shakes out one leg and then the other. While straightening back up, he jogs a nod back toward the thumb drive in Alex's hand. "You just need to unlock all of *that.*"

"Unlock it?" But Alex, more suspicious than curious, doesn't swerve his focus away from my father's face. "The fuck?" But even then, it's as if he knows the answer before asking the question.

"I have the right files downloaded, but most of them are encrypted."

"And you couldn't find a decent security tech to unravel the codes? Even here?"

"None that I can completely validate or trust."

I nod at Lawson but toss my glance to Alex. "He has a point." A solid one. I turn, one hand on my waist while stabbing the other back into my hair. "With the Consortium physically based nearby, they likely own most of the techs in the city. In the *country*."

With new vigor, Lawson approaches me. And for a second, seems to contemplate actual physical contact, a la normal father-son bonding, but nothing about this—about *us*—is halfway close to normal. The recognition grips his features just before he drops his hands, pulls in a grim breath, and then pronounces, "Just to add another layer to the fun, I'm pretty certain the key itself is booby-trapped as well." He chuffs as Alex drops the stick like it's turned into an electric centipede. "The one and only time I attempted to access the files for myself, I took care to hide in the basement of a restaurant owned by friends. Yes, I still have a few of those," he adds while bending to scoop up the key. "But from the second I snapped the thing into the computer, I knew something was wrong. The thing let out some shrill beeps and flashed with a defined pattern of glowing colors."

"Like a code?" I prod.

"Exactly like a code." His scowl tightens as he regards the drive with a longer scrutiny. "Especially because the place was overrun and destroyed by Scorpio henchmen within a matter of minutes."

"Meaning you have *fewer* friends."

Dad ignores Alex's quip. "I escaped through hidden tunnels, but barely."

Alex grunts. "And now you've got a lot of rockets ready to launch, as well as the starter keys, but no flight codes or pilots."

Dad replies with a similar snort. "Simply put, yes."

I lean against the desk. While bracing my hands against the edge, I regard them both with a stare that feels more brainless than it likely looks. At least I hope so. "So how do we access those codes? Or where?"

My father abandons his snort in favor of a full smile. The look brings back some crazy memories. The first—and only—time I made honor roll. The time Tyce crashed on his bike and I carried him a mile home on my back. The night I approached as he and Emma laughed over hors d'oeuvres at the Richards Reaches Out gala, in New York. The seconds in which I kicked ass on the band of criminals who'd crashed the party.

"Not *what* or *where*, Reece," he explains as his smile widens. "It's *who*." And though my comprehension blares as soon as he makes that statement, I wait for him to cross back over to me, hands held up to fully embrace me by both shoulders before affirming, "It's *who*." He squeezes his grip tighter, his gaze warming with deeper pride. "Son, the engine is you."

CHAPTER SEVEN

EMMA

"At what point do I get to say my mind is officially blown?"

Lydia's query brings on a soft laugh from Neeta but a twisted scowl from me. Of course, neither of them have cold goo spread across their bellies—which has been transformed, seemingly overnight, from what I thought was some menstrual bloating to what I now know is my growing baby.

My baby.

Holy. Shit.

I'm going to have a baby.

Reece Richards's baby.

As the truth resonates once more through my senses, I now know exactly how to answer my sister's crack.

"Yours doesn't get blown until *mine* is done." I finish it by flipping my gaze back up to Neeta's face, which is still defined by equal parts awe and astonishment. Like Lydia, the woman's been privy to information that few really know. Reece's junk is supposed to be as sterile as a nuclear meltdown survivor's—and for the better part of the last year, it *has* been. I should know. I'm the woman who's been enjoying the benefits of his otherwise fully functional cock for almost a year and a half now. And, I can attest, who's also been fully functional in my own right, including the regularity of my cycles in *all* their

260

feminine glory. Yes, including the cramps. And the zits. And that lovely, aforementioned bloating...

Until last month.

When I thought all of it had decided to let my stress take precedence over my cycle. I hadn't even bothered with a pregnancy test. I've been happily screwing only one man for a year. After the initial relief that Reece's ion-powered body couldn't kill me, I never considered that his reproductive "stuff" was functional, normal. So we've just been going for it, especially for the last few months. Blissfully fitting in as much protection-free debauchery as we can around training, eating, training, wedding planning, training, reviewing the team's intel on the Consortium, training...

Annnnd that picture's painted pretty clear now.

Just like the one to which I now drop my gaze.

The image, looking a hell of a lot like just a couple of kissing lima beans, that has me choking back a sob and reaching frantically for Lydia's hand.

It's the vision that changes everything.

The change that shifts all of my paradigms.

"Oh, God," I rasp.

"Fuck me," Lydia blurts.

"Hey!" I jerk my hand against hers. "Watch the language around my bean."

"Who still *is* a freaking bean?" she retorts.

"*Well.*" Neeta wields the interjection with exaggerated patience. "If Mommy and Auntie will keep their bickering to a dull roar, perhaps I can maneuver a clearer bean shot for you."

"Oh, yes please!" 'Dia bounces on the rolling stool she's occupying, borrowed from its normal place in the command center over our heads. Yes, we've retreated to the bunker for all this, and we've declared it a no-guys zone until Angie's declaration from two days ago can be proved completely true. "Holy sh—errr, I mean holy guacamole—it's a damn good thing Fershan was able to find this ultrasound machine so fast."

"And that Sawyer was able to procure it," Neeta adds, her smile soft.

"But most of all, that *you* know how to operate it." I reach up my free hand and squeeze around Neeta's forearm. "A woman of many talents, for whom I'm really grateful," I tell her with matching tenderness.

"Well, you can thank my sister," she replies. "All those months of helping her with her certification exams must have rubbed off and stuck to the right brain cells."

Lydia leans forward as Neeta rolls the ultrasound probe over to the other side of my stomach. "I can still hardly believe it," she murmurs.

I shift on the table, trying to disguise the discomfited growl that brings back to my stomach. "Chemistry is a funny thing," I mutter. *Especially when Daddy's a walking lightning bolt and Mommy's uterus has become a solar-powered incubator.*

Facts that haven't left my mind and heart for more than two seconds since Angelique's pronouncement. Right now, trusting any outside doctor, no matter how highly they come recommended for their "discretion," is out of the question. Reece and I asked every single guest at our wedding for the same level of respect—and one glance at the online stats for my "SPF 70 Bridal Meltdown" video are proof of how well *that* went.

So, I've had to take the high—and freaking *hard*—road for two days. Wrestling with my insecurity, uncertainty, and flat-out panic about what Neeta's probe would really find inside my belly. The possibilities have ranged from everything as insignificant as some gas bubbles to full-on absurdities straight out of a horror film fest. What kind of creature doesn't show even a trace of human pregnancy hormones on a pee stick?

At this moment, I don't give a damn about that answer anymore.

All I care about is my little smushed bean.

My magnificent, miraculous, creation of love and light...

"Oh, holy crap!" I blurt.

My bean—with arms I can now see. *Look at that. Holy shit, Planet Earth! Look at that!* One, two. Both there, so strong and mighty and perfect. And now, those precious little legs—one, two there, as well.

Look at him. Look at him!

And yes, I know it's a *him*. I just...know. While science won't be able to back me up on this one for a while longer, I just know this already. My little boy's eyelids and nose and mouth and ears already speak that truth to me.

"Everything seems normal, my friend," Neeta murmurs with her musically accented comfort. "This is a beautiful, healthy three-month-old. *What?*" She discernibly starts as soon as I whip my stare from the monitor to her.

"Th-Three *months*?" I falter out.

Neeta frowns a little. "Three and a half, to be exact," she asserts.

"No. *No*," I argue. "That's not—that *can't* be right. I was bleeding just seven weeks ago. I tracked everything back as soon as Angie made her call in the training center. I-I skipped last month but wrote that off to wedding stress. But before that—"

"You were probably just spotting." Lydia folds her other

hand over the juncture of where I've started gripping her like she's a log in a storm, rubbing over my knuckles in reassuring circle. "You know that kind of thing is common, baby girl."

As I turn my head back to her, I darken my scowl into a full glower. "And *you* also know that kind of stuff's as common in our family as purple warts."

She purses her lips. Glances back up at Neeta. "She's right, damn it. The Crist women have never had any trouble proving our...errrmmm...fertility."

Neeta copies my sister's moue while pulling the probe away. She replaces the instrument by laying her own hand across my center, splaying long fingers that are full of fortitude, encouragement, and a warmth that permeates my skin, seeming to swaddle my bean in love already. Besides the radiance of Reece's touch, I don't think I've ever been so moved by another person's clasp like this.

Reece.

Oh God, I miss him so.

I *need* him so.

At once, as welcome but as cursed as the swell of emotion in my soul, hot tears burn at the backs of my eyes. Neeta and Lydia, holding me in their different ways of comfort and support, let me indulge the deep pain for a long moment. Then, quietly as the night wind echoing through the canyons outside, Neeta rises. Slides a slow nod toward the place where her hand still rests on my stomach.

"Why don't we all get some rest right now—and we will see how things are going with this sweet bean tomorrow afternoon?" Her smile is filled with calm confidence. "This child has already proved he is an extraordinary creation in several ways. If he adds to the list tomorrow, then we will assess the situation and go from there. But Emmalina"—as she bends over, she presses her fingers into my skin, compelling me to feel the outreach of her compassion and strength—"the key word here is *we*." She rivets the bronze force of her gaze directly into mine. "You are not alone in this, my friend—nor shall you ever be. This child was created in love, and in love it will continue to be surrounded and uplifted."

Next to me, there's an obnoxious snuffle. "Holy shit," Lydia finally blurts, swiping at her eyes. "Why don't you have your own talk show or something?" she charges at Neeta, who just rolls her eyes and lets out a musical giggle. "You think I'm kidding?"

"What I *think* is that our little mama and her cargo need to get some dinner and then some sleep." My gorgeous friend re-secures the giant clip holding back her ink-dark hair while beaming a bigger smile my way. "No more ignoring your health to the point of fainting, my stubborn girl!"

"Fine." My sister waves a conceding hand. "But after we're done with all that, you and I *will* be talking about at least a podcast, woman."

⚡

A couple of hours later, I start to fall asleep with a peaceful smile on my lips and the echoes of my sister's enthusiastic chattering in my ears. As 'Dia and Neeta talk, toning down their volume as they watch me drift off, they also cue the speaker system to switch the playlist from "Girl Pop Greats" to "Baby Brainpower." And in the hazy moments between consciousness and slumber, as a lilting piano tune ushers little bean and me into the cocoon of deep sleep, I fold my arms over the middle of my being—of my existence—and whisper a promise only he and I can hear.

"I know you miss him as much as I do, buddy. Daddy will be home soon, I promise."

But the belief of my promise doesn't filter all the way up to my brain—or maybe it does and the damn thing rebels on me anyway, taunting my sleep with strange visions and terrifying ideas. I see Reece racing down narrow, dirty alleys of an old European city. Barcelona? Or somewhere else? Doesn't matter because he's looking for me. I know this because he's yelling for me. Bellowing my name, with increasing fear, down every passage he turns. No matter how loud I scream in return, he doesn't seem to hear me...

I'm here. I'm right here! Please find me, baby. Please come back to us. Your family. Your family...

But he still doesn't stop calling out. He's hoarse and desperate.

Emma. Emmalina!

Damn it!

I'm here! I'm right here!

"Em. Emma!"

"Right here. Just—just look. I'm right—right here!"

"Emma. *Baby girl.* Oh, hell. Dude, she won't wake up."

I reach down inside myself, pulling out more air for the words. Pushing out more volume. "Reece. *Reece.* I'm here!"

"Do *what* now? All right, if you think it'll work."

"Reece." I shriek it now. "Reece!"

"Velvet. *Baby.*"

"Reece!" I palm away the wetness on my cheeks. Oh, God. It's like he's here, but he's not. I can hear him but not touch him. Not smell him. Where is he?

"Bunny," he calls out. No longer lost. He's found me... but now *I* can't seem to find *him*. Where is he? "I'm right here. Wake up and talk to me, my gorgeous Flare."

As he issues that dictate, I fasten my focus completely on his voice. *Wake up.* Why is he saying...

The phone.

He's in the phone. The one Lydia's pressing to my cheek, with pillow lines still etched across hers. Strawberry-blond curls are a sleep-tousled halo around her head, made that way by the light streaming in from the landing outside the ridge's master bedroom.

"Wh-What time is—"

"Two thirteen," she grumbles. "Yes, *a.m.* You weren't picking up, so guess who was next on the call list?"

"Oh, God." That's when everything falls back into place. Reece, leaving for Barcelona. Reece, having to take his cell completely off-grid. Reece, not contactable.

Reece...not knowing he's going to be a daddy.

I impale my sister with my fully alert stare. "Did you..."

"I'm half asleep, baby girl, not half stupid. Of course I didn't tell him."

"Tell me what?"

I home back in on the beloved baritone flowing through to me through the phone line—gripping 'Dia's device with the same intensity I give my other hand, dropping at once to my middle.

Which has swelled from a bad period pooch into a small but defined baby bump.

Yes, overnight.

And no, not a figment of my imagination.

And yes, bringing along a flutter of tiny movement that

I've never felt in my life. So indistinct that if it happened in the middle of the day, I probably wouldn't have noticed it. But right now, in the silence of the very early morning, in the stillness of the bed that's empty without him in it, I know exactly what this is. Exactly *who* this is. My bean has sprouted wings and is now like a small...

"Butterfly." I laugh it out quietly, answering my son's vibrant drumbeat with some gentle circles around my belly button.

"Huh?"

"Errrr. The...uh...butterflies," I answer to Reece's perplexed grunt. "I was just saying that the monarchs are starting their migration a little early this year. They're all over the sunflowers in the canyon." It's not a lie—and neither is the yearning that resonates through my sigh. "I wish you were here to see them, my love."

I miss you so damn much, Reece Richards.

His answering brush of a breath lets me know he heard that part too. Yes, even nearly six thousand miles away, my Zeus still possesses the godlike power to decipher my thoughts. "Well...if fortune favors us today, maybe I'll have a chance to catch the sight, as well."

I push up sharply, adrenaline jolting my every vein. Bolty Bean immediately thrashes out his disapproval of that surprise, but fortunately, he's still too small to dent anything inside. *Yet.* Knowing I won't get back to sleep after this, I know the hours waiting for Neeta to wake up are going to be torture. But I'll cross that long, lonnnng bridge when I come to it. Back to the really cool bomb my man has just dropped.

"What the—how?" I demand. "Did you find her already?" There's more to that, but I can't find the strength for the addendum. I can't find it anywhere inside me to ask if he's also killed Faline, even after all of the destruction she's caused and the pain she's dealt. Talking about death isn't right after the universe has given me the miracle of life.

"Not yet." Reece's tone tightens as he addresses my question. "But we've connected with someone who has all the information we need to do so." His pause is purposeful, and I hear the minor snag in his breath that always goes along with him rearranging index cards in his mind—perhaps even yanking a few out of the deck. While I'm not wholly uneasy about that, I *am* a few ticks past a basic case of nosey.

"Someone...who?" I murmur.

"A contact of a contact."

"So you could tell me, but then you'd have to whack me?"

"Or make *you* whack *me*." At once, his voice becomes as supple and seductive as his finest leathers. With matching speed, I think about him crawling into bed with me right now, clad in those leathers. How amazing and smooth and cool his outfit would feel against all of my nude flesh. I could be that way for him with just a kick of my PJ bottoms and a flick of my T-shirt...

Shit.

The subject.

We *have* to stick to the subject.

Especially right now.

After deep-breathing away my arousal and then rewetting my lips, I clear my throat to steer us both back to the correct path here. "So...what kind of specific information does this 'contact' have?"

"The kind that's been encrypted." He's not hesitant about giving up *that* part.

"Well, damn."

"And can't be decrypted over here." Nor about that.

"Because the walls have ears?" I suggest while propping up the pillows to support me leaning back and settling more comfortably. Holy shit. I must have gained ten pounds overnight, and half of it was in my boobs. At this point, I won't require Neeta or that machine to tell me how far this pregnancy is progressing; I'll simply need to assess my new bra sizes.

"Because the *air* has ears."

While his reply is tense, there's enough of the sarcastic Reece I know and love to make me start breathing easier. He wasn't lying at the beginning of this exchange. He really *is* here. Not physically yet, but in all the other ways that matter, he's absolutely here—and proves it with his gruff laugh, his smooth snark, his loving tone.

And yes...even in the defined weight of his long inhalation, followed by his weighted breath back out. The message, even without words, that he clearly conveys to me throughout the heavy silence that follows.

"So that means...what?" I follow pure instinct in finally issuing the prompt. Sensing he needs me to do it. To all but beat the words out of him now.

"It means..." Yes, another clunky pair of breaths before he finally says, "It means that we can't extract the information here, Emma. And nor can it come home with us in the form it's currently in. The thumb drive it's been loaded onto has been encoded to send out a signal any time it's inserted into a traditional USB port, so..."

No way has he randomly picked that moment to fade off on the explanation. As always, the man knows damn well what's going on in my head right now. The conclusion my gray matter is already closing in on—and, considering the lack of blatant denials from his end, correctly so.

At last leading to the words I *must* blurt out. That I need to hear spoken, by at least one of us, to fully grasp. "So you're going to let them plug it...into *you*, instead."

Another one of his earnest breaths in. Then a decisive *whoosh* out. "Alex thinks that if we hook up an independent USB port to a defibrillator charger and then shock the information into me—"

"*Shock* the information into you?" I say it but still can't believe it. "You mean, like what they do with the dying patients on the medical shows?"

"Only I'm not going to be dying, Emma."

"Thanks for *that* reassurance, Doc."

"I can handle this, Emma!" For several long seconds, our connection is filled with nothing but the huffing force of his fierce breaths. "At least...this part of it."

Everything stops throughout my body. Yes, even Bean Baby's butterfly kicks. My thoughts cease in my head. My stomach quits its incessant growling. Even my nerve endings are still, like wheat stalks gone motionless before a summer storm. "And what the hell does that mean?" I ask it slowly, purposefully—and yes, even suspiciously. A small, silent part of me threatens the man with partial castration if he stalls with those leaden breaths again.

But there are no lead-up whiffs this time. Only his reserved, resigned growl as he finally states, "There's a chance—a slight one—that the jolt from the paddles will dislodge the solar ions blocking Faline's radio waves."

Now I'm taking the lead on the whole heavy-breathing thing. If what my lungs are doing, despite the cinder blocks of anxiety dropped across them, can even be called breathing anymore. Finally, I manage to rasp past them, "Which means... what?"

"Probably nothing." He's fast out of the gate with that, giving away just how prepared he was for my query. "It's just going to depend on how close, and how aware, Faline may be to El Prat."

"The airport?" I clarify. "Why there?"

"Because that's where Alex and Saber will attempt to get this shit done. And, if they're successful, where I'll be directly boarding a charter—and coming right home to you."

I don't feel an iota of guilt about drowning out the last of his assertion with my full, joyous gasp. Reece doesn't seem to mind, either. As he chuckles softly, I level, "As much as I hate the means, that ending doesn't suck."

"No." His utterance borders so totally on a whisper, I have to strain to hear it. But right now, I'll gladly endure this man's means in order to have his ends. "It doesn't suck one damn bit, my perfect Flare." Though he adds, as soon as I gulp so hard that it's audible, "*What*, baby? What is it?"

I rub my stomach, borrowing strength from the little superhero inside to push out my answer. "Wh-What happens if your Plan A fails, mister?"

All the brilliant energy from his end drops beneath a fast fade. "Then we punt like hell for a Plan B," he murmurs. "But either way, Mrs. Richards, I promise you'll hear back from me within twelve to thirteen hours. It won't be weeks this time, okay?"

I swallow again, letting him hear the residual rush of my breath, followed by the sounds of me determinedly fortifying myself. Staying strong is no longer an optional prerogative for me. It's not just *my* life depending on the perseverance anymore. With that determination behind me, it's easier to say, "Okay."

Once again, I can all but hear him mulling over my response. "Dearest wife?" he prompts.

"Yes, my dearest husband?"

"You believe me, right?"

"I believe in *us*, Reece Richards."

So come home...

To us.

Ohhh, yes. I really *did* just leave that spoiler alert solidly in the realm of silence.

Because what will I gain from telling him now—except a husband who's attempting to save mankind from a psychopathic bitch by having her vital intel shock-waved into his bloodstream? Who, in doing so, is willing to expose himself to the possibility of being controlled by her again? Who has given up more than his wedding night to do all this?

Who might be sacrificing life as he knows it for this?

As soon as we disconnect from each other, I get out of bed and throw on a casual sweats outfit, preparing for the interminable wait I'm about to face—

And the thoughts I'll have to confront through every second of it.

The possibility that my husband may get back here and not know who I am or the man he is to me.

The chance that he may come home as a corpse instead of a man.

The potential that he may not come home at all.

What about *then*?

The question slams at my senses, over and over, as I wash

my face, brush my teeth, and prepare to head into what might be the craziest day of my life. And considering the life I've had so far, that needs to be *Craziest*, capital *C*...

A conclusion that, in its own wacky way, supplies my final answer to the query that simply isn't giving up on tormenting my mind, my heart, and my soul.

"What about then?" I challenge back to my reflection in the bathroom mirror. "*Then*, you punt like hell for a Plan B, Emmalina Richards. You punt...and you pray."

⚡

"Okay, do I have permission *yet* to blow up my mind?"

Lydia's crack, its humor layered atop a bedrock of genuine bewilderment, gets answered by Neeta first. "Stand in line," my friend blurts, her chocolate eyes bugging and her generous mouth falling all the way open.

Not that I blame her—because my face probably looks just as thoroughly stabbed by lightning. And electrocuted by amazement. And surrendered to a complete, captivating assault of holy-shit-this-can't-be-real.

But unless we're being really, *really* punked, this is real.

Except that the only suspects for the punking have as much figurative skin in this game as the three of *us* do—at least I'm assuming so, based on Sawyer, Wade, and Fersh's giddy reactions from the second Angelique played preliminary prophet for the stork in the training center a few days ago. Even as we attempted to sneak out of the main house and back down here, into the bunker, the guys spilled out of the laboratory wing to dole out their hugs for good luck—and, to be brutally honest, to gawk at the growth of my midsection. I was happy to stand there and let them, actually reassured by their fascination.

Everyone else's reactions have been the insurance policy for my own. I'm not going loony. I know that every new mother feels like their baby is growing at the speed of light, but in this case, I wonder if that might not truly be the case.

And, thank God, both 'Dia and Neeta seem to be my real-world backups for the argument. Now, it's just a matter of waiting on the hardcore stats from my friend with the smile that blazes so brightly against the dark sienna silk of her skin.

"Emma." She shakes her head, loosening a few strands of her long ebony hair from its claw clip. "This is...remarkable. Look there. The new definition of the face. The fingers and toes, getting longer." She flings her gaze between my face and the monitor. "If I didn't know firsthand that this had happened overnight, I would have marked the difference between yesterday's and today's images at least two days—maybe even three."

"So has anyone done the math here?" Lydia cuts in. "What does this really mean?"

Neeta shuts off the ultrasound and starts wiping off the small mound that is now my stomach. "That our super girl is really carrying a super baby," she declares, beaming a broader smile.

"Yay!" Lydia pumps both fists before swinging her hands down to help me climb off the exam table. "That also means *shopping*." That part is given on her hearty chuckle—as I fight to keep Reece's biggest dress shirt tugged over my distended front. "Lots and lots of shopping!"

"If this kid doesn't decide to make his debut first." I work to make it a joke, but there's not enough there for a true jest.

If this galactic-speed gestation is really going to be half the norm, and six to seven weeks of it have passed already, we have just over three months to prepare for the arrival of the world's newest Richards.

We.

We?

Cart before the proverbial horse, anyone? Or in this case, before the superhero daddy still out there, God knows where, fighting to find and route out the doyen of derangement before she takes down the world with her insanity?

Only now, entertaining a little lunacy of my own.

Thinking *we* is going to even be a thing.

Thinking I'm just going to hike up these steps and find him strolling my way, as well. Actually assuming—even knowing every horrific pitfall of that verb—that the Barcelona Plan A actually worked, when every Plan A we've *ever* had hasn't worked. Okay, so maybe thinking that the Plan *B* worked and will give us the same end result...

And then having to talk myself out of all those thoughts and simply accept that I'll be dealing with Plan C.

That the distinct, beautiful baritone I hear from ground level is just my imagination making hopeful twists on Wade or Sawyer's voice.

That the whiff of orris, cinnamon, and smoke that hits me is just a strange mix of autumn flowers with some concoction Fershan has going in the lab.

That the laugh on the air, so full and throaty and strong, is a figment of my fantasies.

But then I look up.

And see a pair of legs so perfect and muscled and long, I *know* no fantasy can measure up.

And get in an entire lungful of his scent, able to pick out the cardamom and leather notes too.

And raise my head as I climb into the sun...

To take in all of my decadent, dazzling slash of lightning.

My gift from heaven. My miracle of a man. My perfect, grinning husband.

"Welcome home, Mr. Richards."

"Good to be home, my beautiful Velv—"

And suddenly, my unconscious, toppling tower.

"Heads up!" Wade calls out, flagging Sawyer over. "Daddy down! Daddy down!"

SURGE

PART 15

CHAPTER ONE

REECE

Absence makes the heart grow fonder.

Yeah, but since when does it also make a man's wife pregnant?

More crucially, when does it make *my* wife pregnant?

My wife, who has told me so many times that my superhero sterility isn't a deal-breaker for her. Who has let me be her freak-of-nature fuck buddy for over a year, allowing me to take her succulent body in every kinky way I can. Who has been a willing, receptive participant in all that crazy copulation, even during those "times of the month," which have arrived with spot-on accuracy every four weeks.

Except last month.

When she wrote off the interruption to stress...

"Oh, holy shit." The words are the first to tumble out of my newly conscious mind, a fact that hits my awareness as soon as I blink open my eyes, all but spitting up gravel and dirt from where I've passed out cold. Yeah, seriously. Yeah, in my own goddamned driveway.

In addition to the bright blue of the sky over the Northern Malibu canyon, my view consists of five familiar faces. It looks like the gang's really all here. Sawyer, Lydia, Alex, Angie...

And the most vital visage of them all.

The features that suck my breath away all over again. That lush-lipped smile. Those brilliant turquoise eyes. The skin, now glistening with bright gold sparkles, that entices me to reach out and touch, just to confirm she's real. With shaking fingers, I stroke the side of her face and down the column of her neck. Finally, I drop my hand to her sweetly rounded belly. My breath stutters out of me, thick with my astonishment and awe, when the life inside her surges toward my contact. So tiny and tentative but still there. A perfect, innocent vibration...

Blasting me with a depth of feeling I've never, ever known. What *is* this?

Connection? Devotion? Love?

No.

I've known enough authentic versions of these to at least recognize them. But this I don't comprehend. I can hardly fucking handle.

This is deeper. Broader.

More.

"Holy...*shit*." I'm doomed to say it a thousand more times today alone, but I hardly care. Every dazzling light in Emma's eyes conveys that she'll happily hear me out. Perhaps will even join me. Even so, I manage to croak out, "It...it wasn't just stress."

She bursts with a watery laugh. "I guess it wasn't."

I pull in a fierce breath. Of course, that means a throat full of all the dust I just gacked across the driveway, with a fun bonus of pebbles and bugs. Sawyer offers a hand, and I gratefully grab it.

As I sit up, he cracks, "Nice timing, Bolty Boy."

"Tell *her* that." I roll a nod Emma's way, but as soon as Angie and Lydia help her stand, new conviction sets in. This moment needs much more than a goddamned nod.

I shrug off Sawyer and stumble the two steps necessary to be glued to my woman's side—where I swear I'm going to stay until this kid decides to greet me in the more conventional sense.

Holy hell.

This kid.

Holy hell.

My kid.

I'm washed in a new downpour of inexplicable, invaluable feelings. As they flood even harder, I twist a hand into my wife's hair. I practically hoist her off the ground in my need to kiss her. To claim her. To brand her. To worship her.

And now, to whisper to her. "How?"

Another sputter of the woman's gorgeous giggles. "Errrmmm, if you need to ask *that*, mister..."

"No." I buss her firmly. "I mean, how did you find out? Or even know?"

She mellows the mirth into a soft smile. "Well, aside from the obvious"—and then leans back far enough to provide the visual aid in the form of her adorable baby bump. "It was Angie. She was the one who heard him first. Sawyer and I were sparring in the training center, and I felt a little woozy, so Angie just—*Reece*! What the hell?"

But I barely hear her. I'm already whipping around, lunging to grab Foley by the neckline of his faded "Attack on Titan" T-shirt. Appropriate, since I'm beyond tempted to go into attack fighter jet mode on his ass. "You were *sparring* with her?"

The guy flashes a glare through the dirty-blond fall of his hair. That observation, along with Emma's miffed huff, almost has me backing off. Foley really has given up a lot since Alex and I traipsed off to Spain, especially the solitude he and Lydia used to enjoy out at his Redondo Beach place a few nights each week. But since the *team* now includes my unborn baby, every one of the rules has changed. Drastically.

"Seriously?" Foley's growl ramps in proportion to my stranglehold on his shirt. "Do you really think I'd pull that kind of stupidity, knowing there was a damn good chance that Angie's intuition was right?"

As remorse creeps in, I loosen my grip. There's a lot about Sawyer Foley I'll likely never know, though the depth of the man's honor isn't one of them. Of course, I'll also never forget the two seconds he was fascinated with Emmalina in his own right before realizing that she wasn't the Crist woman destiny had in mind for him. Still, his devotion to Emma has never wavered. I have no doubt that if the compound got raided in my absence, Sawyer would have ensured that those bastards had to rip him limb from limb before getting to Emma and Lydia.

"Yeah." I half grunt it while stepping all the way back. "I do know. Sorry, man."

"You're cool, fucker." But he finishes the drawl by focusing a narrow frown just past my right shoulder. I pivot the same direction. Neeta and Angelique approach and then calmly wait. There's a familiar figure with them. He lingers close to Angie, primal protectiveness all but gushing from of his pores for our resident empath.

"Angie." I greet her with a brief hug. "Wade." I bro-clasp him and then follow up with a shoulder bump. "This fucker is glad to see you both."

Lydia slides a sardonic snort into the exchange. "Good

thing you're front-loading those F-bombs now, brother."

"Huh?"

"Juuuust wait."

Emmalina elbows her sister. "We'll talk," she tells me. "Later. For now, you were about to thank Angelique for utilizing her power when she did."

"I was?"

She arches her brows expectantly. "You *were*."

Before I can open my mouth, Angie cuts in with a humble "*Pssshh, C'est rien.*" She colors a bit, and I don't miss Wade's obvious fascination with her. "It really was nothing. The easiest and most joyous message I have ever relayed." She demonstrates the point by stepping over and folding one of Emma's hands between hers. "I hear that strong little bolt getting stronger every day, as well. Be assured of it, *mon ami.*"

"Thank you, honey." Emma's answer is resplendent with all the emotion Angie just invoked—and I can't help but be swept up in the same. Elation, excitement, amazement, awe... They're all here, and at least a thousand more. I never thought I'd compare my bloodstream to a force beyond lightning, but it's really happening now. I'm a walking comet, transcending galaxies and cosmos and universes. I'm more than power, more than light. I'm a freaking god.

No. Better than that.

I'm a father.

As that impact fully sets in, I'm physically knocked back. Dizzy with giddiness. And yeah, digging a hard grip into Foley's shoulder. He lunges over, preventing me from crumpling all the way into the dust again. "You threatening to biff on me again, asshole?"

"Give me a break, choad bucket," I grumble back. "I've

had the breath zapped out of me twice in the last twelve hours."

Alex folds his arms and chuckles. "And I'm pretty damn sure the defib paddles were a walk in the park compared to this homecoming present."

"I'm pretty damn sure you're right," I drawl.

"Yet you're here, coherent enough to recall everything." Fershan, having emerged from the lab right after Wade, inserts himself into the conversation. "Which means that the defibrillator jump worked."

Alex grins. "Better than we thought it would."

I flash a tight glower. "Says the guy who *wasn't* flat on his back in the airport security room, having a thousand volts of electricity stabbed into his chest?"

"Oh, God." Emma's husky mutter makes me instantly regret going so graphic. I yank her close and bury my lips into her hair.

"*Velvet.*" I rub my hands up and down her tense spine. "I'm sorry. I'm so sorry. I'm just slinging shit at Alex because I can."

"And because you took a thousand volts to your chest?"

"Nothing Faline and the lab didn't properly train me for," I assure. "And, as Tex Trestle here has eloquently said"—I nod toward Alex, ensuring he knows that the handlebar mustache will never be *truly* forgotten—"our kill-the-Batman fix for the USB key worked better than we imagined."

I'm about to apologize for the obnoxious slang, but her confusion is so adorable that I linger for a second, giving Alex room to puff up his chest and explain. "One hit of the defib paddles, two taps at the monitor, and three minutes of the download wheel later, we were ready to toss the original key and get the hell out of Barcelona." His cocky expression sobers by a few degrees. "Now, we just pray everything stuck to

Chrome Dome Dexter the way we hoped it would."

Emma crunches a frown full of fresh perplexity. "Chrome Dome *who*?"

"We'll talk." I wink.

She giggles and cuddles closer—and just like that, the weeks of being apart have melted away. Everything is the same between us, yet nothing is the same. Despite the extra buzz in my brain, which constantly reminds me of the dangerous Consortium information that's literally my extra mental baggage, life has gotten a brand-new start. A stunning, amazing new beginning. "We'll talk *a lot*," I affirm, tilting my head to take her lips again. It's a tender, savoring, lingering embrace, and I'm just fine with letting it go on for several more minutes... or hours, or days—whatever this breathtaking creature will bless me with.

When Foley clears his throat with pronounced intent, it's clear I'm not going to get my way.

"So what about the solar infusions?" His scrutiny is just as forceful as his inquiry, as if he can gain the answer just by looking at me. "Can you tell if the ol' hematocytes held up through the defibrillator fun?"

I straighten to blast some thought-clearing air through my own head though refuse to lick Emma's taste from my mouth. I need her there, lingering in my senses with that mix of wind and woman and magic, despite the very real urgency of addressing Foley's concern. "As best as I can tell, the ions held firm." A new scowl. "And Faline's not exactly the queen of subtlety. If she had a viable inroad to my head, I'm damn sure she'd be breaking the metaphysical speed limit to let me know."

"We conducted the download right at the hangar at El Prat for that very reason." As Alex asserts it, he peels off his leather jacket—and it escapes no one's notice that the tight fit of the T-shirt underneath has quietly registered on Neeta's radar. "We assumed the bitch was physically located within a hundred miles," he goes on. "Which was why we got Reece off that table and onto the plane as soon as the download was complete."

"And why inside the hangar and not on the plane itself?" There's no antagonism in Foley's question. He's curious more than anything, clearly expecting that Alex has a detailed answer. He's not wrong.

"The procedure had to go right the first time," Alex explains, folding his arms. As he shows off the ropes of his muscles, I pointedly study Neeta. I doubt anything about Alex will escape her sneaking glances. He continues, "We only had one shot, a first and *only* time. Power and internet issues could've been circumvented, but there were other factors involved with this."

"Like what?" Wade asks, though already seems to discern the answer. "A tracker on the key itself?"

"A damn good one," Alex confirms. "Our contact previously attempted a manual download from a secure underground bunker. Within minutes, he was traced and swarmed by Consortium goons. They damn near made him that day, but his close call turned out to be our lucky break. We already knew what was going to happen if the key's tracker was reactivated—and we didn't want that happening on a plane already in flight."

No more shrewd expectation from Wade. "They would have shot you out of the fucking sky?" he charges, eyes now wide and stunned. "*Could* they have?"

Angelique erupts with a fast chuff. "Yes and yes," she supplies.

"Damn and *damn*," Wade utters.

"Needless to say, we were all over the timing of the operation."

Alex cranks back his shoulders, finally noticing Neeta's increasing admiration. I hold in my smile, letting him have his time in the literal and figurative sun. The guy fucking deserves it. He's gotten no sleep in the last couple of days, even staying awake as I snoozed during the plane ride, insisting that the information we'd just transferred into my gray matter was only going to be viable if I *kept* my gray matter. He alludes to as much while continuing his explanation.

"As soon as we were certain the intel transfer was good, I had Bolt-a-matic's darling ass up the boarding stairs and on the charter. As far as we know, even to this second, Faline Garand isn't aware of the shenanigans at all."

"But she could be at any time." Foley casts a look around, relaying how he hates being the Debbie Downer on all this but is willing to take on the mantle for the sake of necessary truths. "The woman has already demonstrated her penchant—and talent—for teleportation fun. And if your source in Barcelona wasn't completely solid..."

"The source was solid."

I'm stunned Alex jumps on the declaration before I can, but the guy also didn't just get hit with the news he's about to become a father. "He's right," I supply as Foley swings a questioning glance my way. "The source is solid—or as solid as we're going to get, given this new trip down the rabbit hole."

"Or into the lion's mouth."

Alex's quip, referencing the cheesy gallery of wall murals that was our first and only tourist stop in Barcelona, earns my gruff chuckle. What else could we have done when Saber, the tatted underground goon, had ordered us to meet him at the Museo de las Ilusiones? Any slick super spy cred we'd earned to that point had been stripped as soon as we entered the doors of the cheesy place, but our rendezvous point at the roaring lion painting had turned into a symbolically perfect location—considering who showed up as our ultimate trail guide into the darkest heart of the Consortium. A wildcat who proved he might really have nine lives. A predator I didn't completely trust—nor do, even now—but in whom I have to rely.

We have no better choice.

The only other road leads back to square one. *Not* an option. We're racing time itself. In less than eight hours, Faline transformed Emma's own mother into a starry-eyed recruit for her demented cause. Though we've kept a close eye on Laurel and determined she hasn't been imbued with the same transformative abilities, that doesn't mean it isn't possible. That at any time, Faline could activate an insane, secret nation and call her minions into full power.

An army we're still hopelessly in the dark about.

Correction. Not *completely* the dark. We know a few fun facts—*fun* being extremely relative. One, Faline's boot camp is scarily brief. Two, the fresh recruits are turned into starry-eyed automatons that don't remember anything about their own free will, other than how it can be put into Faline's service.

So if the bitch really does call her soldiers to war...

And it *will* be a war...

We'll be marching and flying blind.

On the losing end of that fight.

Not a scenario I'm going to let my child be born into.

Which is why I sure as hell listen, with focus as fortified as Foley's, as he firms his stance and states, "Even if your source was Jesus Christ in the flesh, we can't take chances." He swings his regard back toward Wade and Fershan. "You guys ready to reroute the solar inverters?"

Fershan is the first with a ready grin. "Roger Dodger!"

Wade rolls his eyes, earning himself a charmed smirk from Angie—whom, I notice, is eyeing *him* the same way Neeta's sizing up Alex. "He means we're ready and waiting," he confirms.

"Outstanding. On my mark, then." Foley directs his attention back to me. "Double-checking the solar ionization isn't going to hurt."

"Agreed," I state, pulling in Alex with my own focus. "And neither is hooking me up and yanking all this shit out of my head."

Foley frowns. "You're really up for that too? This fast?"

A terse nod. "The faster the better." I look up, making sure Wade and Fersh are still dialed into our exchange. "You guys are going to want to scrub the files for any more tracers, right? Which will take a while?" After registering their collective nods, I continue, "So let's just get this circus back on the road." I ping one more pointed glance to Alex. "Lions wait on no one—and we've got to figure out exactly where to jab the thorns in this one's paws."

"All righty, then." Foley rolls his head and then cracks his knuckles. "You got it, Bolt-astic."

"Right *on*." Wade sweeps out a fist as emphasis.

"We are ready to hack apart your brain!"

Though everyone understands where Fersh is headed with that, the implication has everyone tensing—most noticeably, my wife. I try to ease her anxiety by teasing him back. "And it's ready for the hacking!" That earns me Emma's smack at my shoulder. Damn hard one, at that. My little fighting flare. Fuck, how I love this woman.

"You coming, hard drive?" Foley issues the invitation from the top of the driveway, near the entrance to the command center.

"You know that under normal circumstances, you'd have a lightning bolt in your ass for that, right?"

Foley reprises the snicker. "And your point is what?"

I growl through my teeth. "Just get your ass inside. I'll be there in a second."

Fortunately, he complies—meaning I finally have the freedom to pivot back toward Emma, who's wearing a bewildered pout. "Why didn't you just give him a third ass crack?" she mumbles.

"Because doing *this* is more important." I'm not done uttering it before I'm demonstrating it, landing on my knees in the dust before her and spreading my hands across the gentle swell of her middle. "Hello there, my little dude," I whisper against her stretched shirt, euphoric when she abandons her stress in favor of this perfect, private moment.

A moment I never thought we'd have.

A moment in which I fully embrace that this miracle is truly real. And once again, sway like a willow in the wind because of it.

Fortunately, I recover in time to grip Emma's hips and lower her gently into my lap. She laughs, settling her weight easily against me before framing my jaw with her fingers and holding me steady for her long, adoring kiss. I moan as our mouths connect, reveling in how she electrifies my body, fills my arms, floods my heart. *All* of my heart. Parts I never knew existed blast open, already brimming with love for her and this breathtaking new person in our family.

Our family.

I get it now. I *finally* get why that word is so important to so many. I haven't even seen my son beyond this small swell in my wife's body, and already I know, beyond a fathom of any doubt on the planet, that I will throw myself in front of any fucking obstacle for them. Will carry a damn mountain across this country for them. Will do anything it takes to keep them safe and happy and protected.

Anything. It. Takes.

And in this flash of commitment, I come to a jarring recognition.

I'll do anything, go anywhere, and sacrifice everything for the sake of my family.

As the vow permeates my spirit, the resolve sinks into all the pressure and passion of my kiss. I don't hold back a shred of the intensity, letting it push into the force of my lips, the drive of my tongue, and the deep resonance of my groans—until finally, when we drag apart, Emma proves just how swept away I've gotten. With bemused blue fires in her eyes, she rubs the tips of her fingers across the reddened surfaces of her lips.

"Hey." She traces the lines of my mouth as well. "Are you... uh...are you okay? With this?"

The hesitant rasp beneath her voice causes a frisson in my heart. "Are you fucking kidding?" I initiate a kiss that doesn't end until we're *both* moaning. "How can you even ask that?" I demand, my mouth still against hers. "Jesus, Emmalina. I'm *not* okay, to be honest."

She yanks back, brows scrunching. "Huh?"

"I'm beyond that, Velvet." I caress the back of her head with one hand and the surface of her belly with the other. "I'm so far beyond okay, I don't think I'll ever touch okay again. And I never want to." With a reverent dip, I brush my lips across her distended stomach. "As long as I have you and our little dude, I never *ever* want to."

My head snaps back up at the burst of her soft sob. While the sound *seems* happy, I need to make sure. We share a rolling, reverent kiss. As soon as we part, she wavers the corners of her gorgeous mouth. The smart little minx already seems to know what I'm looking for—but there's more than that to her expression. I patiently wait.

"You know too," she murmurs. "You *know* it's a boy, don't you?"

I blink slowly, letting the wonderment in her tone imbue my senses. "I guess I do," I admit. "I...don't know how, but I do."

"Me too." The sheen in her eyes turns into a sweet, teary wobble in her voice. Just like that, I'm welcoming a sharp sting behind my eyes. I let the wetness come, along with all the feeling that surges into me with it. The fullness. The completion. And yes, even the fear and the uncertainty—small prices to pay for the enormity of this love.

This love for my girl...

And my boy.

"It's amazing." I shake my head, because the words are fucking ridiculous. Foolish stand-ins for a fullness that will never really find its way into combinations of consonants and vowels. And do I really want it to? This instant, this connection, this woman, our love...

It's boundless.

Timeless.

Our ultimate *more*.

"Yes. It is." Emma's expression confirms her awareness

of the same truth. Even better, her soul speaks it to me. "But... we'll need to discuss plans, Reece." A soft laugh escapes her. "I've already got a few lists..."

"Of course, baby." I slide my hand out of her hair so I can cup the side of her face. "But we've got time. You're—what?— maybe six weeks in?" But as soon as I state it, I cast a quizzical look at her middle. What I've said and what I'm looking at don't seem to match, but I know jack shit about this kind of stuff. Before the Consortium got their hands on every fluid in my body, I was singlehandedly ensuring the condom industry flourished. *No love without a glove* should have been tattooed across my balls, though now it's the largest punchline in my world. Could I have been more wrong about what love really means? About what it truly *is*?

As if Emma has reached into my head and translated my strange trip down Flashback Road, her expression changes into an inscrutable little glance. She backs it up by murmuring, "Like I said, Zeus, there are a few details to go over—but let's tackle this one step at a time, okay?" As she looks up toward the lab, a readable emotion *does* take over her face. She's pensive and not afraid to hide it. "Let's be sure Faline can't find a single crack in your cranium to crawl through."

"Damn good plan."

I give her another drawn-out kiss, making sure she gets every molecule of my soul-deep gratitude. If she were married to a banker or a CEO or even a goddamned rock star, she'd only have to deal with her man coming home and unpacking dirty underwear. Instead, she's taking my hand as we walk toward the room where my team will have to extract computer files out of my head by using shock paddles and dumping solar cells into my blood as an insurance policy against Faline

Garand's radio control abilities.

Just before we get to the lab's door, I scuff to a stop and whirl her in to press against me once more. Emma lifts her head, clearly expecting a kiss, but I hold back for the privilege of taking in all the features that blow my mind, over and over again, with their lush, glowing beauty. The tapered arches of her brows. The thick fronds of her eyelashes. The high crests of her cheeks. Even the gentle jut of her chin, flowing to form the proud line of her neck. I long to smooth my fingers over every gorgeous detail I see as if it's the last time I'll see them. No matter what, that remains a very real possibility. But in so many bizarre ways, I am grateful for that too. It ensures I'll never forget to treasure every damn moment with her. It guarantees I'll always remember...even just moments need to be enough.

With my Emmalina, moments are more than enough.

Because she's more than I ever dreamed of having. Of knowing. Of loving.

Pulling in another breath, making sure I keep that gratitude safe and protected, I drop my hands until they're wrapped solidly around hers again. Then finally, I give her the kiss for which she's patiently waited. I'm slow and sensual but deep and demanding, savoring the feel of her tongue against mine with long, languorous rolls and full, sweeping slides. I don't stop until she's the texture of melted butter in my arms, her body swaying dreamily into mine. Only then do I pull away, meeting her enchanted, sultry expression with a cocky, knowing grin. But my indolence is an act; we both know that. I hate what has to happen now more than a kid having to get his wisdom teeth pulled. I'm not even going to have the Novocain hangover video to show for this.

But if fate is with us—and this time, thank fuck, the wench really does seem to be—we'll have something better.

"This will be worth it, baby." Emma vocalizes the very thought that takes precedence in my brain, sealing the surety with a kiss to the hollow of my throat.

"I know," I murmur back. "And as soon as they suck those files back down out of this big blockhead"—I tick my head forward, just to clarify which hunk of gray matter I'm referring to—"they're going to make sure I'm pumped back full of lots of nice sun rays, for good measure."

"Hmmm." She rocks her head back, flashing me with a mocking scrutiny. "I thought *I* was your sunshine."

"No, beautiful." I lean over and kiss her cheek, since we're now strolling toward the lab's entrance. "*You* are my one and only *flare*."

"Who will always be here to shine on you, Mr. Richards."

As she tucks her head against my shoulder, I lower a kiss into her hair. "For which I'm so damn grateful, Mrs. Richards." But all too quickly, I have to pull away from her to reach for the door to the lab. "And on that note, let's get this shit taken care of."

I hold the portal open for her, but on her way through, Emma discernibly pauses. Then turns, raising a hand to the spot directly over where my heart beats—where it's been beating in full since the moment that hand first touched mine, on that night that seems like a million heartbeats ago. Yet at the same time, it seems just a heartbeat ago. We've come so far since then, but she still soaks every pore in my body with arousal and awareness and life.

"We'll be right here for you, husband." Her promise is joined by a smile dunked in exhilarating life, soaring sentience, and inimitable hope. "*Both* of us."

CHAPTER TWO

EMMA

I promised him that Bean and I would be here—no matter how hard it got.

But shit, it's hard already.

You can do this. You can do this. You can do this.

The words seem to come as much from the little dude in my belly as the big girl in my brain. I greedily accept the rally cry from both—while vowing to stay supportive and strong for my husband. Well, as much as I *can* be. I'm only able to hold on to my husband by one of his bare ankles as the guys prepare him for the procedure with the efficiency of NASA technicians readying a missile for outer space. While I know they don't mean to treat Reece like a cylinder of screws and steel, I wonder if the all-business miens are their version of emotional self-defense: their own steel shells riveted in place so there's not the slightest danger of them screwing up their technical duties.

Because they're messing with something a lot more precious than a rocket ship. Or even my husband's bloodstream.

His *mind* is going to be in their hands.

As if I even need to be reminded of that fact, they give it over in glaring detail—by strapping him down by both wrists and looping a restraining belt around his waist. At last, as

Fershan fires up the lab's defibrillator unit. At the same time, Alex switches on the laptop. Wade stands directly over my husband's head, holding the silicone "connector" that will be jabbed into Reece's ear. With all the machinery revved up and in place, Wade secures his hands over Reece: one gripping his forehead, the other across his chin.

"Unnhhh." It's a visceral reaction, glugging out before I can help it. I clutch my husband's ankle tighter, wishing I didn't pick now to realize I've never told him about my fixation with his sexy-as-hell leg hairs. It's always just seemed so silly—only now, in this purposefully helpless state he's surrendered himself to be in, I feel like he needs to know. *I love you, Reece Richards—down to your beautiful, all-man leg hairs.* But out loud, I say the next thing on my mind. "Guys. *Sheez.* Is it really necessary to lock him down like a tranquilized animal or someth—"

"Yes." The group consensus, given in resounding unity, even includes my husband's voice.

Reece adds, "Now's your chance to call me a stubborn ox and really mean it, baby."

"Or just a hard-headed fucker."

Sawyer's line, along with his presence, can't be more perfectly timed. He adds an encouraging smirk while standing next to me, clamping a reassuring grip around Reece's other ankle—until my husband jerks his head up and impales the guy with a silver glower.

"Hey!"

"What?" Sawyer's scowl is just as intense.

"Clean up the language around my kid," Reece barks back. "Or there'll be a permanent dent in your crotch the size of my ankle."

A spurt of laughter bursts from my sister, waiting along the wall next to Angelique and Neeta. They've come to support their guys as much as me, but I take this moment to lavish my husband's ankle—and its insanely arousing hairs—with strokes of wifely approval.

Letting him know I'm here.

Letting him know I'm not leaving him.

Letting him know that the electric invasion and the slam of pain and the journey to hell will be worth it. That though his mind and body are going to be controlled and corralled by others again, this whole team is worth it. That this cause has been worth everyone's sacrifices.

That once the guys get the information on those files decoded, we're going to see inside the Consortium as we never have before.

We're going to finally have the upper hand in this damn war.

And our child will know a world where superheroes only champion peace.

I pray for this with every cell in my body and force in my soul.

I believe it.

I have to.

I have no other choice.

⚡

Hours later, sometime in the night when the loudest sounds on the ridge are the dancing crickets and the canyon winds, the man's all about stripping me of choices once again.

Only this time, the abdication promises to be a tad more fun.

About seven and half inches worth of "a tad."

Reece curls behind me, rustling the sheets and pillows of our bed, turning even those silken *shoosh*es into erotic foreplay with his steady, seductive movements. Not that my libido needs any more encouragement in that department. He had me at the *hello* of his swollen, persistent length, every inch pressing along the crevice between my ass cheeks.

I'm barely done processing the shudders from that incessant caress against my backside, as well as the tingles it sends through every nerve ending between my pussy and my toes, when the breathtaking bastard goes for some new moves. With the hand he's curled beneath me, he palms and then kneads through my sleep shirt—really *his* old Imagine Dragons concert shirt—making my nipples jab hard at the thin cotton barrier between my skin and his.

A high sigh tumbles from my lips.

A low growl rumbles from his.

With an even deeper sound of pleasure, he drags his other hand up my leg, his fingernails scraping along my knee and thigh. He doesn't stop until traveling his touch past the band of my undies, making enticing circles along my quivering and clenching skin...taking a slow and enticing route for one specific destination...

"Velvet?" His rasp is barely audible, even though he issues it along the bottom curve of my ear.

"Hmmmm." I barely restrain myself from moaning out all of it. "Uhhh...yeah?"

"You awake?"

I let out a soft giggle. "Guess I am now. *Ohhhh!*" I buck my hips as he swipes his long, graceful fingers between the quivering folds at my apex. The layers that are already slick and plumped...wet and pulsing...

"Holy God. I can almost taste you on the air, little Bunny." He works two digits through my lust-drenched center, parting me so he can use a third finger to thrust inside me. "You're dripping already..."

"Mmmmm." With a mewl, I rock wantonly against him. I almost forget that I don't have the same girlish figure he made love to in that lifeguard shack on the Redondo sand. *Almost.* "How can I not be?" I roll my hips, purposely working my sex up and down the decadent rods of his fingers. "That feels...so good. *You* feel...so damn good."

"Not as good as you." He's left the whisper behind, growling with lusty purpose right into the center of my ear. "Not *nearly* as good as you, my sweet Velvet. Fuck. *Fuck*, how I've missed you."

I resort to a growl myself—though my intent is different than his. "*Language*, Mr. Richards!"

He chuckles from low in his throat before biting my earlobe. "I have special amnesty, Mrs. Richards."

"Excuse the hell out of me?" I retort. "From who?" Though I already have a damn good idea what he's going to say.

"The emperor himself." He lowers the hand on my breast to sprawl across my stomach, pushing up the shirt to rub me affectionately. "We have an understanding already, you see."

"An understanding?" I half laugh it. "Is that so?"

"Very so." While continuing his caresses across my belly button, he intensifies his strokes deep in my pussy, clearly pursuing his master plan of turning me into a preggo version of worm-on-a-string. Can I be blamed? He's slowly taking me over, from the inside of my clenching womb to the outer lips of my pouting, pulsing sex. *He's* my damn string. My magical, sensual miracle. "We had a talk," he goes on in a knowing murmur. "And he understands now that when Daddy hasn't gotten to hold or kiss Mommy for two weeks, words come out of Pop's mouth that simply can't be controlled."

I'm breathing hard. My eyes slide shut as I drown in all the lush cadences of his dark, intoxicating voice. "Th-That so?" I manage to blurt.

"Oh, that's *very* so." He slides his lips up and down my neck, sending shimmers of hypnotizing lust along my shuddering, dazzled form. When I pull my eyes open again, the room is spinning around us: the walls are a kaleidoscope of electric blue and dynamite gold mixed with flashes of white light I don't understand, nor want to. I only know it has to be the most beautiful thing I've ever seen...the most stunning, surreal experience of my life.

I'm so swept away, I can't even be bothered by self-consciousness over my changed body. Right now, I'm just the golden ball at the center of this regal vortex of light, a goddess emboldened enough to say, "So...what else might come out of Daddy that can't be controlled?"

Reece's reaction is even better than what I've planned for. After his initial choke of sensual shock, he slides his hand away from my pussy—in order to twist a fierce hold on the fabric of my panties and shove them down my legs. Once they're past my knees, he seizes them in a determined toehold, *thwicking* them past the tips of my toes. While his insanely talented foot is busy, so are his lascivious hands. After shoving up the shirt to my neck, he yanks it all the way off.

And I'm free.

Naked for him.

Bared for him.

Trembling and torrid and hot and eager for him.

And now, sizzling and flaring for him—as he drops his mouth into the curve between my shoulder and neck, and bites me with blatant, bold intent...with primal, brutal possession.

"You really want to know what I can't control around you, Mrs. Richards?"

His snarl is the electrified magma I've missed so much—but in so many ways, there's a new force inside me. It's not just my senses that recognize him now. I feel his heat in the center of my spirit, through every strand of my soul—and acknowledge it in every syllable from my parted, gasping lips. "Tell me," I beg, emphasizing with wanton slides of my ass and thighs—now slickened by the liquid that's seeped through the crotch of his track pants. "No." I reach back and grab at his waistband, which frees his hot, full erection. "*Show* me."

"Oh, fuck."

I'm beyond even attempting a joke about the profanity now as the man digs his hand so hard into my hip, his fingers are like claws. His breaths, erupting in vicious huffs along my shoulder, flow like scalding Santa Ana winds across my torso, making my nipples stiffen and strain.

"That may be happening sooner rather than later, beautiful. *Damn!*" His snarl bursts as his cockhead naturally aligns itself between my throbbing lips, nudging inside the tunnel that's been empty of his force for too damn long. The juncture of our bodies turns into some kind of glowing canyon from an intergalactic war movie—except that the only sensation I'm sure of, as he enters me in one steady, sure slide, is complete and consuming peace.

Even as he swells inside me, stretching me everywhere...

Peace.

Even as all his electrons blend with my cream, rocking me with an orgasm that causes the room to spin again...

Peace.

Even as he starts the primitive pounding that keeps time to the boundless rhythm of our mutual heartbeats...

Peace.

Connecting us.

Completing us.

Binding us with more light and love than has ever tied us together before...

And more desire.

And more need.

And more heat and hunger and...

"Ahhhh!" I toss my head back, slamming it against his chest, as my body convulses in another wave of fire, flight, and fulfillment. My buttocks squeeze in, my thighs tremble, my clit blazes, and my senses detonate. "Oh, holy *shit*! Are you doing this to me again already, Zeus? *Shiiiiit*..."

"Uh, uh, uh." The damnable owner of that miracle penis is actually sing-songing the words into my neck—without missing a single slide of the scissoring strokes he's using to unwrap my senses, ribbon by exquisite ribbon. "Language, Mrs. Richards."

"Fuck you!" I cry. "No. Just keep fucking *me*!"

"With serious fucking pleasure." No more sing-song. He's growling against my skin, locking me to him by sliding his hand from my hip to the plane between my breasts. As he presses into that valley, my nipples stretch and tauten to painful points of arousal. I welcome the tiny bites into my senses, needing them for my sanity. I swear to God, if this man gives me too much more pleasure, I might become a rocket in my own right. If the swirling lights around the room are any indication, I'm probably already beaming brightly enough for the task. If this is what all the manuals mean by the glow of pregnancy, no wonder everyone calls it the best experience ever.

"Ohhhh, my freaking *God*. Th-That's good. Like that. Now d-d-deeper. *Harder*, Reece. Take me harder with that wand of *fucking* heaven between your legs!"

"Christ."

He punches out a gruff sound, a combination of laughter and something else—amazement?—while meeting my demand with carnal, scream-worthy perfection. Dear *God*. Every one of his coordinated hip rolls, ensuring I feel every angle of every thrust, is a direct gift from the universe. Every slide of his sweaty body along mine, forming us into one creature instead of two, is a reminder of why I was put here into this crazy existence. To be his. To make him mine. To remind every molecule in the cosmos of what passion really is...of what love can truly be. Of the light it can truly wield, if it's given permission to be free and wild and embraced and trusted.

"Holy hell, Mrs. Richards." His voice resonates with a third factor now. Pure wonder. "You are one wicked woman, Emmalina Richards."

"Damn straight, Reece Richards." I reach back and twist one hand into his damp, thick hair. "And you love me that way."

"I worship you that way." He glides his hand back down, curving his long, amazing fingers across the small hill of my belly. "I worship you *this* way." Unbelievably, as he sweeps his powerful touch across that stretched expanse, his cock discernibly expands against my inner walls. "Holy *fuck*. You have no damn idea how glorious you really are right now, do you? How I want your golden, ripe body to just keep suckling on my dick? How I want to stay inside you forever, giving you more of my white-hot seed? How much I want to give you load after load of my come as your tight sugar walls flutter around me?"

Oh, holy shit. There's no better soundtrack on earth than this man and his finest slut-guy talk. He's pouring it on thick and hard because he knows how much I revel in it like a kitten in the sun—but in this moment, the gutter gab is rendering a totally different result. I can no more stop it than I can deny it. Knowing I still turn him on like this, though it feels like I'm becoming huger by the hour, guts me to profound and wrenching depths. The tears that flow out are filled with too many emotions to identify. I simply let them come, a confession and a concession and an ultimate exposure, offering them openly from my soul to his.

As they do, I wrap my hands atop his and grip him like he's my life raft—because he is. I cry for him like he's my confessor—because he is. And I climax like he's the comet that's torn open my star—because he is.

As he goes still inside me, his cock bursting with its perfect heat while he surrenders to a long, low groan, I bear down tighter. I compel my walls to hold him as tight and close inside as I possibly can. I cushion him like the most perfect hunk hero husband on the face of this spinning ball called our planet...

Because he is.

So many minutes later—or is it hours, and do I even care?—Reece finally stirs a little behind me. "Mmmmph!" I snort in protest, tugging his arm to keep him wrapped tight and clenching everything down below to try to keep him embedded right where he is there, as well.

"Greedy wench," he accuses, nuzzling my nape before trailing a string of kisses over to the sensitive column beneath my ear.

"Yeah, yeah," I volley. "And you love me that way."

"And I *worship* you that way."

The exchange makes me hope we're already ramping up for more—God knows, my Reece-starved body could use another dunk in his desire—but the second he caresses my belly and palms one of my breasts again, he suddenly stops.

"Okay, so how long *did* you let me sleep after the download was done?" he prompts. "Because I don't know a lot of shit about how the baby-growing stuff is supposed to happen, but I *do* know these fine, *fine* tits—and they were different when I got home last night. Or...*was* it..."

"You've only been asleep for about seven hours, my love."

As soon as he finishes with his puzzled grunt—expected—and clutching his grip on my mound a little tighter—also expected—I calmly go on.

"Remember when I said we'd be talking?"

"Hrrrmmm. Vaguely." He lazily thumbs my nipple, working it into a stiff, aching bud. "Guess I just thought the 'talking' part would come once it was time to get up and make coffee."

"What? You wanted to make *other* things right now?"

"Like whoopie?" He joins his deep chortle to my giggle, circling his hips to emphasize that the dorky slang comes with serious intent. "Or...nookie?"

I laugh so hard, it takes stuffing my face into a pillow to muffle the burst. "Sorry," I offer from the muffled depths of the cushion, "but you did this to yourself, mister. *Nookie?*"

"What?"

He's adorable in his earnestness, which still defines the rugged beauty of his features as I maneuver around to face him. "I'm not sure whether to kiss you senseless or order you downstairs to fetch me some Oreos."

His brows do Spiderman-worthy leaps. "We have *Oreos* in the house?" Then crouch just as impressively. "Does Anya know?"

His reference to our part-time chef, who milks her own goats and knows a hundred soybean recipes by heart, actually gets my indulgent smile in response. At times, Anya's enjoyed her gig for LA's Superhero Stud a little too much, but she has mellowed on the Reece crush since meeting a sexy yoga teacher at Burning Man. Thank God. "She certainly does, but she knows better than to say anything to the feisty pregnant girl," I supply.

One corner of his mouth quirks up, and I get the feeling he's about to jab a fist into the air in approval. Instead, he kicks back the covers and tugs up his track pants. "In that case, Bolt-alicious Mama, I'll be right back."

As soon as he's dashed out the door and is padding downstairs to the kitchen, I chuckle—though finish with a resigned sigh. It's best I get up, as well. It really is better that we talk sooner than later, and doing it over Oreos will make the conversation feel normal. Whatever "normal" even means at this point.

Five minutes later, my husband stands at the door of the upstairs office, where I've wandered. He is such a fantasy vision, I almost wonder if I'm still back in bed, having fallen into a dream. If that's the case, nobody better wake me up. The man is shirtless, burnished, and bearing a tray with three loaded bowls: Oreos, strawberries, and whipped cream. Along with the food are two champagne flutes filled with milk.

I can't think of a better celebratory snack.

And oh yeah, the food looks awesome too.

He looks tasty enough to lick, even though his face falls into a confused frown. At once, I know why. The office isn't so much an office anymore. The desk is already gone, having been moved by Sawyer and Alex yesterday, and half the contents of the filing cabinets have been emptied, thanks to Angie and Lydia. Along the wall, we've separated things into two boxes, labeled *Storage* or *Shredding*. The framed Ansel Adams prints have been carefully removed from the walls and wait next to their padded storage boxes against the far wall.

As Reece slides the tray onto the glass-topped coffee table, he mutters, "What's this all about?"

"The team is moving forward with the nursery," I fill in. After throwing him a gaze that confirms his god status for bringing the food, I gesture around the room with a strawberry. "I had to make an executive decision, circumstances being what they are, and figured you'd agree this was the best place for Bean's nursery."

"Bean?" he echoes while unscrewing two sides of an Oreo. "That's oddly cool."

"Well, it's not going to be permanent"—I toss over a don't-even-think-about-it look—"but it fits. It was because he reminded me of a couple of mushed lima beans...when I first saw these."

And *there's* the appropriate word for the hour. *Mushed* scratches the tip of the iceberg when it comes to the emotion in my voice as I produce the small ultrasound pictures I've brought from the bedroom with me. I knew I wouldn't be able to hold them back any longer, and I'm glad I didn't. I brazenly gawk at every nuance that crosses my husband's rugged face as he beholds our son for the very first time.

Beautiful.

He's *beautiful*.

But the word barely serves the precious perfection of the moment as Reece continues staring.

And then gulps. And then harder.

And finally husks, "Holy...shit."

I borrow his move, gulping to battle the sting that pummels the front of my skull. I refuse to turn into a blubbering mess when this moment is right in front of me for the savoring, the cherishing. I don't even try to grab for my phone, either. A camera lens won't be able to capture this instant. This is a treasure solely for the picture albums of our hearts.

"Gorgeous, ain't he?"

He pushes out a brief laugh in reaction to my light quip but sobers quickly while shaking his head in obvious awe. "No. He's beyond that." He strokes the picture with one thumb as his mouth quavers. His eyes take on the texture of liquid lightning. "He's just...our perfect Bean."

I tuck into his side, rubbing my cheek along his bicep. "He's going to be amazing."

"He already *is* amazing." He gathers me close, inhaling and then exhaling in shaky spurts.

"A little more than you think."

I'm grateful for the subtle sarcasm I'm able to weave into the air again, gaining me traction on wrestling down my emotions. Reece, picking up on the change right away, tugs back far enough to fully view my face. His gaze is steady, his features firm. Good. I'm going to need all the help I can get for the next part of this little "chat."

"Which was why you made the 'executive decision' not to tell me about him until I got home?"

Then again, maybe I don't need the help.

I jerk back by several more inches. Examine him more thoroughly, from the tousled mess of his hair down to where his sculpted torso disappears into his black pants. He's tried his best to wean the accusation out of his tone but isn't so victorious with the stiffness in his stature. But I expected this, so I'm ready with a countermand. "The decision was a little selfish," I concede. "But it was also strategic."

He accepts my assertion—at least the start of it—with a small jog of his chin. Though he doesn't *help* my concentration by prompting with his finest authoritative growl, "I'm listening."

A huge part of me, guided by my newly clenching crotch, just wants to slide to the floor at his feet and let him hand-feed me strawberries for the next hour. But right now, it's time to slide on my imaginary big-girl panties and address the subject at hand.

The *vital* subject.

"Well, you'll be doing that for quite a long while if you're expecting an apology," I assert. "Because I'd do it the exact same way again. No, wait. I'd give away my right leg for the chance to watch you turn into man mush like that."

Though he gives into a small chuckle, his gaze maintains its solemnity. Clearly, he understands now—I wasn't going to give up the chance to watch his wonder and tears, even if it meant a longer wait—but he also knows there's more to what I have to say. Yeah, even if he does go ahead and joke, "I like your right leg exactly where it is, thank you very much."

"Damn good to hear," I quip as he pulls the coveted body part across his lap. As he starts massaging my extended thigh, I add, "But I would have also given up the left one if it meant you'd get to come home *before* agreeing to become a walking hard drive for the Consortium's most important documents."

He stops the caresses. Wraps his hold tighter, imprinting his fingertips into my skin. "At the moment, we're not talking about what *I* did out of necessity."

I pull in a long breath. My shoulders drop as I expel it on a resigned sigh. "Yeah, you're right."

"I usually am, Bunny."

I wiggle my leg, attempting to justify the nickname by giving his stomach a jackrabbit kick. He easily stills me by tightening his grip. The sight of his long fingers splayed against my limb in such blatant power makes me quiver in all the wrong places again. Oh, *God*. The horny pregnancy hormones are setting in with a vengeance.

Refocus. You don't have a choice. He needs to hear this. "So I haven't shared the biggest reason why I held back telling you about the baby."

His shoulders become granite tension again—though he's the freaking epitome of reassuring husband as he sweeps his stare up to capture mine. In the same gallant moment, he wraps his free hand around one of mine, enforcing his assurance with the gentle caress of his thumb over my knuckles. "All right, then. What is it?"

Oh, holy hell. He really does look so earnest, reminding me of Darcy just before Elizabeth takes him down by a peg or ten—the Colin Firth version, because what other version is there?—which makes me swoon and cringe at once, because now I have to be Elizabeth. "Well...okay." I reclaim my leg, as if that's going to help anything. "Mr. Richards—"

"Oh." He hikes up his posture, damn near tugging on an imaginary waistcoat. "It's *Mr. Richards* now?"

I want to giggle. Badly. But I school my features and utter,

"*Reece.* I really need you to be serious."

He dips over and kisses the center of my palm. "Done. I promise, beautiful mama."

I take a second to order my pulse rate into submission. "We've...created an extraordinary child."

"Errrmmm, *hello*?" He nods toward the ultrasound pictures piled near the goodie platter. At once, he turns back into a dreamy-eyed Daddy-to-be. "I mean, *shit*. Really, would you *look* at him?"

"I've all but memorized the image."

My murmur is husky and utterly heartfelt, especially now. I pull his fingers to my mouth and layer fervent kisses across his powerful knuckles. The man even has the hands of a superhero—hands that have wrought such destruction on so many but have brought my senses and my body such pleasure. Hands that can wield a thousand shards of light but then a million molecules of sensual fire. Hands wielding the flames that have brought me here, falling in love all over again with the father of my child. The father he never thought he'd be...

From the depths of that fervent and perfect love, I finally finish, "Just like I've all but memorized *this* one."

And with that, I finally get to bring out the ultrasound that Neeta took less than twelve hours ago.

The picture so different from its predecessor.

Different...to the point of disconcerting.

"Holy blossoming baby, Batman." My husband's stunned sough brings an odd sense of validation to my rioting senses. His shock is a thickening presence on the air as he lines up the second shot of Bean with the first. "And they say infants change from month to month during their first *year*? How about their first trimester?"

I greedily take one more second to enjoy him like this, quietly contemplating the snaps of his little boy, before angling closer to him again. I rest my hands on the ball of his knee, memorizing *this* moment too. The abject joy across his face. The committed focus in his body. But at the same time, the tender adoration underlying both. My fierce god king has finally been subdued—by a couple of fuzzy pictures of the magical creature inside my belly.

Magical, indeed.

"Reece."

"Hmmm?"

"Those pictures were only taken a day apart."

At once, his head snaps up. He searches me with a gaze that, if turned into silver Silly String, would look like a glowing spider web. "Excuse the hell out of me?"

"You're excused," I riposte, feeling strangely lighter already. "But that's not going to change these facts."

He whips his stare back and forth. "Which are exactly *what*?"

I buss the back of his hand again, sensing he needs the extra enforcement. I hate the fact that his reaction keeps bringing me such deep relief, but it's damn nice to be the only one not freaking out from these crazy circumstances. No. It's better than nice. I'm actually the *strong* one here! I've lost track of that knowledge in the midst of all my training, with its tests designed to expose my weaknesses in order to toughen them. It's kind of nice to remember, if only for these few minutes, that I *do* have the emotional stamina to carry shit now too—in addition to the physical treasure I'm hefting.

"Well, number one, our child wasn't conceived in normal circumstances," I profess.

Reece chuffs. "No shit."

I crack half a smirk. "Withhold your applause until the end, sparky." I pause, giving him plenty of opportunity to prepare himself for the whopper. "So now that we're clear about all *that*..." I hold his gaze with my eyes but surround my belly with my hands. "This kid's conception is definitely affecting how he wants to dictate this pregnancy. In short, at the speed of light."

Fortunately—oh, thank God—I've done my duty well. Reece doesn't look as nonplussed at this as he did when I presented Bean's close-ups. "All right. So what's our time frame?"

I lean back, certain I feel yet another new flutter inside my expanding belly. "As much as we can figure"—and that's actually a *lot*, considering Lydia's gone out and purchased every pregnancy development book that's ever been published— "Bolt Junior is cutting his development time in half." I guide Reece's hand across the stretched expanse, as well. If anyone else is going to detect the flutters, it's definitely going to be him. It also feels damn nice to have his touch this intimate and warm, helping me to say for the very first time, "You might just be a daddy by Christmas, Mr. Richards."

I've run this moment through my mind at least a hundred times—and on every occasion, I've come up with a different way that Reece could react. It's a daunting thing for a *normal* guy to be told he'll be a father, and most are damn glad for nine months of prep time. But to be told that one's superhero son is coming in a few months at best? I'm prepared for the man to pass out again. At the very least, to shovel in the whole plate of Oreos at once.

What I *do* get is beyond the best scenes in my imagination.

A smile that reminds me of bold, blazing sun. A hand that he spreads across my middle, lighting up the surface like star fire. But most of all, a star full of such penetrating silver light, I harbor absolutely no doubts about the reality of its intention.

Its gratitude.

Its wonder.

Its elation.

But the man seems to think I need further convincing—evidenced by the determined dip of his head and the fervent clutch of his mouth. He takes my lips with fiery need and adamant desire, until we're both ripping backward just to get half a decent breath of air. I've never felt more revered before. Or cherished. Or deeply, fervently loved.

With all those conclusions still battling for control of my sanity, it's a wonder I get any words out, but I do. Just a few. No more sarcasm in them. Now, only gratitude of my own. "I...I guess you're happy?"

"*Velvet*." Though his tone chastises, his stare all but adores. "*Happy* was me when all you did was wake up."

Twelve hours ago, the man was passed out in the dirt next to our front driveway. Now I wonder if *he'll* be the one calling out for help as he tempts me to reciprocate the favor by swooning into unconsciousness. But I'm damn certain I'll wake up with a smile threatening to take my ears out. I'm lightheaded from joy, replete with happiness, and consumed with thankfulness for this man. My hero. My incredible, sexy-as-hell baby daddy...

And just like that, I'm ready to jump the man again.

And with exactly that intent, I wrap his arm all the way around my body, giving me the space to crawl into his lap...

As a clap of thunder seems to shake the whole house.

"Fuck me," Reece mutters.

"Holy crap," I cry out at the same time...

Before realizing it's not thunder at all.

It's Sawyer freaking Foley. Who, for being a guy who secretly just wants to hang at the ocean and down beers all day, loves to make entrances like he's an entire troop of marauding marines.

"Foley." Reece's bark echoes my perplexity. I follow him out of the office onto the landing overlooking the living room. "You here to collect the dead, asshole? Because I swear to God, you've just woken them all up."

"Sure, whatever." Sawyer plants hands on his hips while flinging back a glare that more than holds up to Reece's scrutiny. "They can come too, if they want."

At once, a wave of tension cascades off my husband. Every inch of his body goes stiff with the same alert dread. "Foley?" he demands. "What the fuck is it?"

Our friend punches a hand through his shoulder-length waves. Completes one wide circle at a noticeable pace. And then makes my blood run cold as he orders, "You probably just need to see this, Reece. Right away."

CHAPTER THREE

REECE

When a guy like Sawyer Foley says there's something I need to see in the command center at once, chances are it's not the latest Rams cheerleaders' rehearsal reel or the hot new piglets-and-puppies Vines compilation.

Fuck.

My gut is an acid lagoon as I follow the guy across the driveway and then into the room filled with more technology than Hank Pym's quantum control room. But surprise, surprise, all the guys look even worse. It's clear that while I was on my ass in bed, *they* were chugging Red Bull and chomping on beef sticks to make *this* happen.

Only I'm still clueless about what *this* really is.

"What the hell am I looking at?" I demand, peering at the three larger monitors bracketed to the shelf above a bank of a dozen smaller screens. What I see on many of the junior monitors is heartening—or as heartening as it can be, considering the images represent the top-secret global kidnapping ring financed by a worldwide crime cartel along with the raided bank accounts of their wealthier victims.

Like I'd been.

I try not to linger too long on those pages, with their endless euro signs and numbers, or on the color-coded maps next to them, comprised of colored hexagons that are keyed by words that make so much sense. *Too* much sense.

Alpha Holding Rooms

Omega Holding Rooms

Labs: Electro-Circulatory

Labs: Electro-Cranial

There are spreadsheets containing names, dates, statistics, and notes that make my head spin and my stomach lurch. So many lives, dwindled to nothing but data in rows and columns. But I use the skill those bastards taught me best and compartmentalize until all I see are the giant images on the large monitors. I can tell they're aerial satellite shots, just like the ones someone would get by clicking Earth View in their favorite maps app, but for the life of me, I don't comprehend exactly what *part* of the globe I'm studying. There's something familiar about the rugged coastline shots, but I don't know if that's a good thing or a bad thing at this point.

I only know that for being a shit ton of intel, none of this is exactly what we're looking for. Not by a long shot.

"Were these all on the encrypted stuff I carried back over?" I charge. "Because none of this terrain is remotely similar to where I was kidnapped." My memory might be off a little from that night, but not by much. Granted, I'd had a lot to drink— but I'd also snorted a lot of coke, balancing out the booze, and had remained fairly alert during that fated drive. The area in which we'd ended up was remote but not the damn Pyrenees. There had been pavement. Street lights. Warehouses. Maybe someplace up or down the coast. A shipping district, perhaps.

But I've shared all of that and more with the guys already.

They know this.

So why am I looking at aerial images of sweeping foothills and sprawling canyons?

Unless this is the area in Spain where the fuckers are thinking of permanently moving the Source?

But even if we know that for certain, we can't just wait for the move to happen. That would require lying low again, basically sitting on our hands waiting for the Consortium to make their move. It's a Pause button we don't have time for, considering Faline's given us the message, loud and clear, that she won't stop at any boundary, including our own families, to harvest souls for her mob of mindless idolaters. At this point, we're flying blind about even that and what she hopes to achieve. Why the brainwashed army? And why now? What's her plan? My gut has no damn answer except haunting flashes from my confrontation with Dad in Barcelona.

In the end, death is going to be better for all of us...than what those moon pickles have planned...

They're whack jobs on a mission...to wipe out humanity...

I was a mixed-up asshole...who really bought into their illusion of a master race...

Chilling pieces of a bomb—but still no cohesive detonator for the damn thing.

What is going to be that bitch's trigger? And just as importantly: *where* and *when* will it be?

Without those answers, even the information we've got here might be too little, too late. Information both Dad and I have risked so much to get...

But this is no time for wallowing. I shore up my demeanor as Foley moves next to me, though I don't miss the bug of his eyes at the bulge of Emmalina's middle. Quickly, I replace my moroseness with a full-on gloat. *Yeah, man. I did that shit. Just call me Super Sperm from now on.*

While it's tempting to go there, I refocus all my attention to the monitors up top. Foley follows suit.

"As you can see, we've been busy," he starts in. "Except Alex, who got ordered to quarters for R and R. Dude looked like burnt toast with chunky butter in his cracks."

"Smart call." And that's that for craving toast anytime soon.

I tap a nod back toward the mystery satellite shots. They're clearly what Foley came and got me for, since they're blasted across all three of the large screens, but the guy's dancing around actually answering me about them. "So what fucking gives?" I charge again. "I'm still looking at terrain that makes no sense to me, and you're playing as coy as Taylor Swift with the details."

In the moment I take to let the accusation set in, Emma squirms a little next to me. Then again. I look down, concerned she's copied my barefoot state and is now battling the biting chill of the early morning. Negative. Unlike me, the woman was smart about slamming into a pair of pink Ugg-style boots. The footwear has floppy bunny ears sewn onto the sides, making it official: she's sexy as fuck *and* cute as hell.

Even if she's also clearly unnerved joining us in perusing the images across the monitors as well.

"Oh, holy shit."

Astonishment drenches her murmur so thoroughly, I tug her closer and demand, "What?" I examine the harsh concentration etched on her gorgeous profile and grind my brows down before reiterating, "What do you see, baby?"

She wets her lips. "Better question is what I *don't* see."

Unconsciously chews the inside of her lip. "And that answer is, nothing that's unfamiliar."

It takes a couple of seconds for her statement to soak all the way in. Or maybe not. "What?" I prod again. "I don't get—"

"I know this," she breaks in. "I think I know...*all* of this."

"The terrain of the Castillian Coast?" I rebut.

"No."

"No?"

She steps away, moving closer to the monitors. Takes a second to give encouraging shoulder squeezes to Wade and Fersh, who have barely glanced up from their decoding duties even after we walked in. Then pushes up into the unoccupied work bay between them so she can get closer to peering at the terrain on the screens. "That triangular jut into the ocean there,.." She points to the spot she's referencing. "That's Point Dume. North of it, this stretch here, is El Matador Beach. And this little bump... That's Sequit Point, where Mulholland meets PCH at Leo Carrillo State Beach. Back over here...all this green...is Pepperdine. And here's the market where Anya works, next to the yoga studio where her new stud is employed."

Despite the somber angles beneath his amber stubble, Foley snarks, "Somebody had to get *that* part in."

And me? I'm just damn glad there's two empty recliners along the back wall—necessities for the guys on weekends with huge game releases and side-by-side play is a must—allowing for me to park my stunned ass on a cushion instead of the floor. I shoot an openly dazed gaze around the room, really wondering how twenty feet of a rock mountain just opened up to let a lightning storm in here. Yeah, the one that's just jolted every inch of me.

Holy freaking fuck.

The words bounce off each other in the back of my head as I wrestle my front lobe around the ability to form words again. "That's...the *Southern California* coast?"

Foley rocks back, shoving air out through his nose. "Seems to be the case."

I really yearn to argue the point, but he's not the one drawing the conclusion here. It's my wife, the Southern California native. The woman who knows this coastline so well, she's taken me to a bunch of its locals-only dive bars and hidden-secret burger joints. Who knows the nicknames for all the coves and the best beach access points like the back of her hand. Who now stands there between her friends, staring at the satellite images with as much stiffness in her spine as the guy who carried out the damn Thunder Cats entrance on our upstairs office—*nursery*—a few minutes ago.

Now, Foley's behavior has a much clearer explanation. A much more troubling motivation.

Troubling?

Who the hell am I kidding?

Troubling is for shit like flat tires on the way to the airport or employees making out on the job.

This is full-blown terrifying.

But the truth, nonetheless.

A reality that needs to be verbalized. By me. Right now.

"So...I let Trestle hit me with those paddles, *twice*, to carry back maps of our own fucking backyard."

Foley tilts his head back, letting the long blond layers fall backward out of his face—and while he's at it, likely seeking a little guidance from the big guy upstairs or whatever higher power he communes with on a regular basis. He must have somebody looking out for him in that regard. Nobody maintains that kind of Dalai Lama vibe when hit with this level of a Joker-style twist, especially after staying up all night after days of dealing with their boss's newly pregnant wife. He's got a giant dose of metaphysical help, for sure.

My helping isn't as large.

Admittedly, that's due to a self-inflicted distance—God wasn't my favorite guy even before my time at the Source—but a good chunk of my soul is calling out to the big man now, an inner combination of desperation, exasperation, and rampage, as I jolt to my feet in a furious rush. Then, because it's there and I can, I send out a pulse to raise the other easy chair to waist height and give it a not-so-easy death against the cinderblock wall.

In the silence that follows, all I seem to hear are my own breaths. Shallow. Shaking. Protesting the confines of my chest as my mind counterattacks a vision of my ass on a platter—which is about what's just been handed to me.

By my own father.

"Mother. *Fucker*." The syllables burn my throat worse than a surge of bile.

The nausea worsens when I widen my thinking about this fuckery.

What if Dad fed us this file...on purpose? Knowing all the while what was really on it? What if his rage, his remorse, and his bid for redemption were just devices to keep me in the room without killing him first? What if the meeting in Barcelona, and the whole story about needing to shock the files into me, was just a way to get something *else* into me too? Some other form of tracking device? Some ability to spy on us in *another* way?

What if my father faked his death...

Because of Faline Garand, not *in spite* of her?

"So." Foley wheels around, hair dropping into shaggy waves around his face again. His face, emblazoned with an obvious and open scrutiny—as he tucks his arms in, conveying the exact opposite message. "About this 'solid' resource of yours..."

So much for wanting to squabble with him anymore. I full-on yearn to deck the wiseass, but there's the not-so-tiny issue of admitting he's right. And that every inch of my fuming face probably already betrays that—before I spin around, patting myself to locate whatever secret stash I've found for my Spanish burner phone this time. I should have ditched the damn thing before we even took off out of El Prat, but a tiny schism of instinct had warned me not to. Had known, despite the crazy risks Lawson Richards had taken for me, that snagging the golden goose he'd promised wouldn't be as easy as a mental download and a transatlantic flight.

Because the golden goose always comes with a giant to take down too.

Why didn't I keep my eye on that goddamned caveat? *Why* had I let Lawson talk me into accepting those files as one easy zipped doc instead of demanding to see every damn one of them first?

I already know the answer to that. And have myself to blame for it.

We hadn't asked because it had been my fucking *father*. Because for once—for the first fucking time in my life—I wanted to be the kid who looked at his dad and saw the guy he could ultimately trust. The guy who had told him the truth. The guy who had made him a promise and kept it.

The guy I didn't have to hang on to the cell phone for.

But the reason I did anyway.

I find the device in my left pocket and swipe the screen hard and fast. "I have to make a phone call."

But as I say it, the phone buzzes angrily against my hand. The screen flashes to even brighter life. An incoming call from a number that causes Emma, who's now slid up beside me once again, to gasp like she's leapt from a pond after being submerged for ten minutes.

"Reece?" she sputters. "Why the hell does that say an *L Richards* is calling you from Barcelona, Spain?"

There's the five-million-dollar question. I can't give it to her because I'm doused by the same perplexity—which feels like an acid rain shower at the same time. If I can see the name, number, and location of the caller, then so can a lot of other people. A lot of people who supposedly think my father is dead.

Supposedly.

Screw the acid rain. The stuff is now the flow of my bloodstream, turning my fingers into neon rods as I stab at the green button on the phone screen to answer the call.

"If this is another Mufasa and Simba moment, save it." I grit my teeth until they hurt, my only way of holding back the *fucking asshole* addendum. At the moment, Lawson Richards isn't worth it. I can barely believe I'm wasting breath on him as it is.

"Reece."

"I said *save it*, asshole." Fine; it slipped. *I* slipped. Trouble is, it's just the plug in the dyke. There's a torrent of other things I long to roar and snarl and spew but must shove back. Shove down. Turn off. Just like it's always been with Dad.

Except worse.

So much worse.

Especially because the bastard doesn't let a second go by before his gritted return.

"Listen to me!"

Well, *shit*. The triple syllables help me hear what I didn't before. The hoarse grit of his tone. The urgent speed of his delivery. The muffled rustlings that surround both, as if he's calling me from a zipped-up snow parka. "You *need* to listen to me!"

"The same way I *listened* and helped you dump all the data off that USB?" I whirl to face the wall, focusing on my rage instead of the stunned stares from my wingman and my wife. They've started putting the details together despite barely believing it for themselves. While I understand their reactions, I have to deal with this shit one fire at a time. "I bet you and Faline enjoyed a few laughs about this last night, yeah? Maybe even cracked open a bottle of sangria and then had some steaks, celebrating how you snowed your own son once again by feeding him shitty intel?"

There's a sharp hiss from Dad's end. I'm too worked up to interpret what the fuck it means. "If I was still in league with her, would I have even let you leave that room at the Museo?" he spits back. "Then would I have called in every favor I have with every connection at El Prat just to help you leave the country so fast? Would I have done all of *that*, Reece, if that bitch still had her hands on my dick?"

I slam the wall with my free hand while my mind swims in deeper confusion. With my head ducked, I finally snap, "You remember the way Mom used to take out those ant colonies in the garden? Rather than trying to kill the bastards that were right in front of her, she had those traps with the poison in them. They'd swarm the thing, thinking it was the best gift they'd ever gotten—only to find out they'd brought the killing blow back to the nest with them."

A louder hiss through the line. I recognize the sound is actually part of Dad's frantic breathing pattern, as if the parka is buttoned and zipped up all the way and suffocating him. "The...The keys were switched—"

"Thanks for the news flash. I'll let the ants know."

"But I swear to you, on your mother's life, I didn't know until a half hour ago. I *swear* to you, Reece—"

"Do *not* fucking qualify that with Mom's life again, or I swear to God, I'll hang up."

Why the hell haven't I done that anyway? Why the living *hell* am I giving this son of a bitch one more *second* of my time and attention? But I am and I do, compelled to stand here with my stomach full of bile, my spirit full of betrayal, and my system full of fire. My eyes burn so badly, I'm sure my irises are about to bore holes through the concrete wall. Even tears would be better than this agony, but I'm beyond the ability to shed them. This hurts too much. Worse than every afternoon the man had to cancel out on playing catch with me. Deeper than every school pick-up he sent the driver to instead of going himself. Harsher than the times he growled that I'd be transferred to a new school instead of taking the time to look into why I had disciplinary problems at the current one.

"Don't hang up!" And just like that, he supplies the reason I'm still gripping the fucking phone. The choppy urgency in his voice...the real fear vibrating through every syllable... Shit. *Shit.* Even if he didn't relay the truth about the material on the USB before, he's too terrified to be lying now. Either that, or the man missed his calling in life and should be a goddamned actor.

But right now, he doesn't sound concerned about his life's calling.

He sounds like a man about to *lose* his life.

Though I probably sound like a bear in a trap myself, I force my emotions into a mental lockbox and then weld the damn thing shut. Whatever Lawson's going through, I can't directly help him—and for whatever reasons he has, he's calling to help *me*. I have to focus on the questions that'll assist him.

But first, the most necessary inquiry.

"How did you find out about the switched keys?" I demand. Not-so-subtle subtext: *how the hell did you not know about that to begin with?*

"Because I killed the bastard who did it."

Fuck. I was afraid of that. "A death throes confession?" I snarl. "Did he even cackle it in glee as you twisted the knife in?"

"Something like that." He's still rasping heavily.

"And you believed him?"

"Didn't have any reason not to." He pauses, but only for a few seconds. "He was the friend who helped me sneak away in Paris, after I faked the death in the catacombs."

"So he was Consortium," I spit.

"Yes, but one who shared my revulsion at how far Faline was taking things." He huffs hard, and there's a rustling as if he's impatiently shifting. "Or so I thought."

For a long second, I offer no feedback except my leaden silence. There's no use in calling him names anymore or even tearing him down for choosing to trust the "friend" he had to kill. I've been in similar spaces before, on all fronts. Believing people based on the "sincerity" of their word. And yes, even having to drive a life-ending stab into a friend. "So he was likely reporting back to them on everything you did since the events of Paris."

"Like the good little minion he was," my father grates back.

"And they let you relax, lulled into thinking you'd really given them the slip," I go on. "Knowing that eventually, you'd try to get that stolen drive to me."

As soon as I utter the last of that, Dad's breathing hitches. I almost don't believe the sounds that replace his petrified gasps. Sobs. Heavy, tattered, desperate. "I'm sorry, son. I'm so, *so* fucking sorry."

I grit my jaw tighter. Punch fingertips against my eyelids, attempting to order the lasered lightning away from my stare. *Don't call me* son. But at this moment, I've never longed to embrace my father tighter. He's doing the right thing—or at least he's fucking trying. So little, so late...

Why couldn't you have just tossed a ball with me in the backyard?

"So..." I clear my throat, shoring up my composure. "All the intel we've been pulling apart for the last ten hours..."

"Is probably bogus."

I whoosh out a breath. Okay, so bad news that's expected is still crap on a stick.

"But Reece—" Dad's voice rushes into a different octave, accentuated by more restless scuffs and rattles than before. "Son...there's more."

"*More?*" I retaliate. "Than *that?*"

No more teary sighs from him. Not one stressed huff. Definitely no more jittery shuffles. Just his instant reply, hardened to the point that I'm reminded of the punishing speeches he *did* take the time to dole. "There are satellite images on that disk. Ones you probably recognize."

"You really think this is the freshest intel I've got, James Bond?"

My gritted spew earns me his silence. Right now, that's probably for the best.

I'm silent again—but this time, only halfway because I want to be. Air is passing up my throat through a fucking pinhole of space, and my lungs have shrunken into raisins. Worse, I don't even want to know what it would feel like to take a normal breath again. That would mean fully confronting what he's just told me.

It would mean having to grasp what he tells me next.

"You've been damn good about hiding out so far, son— but I guarantee you, they're getting closer by the day. They've narrowed down the search. One day, likely soon, they're going to pinpoint it."

And *now* the fucker takes a second to readjust himself inside the parka or wherever the hell he is... As I stand here, airless and motionless and senseless, he's taking a moment to get more "comfy?" *God damn you, Lawson.*

Finally, he clears his throat. At least that's what his thick gurgle sounds like. *Shit.* There's a chance, a damn good one, he might not have emerged unscathed from the confrontation with his "comrade." But that can't matter right now. I have to focus on what he's telling me, not on the price he's paid to do so.

"They're...they're going to find you, Reece," he finally stammers on. "If...if you've heard nothing else I've said r-r-right now, then hear *this*. Faline...she won't...she'll never fucking stop. She will find you, where you live, and then—"

He cuts himself short with a brutal snarl, which is in turn interrupted by a brutal creak of a sound. I push off the wall and spin around, as if my motion here in California will stop the intruder on whatever hiding space he's in.

"Dad?" Once more I obey instinct, muttering it instead of yelling it—only to swallow against saying anything more because of the sounds that pierce the receiver next.

The violent zings of bullets being shot through a suppressor.

The guttural poofs as they solidly hit their target.

CHAPTER FOUR

EMMA

"Reece!"

Twenty minutes after my husband first led the way out of the command center looking like the phone in his hand had turned into a ticking bomb, I'm still having to nearly yell every word before he notices me. Even now, in the haven of our bedroom, he's acting like Armageddon's looming and he's just been filled in on exactly when.

But that's just a hunch.

All right, maybe more than a hunch.

"Reece."

He finally stops, pivoting between our bed and the bathroom, and looks at me. This time, really looks. I'd say the action was a nice change of pace, considering all he's done since getting off the phone is race back up here and yell orders at me, but his stare gives me no more reassurance than his crazed-out energy.

No.

It gives me even less.

The last time I saw him like this—as if he's yanked out his mind and played a sudden-death round of rugby with it—he was barging into Faline's lab at the mansion in RPV and fully absorbing what the witch had chosen to do to me that night.

Like then, I wonder if he's preparing to zap the roof down around our heads. His body is a massive throb of violence. His teeth are bared, exposed by lips fixed in a feral snarl. His hands are like Tesla coils molded into fists. His eyes are twin reactors of nuclear-force fury.

Now that I've pulled up the memory, I'm forced to realize it pales to the present moment—which finally prompts sound to my lips again.

"Reece?" I take a tentative step forward as he returns to his previous task: shoveling everything out of our dressers and cabinets into the three huge suitcases on the bed. "You're scaring me."

"Good." The shoveling continues without a falter. "You *need* to be scared."

"Wh-What's going on?" Instinctively, I grab at my belly. "Reece. *Damn it.* I'm your wife!" When he still doesn't stop, I march across the room to bodily park myself in his way. I stand firm, planting my hands on the middle of his torso. "Who the hell was on the phone? And why did the caller show up as your father?"

He dials back his tension by a few degrees but only by visibly forcing himself to do so. I'm only getting a short—*very* short—reprieve from his mania. Or whatever the hell this is. "It doesn't matter anymore." He grabs my jaw in an urgent hold, snapping my face up for the intrusion of his adamant kiss. And I'm such a puddle, even after just five seconds of that perfect penetration, that I'd even let him tackle-crush me to the bed— except that the whole thing is consumed by the damn luggage. "He's dead now."

Well, duh.

Except that I can't claim the thought completely—not

while witnessing how he tenses as if he's just walked through a blood bath.

And I have to embrace my stronger impression—my certainty now—that he isn't referring to the moment Lawson was supposedly blown up in the caverns beneath Paris along with his middle son.

I was standing beside Reece when Tyce made that detonation happen, and I was practically in the same position when he took that call today. The moments were markedly different but scarily similar. Today, when Reece's phone call ended so abruptly, I wasn't watching anything but him. I stayed riveted to the expression on his face. There was grief, real and raw, mixed in with his fury, confusion, disbelief, and dread.

More than anything else, his *dread*.

The same awful stuff that coats every inch of his face now—right after kissing me like it was the last time he'd do so.

No.

No.

Now I'm the one reaching and framing his face, fighting off terrible trepidation. My mind spins but rivets on the inescapable fact that he's pouring stuff for *both* of us into the suitcases. Whatever's happening, it's clear he's not planning on doing it without me this time.

A conclusion that should be more uplifting than it is.

But he's letting me keep him locked like this, with his head dipped and our thighs pressed and his stare raking my face, so I dig my fingers tighter along the beautiful square of his jaw. If he's offering, then I'm taking advantage for as long as I can.

"Zeus," I plead in a whisper. "Come on. You need to throw me a bone here. And I don't mean the one between your legs, but if that'll help..."

He kisses me again. It's softer this time but seems to carry more significance—if that's even possible. But I know it is, because the intent in his gaze impacts me so much deeper than before. There's a resonance inside of me, reaching out to the disturbance inside him. Though it's always been this way between us, the connection is even stronger now.

In a flare of insight, I realize completely why.

Our circle of communication has become a triangle—with one of the three points still contained inside my body. It's awestriking and amazing, but at the same time it's troubling and painful. I can't just tell Bean to get off the furniture. Right now, I *am* the furniture.

"Don't think I'm not going to take you up on that, beautiful." The storms in his eyes gain thicker intent, responding at once to my saucy sarcasm. "But at this second, not a fucking thing matters more than your safety." He slides a hand down, pressing it over my stomach. "And his."

I mesh my fingers with his. "And I'd like to help make that happen—but you've *got* to fill me in on the story so far, buddy. You're jumping me in at volume ten of the series, but you're hoarding one through nine."

For a second, I almost sense I'm about to get my head ripped off for that. His nostrils flare, and his fingertips pulse like he's about to head out and be the LA rave club king for a few hours. But then my senses start to resonate again, pulled by the intense conflict of his...the overwhelming pieces of him being torn in a thousand directions at once. I feel it all. His commitment to be brave but his temptation to crumble. His anger warring with his fear. His suspicion and his desperation and his apprehension...

But most of all, his determination.

The part I want to help the most. The kernel of courage that I see in his eyes and feel from his heart and desperately need to help him grow—if he'll let me.

I'm your wife, Reece.

Let me in.

A hard breath shudders in and out of him, as if those very words have slammed into him. Imagine *that*. He pulls in two more, a hard inhale and a matching rush out, before finally capturing my hands between his. He lifts them and then smashes them against his lips. His pressure is fierce. He squeezes his eyes shut until deep crinkles are etched into his taut temples.

"You were right," he utters. "About the satellite images we decoded from the files. What we expected to be specific neighborhoods in Barcelona is actually the Malibu and Ventura coastline."

I examine him closely. "Which means...what?"

"Number one, that the key we were given was switched with another drive at some point." He twists his lips, and his gaze turns to twin electric storms. "I don't know the details. Nor do they matter."

"And number two?" My nerves are prickles of panicky pain as I issue the prompt, already sensing what he's going to say. No. Already sure of it.

"That Faline's putting information together and guessing where we live." His grip tightens as I give in to a whole-body shiver. "She obviously doesn't have anything concrete, especially because the complex simply looks like a solar-powered industrial facility from the air."

I attempt a heartened nod. "Thank God we've got the full awning over the pool deck too."

"And we've built everything to be innocuous from the road, as well. *Fuck.*" He surrenders to a burst of frustration, letting go of me to drive a hand back through his hair. One thick lock escapes his clench, invading the space between the glowing violence in his eyes. "I'd give my left nut just to live one *day* without looking in my rearview every ten seconds."

I slide out a sardonic glance. "I think the Bolt Bean might have something to say about that."

He rubs a hand across my belly with silent remorse. "Wade and Fersh are scanning back through the video and motion-detector footage from the last six months. So far, all they've found are ground squirrels, deer, opossums, and hawks."

"All right." I'm steady and encouraging with it, but my follow-up isn't as stellar. "So where does that leave us?" I plop down on the one clear corner of the bed, needing to give my fear-zapped legs a break. "*Holy shit.* Where does that *really* leave us?"

"Sssshhh." Reece pushes forward, wrapping my head and shoulders in a fierce hold. He dips in, wrapping his entire upper body around me. This reaction, he's been ready with. This comfort, he's had really ready to go. As I wrestle with whether to be joyous or troubled by that, he murmurs, "It's all right. We're going to be okay. I've already set the contingency plan into motion."

"You have a contingency plan?" Once again, should I be elated or uneasy?

"Since the day we moved in here," he affirms, letting me nuzzle closer and cherish the thrum of his heartbeat against my cheek. "I wasn't about to fuck around with protecting the reason I live." He scoops a hand up through my hair, bringing me even tighter. "And now, the *two* reasons I exist."

His declaration is punctuated by a rap from the bedroom's entrance. We break apart by a few inches, looking toward a firm-faced Sawyer in the doorway. While this is a marked change from the guy's battering ram method, I'm back at not being unable to decide on a reaction. The two men, nodding at each other like they've actually rehearsed this scenario a bunch of times, should make me feel shielded and assured. Instead, I'm shocked and disturbed. Have I been living a complete illusion? Even after everything that bitch has done to stalk my man, alter my body, and poison my life, have I been just pretending the ridge is our haven of safety? And if it's not, then what place—if any—will be ever again?

But those questions have to be shoved away. I have to pack them in and zipper them off just like all the stuff I'm cramming into these suitcases. Just like I'm locking away the most vulnerable parts of my heart and spirit. I have no choice. This isn't about protecting just myself anymore.

Or even the man who reluctantly pulls away from me to approach his right-hand man. "Everything looking good?"

"Affirmative. Alex wigged and make-upped the crap out of Lydia and Angie, and they're on their way to stock provisions at the house. He's gone with them and will be double-checking the perimeter as well as the security system. It's a weekday during off-season, so you shouldn't have too many neighbors poking around or doing the lookie-loo bit."

I jerk my attention back to Reece, toppling a chunk of the bun I've formed with a pencil and a bobby pin. "The *neighbors*?"

"Safety in crowds," Reece explains. With a new look at Sawyer, he charges, "The M5 is ready? With new plates?"

Sawyer dips a brisk nod. "The ownership is now totally

untraceable to you. To anyone bothering to look, the car belongs to Dr. Stephen Sarsgard."

I groan. "Cripes. Sounds like someone my parents would hang out with at the tennis club."

The men exchange a glance that's brief but loaded. Before I can even try to decipher it, Reece mutters, "We'll be right down. Thanks, Foley."

Thanks, Foley.

Not *Arigato, asshole.*

Or *TY, Mr. KY.*

Or *Spasiba, spaz-nuts.*

Which makes me plunk back down on the bed again—and then shoot out a hand, hooking Reece before he can pass. With a take-no-prisoners snort, I yank him down next to me. "Okay, mister. I know we're all jump to light speed with our hair on fire here, but you need to crank down the hyperdrive for a hot second." I drag his hand to the spot on my stomach that's noticeably lurching. "I'm not the only one who's asking."

I watch, temporarily enraptured, as the face of the man I love is transformed by the same sentiment. I know this not by just watching him but feeling him. My breath catches, along with his, as the energy from his bright-blue fingertips flows through every layer of my skin and tissues, spreading into places neither of us can even see from the surface. Permeating into the new life inside me.

Speaking directly to our child.

And receiving a vibrant answer in return.

A feathering touch. An adamant kick.

Then my breath, escaping me in jolting spurts.

Then Reece's, leaving him along with a dazed, beautiful smile.

"What can I do?" he finally asks, continuing to circle his hand across my womb. "For both of you?" He raises his head, capturing my gaze with the azure energy of his—and the neon sign of his nonverbal message.

Anything. I'll do anything for you and him, Velvet Bunny. Any fucking *thing.*

But now that I have his full attention, I'm back to uneasy-ville. With a vengeance. Less than a month ago, I was sprinting across the top of Rindge Dam and frying any "bad guys" that got in my way. Four days ago, I was dictating Sawyer Foley to call me his daddy, on the verge of finally besting him in a hardcore training session. Less than a week later, I'm starting to swell with a kid determined to buck every law of human biology and wondering if and when I'll ever again see this place where I've imagined, so many times, Reece and I getting to grow old together.

Superheroes *protect* the fairy tale endings.

That doesn't always mean they get to have them for themselves.

But I need to just suck my shit up, get the hell over myself, and accept that fact as my reality.

Because he's worth it.

No matter how many fairy tales I have to give up, dreams I have to change, or expectations I have to set aside...

Worth it.

This man, dark and rugged and beautiful and noble, is worth every second of this odd and crazy and capricious life.

I tell him so by lifting my face and then pulling his down for a desperate meeting of our lips. He tastes like everything that's become precious about this home of ours, mixing on my tongue as if to comfort me one last time. Wind and dust, sage and leather, lavender and love, my man and my *more*...

But *that* part's not going to go away.

From now on, *more* will simply taste differently. Once again. As it probably always will.

As soon as we pull apart, I whisper to him, "You know I love you, Mr. Richards."

He smiles while pushing some tiny hair strands away from my face. "As I love you, Mrs. Richards."

"All right, so..." I nibble nervously on the inside of my lip, treasuring how he stares at every iota of the action. "Where *are* we bound for this epic contingency plan of yours?"

Only then does his expression depart from its sultry confidence. Instead, looking a lot like he did during that weird "look" he and Sawyer just shared, he firms his lips, takes my hand, and states, "I'm going to let that be a surprise for now." And then squeezes my fingers tight. "For now, I just want you to promise me you'll keep an open mind."

REECE

"Holy. Shit."

She blurts it as soon as I guide the Range Rover off the 73 Toll Road at Macarthur Boulevard.

"Bunny."

"Do *not* with the *Bunny*," she snaps, at last reclaiming her stiff hand from my stubborn clasp.

"You agreed to be open-minded."

"Open-minded, yes. Freaking insane? Hell to the *no*."

So this is going well.

Okay, maybe not "well." But better than I imagined, especially now that she knows exactly where we're headed and hasn't tried to throw herself out of the car.

Yet.

"You are out of your *mind*," she grumbles as I turn into Newport Center. Just ahead, workers are fixing bulbs on some holiday decorations in the Fashion Island parking lot. Though Halloween's still a good ten days off, the bastion of Southern California consumerism merrily glows in its solid middle finger to the calendar. Not that Emma is noticing. "*Newport Beach* is your idea of *hiding out*?"

As I brake the car in the nearly empty back parking lot of the Big Newport movie theaters, I pour all my most alluring charm into a fast wink. "Nobody will suspect you *want* to come here."

"You've got that right." As she drops back against her seat, seething her ways through folding her arms, I decide to drop the Jason Stackhouse and keep my balls. It's quickly a nonissue anyway, as a couple tumbles out of a brand-new Audi nearby. The man looks like a mustached Don Draper, with glossed black hair, vintage shades, and a natty *Mad Men*-style bowling shirt. The woman is a va-va voom knockoff of Peggy Lipton in *The Mod Squad*, except in updated clothes and clunky boots. She's also sporting semi-vintage sunglasses, and her come-to-mama pout is lipsticked in cherry red.

"Perfect timing," I mutter, powering down the car.

Emma ping-pongs a wary look between them and me. "For what?" But the next second, pins her wide eyes on the approaching duo. "Wait...a...second. What the hell?"

"Hiiiii!" the blonde calls out, giving away her identity at once.

"'Dia?" Emma shoves her door open and hops out of the Rover. Yes, before I can scan the whole area for any dogged onlookers. Yes, before I can utter a syllable of caution for her to do the same. But as soon as the sisters embrace, I decide to stand down and motion for Alex to do the same. At least I'm pretty sure it's Alex. I'd know the guy by his nearly perfect fake facial hair anywhere.

"Look!" Lydia exclaims, modeling off her whole ensemble. The mini skirt, resembling a ballet tutu with its springy layers, fans out around her stockinged legs. Her hair flings out like blond helicopter blades. "I get to be Princess Daenerys!"

"With a skirt like that?" For the first time in the last couple of hours, my wife openly laughs. I've never been more grateful for the medicine called Lydia, even if she does brandish an open pout at Emma.

"Hmmpphh. It's a new look for her."

"The dragons will go berserk," Alex cracks, bringing me an excuse to refocus on him.

"I'm almost afraid to ask what you concocted for us," I charge.

"Us?" Emma jerks away from her sister and then skirts the car's hood in her rush over to my side. "*We're* getting disguises too? But why?"

"Yours are the most important ones," Alex interjects. "I've been working on them for a while. You have full wardrobes waiting at the safe house."

Inwardly, I cringe. I've avoided calling the place a "safe house" due to every connotation that exists for the term. *Cage. Coop. Jail sentence. Hard target. Imminent danger. Inescapable prison.*

None of that applies or will apply. I've taken *a lot* of precautions to make damn sure of that for Emmalina.

"It's the only restriction we've got at the place, Velvet." I reach for her, more ecstatic than I let on as she slides her hand into mine. Her grip is warm and trusting, at least for now. I hope she'll be all right with this—at least until we know more about what Faline's latest fuckery is and how close the bitch is to truly discovering where we live. "It shouldn't be too awful when it's just us inside the house. This is only for times we need to avoid going stir-crazy."

She pours a gallon of starch into her stance. "Too late," she mumbles though finishes with a stiff nod toward Alex. "All right, then. Let's see it, Trestle. What'd you concoct for—oh, hell. What's our last name again?"

"Sarsgard," Reece supplies though adds an adamant glower at Alex. "Who'd *better* not have any chrome domes in their heritage, man."

"Huh?" the sisters blurt together.

"Just one of those inside jokes from the trip to Spain," Alex explicates with a chuckle. "I can probably be bribed to find some pictures on my phone..."

"*No.*" A brutal glower has never felt so good. "He *can't.*"

After indulging half a chuckle more, Alex reaches into a duffel and hands me a smaller bag. "There's no chrome dome action this time around," he assures. "Everything is designed to be put on fast, in case you're farting around the house but need to get into character in less than a minute." He hands a bag to Emmalina. "Sorry, girl. This means you don't get to turn into the Mother of the Dragons too."

"You get something even better." Lydia's back to being the life of the party, and my gratitude for her can-do attitude doubles. "We're going to make you...a redhead!"

As soon as her sister pulls out the double boxes of a shade that can only be called "Jessica Rabbit Red"—which is ironic or tragic or perfect. Emma's expression explodes so wide, I'm certain her mind has detonated. As anxious as I am to get into whatever getups Alex has conceived, whether it's Dr. and Mrs. Sarsgard or Mr. and Mrs. Jackrabbit, I realize that for the moment, I've got to cool the fuck down on my let's-get-into-hiding jets. My wife's just been pulled out of her home, away from her life, and into the land she often calls hell on earth. Making her become someone else entirely is probably like stripping an angel of her wings.

When all I want to do is make sure she's alive to fly another day.

But that means protecting her heart, as well. And at this moment, that means giving her a few minutes to get used to the concept of her new normal—at least as it stands right now.

But with God as my fucking witness, not forever.

Not. Forever.

"Why don't we get to the house first?" I suggest. "It's two p.m. on a Wednesday, and we're in Newport Beach. If any of our 'new neighbors' are even around right now, they'll barely lift an eyebrow to take notice of our arrival. We can break down the new wardrobes and backgrounds for 'Steve' and 'Sophie' in more comfortable surroundings."

At once, Alex nods his concurrence. "Outstanding plan."

Lydia pumps a thumb. "The sooner the better for Operation Sexy Redhead."

Next to me, Emma folds her arms and then curls her hands around her shoulders. "Sure. Of course. Just don't ask me to call any part of this *comfortable*."

CHAPTER FIVE

EMMA

I blink hard at the mirror. Then again.

Am I me?

Or is this just the dream where I become the redhead of all redheads, having landed—appropriately—in the heart of hell?

But everything feels so real. The shiny marble floor beneath my bare feet. The enormous bathroom, complete with a timed spritzer to inject more custom scent, "Eucalyptus-Sage Serenity," into the air. The salt and sounds of the crashing waves, literally only a hundred yards away.

"Ohmygawd. It's *so* effing cute!"

Oh, yeah. And the ecstatic-out-of-her-mind shriek of my big sister. That too.

Just in case I couldn't hear it the first time—though who on the entire block along Ocean Boulevard didn't?—'Dia cuts loose with yet another scream. Or maybe that one's just for fun, because the girl has clearly missed her true calling in life. Screw the semipro tennis circuit; my sister is in her wheelhouse when getting to use grown women as real-life dress-up dolls.

"Do you love it, Baby Girl?" She steps up behind me, seizing me by my shoulders. "Tell me you *love* it!"

I swallow. Hard. I can't ruin her moment, no matter how disconnected I'm feeling from all of this. I do my best to model her adventurous spirit, if only for Reece's sake. He wouldn't make this drastic call without assessing the ramifications, despite clearly being ready to pull the trigger on the plan whenever he had to. Still, none of this can be easy for him. Giving a cover story to the world about our disappearance, asking for the media's "respect for our privacy" as we enjoy our "belated honeymoon." Suddenly bringing "Stephen and Sophie Sarsgard" to life with false IDs, bank accounts, and searchable internet information. And most grueling, having to leave the rest of Team Bolt behind at the ridge, knowing damn well they might be sitting ducks for a house call from Faline at any second.

And here *I* am, in my marble-lined bathroom, picking up a used hair coloring comb and then singing off-key in an impish soprano voice, emulating the most iconic redheaded mermaid on the planet.

"Ohhhhh!" Leave it to Lydia to clap like I've just made the best holy-shit-it's-really-red reference in the world. "Yes! Perfect! I'm going to blow it out and give you gorgeous princess curls. I'll tell Alex to look for a teal-green jumper for you too. And themed bows with the flounder and the Jamaican crab!"

My sister. True calling. Enough said.

"Curls, yes," I state. "But bows, *no*."

"Oh, come on. If you hate them, and then you have a daughter—"

"I'm not having a daughter."

A fresh gasp from her. "Did Neeta see something on the ultrasound?" she all but squeals.

I shake my head. "Neeta didn't tell me a thing." I smile and place a hand over my belly. "I just know. So does Reece."

"Ah. Got it." She flicks a heavy dose of skepticism while

opening her phone and typing in a search for bows. She's in the same boat as the rest of the world. They don't get it. The connection among the three of us already, as tight and permanent as real bonds... Perhaps it's a biological thing because of the electricity in our veins, but it feels like more than that. So much more.

But for now, I give up trying to say anything more. Which is probably a good thing, because it's time to really shut my mouth lest something snarky spills out. Okay, so they *did* have to finagle a last-minute switch-up of my alter-ego's key wardrobe staple due to Bean's prominent appearance, but *jumpers*?

Sure, there was a time in my life when I really liked jumpers. I was twelve.

An hour and a half later, donned in one of those hideous things along with a matching pair of thick eyeglasses, I follow 'Dia downstairs. We head for the rec room, where Sawyer, Alex, and Reece are setting up a command post on the billiards table. I'm puzzled by this since this place seriously must have a decent office tucked somewhere. According to Lydia, there are eight bedrooms and an equal number of bathrooms, a casual and formal dining room, a kitchen with a walk-in freezer, two libraries, a screening room, a couple of sun decks—one with a pool and one with a sauna—as well as a solarium and a night-sky observatory. Honestly, she had me at the "two libraries" part but was on such an excited roll, I didn't have the heart to stop her.

As hideouts go, it doesn't exactly suck.

But right now, that's as close as I'm getting to admitting that hell might be mildly tolerable. For a little while.

When we get to the ground floor, the smoky, briny smells

from the beach are more noticeable. I allow myself the hint of a smile, realizing I've missed the surging energy of the Pacific as a constant presence in the air. It's late afternoon, meaning the wind's starting to kick up as well. It'll be heralding a sunset painted in all the colors of the season—pumpkin spice, harvest amber, maple brown—and now that I'm in full "Sophie" regalia, I wonder if I can talk my husband into breaking away from his war room for a walk along the sand.

His war room.

Did I really just call it that? And so damn easily?

For the first time in a long time, a distinct chill assaults my spine. I lob solar heat up and down the column, chastising myself for borrowing 'Dia's melodrama. But is it really that? We're in a secret safe house, setting up false identities, deciding on defensive strategy against an enemy constantly two moves ahead. And who, oh yeah, is amassing an army of mindless followers on the side, just in case she needs a little backup.

Morose thoughts like this belong to another woman. *Not* the badass redhead who, even deep in disguise, could make an Amazonian princess cry.

Suburban jumper wonder powers, activate.

Using the credo to sheath myself in imaginary armor, I pull in a deep breath before following Lydia across the living room, through the breakfast nook, around a corner with an interior waterfall and koi pond, and then into the rec room.

Where the sight of my husband has me expelling that air in a series of shocked spurts.

Then a couple of captivated gasps.

Then one hell of a dumbfounded smile.

I never thought I'd live to see this day. My husband, who's rocked my hormones with every look from a T-shirt and sweats to a bespoke formal suit to leathers and shitkickers, has actually found a new way to make the angels in my libido break into soaring choruses.

Move over, Clark Kent. There's a new hot geek on the block.

And Lois Lane? Don't even think about it, wench.

I stand and simply gawk for at least another minute. His big feet are encased in polished Oxfords. His waiting-for-a-flood pants make his long legs look like an oversize wishbone. The argyle sweater vest atop the rumpled French blue button-down is rolled to reveal forearms that provide mental foreplay all on their own. But the best part of it all is *above* his shoulders, where his mad scientist hair, an obnoxious soul patch, and a pair of thick eighties checkered glasses provide the mismatched *pieces de resistance* for the look.

Only then, on about my fifteenth drooling appraisal, do I peer past the glasses into his eyes—to realize *he's* eyeing *me* with the same stupefied delight. Holy crap. We're two peas in a seriously fucked-up pod. But isn't that what life's all about? Finding the other pea who fits in your shiny husk?

Not in any other moment, even the one in which he smiled down at me while whispering "I do," have I been happier to have this man as my fellow pea.

"Well, good afternoon, Mrs. Sarsgard."

Okay, correction. *This* moment, as he saunters toward me with Joey Tribbiani charm, is my happy peapod place.

It's never been a huger joy to giggle at the man's antics, though I manage to get out between titters, "And good afternoon to you too, Dr. Sarsgard."

Reece's glasses slip as he gathers me close for a long, languishing, tongue-filled kiss. While I logically know we have bigger worries than the clamor of my hormones and the throb of my pulse, I table the stress for later. Right now, it's all about him. The man making the world go away. My existence is about nothing but my breathtaking nerd god. Letting him turn my knees to mush and my senses to mindlessness...

Until my sister's protesting groan punches the air. "You two want to have a little mercy on the rest of us—like getting a room? There are dozens to pick from. Literally."

Reece releases me, and I give my sister my impish grin. "Says the girl who *doesn't* look like an extra from *Dawson's Creek*." While 'Dia stews over that, I use my hold around Reece's neck to nudge at the back of his head. "Speaking of rooms, why are you turning *this* into the forward operating base?"

His expression darkens. "Because Sawyer and Alex decided to have a little fun creating the good doctor's back story."

I flare my gaze. "Do I dare even ask?"

"Probably not." He starts tugging me down an arched hallway I haven't been in yet—but I skid to stop nearly immediately.

"Oh, crap," I spew with authentic fear. "Did they make you an entomologist? If you're about to show me a room full of things with more than four legs..."

He shakes his head. But the chuckle I expect as accompaniment isn't happening. He actually growls and rolls his eyes before muttering, "It's worse."

I bug my eyes. "Huh?"

He continues yanking me down the passage to the pair of double doors at the end. He unfurls another low growl, filled with more exasperation than vexation this time, while twisting the knob. I precede him into the room...

Where I let my jaw drop all the way.

I turn in a full three-sixty, gazing at the strangeness in every corner of the spacious room. Only I'm having trouble calling it a "room," let alone the office for which it was clearly intended. There are built-in bookshelves and a desk alcove, though there's not an inch of space for that desk now.

"What...the freak...am I looking at?" My combination of confusion and fascination helps me extend nearly every vowel.

Reece, still standing near the doorway, looks ready to jet any second. He's jammed his fingertips awkwardly into his back pockets. His pants are too tight to allow anything else. "The Double Jeopardy answer for that would be...what are aliens?"

"Aliens." I don't attach a question mark to it but sure as hell want to. Still, as if I've really been sucked in by a round of the game show, I can't stop gawking. I take in everything from the stereotypical bright-green dudes with the oval eyes, to blueberry-colored plastic toys adorned with jeweled faces, to creatures handcrafted in everything from paper clips to modeling clay to red raspberry satin. No, really. Satin. With eyes that look like almond-shaped disco balls.

"And you thought you had it bad with the jumpers?" he finally utters.

I spurt out a laugh. "Well, they haven't filled me in on *Sophie*'s hobbies yet, so—"

My words are stolen by the crush of my man's lips, sweeping down and then in as he traps me in the corner beneath an inflated UFO. I let him in, at once recognizing the weirdness of having a thousand "extraterrestrials" as our voyeurs, but I can't help myself. His power over me, even in Dr.

Alien Nerd form, is the most beautiful thing my senses have ever experienced and my body will ever know. I want him, even here. I crave him, especially now. I open readily for him, sweeping my tongue out to match the greedy assault of his—

Just as the front doorbell rings.

We break apart like a pair of teenagers caught at second base in the rumpus room. The feeling only worsens as Lydia dashes in, her face fixed in a gape. "There's someone at your door!"

I pin her with a *duh* glare only a sister could get away with. To Reece, I demand, "What do we do?"

He pushes his glasses back up his nose and reaches into one of his front pockets to produce a pair for me. Though the spectacles are definitely props for a grandma, I still wonder how he fit them *and* all of his lower half—including the important junk—into the skintight legwear.

He opens the glasses and jams them onto my face. "No time like the present to see if these getups are really going to work. Come, *Sophie.*" He smirks, so irresistibly geeky and gorgeous at the same time. He scoops up my hand and leads the way toward the main entryway.

"Shit, shit, shit, shit," I hiss as he double-checks my ensemble as well as his. Then he turns and grabs the heavy iron handle of the massive front door, pulling the portal open wide.

I hold my breath, hoping for simply a misdirected delivery guy, but no way am I getting that lucky. Not by any kind of a longshot.

Because the Ocean Boulevard welcome wagon has really and truly arrived. In every horrific way possible.

The couple standing on our porch looks like they jumped off a video monitor from the lobby of a plastic surgeon's office—

not an unlikely scenario, considering there are more altered faces than Starbucks stops in this neighborhood. The man is tall and sturdy, with bright, eager eyes and swoopy dark-blond waves into which a gallon of product has been dumped. The woman is petite, curvy, and rocks a matching serial-killer glint in her gaze, despite her traditional brunette bob and heirloom pearl earrings.

As soon as Reece fully opens the door, the Bradley Cooper look-a-like softly finishes his eight-count.

This isn't going to be good.

They launch into a version of "Rock Star" that sounds more like a cheerleader chant than a song. I'm not quite sure how to tell them their welcome-the-new-neighbors spiel probably needs to be replaced with a pie and flowers, especially as they punctuate the number with spirited moves that rival any pro cheerleading team on the continent.

I'm almost glad when their coordinated moves nearly take out the porch light, giving Reece a perfect excuse to halt them by holding up both hands. Well, *tries* to. When he adds some valiant applause to the quest, I readily join him.

Success at last. Sort of.

Because thirty seconds later, we're still clapping. Annnnnd clapping. Then even more clapping, as the duo accepts our "praise" like Broadway stars basking in three—now four—standing ovations.

Finally, after exhorting us to stop, they chuckle and straighten their matching V-neck sweaters. I'm positive they picked out the garments from some high-end catalogue in which the color was listed as "Serious Squash" or "Hunter Rust" rather than simply "orange." It fits right in with their quirky schtick.

"Well, good afternoon, sir." The man gives Reece a hearty handshake. "We were happy to see some life over in this quadrant of the neighborhood and thought we'd roll on by with the welcome wagon. Left the ol' gray mare at home, though. Oh, wait a second"—he wraps his opposite arm around his woman—"she's right here!"

"Oh, *Mel.*" The woman's smile doesn't reach her eyes. She bats the center of his chest with a hand adorned by three egg-sized diamonds and a wrist accented with three pearl bracelets. She steps toward me and extends the bejeweled hand. "Hi there. Maddie Makra."

I grit out a smile while clutching my new curls with a free hand. "Nice to meet you. Em—errmmm—*Sophie.* Sophie Sarsgard."

"And I'm Dr. Sarsgard." Reece shakes the woman's hand, flashing a smile that matches the façade of mine. Not that Maddie notices. Or perhaps doesn't care. Her stare oozes I-want-to-climb-you-like-a-spider-monkey intent, and I have to stab *my* gaze to the foyer floor at once to hide my rush of jealousy. Hopefully the expression comes off as shyness and don't-even-think-of-touching-my-husband-ness. We've already given the Makras tons to relay about the "new eccentrics" on the block. Adding a girl fight to their "juicy details" is pouring on one idiosyncrasy too many.

"Nice to meet you, doctor." Thankfully, the woman is cordially respectful. "Stephen and Sophie," she repeats, as if mimicking one of the YouTube courses Mom used to play about effectively remembering peoples' names. "Now isn't *that* fun? Your initials together are *sssssss.*" She makes a snake-worthy torso wiggle. "And ours are *mmmmmm!*" And then some slinky moves that might be an attempt at a sexy cat.

Or a dying jellyfish.

Kill. Me. Now.

"That and fifteen bucks will get you a cupcake at the new bakery up on Orchid, dear."

On the other hand, maybe I'll just kill *him* now.

Reece ropes a hand around my waist and then squeezes at the top of my hip—a silent warning that my solar "magic" is in danger of showing. I plaster on a smile, channeling as much of my fake-it-till-you-make-it prowess from the tennis club days. Shocking how all this shit-shooting is like riding a bike. A few pedal strokes in, and I'm already back to the rhythm of pretending that fifteen-dollar cupcakes are the most exciting thing in my day.

"So you two live...where?" As Reece smoothly changes up the subject and the mood, I notice that he's also modulated nasal overtones in his voice. I curl a hand into the back of his vest to keep from giggling. But hilarious or not, the idea of a slight vocal change isn't a bad idea. I'll never be able to pull off his tribute to *Napoleon Dynamite*, but borrowing from the summer 'Dia and I went through our British obsession might just come in handy a bit.

"Oh, we're just two doors down, Doc," Mel says smoothly. "But we're usually out and about in the neighborhood a couple of times a day. You'll be seeing plenty of us."

Oh, goodie.

"I have to say, everyone's pretty excited," Maddie injects with enthusiasm. Imagine *that*... Local gossip is right in the woman's wheelhouse. "You two are already pretty big news—and just look; it's soon going to be *three*, yes?"

I obey instinct and flatten a hand over my belly. "Oh, yes. Soon."

Mel swings a sound punch into Reece's shoulder. "Nice work, Doc!"

Reece smiles from his lips but glares from his eyes. "It... was a team effort."

"You'd be the one to know, bro," the guy finishes, clearly preening as if he reinvented poetry with the rhyme.

Maddie executes a little pivot to mask her pivot away from him—and closer to me. "So, errrmmm...when are you due?" she queries.

"By Christmas," I answer.

"A few months," Reece says at the same time.

"Nothing like a little synchronicity." Mel flashes another I'm-the-funniest smirk, even before adding, "And that was *nothing* like a little synchronicity." He narrows his eyes at Reece. "You *are* a doctor, aren't you?"

"Not medical." Reece's answering drone is so spot-on with the nasal overlay, I'm sure he's already practiced this part. "I hold several PhDs. Astronomy, Astrobiology, and Earth and Spaces."

"Oh." Mel blinks. Then again. "And...what does all that mean, exactly?"

"I study aliens. And UFOs." He doesn't let on that "Steve" has an entire room full of them in plastic and plush form, and with any luck, we'll keep it that way—though I'm pretty sure the Makras couldn't wear worse gawks than they do this second.

Thank God for Bean. I have the perfect excuse to change the subject. Or in this case, get back to it. "We're both...uhhh... just really excited," I offer. "He's our first baby, and keeping up with the details..." I jerk a convincing shrug. Hopefully. "It all seems to be going by in a big blur."

That part's definitely believable because it's not really

a lie—though I certainly can't share that our last "prenatal checkup," barely over twenty-four hours ago, ended with the baby daddy returning from hunting bad guys in Barcelona and then dropping into a dead faint.

I'm pulled from the memories by the abrupt change in Maddie's demeanor. I watch, semi-fascinated, as the energy glow around the woman's head changes from dark amber to midnight blue. Rarely have I witnessed such a fast switch, which matches the drastic change across her face. From perky cheer to misty melancholy inside five seconds. "Well, enjoy the big whirl," she murmurs. "Before you know it, they're off all day at soccer practice, tap class, ballet technique, or sewing social club."

"Sewing social club?" I try to lighten her mood with genuine curiosity about that one.

"Our oldest is into 'cosplay.'" Mel surrounds the last word with air quotes and a disapproving grimace.

"Now, honey."

"Don't 'now honey' me, Madeline," he spews, though I instantly want to hug Maddie for firming her stance and standing up for her child.

"It's just another form of theater," she declares. "In which she participated before all this—and you were perfectly okay with."

The assjerk—why not, because he's well on his way to earning the assignation—harrumphs. "There's a difference between shoo-bopping as Sandy and trouncing around with a bloody spear as Warrior Queen of the Shadow Valley."

"Certainly is," Maddie counters. "One turned herself into a skank for a man, and the other eviscerates races who want to subjugate her people."

"Sounds perfect." I add a sincere grin, which is mirrored by Maddie.

"She goes to events and masquerades with her friends from college," she adds. "And sometimes they even get paid to promote upcoming movies or books featuring the characters they portray. They're even thinking of forming their own little company, with an LLC and everything. They all have several costumes. Everything from cats and unicorns to warriors and superheroes."

Reece digs in his fingertips at my hip, though the only thing that changes about his outward manner is the tumble of hair against his forehead, blown by the increasing twilight wind. "Superheroes?" He conveys nothing but nerdy eagerness. "You don't say."

"Oh, but I do." Maddie lifts her head higher, clearly beaming with pride. "I'll have to show you some of her latest creations sometime, especially the beautiful Bolt leathers she designed for her boyfriend."

If the seaside breeze turned into a polar gale force, I'd be fighting less to keep my composure. But even if I had full freedom to express myself, I'm not sure what I'd pick: a bemused gape or a happy grin. Maybe it's a good thing I'm forced to focus on my façade of suburban pleasantry. "Bolt leathers." A quizzical look, praying I've got the right mix of inquisition and interest. "What's that all about?"

"Oh, he's all the rage with the kids." She pushes up her hands in wide, sweeping fans. "You do know who I'm talking about, right? *The* Bolt? The Hero of Los Angeles? The one leading the charge against those lunatic terrorist scientists? The Consortium?"

Reece shifts his weight and ducks his head, camouflaging

his choke into something more like a rough throat clearing. "Yes. We're, uh, familiar with the general details."

"Well, my Bethany outfitted her Ash in an amazing ensemble for an early Halloween bash last Friday. He even had battery-operated lights in his hands, simulating lightning bolts. Just like the real thing, if you ask me."

"Except that he wasn't chained down and tortured first," Reece growls for my ears alone.

"Pardon me?"

My husband's dorky grin falls back into place. "I was just saying...what a *change* from the days when we dressed up in plastic costumes or old bed sheets for the holiday."

"*So* true!" The woman glosses over Reece's bumbling—or his epic save, depending on the perspective—as if he's spouted the wisdom of Obi-Wan Kenobi. I know I should leap on this prime opportunity to change the subject, but I can't help myself from asking my next question, mostly because I actually *can*.

"So have you seen the real thing?" I query Maddie. "Bolt, I mean."

"Oh, gosh no." She giggles and swipes a dismissive hand. "I mean, wouldn't *that* be something, though? Several of my friends were at the party up at Pelican, when he outted himself to the world."

"Seriously?" Reece is bold and brash about his perplexity over that, but Maddie goes on as if he hasn't spoken.

"The only other place I've seen him is in some personal pictures."

"*Personal* pictures?" Now I'm on the astonishment bandwagon—until realizing I've clearly played right into the woman's narrative.

"*Family* pictures." The woman inserts a smug nod. "One

of my dearest friends has them proudly displayed in her home. You probably saw her in some of those craaaazy leaked videos from the couple's wedding, yes? Her name is—"

"Laurel."

At first, my husband's spurt has me whipping a what-the-hell stare up at him.

But only until I see that *his* expression has trumped mine for sheer shock.

"How'd you know?" Maddie returns—during the last moment my system gets to enjoy its last fragments of normalcy. And my guts get to know something besides complete chaos. And my mind gives my body at least an illusion of balance.

Because the second I follow the route of Reece's stare, past Mel and Maddie's shoulders and out to the middle of the front walkway, every shred of that familiarity and that stability are stolen from me.

Just like Faline seized my mother from the middle of my wedding reception.

And to this day—to this *moment*—never really brought her back.

Because even though the woman is physically standing eight feet away from me now, donned in Balenciaga ankle boots, leather leggings, and a flowy silk top with an equally stylish scarf, she's only Laurel Crist on the surface. Two seconds into this catastrophe, and I can already tell. There's that surreal gleam in her brilliant blue gaze. That eager slant of her beyond-bleached smile. That restless bounce in her stance, as if she's waiting to get up and do the Macarena any second.

My mother hates the Macarena.

My mother *used* to hate the Macarena.

I have no damn idea who *this* person is, and I haven't since she and Faline disappeared for those insane hours during our wedding night. To this moment, no amount of questioning the woman—and everyone on our team has tried over the last three weeks, Lydia and myself included—yields any answers but similar phrasings of what Mom first relayed after Faline mysteriously threw her back at us. *It was a wondrous place. I was shown all the magic, and now I believe in all the magic. Only the strongest will survive to see magic happen again in our realm.*

What's the best way to say that your own mother is a total stranger to you?

And worse, that you pray you'll be as much a stranger to *her*?

"Hey hey hey!" she calls out in that sing-song voice I should be used to by now but will never fully accept. That's the voice she's had since my wedding day. The voice Faline Garand gave to her.

"Well, speak of the devil!" Maddie croons before welcoming her "dearest friend" with darting hugs and fast air kisses. "But I see the devil can still read. Glad you got the note on the door, early bird."

"And good thing I did too," Mom volleys. "You said you were down here to meet the new neighbors?"

"Certainly did. Certainly are."

Maddie's sally corresponds with Mom's smooth swivel, at last exposing Reece and me to her full scrutiny.

Crap.

Ohhh, *crap, crap, crap.*

I'm so damn glad that Maddie starts in with the social jabber again, making it possible for me to audibly hitch my breath without worries. "Laurel Crist, please meet our newest arrivals to the neighborhood. This is Dr. and Mrs. Stephen Sarsgard."

"Errrrmmm, Sophie." I'm stunned at how ably I interject it. I even manage to hold back from overdoing the accent, while following up with an extended hand, "Very nice to meet you."

"Lovely to meet you too, Sophie." Mom's cordial about taking my hand, not even pausing when I use the tips of my fingers to return her clasp. I hope she'll write it off as a quirky British thing, though my true goal is as little contact between her skin and mine. Anything to avoid even a schism of recognition.

Though as the seconds tick by, my nerves knot from the fact that there really aren't any.

Not a single befuddled blink.

Not the tiniest puzzled tilt of her head or intensity of her stare.

Nothing more than the casual interest of a complete stranger.

So a new hair color, a tent dress, some glasses, and a makeup-less face are all it takes for my own mother not to recognize me.

As I vacillate between being relieved and perturbed, especially as Mom displays the exact same reaction to Reece, Maddie is the conversational savior once more. "Your timing *is* rather remarkable, Lau." She's oblivious to Mom's wince at the nickname, which even Dad isn't allowed to use. "We were just talking about your exceptional son-in-law."

Mom forgets the grimace in favor of her moment in the suburban neighborhood sun. "And isn't he just? Exceptional, I mean. And now, my daughter too, you know. *Not* Lydia. I mean, she's a love, and the tennis is going well for her. But my *Emmalina*. Can you *even* with my incredible Emmalina?"

I plunge my hand against Reece's, clenching with pressure that would surely snap the digits off a lesser man's body. In this moment, my only intent is to pulse all the pressure of my emotion through the contact of our skin, praying I can keep the visible flare of my emotions away from the air.

So many damn emotions...

Stupefaction at hearing my mother speak of me with pride again. Indignation at how she's blithely written off Lydia like that. Fury that she only sees my power as beautiful because of her strange field trip with Faline. Even more outrage because of the bitch's continuing hold on her. So much confusion because of the questions *that* brings.

What the hell did Faline do with my mother during those hours after they vanished? Where did they go? And why has the mental honeymoon for my mother not waned at all since then? Though she didn't return from the trip with powers or abilities of her own, has she been permanently changed into Faline Garand's minion for the rest of her days? If so, how does this affect everything from my day-to-day reality with her, which includes telling her she's going to be a grandmother?

Ohhhh, crap—the completely horrified sequel.

Instantly, I battle to shut my mind down. To stave my system's reaction to that query, slamming so hard and fast I even shove away from Reece because of it.

Because the vision, like a memory of a trauma instead of a what-if about the future, permeates my mind, snakes down through my sinuses, and even slithers down my throat. It cuts off my air. Squeezes the life out of my heart. Freezes my veins.

Damn it. *Damn it.*

My distress permeates even Bean's safe bubble. He kicks at my insides in protest. Despite that, I can't halt the horror. I can't unsee the nightmare my brain has just supplied.

The scene of my mother standing next to Faline—and proudly showing off her infant grandson to the witch.

Meanwhile, back at the corner of Ocean Boulevard and Torment Lane, the two women on the front stoop are going on as if my world hasn't just been permanently, horridly altered.

"So the videos from the reception were *real?*" Maddie is prodding Mom with wide eyes. "*Emmalina* has superpowers too?"

Mom firms her stare. "Not 'superpowers,' darling. That's the way the world chooses to trivialize them. As my friend Faline explained it—"

"Of course." Maddie's lips are flat with the interruption. I watch the glow around her head turn as crimson as blood. "Faline. Your *friend.*" And there's the explanation for her vampiric aura. "The *friend* we have yet to meet, hmmmm?"

Mom quickly flaps a hand. "As I *have* repeatedly informed you, dear, Faline is an important individual. She doesn't have three hours to stroll through Fashion Island or even a spare moment to just grab lunch."

"Yes," Maddie snips. "As you have *also* informed us."

"*Madeline.*" Mel's terse murmur hooks enough of his wife's attention for him to fling an explicit look. *Don't provoke the crazy lady.*

Maddie wriggles through a delicate *hmmmppph.* "Well." Purses her bow-shaped mouth. "It certainly looked like Emma had superpowers to *me.*"

The moment she takes to add another huff is all Reece and I need to trade a what-the-hell glance. I'm not even sure we've disguised it as anything else. I'm sure neither of us cares.

"*Not* superpowers." Mom's patience is clearly dwindling. "Madeline, my daughter *isn't* a 'superhero.' She is an elevated being. An enlightened creature, chosen to become part of the new age of the world. We could *all* choose to become that fortunate. To endure the crucible and—Sophie?"

She interrupts herself by reaching for me, though I'm not certain what she does after that. By this point, I'm fully doubled over. Whimpering. Swallowing hard as bile surges up my chest and stamps an ache into my jaw. Leaning on Reece again, I desperately grab at the middle of his vest.

"Oh, Lordy." Maddie's exclamation whips through the air over my dropped head, full of high-pitched concern. "Have we overwhelmed you, dear? I think we've overwhelmed her."

"I'm—I'm going to be sick."

"Oh, dear! Well, you know what they say. It's not *really* morning sickness at all now, is it? Maybe we should just leave you kids be and get off to dinner now..."

Reece stammers out fake niceties, but the words are meaningless to my ringing ears. He closes the door with a resounding *whomp* and supports my feeble turn back into the foyer. Thank God there's a small guest bathroom ahead, to which I shuffle like a destroyed armadillo.

"*Velvet.*" Reece's thick baritone, normally just the medicine I need, feels like a serrated scythe on my senses right now. "Let me help—"

"No." I slam the door in his face—the very first time I've ever done so—and already hate myself for it. But I hate even considering what my meltdown would do to him, especially after everything he's done to keep me safe. And now, to keep Bean safe too. Today more than any other, he's been my steadfast protector, my resolute knight, my true superhero. And not once did he fire up his lightning and thunder and power pulses. He's saved me—he's saved our *family*—by being true to his conviction and following through with his backup plan.

Despite the fact that I've now locked myself in a bathroom, puking and sobbing because of it.

And unable to stop myself.

Whoever *myself* is anymore.

A woman who, a week ago, was sliding into leathers in order to be trained as a new badass on Team Bolt.

A woman who now can't call her husband an ox because she's bigger than one. Who's not recognizable to her own mother. Who's going to *be* a mother.

Who can't stand to think about the world awaiting her baby son.

"Emma!"

Reece's voice is full of anguish, cutting through the noise of my third hurl into the toilet. Hearing his heartache only makes mine worse, and I cry harder as I flush away all my sick.

"God*damn*it, woman!"

"Reece. *Stop.*"

"We can talk about this." The thud of his fist against the door sends tangible tremors through the walls. "We *need* to talk about this."

"Right now?"

He huffs heavily. "*Shit.*"

I force enough air to my lungs to back up my words with some volume. "Baby...please...go away."

Not forever.

Just for a second.

I just need one damn second.

Okay, maybe two.

But a much longer pause goes by, dripping with the continuing tension of his presence outside the bathroom. He lingers with shallow breaths and potent hope...

"I love you."

And finally, with his soft-growled surrender.

I swallow hard. Swipe the wetness off my cheeks. Curl myself against the wall, if only to feel the relieving cool of the marble on my forehead and cheek. "I—I love you too," I finally rasp. "But I just need a little space, okay?"

"Okay."

I almost call him out on it. He believes in those syllables about as much as he really believes in aliens. The grate of the tears in his voice proves that as thoroughly as the leaden sigh he releases—before finally stepping back and then walking away.

But he won't be far.

For which I love him even more.

⚡

I've been out of my mind for three damn days, ever since plummeting to the tile in that bathroom and praying to the porcelain god. After I shut my husband out of my grief. As I promised him, nearly a year ago, that I wouldn't do again.

I'm not proud that I'm back in this space—wherever the hell *this* is. I recognize it less than the bathroom where I'd finally lost my lunch, my composure, my hope...

Myself.

The normal fixes haven't helped me sort through the

mental Lost and Found bin. I've tried them all. Exercising. Rereading my favorite Sherrilyn Kenyon series. Bingeing every season of *Agents of S.H.I.E.L.D.*, *Arrow*, and—when in Rome, right?—*Real Housewives of Orange County*. I even let 'Dia talk me into a try at adult coloring books.

Laughably thin Band-Aids. For a slice in my soul that's no laughing matter.

And wider than I want to admit.

Much wider.

This is a crisis of my damn identity.

Which is why I've gone ahead and done this really dumb thing. Told everyone I really need a nap, but instead slipping out the back gate and quickly making my way to the south end of Ocean Boulevard, where the paved footpath down to Little Corona Beach begins.

At the halfway point of that path, there's a little overlook with a stone bench, surrounded by the glory of year-round wildflowers contrasting with the rich azure of the Pacific waves. I used to call the overlook my "secret spot," since it was a perfect place for imagining the day I'd escape the confines of the cookie cutter and see the world beyond the OC. I'd come down here with my journal and my thoughts, always hoping the bench would be unoccupied so I could scheme and dream in private.

Today, there's someone already sitting there.

For the first time ever, I'm so freaking glad.

I slide onto the empty side of the seat, taking care to keep my head well tucked into the hood of my jersey. 'Dia managed to find some cuter things for "Sophie's" closet, including this dress/hoodie combo in a surprisingly decent shade of blue. I borrowed her Vans slip-ons to finish the look, mostly to better blend in, but none of the hardcore surf crowd comes to the "little" side of this beach. At this time of the day, it's just families with infants tromping by. I could be wearing bedazzled disco wedge pumps, and none of them would care.

For a second, I study those passing bunches of domestic bliss with a wistful smile. It's surprising and sweet to see a lot of dads in the mix, even in the early afternoon. Without hesitation, I envision Reece in their midst. Without reservation, I know he's going to be as much of a hands-on father with our Bean.

Without warning, the backs of my eyes burn with tears.

Like they have been for nearly a week.

Stupid, stupid, stupid.

Not only the way I've been feeling—but what I've finally chosen to do about it. And especially whom I've sought out to talk about it.

"Hi, Dad."

As I've asked, he doesn't openly gesture to me. He keeps his profile, still a collection of youthful angles, directed ahead toward the waves. I compel my sights that direction, maintaining the charade on the off chance I'm being watched. The view is typical for an autumn afternoon along the coast. The morning haze has burned off a little, leaving a languid layer of lavender cotton along the horizon, which blurs the break between sea and sky.

I can't remember a time when my psyche and surroundings were so ideally matched. My emotional state is just like that nebulous mash. I acknowledge the fact but then push the mess away from my heart, caging it solely inside my head. I took this gamble in the hopes of getting some perspective—and I pray like hell that the first man in my life can help me with all the tangles around the last one.

"Hi there, honey."

He's still on the opposite end of the bench, but his greeting swaddles me like a preheated blanket. Like the warmth of home. Of family. Of unconditional love. *Oh, God.* I get it now. I get why he sacrificed so much to lavish so much. I'd seen all of it—the big house, the cars, the clothes, the jewelry, the club memberships—as a trap. But we'd all done with so little for so long that when the money rolled in, Dad had flowed it right back out to the three of us. As the realization hits, I glance at him again. He's wearing a hoodie too: the same one he's owned for fifteen years. The only new things he ever gets for himself are suits for the club—because Mom insists on it.

At least she used to.

And suddenly, despite everything I've come here to talk about, I go ahead and jump subjects. Drastically. But if I doubt the judgment, Bean's brutal kick to my ribcage dispels the uncertainty. My son is my first priority—which means keeping tabs on my mother has to be as well.

"So how's Mom?"

Dad jerks his head up, shooting over a narrowed glance. Clearly it wasn't the lead-in topic he expected, either. "About the same," he murmurs. "Still president of the Faline Fan Club and proud of it. Still flighty and flirty. On one hand, I feel like putting cult deprogrammers into my speed dial. On the other, I've never had a better sex life."

"Oh!" I exclaim. "*Todd.* Ew!"

He throws a hand over his lips to mute his snicker. "You did ask."

"And you sure as hell answered."

As I speak, he peters out the laughter. We settle into a relaxed stretch of silence before he finally asks, "*Do* I need to think about that call, Lina? To the cult people?"

I curl the tips of my fingers around the front of the bench. I'm grateful for the rhythmic rise and retreat of the waters below our promontory, helping to soothe the tattered, exhausted edges of my mentality. "It won't help, Daddy." I swallow, and it hurts. Not physically. The pain is deeper than that. And the fear... It's been ingrained in the very cells of my blood since the second I watched Mom disappear in front of my eyes. "Faline isn't starting a cult." I shake my head. "She's—"

"Forming an army."

The air halts in my lungs. Squeezes them to agonizing compression. "How...do you know..."

"Oh, sweetheart," he chides. "None of this is rocket science from where I'm sitting. From the second you confronted that woman at your reception, it was clear she wasn't just a rogue reporter. The shit that ensued with your mother... I was stunned but not surprised, if that makes any sense."

"When it comes to Faline Garand?" I countered. "It makes too *much* sense."

"Since then, I wish I could say your mom's been simply acting like she made one too many trips to the weed dispensary, but I'd be lying." He pretends to stretch, but the tension along his arms, even beneath his hoodie, is all too blatant to me. "She's saying things, Lina. Things that, quite frankly, worry me." He stands to take another pretend stretch, as if preparing for an afternoon jog. "Needless to say, I was damn glad you asked to meet today—for more reasons than missing my little girl like crazy."

As wonderful as it feels to hear the second half of his statement, I focus on the first part. "Saying things like what?" I press.

"Like the kind of crap fundamentalist followers pepper into their everyday language," he explains. "The kind of nonsense that guys like Mussolini, Jones, Hussein, and Bin Laden prompted their disciples to spew."

Not even the ocean succeeds in easing me. "Well, as a wise man once said, I'm stunned but not surprised."

Dad's nostrils flare. He whooshes out a heavy breath. "So this person is darn bad news."

I almost slap myself for spurting out a full laugh, despite being grateful it's still possible. My spirit hasn't been this light, even temporarily, for three days. "Guess what, Dad? I've had a few grains of salty language tossed at me by now." As he turns a little, indulging me with a loving smile, everything stays warm and effortless. For the first time this week, I feel a little like me again. Yeah, despite the mermaid princess hair, the color-coordinated eyeglasses, and the body occupied more and more each day by the not-so-little dude with whom I'm already in love. "But if you're going to let a doozie fly"—I turn more too, spreading my fingers across my stomach—"try to keep the volume low so *this* guy doesn't hear."

So much for us keeping up the façade of not knowing each other. But so much for giving a shit about it, either—especially as my father takes in my bump and instantly tears up, complete with a trembling chin and an awestruck gasp. Only Reece's faint can top his for the most perfect reaction I can ever desire, so I dissolve and blubber too.

We slide toward each other, unable to help ourselves. Dad gathers me close and tight—and doesn't let go. And still doesn't, even as my emotional crack turns into a full split, and I let out racking sobs against his shoulder.

"Oh, Lina-Bina," he croons, rocking me with the magic

that belongs to him alone. Surrounding me with his arms. Engulfing me with his love. Drenching me with his acceptance. "I'm so happy for you and Reece." But when my tears won't stop for another full minute, he prompts, "But only if *you* are." There's an audible snag in his breath. "Emma? You and Reece *are* happy about this, right?"

"Of—Of course." But his implication otherwise has me scrambling to put my shit back together. With snotty sniffles and big palm swipes across my cheeks, I pull back enough that he can see my valiant effort to regain composure. But just as fast, I really want to chuck the effort. "Things are just...such a mess, Daddy."

A *mess*. Four little letters having to bear such huge meaning. The depth of my love for my husband. The lunacy of the woman obsessed with destroying him—and enslaving a whole army to do it. The lengths to which I'll join him to stop her—especially if she so much as sniffs in my son's direction.

Even if that means I have to take lives.

Even if that means my own mother's.

But how do I tell my *father* that? Especially when the man tucks a finger beneath my chin and then searches my face with such soul-stopping tenderness, affection, fortitude, and pride?

With all the things I didn't think he'd ever openly express to me again...

So what's the next step up from *mess*?

"The greatest adventures often cause the biggest messes, sweetheart," he murmurs. "And many say true love is the greatest adventure of all."

I narrow a mock glare. "You still trying to be an Obi-Wan here, dude?"

He smirks. "Your friendly neighborhood Jedi, at your

service." After we share wry chuckles, he goes in at me with a new stare of fatherly intensity. "So...this mess. Is it why you texted me from 'Dia's phone, darted out here like a fugitive rabbit, and are dressed in a color I haven't seen since you girls were into *Friends*?" As I wobble out a nod, he adds, "Just please tell me *Lydia* picked out that hair color and not you."

I roll my eyes. "What do *you* think?"

Seemingly reassured about *that* world-changing information, he chuckles and tucks me back against him. We gaze out over the waves and cavorting seagulls as I take a few more seconds to organize my thoughts. If that's even possible.

Doesn't take me long to realize that it isn't.

Still, I need to try.

No. We're Jedis today. *There is no try. There is only do.*

And I need to do this. To figure this shit out.

With a weighted breath, I try to figure out the best place to start firing up the lightsaber.

"So...you're right," I finally murmur, not faltering my stare away from the ocean. "Faline is *not* good news. Not in any time, realm, or galaxy."

Dad chuffs. "Those murder weapons doubling as her shoes at the reception *were* a huge tip-off."

"You should see them with a black latex catsuit."

"I'll just take your word for it."

I give him a little side-smush of affection. "As you've probably figured out, she's part of the bigger picture at the Consortium. She's been one of the ringleaders since the beginning—but while the others in the outfit might be after scientific research, she's got some extra issues, especially where Reece is concerned."

"Issues?" His echo isn't just about curiosity. There's a

spike of alarm, probably because he senses where I'm about to go with this. For a second, I think about softer ways to say "sadistic bitch," but I'm here for the sake of brutal honesty. About *everything*.

"She's sick, Dad," I go on. "The power, the control... dishing out all that pain..." I give in to a wince as I'm blasted by memories of my personal agony on the woman's lab table. "I can't even say it's a fetish or an addiction for her. It's different. It's...more."

I fall into silence with a frustrated huff. I'm still not saying it all right.

"It's evil."

Okay, *that's* saying it right.

I try to tell Dad that with my long exhalation, but by expelling the air, I've somehow just made room for more dread in my heart. "Shit," I finally mutter. "I guess I didn't want to admit it. Or...*believe* it."

"Because you always want to believe there's a chunk of gold inside everyone, no matter how deeply it's hidden. You've been this way forever; you'll be this way for always." Dad busses the top of my head through my hoodie. "It's one of the things that makes you so special, honey."

While I'm able to absorb and treasure his words, they do nothing for my spirit's deep dilemma. "So what happened to Faline's gold?" I rasp. "Because, Dad...it's *gone*."

He sighs heavily. "Evil is the child of rage, and rage is the child of fear." Another long breath in and out. "And fear is the child of pain."

"But...*that* much pain?" I'm truly perplexed. There must be more to Faline's story than the basics that Angelique relayed to me months ago. What else was the woman subjected to that's turned her into such a vengeful succubus of superpowers and hyperdrive for hate?

And at this point, do I really want to know?

Dad, suddenly reading my mind with Reece-level aptitude, utters, "Will knowing that answer change anything about the situation now?"

I separate far enough to sit fully upright again. The motion helps my resolve. "Probably not. *Ugh*." I underline that with a growl. "No. *Likely* not."

Dad ticks out a nod. *This* behavior, I recognize at once. It's part of his all-business protocol and gives me insight as to why he's risen so far in the high-end corporate ranks. With two seconds of action, he's already instilled me with a new world of confidence. Maybe I really *can* do this...

"So what does this mean for forward motion for you and Reece?"

And maybe I can't.

Because just like that, my chest closes up. My nerves turn into needles. I straighten and tug away a little before muttering, "I think that's what I need help figuring out."

He doesn't nod this time. His attention is the same, though. Quiet, steady, strong. A rock. Exactly what I need. "Because right now, there's no forward motion?" He cocks his head as soon as I answer that with a frown. "Or is the motion just not the direction you were ready for?"

As soon as he says it, with such firm calm, I want to cry a new bucket of tears and then nosedive into it. He's so right. Why does he have to be so damn right? And why does it have to feel so scary?

"But...I *should* be ready." A sob sneaks in while I'm busy trying to form words. I pound the seat, as if the motion will help beat it back. "*Damn it.* I'm not a victim here! I *knew* what I was getting into. I *knew*, when jumping in with this man, what I was signing on for."

"So that automatically makes you completely ready for everything?" He's half teasing, like the days he used to chide me for getting ticked off about Skips in family Uno games. "My little Lina-Bina, let me tell you a secret." With his arm draped across the back of the seat, he curls a hand in to gently massage my nape. "If everyone, us 'mere mortals' included, waited until we were a hundred percent 'ready' for every twist of life, no business would ever get accomplished. No art would be created. No babies would be born. No lives would be saved." He tips his head a little closer, emphasizing his follow-up. "The truth is...*nobody's* ready, honey. Not really. Not a thousand percent."

I pout. "I'm not asking for a thousand. Or even a hundred."

"But you have a figure in mind already, don't you?"

Bigger pout. "I'll settle for anything north of fifty at this point."

"And maybe you'll get it." He extends his free hand, turning it over as if to catch raindrops. "And just maybe you won't. But Emma..." His expression takes a turn for intense and inquisitive. "When has that ever stopped you, honey? *Ever?* Not when you opted to try out for plays at school instead of the tennis team at the club, despite your mother telling you to get your own rides to rehearsals. Not when you blazed your own trail about moving to LA, insisting on paying your own way for everything. And certainly not when you fell in love with a guy who shoots lightning out of his fingers and turns into a radioactive Smurf when he's pissed-off."

His last sentence brings a soft quirk to my lips—and a

consuming heat in my soul. "Well, you're not wrong."

"I'm usually not, honey."

The heat ruptures into a full laugh. Has my dad just stolen a page out of my husband's playbook? And if so, should I be scared or delighted?

Before I can come to that decision, he goes on. "But the most important part about this whole equation is that Reece Richards is just as deeply and fully in love with you." He's the one resting back now, as if purposely giving himself some space to study me from a distance. Only when he fortifies his stare and firms his jaw do I realize the opposite: that he wants *me* to be seeing more of *his* determination. "He's the man destiny brought for you, Emmalina Paisley," he asserts. "I'm as sure of it as I am of the gravity holding us here and the forces pulling the tide to that sand down there. That man sees the Emma *you* don't even see yet—the woman *I've* always known you are. The person with so much more strength, resilience, and beauty than you've ever given yourself credit for." He leans back over to engulf one of my hands with his. "And the beautiful human who's going to be an amazing mother to your miraculous baby."

Well, freaking hell.

And holy shit.

And screw the subtleties of keeping up this pretense, because now all I want to do is throw myself at my beautiful, courageous father and sob in his arms. And that's exactly what I do, clinging to him as the waves crash on the shore, the children laugh on the beach, and my spirit finally, *finally* starts to speak to my soul again.

And my heart reclaims the truth that it's so desperately needed—but that Dad speaks for it anyway.

"You two have the bond of a lightning love, honey. It

strikes true so rarely, but when it does, it's capable of incredible things." He murmurs it as I pull back, even more lousy with snotty sinuses and streaky cheeks than before, but he frames one side of my face with one hand anyway. "Nothing is going to change that reality, Emma. Not that bitch Faline and her legion of lemmings, and certainly not Strawberry Shortcake hair and a dress in a color I haven't seen since you were in junior high and praying Tony Kemper would invite you to the fall formal."

I accidentally spray him with laughing tears. Serves him right for invoking a cartoon character inspired by a gooey dessert. "Thank you, Daddy," I rasp. "For all of that. For all of... everything."

I'm not sure I'll ever be able to express every speck of that gratitude—because now more than ever, I begin to really understand what *everything* truly means—but I know that I'm really going to try. Right now, that means claiming the new strength he's shown me. Embracing the new light he's given me. Being the person he sees in me.

The person that Reece sees too. More than *anyone*.

I snuggle against him once more, burying my nose against his shoulder. "You're right, you know," I mumble. "About all of it."

He wraps his hug tighter. "I usually am, my sweet girl."

I giggle and then let the sound trickle into a deep, contented sigh. A new peace settles over me, as certain as the cliff below us and as vast as the sea stretching before us.

And as bright as the new light flaring in my heart and spirit.

CHAPTER SIX

REECE

We're taking some space.

It's a term I've heard so many times before, from acquaintances male and female alike, usually in response to efforts at small talk neither one of us really means. Of course, most of those occasions were behind velvet VIP ropes at high-end nightclubs, when said "friends" were joining me for a night of forgetting the loneliness behind those words—and I was all too happy to oblige them, as fast as I could. I was always fascinated to watch it on their faces. Fascinated but terrified. Did the bottom even exist? And did it hurt when they finally landed there?

Somewhere along the line, I'd tempted karma too many times with that damn well.

Because now, I've hit the fucking bottom of it.

And it's really as dark, disgusting, and painful as I always thought.

Especially because ogling the dance floor dollies from a couch behind the velvet rope is *not* going to be my rope out of the well, either. I have a sick feeling about who'd be lining up to give me that advice too. Every single friend who joined me in those nights of depraved avoidance therapy.

Memories that make me sick now.

Reminisces that make me shudder.

So much time wasted, for so many years.

So why do the last three days feel like five times longer? And a hell of a lot emptier?

No. That's not true.

Not emptier.

Because I look down and still see the ring on my left finger. I can still feel my wife's energy on the air throughout the house. I can still smell her when I wake up in the morning, as warm as taking a breath of the summer's first warmth. At this very moment, I gaze across the master bedroom and still view where she rumpled the bed last night. Granted, she went to bed without telling me, and since it's a California king mattress, we were probably sleeping in separate zip codes, but she chose to sleep in here over the dozen other bedrooms in this place. I'm taking it for the win.

I'm taking anything I can get right now.

I'm taking *everything* I can get right now.

Every stolen peek at her. Every cherished sniff of her. Every confirmation, however small, that she's still choosing to be here with me, no matter how hard that choice has become for her every day. Maybe every hour. Perhaps every minute.

So yeah, she gets the "space." No matter how painful it is for me to make *that* choice. Every day. Every hour. Every fucking minute.

Only in *this* minute, I give up on reading the reports Foley has brought down from his trip to the ridge today, returning them to the nightstand with a frustrated smack. Though I've been waiting for the intel—the team's compilation of any noteworthy news stories, communications, transactions, or security camera footage from Spain over the last week—I feel like Skywalker trying to lift his X-wing out of a Dagobah swamp. Mentally, I'm covered in sludge. Physically, I'm impatient for action. Spiritually, I long to reconnect with my Force.

My *more*...

"Three days," I snarl at myself. "It's only been three days, asshole. Cool the fucking jets."

On the other hand, *three goddamned days*.

The last time Emma and I were apart like this, I *didn't* "cool the jets." I got my ass on an airplane and then located *her* adorable ass in New York City.

When I was there for her when she needed me most.

All right, so Foley and Angie had tipped me off about the danger. And I *did* have to approach the whole thing like a stalker, which Emma still delights in reminding me of from time to time. And I *have* been nearly doing the same damn thing to her this week, except in closer quarters. And I'm prepared to keep doing it if necessary.

For twenty-four more hours.

I answer the conclusion with an approving grunt and then take a sip of my Scotch to commemorate the decision. "Twenty-four hours," I grit to the empty room, accepting that I sound more like evil Anakin than moody Luke right now. But the ultimatum still feels right. She asked for space. I've given her seventy-two goddamned hours of it. Three days of exchanging nothing but surface pleasantries, basically being nothing but her roommate, is a generous allowance. But come tomorrow, I'm going to nail that woman's jumper-clad body to the couch—or the bed, or the dining room table, or wherever else I want—and demand answers about what she feels she has to muddle through without me.

I reward myself for the verdict with a longer drag on

my Lagavulin. I consider continuing the celebration with a shower, since I'm still in my sweats and tank from a punishing three-hour session in the gym downstairs, but a strange sound from the bay window has me snapping a curious stare that way. When I hear the same light ping against the glass, I swing to my feet, stride across the floor, yank back the curtain...

And nearly swallow my tongue.

The window overlooks a private side garden of the house, small and protected by the spreading boughs of a huge oak. There's a canvas hammock swing suspended from one of the tree's limbs, next to a small natural rock waterfall and a tile-topped table for two.

Strewn across that table right now is every stitch of Emmalina's clothes.

I know this because she's sitting in the swing wearing nothing but a smile, dangling one playful toe into the pool beneath the waterfall.

And readying to lob another pebble at the pane rapidly fogging over with my aroused huffs.

Holy. Fuck. *Me.*

As I repeat all three words aloud, she reaches beneath the swing and pulls out a large piece of poster board. I have no idea where she got that, nor do I really care, as she flips over the card to expose the writing on the other side.

What's a girl gotta do to get Bolted around here?

I pause long enough to slide open the window. To let my arms stretch out, touching the sides of the encasement, making sure she knows exactly how serious I am about the words I issue.

"Don't. Move."

EMMA

"You moved."

The sensuality beneath his rumble is almost worth the price I'll pay for noncompliance, but that's not why I got up to wait for his arrival, standing utterly nude in the middle of the garden's small patch of grass.

I need him to see me.

To see I'm ready to reaffirm my truth to him, here and now.

To live *our* truth again. To its fullest. To its strongest.

Like the lightning strike we really are.

"I needed to." I step forward, the cool grass tickling my ankles, before I scoop up his hands into mine. I finish the action by channeling the flare of energy inside me. Letting him see the soft, steady light with which he fills the deepest parts of my soul...the hugest embrace of my heart. "I'm sorry."

"Oh, that's all right, sweet Bunny." My husband hitches a corner of his full mouth, flashing the smirk responsible for selling countless gossip magazines through the years. "It'll be so much fun...disciplining you."

"No." I laugh lightly before catching the inside of my lip beneath my teeth. "*Reece*. My patient, magnificent husband." I stretch my fingers out across his wrists, needing him to feel even more of my intention—of what the last three days have taught me. "I mean that *I'm sorry*. For...all of this." I drop my head and take a second to recalibrate my thoughts. "I'm sorry for running from you again. And for—"

"Ssshhh." He leverages our hold to yank me against him, at once smashing his lips onto my forehead and then along my hairline. "You didn't leave me, Velvet."

"But I did check out. It's true."

"Won't argue," he drawls.

"I...I just felt like..."

"We went from Mach Five to Mach Hundred in one damn day?"

I wrap my arms around his neck and tuck my head into the dip between his biceps. The contrast of his hard, heated skin and the cotton of his tank is doing naughtier than normal things to my sex drive. *Holy crap.* My hormones are all over the place, meaning I haven't missed my man in just the mushy ways. There are already parts of me that ache and throb and *need* him...

Not yet.

Not much longer, *but not yet.*

The words first. My declaration first.

He needs to hear it as much as I need to give it to him.

"You did what you had to do, husband. You didn't make your call lightly or rashly—but you were clearly ready to ignite the engine and put the wheels in motion in case you had to." I lift my head and press closer to him, knowing he's got to feel the energy of our child at this point too. I revel in the intensity that takes over his ruggedly beautiful face, indicating that he does. "You made the responsible call for any man in your position. Any *man*, Reece. Any father, friend, and leader"—I sweep my hand up to the crook between his jaw and ear—"not some boy playing with the new Bolt game on his PlayStation, thinking he can restart at the beginning if everything goes batshit. But we're not in that reality. We're in the one where life—and Faline, and whatever sick game she's up to now—aren't going to permit *any* restart button."

"And thank fuck for that."

As soon as he issues it, he tacks on a wolfish smirk and turns his head to nibble at my knuckles.

Still, I challenge, "Excuse the crap out of me?"

He softens the pressure of his mouth but doesn't release me from it. Refastening his gaze on me, he murmurs, "Life has given me a hell of a lot of restart buttons, Emmalina Paisley. Some of them I've welcomed, and God knows, some of them I haven't—but I swear to you, with this sky and these stars as witness, I will fry any of those switches I'm ever near again." He traces the little hills across the back of my hand with his tongue, his stare remaining intent...resplendent. "No more resets," he husks. "No more do-overs. No more blank pages, and no more new races. I don't want the *start* with you, woman. I want the *now* with you. All the good times and the bad, the joys and the tears, the memories and the messes..." He stops to inhale deeply, as if his next words need an extra effort. "And yeah, even the times when you need a little space."

I match his long, measured intake. As I release the air, I shuffle backward by a reluctant step—ensuring he sees all of me. "And...the times for being naked."

He jogs up both his brows. Reprises his rogue's grin. "I'll never argue with naked."

"I mean in *every* way," I chide.

"So do I," he volleys.

"All of me, Zeus," I persist. "My soul, my spirit, my mind... my body."

"Just as you have all of me, Velvet," he husks. "As you have since the night we first met."

"I know." I catch the inside of my lip again, using the gesture to help my coy glance. "You were juuuust a little bit clear."

"A *little*?" He flings a mock glower. "I don't recall the word *little* entering the conversation at all that night."

"Damn good point, Mr. Richards."

I've barely completed the quip before he's covering the distance between us again, consuming my personal space and then smashing my lips beneath his with relentless, mindless, limitless demand. *Oh, God. Oh, yes!*

I let my throat vibrate with a husky mewl, betraying how deeply I crave him...how thoroughly I've missed him. He layers his greedy growl atop the sound while sweeping in again, plunging his tongue deeper this time. I let him in with eager, erotic abandon. My sighs escalate into soprano-register pitches. No surprise. My body isn't my own anymore—nor do I want it to be. I need the reconnection to my husband. I pray for all the circuits that are purely, perfectly *us*. The last three days, I haven't known myself—and now, the reason is so clear. I am him. He is me. We are spark and electricity. Thunder and lightning. Bound and sealed and entwined and real with each other...*because* of each other. To an outsider, it must sound dysfunctional as hell—one of the reasons I fought it so hard for the last three days, until I forced myself to surrender and recognize the truth.

Not dysfunction.

Destiny.

As simple and sublime as that.

It just took the universe a bit of time to let us in on the secret.

But now that I know it, I'll never let it go. Right now, I even wonder if I'll explode from the sheer glory of it. Of *him*, so mesmerizing as his fingers start to glow. Of *me*, producing a string of wild whimpers, as if his assaulting lion act has summoned a matching creature from some primal place inside me too.

An animal pushing harder at my composure with every passing moment—especially as Reece slides one of his beautiful hands up and over my aching breast. He plucks my throbbing nipple with insolent ease, making me yelp with heightened heat. I cry out as he travels his touch to the other peak, lavishing the same perfect pressure to my other erect nub. He watches my every aroused wriggle with his heavy, lusty stare. There's no more of his charming rogue act. He's tossed out subtlety in favor of need, dignity in favor of desire.

So much pounding, delicious, desire...

"So as long as we're on the subject of *points...*" His growl reminds me of a rising tide conquering massive shore rocks of control, eroding the bastions with every surging pass. He rolls his hand down and then in, pushing up my breast for the full attention of his greedy mouth and lascivious tongue.

"*Fuck*, Emma." He mixes his heated words with my supplicating sigh. "Look at this." He scrapes my swollen bud with his thumbnail before closing his mouth back over it. His hunger reminds me of a kid gorging on ice cream. "Look at *you.*"

I swallow hard. My mind instantly whips up a thousand fun comebacks, all addressing how *he's* the arguably better sight right now—*hello*, girl with the fast-rise baby dough in her stomach—but my superhero lover is determined to burn all my protests at the stake.

And, while he's at it, set all my senses afire, as well.

Turning me into his burning beggar...

Holy *God*, how I need him...

I'm parched...

Starving...

Overheated. Underfilled. Empty. *So damn empty...*

"Ahhhh!"

Yet not any of those descriptions finds footing on my lips, eclipsed by that desperate shriek. The scream turns into a whine as soon as Reece dives his lips across mine again. I submit without thought, letting him silence me completely. And yes, I realize that marvelous Mel and Maddie might be waiting around the corner, perking their ears for sounds like this from the new kids' backyard, but my decision is about more than that. It's greater than our freaking "appearances." We'll put up with the Makras' busy-body interrogation tomorrow if we have to. But tonight, I have to have the drowning of his merciless passion, the suffocation of his sexual worship, the surrender to his perfect, carnal command.

And holy *shit*, what command. It permeates his measured twists around my nipple...and then the force of his other hand, gripping my ass so he can grind my core tighter against his...

"Ohhh!"

And maybe Mel and Maddie will get their jollies after all. But I can't be blamed; not when my husband starts huffing as hard as me and our passion reminds me of mating dragons in a mythical dungeon. If that's the case, then drag me faster to the castle, please.

"Oh, please..."

Vaguely, I comprehend that I've rasped that out loud. But I'm damn happy I have as soon as Reece utters back, "You like that, Velvet? When I pinch your tits this hard? And grind against your pussy this deep? When I start turning every inch of your delectable body into my perfect, gorgeous little plaything? To do *any* damn thing I want with?"

He keeps his face a few inches above mine as he unleashes the filthy, flawless litany over me...into me. Yes, I feel every searing impact of every carnal syllable and absorb it with greedy urgency. He's tormenting me, and I welcome it. He's taunting me, and I love it. *I love him.* His words. His command. His dark, carved face. His blazing, seizing gaze. Whatever fire his kiss hasn't already enflamed through my body, his stare takes damn good care of now. From the roots of my hair to the crevices between my toes, I'm a white-gold beam of turned-the-hell-on—especially as he leans in, his breath filled with lust and his touch filled with purpose, and spits, "*Answer me,* Emmalina. Give me the fucking words."

At first, I can only squeak. But his words have me rallying to meet his demand. There are so many beautiful elements beneath his gritted growl. The desperation. The question. The apprehension. The statement he's *really* trying to give me...

Give me the words, Emmalina...

Because I need them.

Because he needs me that badly. To open me that fully. To take me that deeply. But not without knowing that I—and Bean—can handle it. All of it. All of him. In every possible way. With every incredible repercussion.

And if my pussy wasn't soaked and ready for him before, that recognition just accomplished the job.

Past a frantic nod, I finally manage, "Uh...huh."

His whole form stiffens. "*Words,*" he orders again through gritted teeth. "Give me *coherent* words, Bunny. I need to know you're still with me." His glistening gaze dips to my mouth. "For now."

For now. The words are my undoing but my salvation. He's really planning on sending me into space—and I'm completely going to let him. That means giving him everything he demands. Showing him every inch of my trust. Opening everything I am to him again.

No. More than that.

The woman *he* sees in me.

The beauty in his bolt. The partner of his power. The flare to his fuse.

"I like it," I whisper, jogging my chin up so his stare has to follow—so I can behold all the sorcery in his gaze again. "No. I *love* it," I rephrase as my senses career like comets in the wake of his commanding stars—and carry the last of my inhibitions along with them. "When you pinch me like this." I thrust my breast up, molding it tighter against his broad, brutal palm. "And suck me. And bite me."

His stare darkens and thickens, turning from star glow into a pulsing meteor shower. "And then tell you I can't wait to fuck you?"

Yep. I'm soaked. Beyond even that. I'm dripping for him. Throbbing for him.

Glowing for him...

"Oh, yes," I pant, coiling a golden fist back into his knit tank. At once, my touch makes the fabric sizzle, but I'm beyond caring. I'm beyond craving anything but more of his burning touch, his raw and rugged lust. "Oh, God. *Please.*"

He unfurls a low growl, clamping his hold harder. I answer with a taut whimper, grabbing him just as tight. I want to go tighter but know the man could use a few clear moments for stripping his pants off—or at least ordering me to do it for him. At this point, I don't care how it happens. I just need that pounding ridge beneath his sweats to be the naked, nuclear flesh in my hands. Or between my lips. Or buried inside me.

Anything other than this acute edge of hot torment...

We're a moment closer as soon as he scoots me backward, directing me to sit in the swing. The hanging apparatus is more like a stiff chair than a dangling hammock, which garners his satisfied grunt as soon as he plummets to his knees, sending the leaves in the grass flying.

And gushing more arousal through every drenched, quivering inch of my sex.

And then dipping forward, taking up all the space between my thighs.

And then pushing me wider, opening my most intimate core for him. Exposing the hot, wet folds of my throbbing, pulsing center—and turning them into fire with the power of his penetrating stare.

That's before he even touches me. Scorches me. Makes me cry out all over again as soon as he swoops down a pair of elegant fingers and masterfully caresses my slit.

"Holy ssshhh..." My voice fades into a croak as my body shakes beneath waves of astounding heat. Okay, forget surreal. This is sheer magic. This man and his mystical strokes, spiraling liquid lust into every cell of my being, make me wonder if he's already projected me to another stratosphere. I lift my head, actually wondering if it's so—to be showered in a stare of iridescent silver worship, beaming at me across the prominent rise of my belly. The moonglow on my skin, along with the lightning fire in my husband's eyes, moves me to soul-deep tears.

He gave my life more.

And then he gave me *life*.

And always, *always*, with the devotion and fullness and brilliance and completion of his love.

The same love that tangibly flows from him as he raises his free hand, swirling those long, beautiful digits back and forth across my stomach. He lavishes my skin with the same worshipful attention he keeps giving my pussy, and I cry out with need once more—until he interrupts with his heartfelt husk.

"Holy fuck, Emma. You're the most exquisite female I've ever laid my eyes on."

I believe him.

Every word.

There's no more doubt in my mind or fear in my heart. We're going to get through this crazy twist in our journey the same way we've navigated all the rest: by fusing our hearts and fully trusting our love.

And I couldn't be filled with more excitement.

Or gratitude.

It twirls and pushes and fills me until I can't contain its explosion, meshing my light with his until it manifests along every inch of my quivering nudity. Inside, I'm a mesh of yearning and fire, desire and hunger, thankfulness and awareness. Outside, my skin swirls with intense shades of sunset gold and moonrise blue.

"*Reece.*" I lift my arms toward him, sighing as he glides his brilliant blue touch through the glowing amber tides along my body. Everywhere he touches, I ignite even brighter. Every time he pauses, I sigh even higher. There's even a part of me that wonders if I've fallen asleep in the swing and am just dreaming this dazzling sensuality, but when he twists his lower hand, driving his fingers deeper inside my channel, I joyously accept the full reality he's gifted me with. "Ohhhh, damn! *Damn!*"

He responds with a rougher rush of air threaded with

guttural emphasis. Hearing his arousal inspires mine to flare, and my skin pulses brighter to prove it. But I dim by a few watts, surrendering to a blissful shiver, as he pulls away far enough to tug at the tie on his sweats. Though his face is set and firm, his movements are fast and frantic—so much so, he singes the fabric in his haste. Not that I'm complaining. If he's fried off every stitch south of his waist, my win is bigger and better.

So much bigger.

So much better.

I gasp, trembling harder, as I finally take in the flawless sight of him. *Heaven*. His perfect penis is finally free, the muscled length extending from his rippled abdomen, a beacon of pure masculinity. Just beneath the stretched, burnished skin, his veins are like electrified express lanes for the blue flames of his hot essence.

Elixirs I need inside me.

Magic I crave to be a part of.

"Reece." I'm truly begging him now and rejoicing in my greed. I've never craved him more. Lusted for him harder. "Oh, please!"

He leans over, fisting one of the swing's ropes to mash our bodies even closer. Slowly, he withdraws his other hand from the depths of my body. I whimper again, damn near pitching the sound into a keen, as he slowly lifts his fingers to his lips. Dear *God*, how beautiful he is, sucking on the shimmering evidence of what he's done to me. Rapture takes over his face as he pumps them in and out of his firm, full lips. He closes his eyes and tilts his head back.

When he opens his gaze again, there's nothing but pure lightning in his eyes. I react with a stark gasp. He answers with a slow smirk. "Just a preview," he husks, "of what my cock is going to do to your sweet, sopping little cunt."

"*Yes.*" I rasp it as he centers himself, circling and adjusting, finding the ideal place to notch the throbbing head of his sex against the quivering slit of mine.

"This what you want, little Bunny?" He doesn't wait for my high, confirming gasp to shuttle in again, penetrating the first couple of inches of my quaking cavern. "This right here?"

"Mmmm!"

I feel my head fall back again. The surrender is too good not to. I want to fly and almost wonder if I am. The extra buoyancy lent by the swing is an extra shot of freedom and adrenaline, resonating at once in the zapping, racing tissues throughout my sex. Oh, hell. I'm gushing and throbbing and constricting and *ready*.

So...damn...ready...

"Mmmm," I let out again. "Mmmm-hmmm!"

"*Words,*" comes his virulent growl in my ear.

"Yes!" I obey at once. My clamoring pussy doesn't give me any other choice. "Yes, I want this."

"*Words!*"

"Your cock!" I'm snarling too, leveling up to his savagery. It feels so damn good. No, it feels freaking *amazing*. My air comes in animalistic spurts. My blood races with a hotter crisis. "This bunny needs her beast's beautiful, swollen cock."

As he trails bites from my ear to my nape, he adds a sleek, intense underline of low, lusty thunder. "Inside her wet, welcoming cunt?"

"Y-Yes," I pant. "Deep...inside. *Please.*"

I brace myself—a little mentally and much more physically. If my confession fully unleashes his savagery, as I hope it will...

But it doesn't.

Instead, he's tangibly debating with himself. Expelling harsher breaths against my neck as he weathers the significant swell of his erection against my dripping walls. "I don't want to hurt you, Emma. Or him."

I want to scream. I almost do. "You won't. *You won't...* Seriously." *Oh God, please take me, seriously.*

But he doesn't. I see it in the conflict contorting his lips, still shiny with my cream. I confront it in the doubtful shadows that haunt the backs of his eyes.

"*Reece.*" I snatch up his hand and guide it back over my belly. My skin is still a wild mix of amber and blue shades, but as his fingertips touch down, the whole swell turns the color of a massive lapis gemstone. "This is *your* child, Zeus man. You really think anything short of a Mount Olympus eruption is going to dent him?"

He releases a new scowl, but his answering mumble is wry. "At the moment, I'm really feeling like that damn volcano myself."

"Show me."

"*Shit.*" He grits it as I purposely thrust myself higher—welcoming his cock deeper. "You're not being fair."

"We're girding ourselves for war, aren't we? And you know what they say about love and war."

"Fuck." He looks ready to laugh. Or cry. I'll take either, as long as he's inside me at the same time.

"Show me, Reece."

"Damn it. Emmali—"

"*Show me.*"

And then, at last, he does.

And I'm not just gazing at heaven anymore. I'm flying up

into it. Carried and caressed and consumed by endless rays of light that stretch along my veins like fuses on magical dynamite leads. I'm sizzling, burning, screaming out for the TNT to blow—and God, how I need to blow. My senses are thrumming and clamoring. I need that ultimate, releasing blast...

But at the same time, I can't ignore the fireworks in my mind. The wonderment of the truth Reece has been so patient about letting me see this week, despite the agony I know all the "space" caused him. But I got here *because* of the space. I came to this crux because of realizing one inescapable axiom. The clarity of what will always and forever be true for us.

That no matter how hard or strange or bizarre or dangerous this journey may get, we have to face it together.

We have to fight with each other.

We have to fight *for* each other.

We have to fight to always, *always*, get back to this.

Our fusion.

Our connection.

Our union.

Our love.

The love he's making me see, in every bright and blinding and glaring and glorious senses of the word, as he thrusts with the intention of knocking my damn hair out of my follicles. And it's paradise. Nirvana. A light-speed ride to a crazy, carnal cataclysm. Stars start to appear behind my squeezed eyelids. Lightning shoots to the center of my being, and my senses spin faster and faster out of control. My clit tingles. My buttocks tighten. My thighs ache. I'm fully pressurized, ready to blow any second...

"Reece!" I finally find the strength to gasp out.

"Yes, goddess," he growls. "I hear you. And I know. I *know*."

I whine like one of those pathetic piccolo fireworks, hard and horrifically. "You don't know. You *can't* know."

"Almost there, baby."

"I...I can't..."

"You can." He yanks harder on the swing. At once, my channel is lodged tighter around his cock. I've never felt more ready to split into two. Into *four*. Into a *million*. "And you *will*."

His command makes me hotter and angrier in the same agonized, galvanized moment. "It's...it's coming..."

He dips his head and shoulders, staring ruthlessly while I pant through gritted teeth. "Good," he snarls. "Let it."

"I—I need to...I'm going to..."

"Do it, Emmalina. *Do it*."

"And—and you too?"

His face, consumed by brutal lust, surrenders to a warmer expression. He drops his head, capturing my lips with what 'Dia and I used to call *Titanic* kisses. Dueling nose tips, Crashing lips. Thick, mingled breaths. The kind of stuff a guy—and for that matter, a girl—would let go of the floating door in the ice for.

Only after he curls my damn toe hairs from the contact do I remember our floating door is a canvas swing in the middle of a secret garden. But most awesomely, that he hasn't let go at all. He's actually secured both hands to the swing, fisting the fabric panel to make it move faster...to fuck me harder. He drives my body onto his in a ruthless, ravenous, skin-smacking rhythm, spreading his thighs farther to open me even wider.

I gasp like a wild woman. I'm transfixed by the untamed wonder of him. With his lower body pounding me and his upper body drenched in sweat from the exertion, he's nothing short of breathtaking. So powerful and carnal. So hedonistic and hot. Easily the most beautiful husband who ever walked this planet. Who existed in this *cosmos*.

And, by some incredible blessing of fate, he's mine. Forever. But especially in this perfect, erotic moment, as he bares his teeth like an avenging demigod and growls, "Oh yeah, Velvet. Me too." Then ensures my heart flips end-over-end once more, dragging my lips into another *Titanic* kiss.

I'm open and ready for him again—only this time, I refuse to passively accept his desire. He's worth so much more. I'm determined to make sure he gets it.

I delve my tongue inside his mouth, savoring every drop of his whisky and sweat deliciousness. I suck him back into mine, delighting in his stunned grunt of reaction. I mercilessly twine my tongue against his, bringing along every essence of our breaths and lusts and desire, until suddenly he's the one breaking off with a growling moan.

But only long enough to make sure I hear his nerve-igniting growl.

"I'm with you, baby. All the way. Giving it all to you. Every. *Fucking*. Inch."

"And I'll take you." I almost lose the lock on my control, but forming the words helps me hold back the heat a little while longer. *A little while.* "All of you, Reece. Yes. *Yesssss*."

"All of my cock." His face becomes granite again. His voice is carved in matching hardness. "*Say it*, Emmalina."

"All...all of your...cock." Okay, that one's tougher. *Much* tougher. Good freaking *God*, how this man knows exactly how I like to be taken. Torn apart. Cracked open. Mashed from the inside out, until I'm raw and exposed and blinking at bright gold outlines around every living thing I see. Especially him.

Oh, *especially* him.

"And all of the come in that cock."

My brilliant, haloed angel...with a mouth of such nasty devilish intent.

I really am the luckiest girl on the planet.

"All...all of the..." But I gasp out my own interruption. "Oh, God!" He's pounding again, so hard and deep and perfect. He's locked me in his stare, blazing with lust and lightning. He's not going to stop. He's not giving me any mercy. Not this time. Thank *freaking* God.

"Say it, Bunny." His dictate is as merciless as his tough, erotic thrusts. "Form your pretty mouth around that sweet filth." He rams his mouth against the base of my neck. "Take every syllable into your mind and soul, just like you're taking me in your gorgeous little cunt."

His words, debased but desperate, are the perfect key in the lock of my self-control. "All of the come," I surrender with matching urgency. "I need all of the come in your cock, Reece."

At once, his drives grow fiercer. His face does too. Commanding me but surrendering to me. Lighting me with his storm but drenching me in his rain. Demanding to screw me but needing to love me. "Dear fuck," he spits. "Dear...*fuck*."

And just like that, I *am* his bold, naughty bunny. "All of it," I issue, clearly challenging this time. "Every glowing, hot drop."

The amber light around his head thickens. It's contrasted stunningly by his dark, messy waves. "You're going to rip me apart."

I flash him half a smile. "Then that'll make two of us."

He releases the swing. Seizes his hold on my waist instead. "Together."

"Together."

"I'm ready. *Fuck*. Emma!"

I frantically lick my lips. Already, I can feel the telling thumps in his balls. And then the mighty surge up his shaft. Still, he pumps into me with a wild, electric, superhuman pace. "Give it to me. I'm ready too. I'm...I'm..."

I'm not capable of words anymore is what I am. A scream forms in my throat, claimed at once by Reece's ruthless lips. He groans in erotic glory, giving back every shred of the energy I've erupted at him, until he suddenly stills...

And then explodes.

He floods me with so much heat and light and energy, I have no choice about letting my orgasm break in. And break me down. And splinter me apart. And shatter me whole. But in the same incredible collection of seconds, I'm also put back together again—at least enough to acknowledge the fireworks along my skin, the sunbeams through my blood, and the frantic, fiery flutters invading every inch of my thrumming, glowing womb. Okay, so I have to accept that last part in good faith from all my senses in that resplendent space. That's sure as hell what they're telling me everything feels like...

I'm drenched in gold.

Awash in light.

But most of all, I'm filled to the brim of my existence with love.

⚡

Apparently, when a girl is carrying a superhero baby with sun and lightning in his DNA, being filled with love gets followed real fast by being filled with exhaustion.

Especially if her half-naked hunk of a husband has just

screwed her into orgasmic oblivion, only to roll over, keeping her sex fully locked around his even in a freaking hammock swing.

That's just the start of the man's postcoital amazingness.

I sigh in bliss as Reece wiggles a little, noisily digging his toes into the grass, gaining purchase so he can push the swing in a gentle back-and-forth. My sigh becomes an elated moan as he matches the tempo with rhythmic scrapes along the length of my spine. But I let myself fade into silence as sounds vibrate out from him. It's music, flowing from the center of his chest and all the way through the amber glow of my being.

The tune?

"Electric Love."

Like I said...amazingness.

I smile into the expanse of his chest. Let myself melt a little more, absorbing the sounds that mingle with his rumbly serenade. The swing's ropes creaking against the tree's bough. The coastal wind rustling through the garden. The mighty crashes and tidal swooshes of the nearby sea.

The beat of my man's heart, so close and tight with mine.

As it should be.

As it needs to be.

I breathe in his masculine musk, mixing with the leather and spice of his intoxicating scent, while letting myself be lulled by the gentle rocking of our bodies. As every minute passes, sleep is harder and harder to fight—and I finally don't. I'm carried along through subconsciousness by the strains of Reece's song, with his melodic promises of lightning in bottles and drowning rain, until the notes swell around me like Pacific waves. Hypnotizing me. Transporting me. Music that becomes a stretch of dream-borne satin covered in stars.

But then the slick dream fabric folds up around me, caressing my naked skin. It billows around me like a red-carpet ball gown, only it's not.

What's going on?

Reality starts to return.

Sheets.

The softness of my dream was emulating bed sheets. More specifically, the linens of the big bed in Newport where Reece and I have been sleeping together for three days. But *only* sleeping. That's been on me—or the person who hasn't really been me—since we got here. And maybe attempting to shut *me* down was simple survival on my part. In a matter of days, an alien took over my belly, the nineties took over my wardrobe, a redhead took over my own reflection, and I relocated from the ridge in our heavenly canyon to a vague semblance of hell on earth.

So yeah, I'd cashed out. Sealed myself off as solidly as possible without physically leaving—because I was hurting, not stupid. Just because I hate having to come here doesn't mean the necessity has eluded me. The dangers we face, and the woman responsible for them, are still very real.

So, yeah. Hell it is.

Though at the moment, hell couldn't feel farther away.

As a matter of fact, I'm inching closer to heaven.

Not a difficult stretch of possibility as I look down to where my husband's dark head stirs against the rise of my belly. As usual, Bean responds to his dad's proximity with a few steady kicks, but I focus on breathing as shallowly as possible. The last few days have been as trying on Reece as me, probably more so, and he also went through the effort of carrying me all the way out of the garden and then up a dark flight of stairs. Or at least I think so. I'm so warm now. So safe. So willing to let him be in the lead...for a few minutes, at least. Most importantly, it's good that my astounding, steadfast hero is finally and fully resting.

"*Dude.* You've got to chill with the kicks. You want to wake your mom before I get to the good stuff?"

Or...not.

I press my lips together to keep myself from giggling at my husband's conspiratorial whisper. Oh, God forbid the boys wake Mom up. Besides, I have a distinct feeling I'll hear juicier stuff if I feign the snoozing. I even shut my eyes, making everything look authentic, as Reece rubs a calming hand across the tiny bump where his son still persists in pressing a foot.

"So like I was saying, you get more flies with honey, okay? *Share* the puff bites with the girls first, and you'll get twice as many in return the next day. Same goes with the initial hook. You're not going to get anywhere by saying her Wonder Woman lunch pail is cool. You've got to tell her *she's* cool. She may deck you at first, but she'll come around. No risk, no reward, son. I'm going to hold you to repeating that for me once you're out here on our side of the world."

He pauses then, rubbing lightly across the swell and then kissing Bean's persistent foot, which gives my composure just enough time to catch up with my swelling heart before he goes on.

"Speaking of that shit—well *shit*, I just said—oh, *fuck*—all right, so that's going to be our secret, okay? What your mom doesn't know saves my mouth from having to chug a melted bar of soap. As long as we're on that subject, we've got to discuss your nursery décor. This is code critical, son. Your mom has dog-eared some pages in the catalogues. I have to pretend this shit isn't important, but you *cannot* let her pick anything with cartoons or *Doctor Who*. Buddy, I'm as much a *Who*vian as the next guy, and I'll watch it with you all day long, but we're talking about the place you're going to *sleep*, man."

My brows knit before I can stop them. I bent the page for the *Who* theme especially for Reece and thought we'd have to toss a coin on the whole matter. It's good I know about the cartoons, though. Sheez, who doesn't love *The Incredibles*?

"All right, that's the preliminary stuff. I'll probably think of more later. But there's just one more thing I've got to let you know about here. *This* is the *really* important stuff, so listen up."

With practically held breath, I do the same. He's half an octave shy of secret-agent-man intense. This isn't going to be pointers on tying a perfect Windsor or staying away from the green baby-food flavors. Oh, hell...

"I've got to ask you to take it easy on your mom, Bean. I mean, you *are* you, so I get it. She makes you happy. Shit, she lights *me* up like the Super Bowl when she simply walks into a room. But hear me now and hear me true: if you know nothing else about your spectacular goddess of a mother, it's that *she's in charge*, buddy. That's another one you'll be repeating a lot once you're out here in the big bright world."

He twists his head again, feathering a kiss across my stretched skin that causes me to shiver before I can help it. Exactly like the tears that prick, surge, and well over, trailing harder down my cheeks as he rolls his head the other way, bringing his sights into line with mine.

Without deterring that breathtaking azure regard, he finally murmurs, with a grate as intent as it is emotional, "And my Bean...my boy...your mama and I can't *wait* until you're really and truly out here."

I drag in a graceless sniff. Dive a hand into my husband's unruly waves, ensuring his stare stays put as I answer in a hoarse whisper. "In the big, bright world."

The corner of his mouth kicks up with that mix of roguish power and worshipful need that never fails to flip my senses inside out and vanquish every drop of my heart in fierce desire for this man. "Where Mom's always in charge."

I let a watery laugh slip out. "As long as we're all together." And then form my other hand over his, twining our fingers atop the place where Bean clamors to join the Team Bolt high-five, as well.

"Kicking ass, taking names." Reece's smirk is a broad ribbon of cocky white, bursting my libido and billowing my soul until I'm gazing at him through a haze of tears again— but I don't freaking care. We're here together, ready to take on anything together, because we have the greatest power in the world on our side. Love has bound us together, carried us through, and created our beautiful light of a child—even if he *does* seem determined to crack a few of my ribs before he's done incubating.

And that's all right too.

After I get done with a soft "oof," I turn a wry grin up at my husband. "I think your son's already gotten the 'kicking ass' memo, Mr. Richards."

Reece chuckles. "Would you have it any other way, Mrs. Richards?"

I tighten my hold on him, coaxing his face toward mine for a long, deep kiss he's definitely going to remember. "Not for every lightning bolt in the sky."

Because I've got the only bolt that matters...right here.

Continue the Bolt Saga with

Light

Coming Soon!

ALSO BY ANGEL PAYNE

The Bolt Saga:
Bolt
Ignite
Pulse
Fuse
Surge
Light (Coming Soon)

Honor Bound:
Saved
Cuffed
Seduced
Wild
Wet
Hot
Masked
Mastered
Conquered
Ruled

Secrets of Stone Series:
No Prince Charming
No More Masquerade
No Perfect Princess
No Magic Moment
No Lucky Number
No Simple Sacrifice
No Broken Bond
No White Knight
No Longer Lost
No Curtain Call

EXCERPT FROM
NAUGHTY LITTLE GIFT
BOOK ONE IN THE TEMPTATION COURT SERIES

CHAPTER ONE

Mishella

"Dear, sweet Creator. That man's ass needs its own web page."

"Right?"

"Maybe it already has one. Have we tried looking it up? What would that search string even be?"

"*Cassian Court's Glorious Glutes?*"

"Sounds about right."

I scowl at the exchange between my best friend and my princess of a boss. Debate adding a huff, though that might make them giggle harder. As it is, Vylet lifts her head, lets the wind blow her black waves as if she is shooting a scene for a movie, and slowly bats the thick lashes framing her huge lavender eyes.

"Is there an issue, Mistress Santelle?"

Her purposeful drawl on the *s*'s turns her query into a tease—though before I can properly purse my lips, she is answered by a long, snorting laugh. I add a groan to my own response, stabbed at the sound's source. Brooke Cimarron, Princess of the Island of Arcadia, might have the loyalty and love of thousands across our land, but her royal in-laws are not in that legion—and outbursts like that are no help to her cause at all.

The groan might be forgotten, but the sigh is not. Even after three months in her employ, my work is still clearly cut out for me. In my princess's own words, I am to do everything in my power to "whip the royal decorum into shape." Some days, the task is easy. Some, like today...are entries in the *Sweet Creator Help Me* journal.

I have one of those. Literally. Though on the outside, as I observe right now, the book simply says *Action Items.*

Despite the lists taunting me from the pages of said journal, there are many more checks in Brooke's "plus" column than not. Brooke has a good heart, a willing spirit, and a loyalty to Arcadia rivaling that of many native-born to the island. If I can only work out a way to keep Vy from enabling the woman's snarky American side...

Not likely anytime soon.

Most certainly not during this week.

Cassian Court's arrival in Arcadia has sealed that certainty solidly enough.

Cassian Court. Just rolling my mind over the man's name jolts me with such intense heat, I wonder if the Earth has rolled too quickly on its axis, shifting my chair into the sun instead of beneath the table on the Palais Arcadia lawn. That only forms the start of how he has upended my world in just two days.

Two. Days.

Cassian Court.

I cannot help myself. The syllables are synonymous with so many other expressions. *Engineering genius. Corporate wizard. Billionaire icon. Consultant to kings.* Yes, that includes the leader of our land, Evrest Cimarron, who has invited his friend for a "modernization think tank" with Arcadia's leaders. Yanking a kingdom forward by two hundred years in two days is no small feat.

Two. Days.

World. Upended.

Not to mention my thoughts. And my bloodstream. And the very wiring of my nervous system...

"Mishella?"

Vylet's playful prompt is perfectly timed. "Hmm?" I am grateful to leave behind a memory that has been taunting, of the man in his formal wear from the party King Evrest threw for him last night. Out of respect for Arcadian tradition, he wore a doublet-style jacket with his tailored Tom Ford pants, everything flawlessly fitted to his tapered torso and long legs. The black garment had featured one modern touch: a moss-green zipper instead of buttons, drawing out the same shade in his eyes. Matching zippers had adorned his hip boots, making him look very much "at home" in the ballroom's courtly crowd...

"You truly have no comment?" The edges of Vy's lips curl up. Little wench. She knows I would sooner watch a storm come in over the sea than have to look at the body part they've referred to on Cassian Court's incredible form.

Incredible.

And magnificent.

And breath-stealing.

And, in just two days, has made me painfully aware of how small my island home truly is. The man and his magnetic pull have actually made me yearn for a land as big as his, though the expanse of America still does not seem big enough for all these new feelings he inspires—sensations that sweep in again as I gaze upon him training at swords with Jagger Foxx on the palais lawn.

Dizzy.

Giddy.

Hot.

Needy.

No.

I cannot. I will not.

Instead, I compress my lips harder. Swing another censuring look at my friend. "I was being courteous, in deference to Her Highness."

"Oh, here we go again," Brooke mutters.

Vylet hides a laugh behind her elegant fingers. "But Mishella wants to practice her protocol, *Your Highness.*"

Brooke glowers. "Am I going to kick *your* ass about this now too?"

"Not in that pretty tea frock, missy."

"Oh, even *in* this rag, ho-bag."

"Who you calling ho...*ho*?"

"Say it twice because I own that, baby." Brooke swirls and then stabs an index finger. "Especially after last night's marathon under that man of mine."

"Ohhh!" Vy roller coasters the syllable with knowing emphasis. "And I thought you were just walking funny from the platform pumps."

"See how I did that? Gotta have a cover, girl."

They snicker harder than before. I fume deeper than before. Attempt a prim glance down at my lap but only get two seconds of the reprieve. A fresh punch of testosterone hits the air, swinging all our stares back up.

By everything that is holy.

The masculine energy is well supported. Even a hundred feet away, the two men are like gladiators of old, shirtless bodies lunging, gleaming muscles coiling. Jagger Foxx, the Arcadian court's lieutenant of military operations, does not give his American guest an inch of visitor's courtesy—a handicap Court would take as an insult anyway.

The result is...

Glorious.

Slanted forward, his body forty-five degrees from the lawn, Cassian Court is a breath-stealing study of sinew, strength, might, and motivation. His thighs, clearly etched beneath his white fencing pants, wield the force of a stallion. His torso, the color of a lion in the sun, coils with equal power.

Their blades clash. Metallic collisions *zing* the air. Jagger stumbles back. Again. Grunts hard—though not as deeply as the man besting him. Just like that, Cassian Court turns into an even more exhilarating sight. His beauty is meant for the glory of physical triumph.

All the heavens help me, I cannot stop staring. Or wondering. What would it feel like...to be held by those massive arms? What would it be like to lie beneath that beautiful body? To spread my legs, allowing his hardness against my welcoming softness...my tight readiness...

My throat turns into the Sahara. I swallow, coughing softly as the moisture clashes with the dryness.

"Holy hell," Brooke murmurs.

"Which has to be where I'm going, after what I just imagined about that man."

Vy's confession welcomes new knives of confusion. Logically, I should be reassured. My reaction to Court is not unique or special. But another part, new and foreign, fights the urge to think otherwise. To scratch her eyes out for sliding into my territory.

As Brooke would eloquently put it: *what the hell?*

Men are a complicated subject in my life—contradicted by their very simplicity. They are like clothing or cars or office tools: needed but not coveted, functional but not desirable. Yes, some exist in higher-end form, but I do not think of them longer than the time it takes to interact with them. I do not dare. Father and Mother will eventually use me as a pawn to gain what they want from one. It might be the twenty-first century, but politics are politics—and world-changing decisions are still made by the heads between men's legs, not the ones on their shoulders. I have to be grateful for reaching my twenty-second year without having to bother with it yet.

But I will.

And lingering lustings for Cassian Court will not make it any easier.

This story continues in
Naughty Little Gift: *Temptation Court: Book One!*

ACKNOWLEDGMENTS

Wow! What a journey! What a lightning ride! And it's been so much more thrilling because of the love and support of so many. Thank you to all!

Scott Saunders and Jeanne De Vita, you are the most amazing editing team on the planet. I'd be rocking myself to sleep in a padded room without the two of you there, letting me know that all the weirdness is great—but importantly, helping to make it better. THANK YOU!

Meredith Wild, Jon McInerney, and absolutely everyone on the Waterhouse Press team: Bolt is possible because of you. Thank you for caring about my superhero "baby" as much as I do and for not giving up on this dream. Jesse Kench, Haley Byrd, Jennifer Becker, Yvonne Ellis, Kurt Vachon, Amber Maxwell—I am blown away, on a daily basis, by your dedication, heart, positivity, and support. Thank you for being the wind beneath Bolt's electric wings.

Extra special thanks to the marketing goddesses who continue in your superhero strength to spread the Bolt-alicious love throughout the world! Robyn Lee and Wendy Shatwell, I have no words for how much I adore you both.

Every single incredible member of the Payne Passion crew: thank you for all the love and encouragement you lend me on a daily basis. You are my lights!

Martha Frantz: you keep all the gears turning, and

sometimes I have no idea how. You're amazing and such a blessing to me. Thank you!

Victoria Blue: you have made me a better writer and a better person. I love you more than words can encompass.

Special shout-out to the real Corinne: Corinne Akers, your nonstop and diehard love for Bolt has meant the world. I hope to be knocking over more displays to hug you again soon!

All the geeks and freaks and "different ones": as always, and more than ever, this Bolt is for YOU. As I've met you at all the Cons—romance as well as pop/comic culture—it's been a blessing to hear your stories and share your joy in celebrating your differences and living out loud with your quirks. Here's to accepting our differences and taking pride in our truths. I love you all. Be real. Be kind. Embrace love. Do you, in every bright and beautiful sense.

ABOUT ANGEL PAYNE

USA Today bestselling romance author Angel Payne loves to focus on high-heat romance starring memorable alpha men and the women who love them. She has numerous book series to her credit, including the popular Honor Bound series, the Secrets of Stone series (with Victoria Blue), the Cimarron series, the Temptation Court series, the Suited for Sin series, and the Lords of Sin historicals, as well as several standalone titles.

Angel is a native Southern Californian, leading to her love of being in the outdoors, where she often reads and writes. She still lives in Southern California with her soul-mate husband and beautiful daughter, to whom she is a proud cosplay/culture con mom. Her passions also include whisky tasting, shoe shopping, and travel.

Visit her at AngelPayne.com